GOLDEN HARVEST

"Here it is," she announced, rolling up her sleeves and leaning over the boat. She peered into the shallow water. "Aren't they magnificent?"

Although Zach had always had an inquisitive mind, he had to admit to himself at the moment he was much more interested in Eugenia Whalen and the inviting, full-curving figure she cut leaning over the boat than the clusters of oysters in the Whalen whack.

"Magnificent," he answered, but he was thinking about Eugenia.

She glanced back over her shoulder at him. "Here, roll up your sleeves and lean over next to me; you can see better."

Zach inched over until they were shoulder to shoulder, bare arm touching bare arm. Her smooth skin made the hairs on his arms stand up on end, he was so tuned in to her nearness. She smelled of fresh soap and rose water. And her shiny auburn hair was threatening to escape the pins at the nape of her neck, a neck he would thoroughly enjoy nibbling at the moment.

He was beginning to burn for her until she reached over the side of the boat and plucked an oyster from the water.

"What do you think?" She plopped the dripping bivalve into his hand. "They are so near the surface that I do not have to use tongs to harvest them."

Zach looked down at the hard shell, then back at Eugenia. It was not at all what he had in mind having in his hands at the moment. . . .

GWEN CLEARY

PETTICOAT PIRATE

ZEBRA BOOKS
KENSINGTON PUBLISHING CORP.

ZEBRA BOOKS are published by

Kensington Publishing Corp.
475 Park Avenue South
New York, NY 10016

First Printing: January, 1994

Printed in the United States of America

*To the people of the peninsula
who are fortunate to live in God's country.*

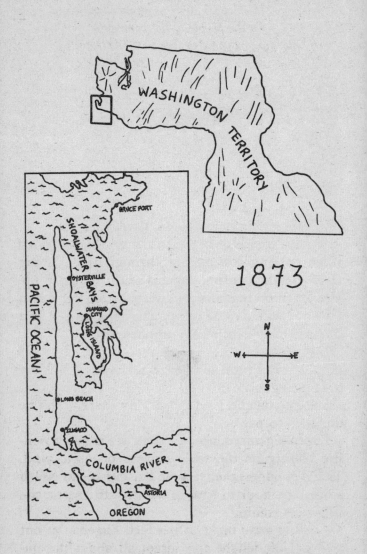

WASHINGTON TERRITORY

1873

BRUCE PORT

SHOALWATER BAYS

OYSTERVILLE

DIAMOND CITY

LONG ISLAND

PACIFIC OCEAN

LONG BEACH

ILWACO

COLUMBIA RIVER

ASTORIA

OREGON

One

"Eugenia Huntley Whalen, how could you!"

At the screech of her aunt's angry, high-pitched voice spiking toward her through the roaring flames of the bonfire, Eugenia's head snapped up. Her attention temporarily diverted from her quest, an unexpected wave crashed at her knees and threatened to sweep her from her feet.

"What do you think you are doing? You get out of that ocean right now!" Iris shrieked, advancing toward Eugenia.

She was caught. Found out. Now there would be the devil to pay.

Eugenia glanced around. Hers was the only bonfire blazing on the wide expanse of white sand. Thank goodness there was no one else on the beach at this late hour to witness the dreadful scene she knew was coming.

Another wave broke at her feet. Eugenia let out a squeal of delight and forgot all about the impending confrontation with her aunt. Darting through the foaming waves, Eugenia hurriedly scooped up the wiggling grayish-green fish which had come in with the surf.

"Eugenia!" Iris screamed and jumped back from the high tide mark as the school of six-inch fish burrowed their tails into the wet sand.

Eugenia ignored the slender, older woman's caterwauling and gleefully bailed the silver-banded fish into the bucket strung over her arm. The waves retreated, the fish with it. Grasping a squirming fish in each hand, Eugenia trudged over to the bonfire where her aunt now stood. There would be no escaping her aunt's carping.

"Just look at you!" Iris spat and slapped her palms to her cheeks. "How could you! You have utterly ruined one of my favorite gowns."

"Me?"

"You are the only one here, aren't you? And the one who is wearing my favorite silk, I might add!" Iris's gaze shot down the length of Eugenia's skirt.

Eugenia followed Aunt Iris's line of vision to the dripping hemline of the emerald silk. It clung against her bare legs, limp as her auburn curls in the misty salt air. Wet sand clumped in beige, sticky clusters along the hem. She glanced up at her scowling aunt.

"Watered silk perhaps?" Eugenia ventured with a sheepish grin.

"I beg your pardon," Iris sniffed.

Eugenia gave a guilty shrug. Unable to stop herself, she ventured, "Salt-watered silk?"

"More like ruined silk thanks to you and your

foolishness, young woman. Where is it going to end?" Iris dropped talon-like hands on her hips. "With you disgracing the entire family? Thank goodness no one but your Uncle Eduardo and I saw you sneak out of the party tonight."

Iris's vision caught on the wiggling creatures Eugenia held. Her eyes rounded. "Good Lord, those dreadful things are alive! What pray tell have you got this time?"

Eugenia held out her hands, the fish squirming frantically. She forced a weak smile. "Grunion."

"Grunion?" Iris mimicked in disbelief.

"At the party earlier Miles Dobbley told me the grunion were running late tonight. He explained how they come onto the beach to spawn. They lay their eggs and then catch the next wave out to sea." Eugenia shrugged. "I had to come down to the beach and see for myself if what he was saying was really true," Eugenia said as if it were the most natural thing a young lady of breeding could do.

"Get those disgusting things away from me." Iris shivered with revulsion, then dragged her eyes from the small fish and rolled them toward the full moon.

Eugenia's lips drooped, and she lowered her arms and head. Her aunt had no appreciation whatsoever for nature's creatures.

Iris let out a labored sigh and returned her vision to her niece. "Your father sent you down here from Washington Territory, trusting that I would take you in hand and send you back East to school with your Cousin Mildred. But he did not warn me that you were incorrigible."

"Daddy would not think that of me," Eugenia

insisted. "He would be as interested as I am in marine life, since he makes his living from the sea."

Iris rolled her eyes again in utter exasperation. "An oyster farmer in Washington Territory. I do not know what my dearly departed sister, God rest her soul these last twelve years, ever saw in a man who gets his hands dirty, harvesting oysters, of all things."

Iris fanned herself from the heat of the flames, ignoring her niece's stiffened pose. "Get rid of those frightful fish before you cause me to have an attack of apoplexy."

Eugenia swallowed a retort in defense of her father. He had warned her that she would never win an argument with Aunt Iris. "Just stand there quietly and let her blow off steam. The old serpent means well. Let it go in one ear and out the other, like your mother did when she chose to marry me, child," he had advised. Shortly after arriving at her aunt's home outside of Los Angeles, Eugenia had learned the hard way to do just that.

Eugenia held in a baleful sigh. She always seemed to be learning the hard way.

She had seemed to provide her aunt with a constant source of censure since her arrival, whether it be her dress, manners, speech or actions. Eugenia had been unable to please the woman.

Without a word of protest Eugenia flounced back to the water's edge and cast the fish into the sea. Swinging the empty pail easily to keep from letting Aunt Iris see that the forceful woman had daunted her, Eugenia returned to where her aunt stood.

"I never meant to keep the grunion, and I was

perfectly willing to give them up. But it would have been nice to study them first."

"Need I remind you that proper young ladies do not engage in such activities?"

"No, I suppose not," Eugenia mumbled, reminded again and again of the unacceptable choices she made. "They sit around all day in the parlor and practice the fine art of ladylike pursuits."

"Exactly. Just as does your Cousin Mildred." Iris raised her chin, ignoring the girl's sarcasm. "And considering that you are a year past your twenty-second birthday and should know better by now, I should think you would be grateful to me for arranging for a school to accept you at your age, so you can finally put aside such outrageous pastimes. No simple task, I might add."

Feeling she had properly chastised Eugenia, Iris directed, "Now, gather your slippers and stockings and come along with me." Iris waited, then ringed an arm through Eugenia's. "My carriage is waiting. I must get you back to the house before somebody catches sight of you in such a disgraceful state. And I shall not have you embarrassing your Cousin Mildred.

"You are just fortunate that she pointed out to Eduardo and me what you were up to, so I could come fetch you before you became a public laughingstock. The dear, sweet girl gave the party in your honor, and presently is back at the house doing her best to soften the rudeness of your disappearance. I shall not have you humiliating her," Iris added for good measure.

"I would not think of it, Aunt Iris," Eugenia said

11

with just the right amount of humility to satisfy her aunt's rage. Secretly, Eugenia thought Mildred was a total bore, incapable of independent thought.

"Good." Iris climbed into the carriage and held her satin skirts until Eugenia was seated, then she leaned forward. "Driver, tie the girl's horse on behind, then head home. And do not stop out front. We shall require to be taken around to the rear entrance."

Eugenia stole one last longing glance at the ocean, while Iris leaned back in her seat, and the driver secured her horse to the rear of the coach. The squat Mexican climbed back into his seat and snapped a whip over the roan's rump. The carriage lurched forward, and the seashore with its roar of waves faded into the distant moonlight, mixed with the dying flames of the bonfire.

Hot curls of sunlight snaked into Eugenia's room in the spacious two-storied adobe house owned by her aunt and uncle, awakening her from dreams of home and happier times. Eugenia had overslept. She leaped from the bed and threw open the shutters. The sprawling house sat upon a hill above a fragrant orange grove, and she had a clear view of the ocean and harbor from her window.

A familiar schooner bobbed in the shimmering blue waters. Excitement stretched in Eugenia's chest, and she hurriedly tossed off her cotton nightgown and slipped on the pale yellow morning dress her aunt had provided. She dragged a brush through her unruly curls and tied a yellow ribbon in the untamed mass.

Foregoing the decorum her aunt had insisted upon since her arrival, Eugenia rushed from her room to the top of the stairs. She gave a conspiratorial glance around. No one was in sight. Aunt Iris would be livid if she knew what Eugenia had on her mind.

Eugenia knew she should curb the urge overtaking her. But her father never banned it. He used to laugh and encourage her to indulge in life's small pleasures when they presented themselves. It was Aunt Iris who insisted that Eugenia refrain from so many of the simple enjoyments she had taken delight in at home.

"Do I dare?" Eugenia ran her fingers over the smooth, polished wood surface. It was so tempting. And if no one was around to see her this time, such a harmless indulgence could not be wrong, she reasoned. Unable to stifle the forbidden desire any longer, Eugenia grinned to herself, bunched up her skirts, and straddled the banister.

With a push Eugenia was off.

She slid down the entire length of the banister with a delighted squeal.

Her pleasure ended abruptly at the bottom of the stairs. She collided with a hapless servant who was carrying a silver coffee service into the dining room and had failed to glance up.

The silver service went flying and clattered to the floor, bringing Iris, in a state, and the dining room's other occupants spilling from the room.

"What in God's name is going on . . . ?" Iris's

13

voice choked off when she sighted Eugenia in the middle of yet another disaster which had befallen the family since that young woman had abruptly intruded into their peaceful and orderly lives.

"Eugenia! What is the meaning of this latest calamity?" Iris swooped out an arm to encompass the wet mess strewn about her elegantly tiled floor. "Wasn't last night's near debacle enough for you? If Mildred had not deflected the guests' attention while I spirited you upstairs, you would have disgraced us all. And now here you are a mere eight hours later in the midst of yet another disaster."

The servant scrambled to collect the silver service and clambered from the room. But Eugenia just sat there, big as you please, in the middle of the dark brown puddles, her dress stained, her hair escaping from the yellow ribbon.

Eugenia shrugged, a slight impish grin hidden underneath her downcast eyes. "Milk and sugar?"

"You incorrigible ingrate!" Iris hissed.

Eugenia did not dare look up as she listened to her aunt's latest tirade. She stared at her aunt's tapping toe, peeking out from beneath the hem of the fine linen skirt. Her vision caught on heavy boots which came to stand next to her aunt. Only then did she venture a glance upward.

The battered old boots belonged to someone who was on her side!

She immediately scrambled to her feet and flew into the heavily bearded old sailor's arms.

"Captain Derrick!" Eugenia cried and hugged the white-haired sea captain, ignoring Aunt Iris's censuring scowl and Cousin Mildred's sly grin. "I thought that looked like Daddy's ship in the harbor. I am so happy you are here. Did you come to take me home?" she probed before Iris could chastise her further.

Iris stepped forward to dash her hopes before the meddling captain could answer. Her spectacles, dangling at her shriveled breast, danced in beat with her scolding finger. "You can get those thoughts right out of your head, young woman. Now, before you attempt to get out of yet another fiasco for which you are responsible, I demand to know exactly what you were up to this time."

Eugenia hadn't meant to give away such a slight infraction so easily, but at her aunt's mention of this latest infringement on family propriety, Eugenia's gaze unconsciously shifted toward the banister.

Iris followed Eugenia's line of vision. Horrified and exasperated, Iris huffed, "You were sliding down the banister again, weren't you?"

For minutes no one spoke until Iris broke the silence with, "I knew it!"

With sarcasm melded into her voice, Iris said, "I suppose some young swain at the party last night mentioned the banister, too."

Eugenia opened her mouth to present her reasoning, but Iris waved her off. "Do not bother to try and conjure up another tiresome explanation. I have heard all your excuses before."

Clearing his throat, Captain Derrick stepped forward and said, "I be sure Miss Eugenia will stand 'er full height and take your floggin' tongue like the able sailor she be."

Her wrath mushrooming under the perceived

slight to her person, Iris's rage swooped down on the captain. "I shall thank you not to attempt to intercede on the girl's behalf at my expense, Captain Derrick. Eugenia has been nothing but a constant source of trouble since you brought her to us last spring."

Not one to be cowed by the old albatross of a sister of his boss's dearly departed wife, Captain Derrick's expression tightened through his white whiskers. "Aye, but I be 'fraid I must, ma'am. You see, I know Miss Eugenia meant ye no harm."

Iris raised her chin. "That, Captain, remains to be seen."

"Aye, so it does. So it does. Since me presence seems to be weighin' heavy on your anchor the way it be, ye might as well know now that it be the lass's own father who sent me here with a letter written in his very own hand." He rummaged in his breast pocket and pulled out the missive.

"Let me have it," Eugenia said and made an ungracious grab for the envelope. She was not quick enough. Iris snatched it from the captain's grasp and settled a disapproving frown on Eugenia.

"I shall take that," Iris announced triumphantly and returned to the dining room. She took her seat at the head of the enormous carved table running the entire length of the opulent room and set the pair of spectacles to her generous nose.

While Aunt Iris tore open the envelope, Eugenia meekly traipsed behind the others and gingerly took her place at the table, next to Captain Derrick. Cousin Mildred quietly sat across from her in all her off-white dainty finery, although Eugenia could

16

have sworn that the petite blonde was grinning at her.

Iris read the letter, then set it aside. She looked up to see Eugenia staring in earnest at her. Without a hint of emotion, her gaze shifted to the captain. "Captain Derrick, I presume my brother-in-law has shared the confidence of this letter with you?"

The captain nodded in response. "Aye."

"Of course he did," Iris said with the sharp edge of distaste to her voice. "In that case, my husband and I shall take its contents under advisement and deliver our response to you at your ship before you sail in the morning."

"What response?" Eugenia blurted out, unable to stand the suspense any longer. "Please, Aunt Iris, may I read Daddy's letter?"

All eyes in the room turned to Eugenia, and she wanted to shrink under the heavy weight of admonition mirrored there.

"Ye might as well let the lass see it," the captain suggested. "She has a right to know."

Eugenia scooted to the edge of her seat and leaned forward. "Know what?"

Iris heaved a sigh. "Oh, I suppose you are right for once."

"Right about what?" Eugenia urged.

"For heaven's sake, Eugenia, can't you ever be patient?" Mildred said.

Eugenia shot her cousin a frown but remained silent. She knew impatience always had proved to be a character flaw in her nature, but she did not need Cousin Mildred's constant reminders. "Aunt Iris?"

"Since you cannot seem to observe decorum and

wait until you are addressed, if you must know, your father appears to have suffered severe business losses and has requested your Uncle Eduardo's financial assistance again."

Ignoring etiquette and fearing that her father desperately needed her, Eugenia captured the letter.

"Eugenia!" Iris sputtered.

Eugenia disregarded her aunt's bellow of outrage and scanned the letter. Her father stated quite clearly he did not want to concern her. She read further. Her father seemed to be suffering unexplained financial reversals again, which she had difficulty understanding. While she had been helping out with the business, they had been doing well in the highly profitable oyster business.

Her father's letter translated into only one thing in Eugenia's mind: He needed her. Now.

Determined to remain calm, Eugenia looked up and turned her attention to the captain. "Captain Derrick, how soon are you sailing?"

"As soon as I get your uncle's answer, lass, and the tide allows."

Her strained efforts at regaining a cool, ladylike demeanor snapped. Shooting to her feet, Eugenia announced with conviction, "I shall be returning with you."

Shooting to her feet in concert with her troublesome niece, Iris stated flatly, "And I shall endure no further insubordination on your part, young woman! You and Mildred shortly will be on your way East to school, and that is final."

Two

"Will you hold on to the line?" Eugenia hissed at Cousin Mildred.

The small dinghy bobbed precariously in the inky ocean waters against the schooner, and Mildred had to fight to steady her stance. "I am doing the best I can. Will you hurry up and climb aboard so I can get back before Mother and Father miss me? If they find out that I am helping you stow away on your father's schooner, after they specifically stated that you could not return to Oysterville on your father's ship, they will be livid."

Eugenia ignored Cousin Mildred's attempts at self-canonization, tied her skirts back, and scrambled onto the ship.

Once on board, Eugenia lay belly flat on deck and leaned over the edge facing Cousin Mildred. "I have given you every cent I had saved. It is not as if you are doing this out of the kindness of your heart. Furthermore, it is late, and they will not miss me until morning. By then you will be safely back in your own room, and they will not be any the wiser that you helped me. So quit complaining, be quiet before the man on watch catches us, and throw me that rope so I can help you up."

"A quick look around, then I must get back," Mildred whined. Curiosity overtaking her better judgment, Mildred allowed Eugenia to help her onto the deck of the schooner.

Soft lantern light, swaying with the rocking motion of the ship, caused shadows to shift about the deck as the two young women gained their feet and explored the deck of the graceful schooner.

Mildred had never so openly gone against her mother's dictates before, and forbidden excitement filled her breast as she took in all the nautical wonders. Secretly she was quite happy to help Eugenia. Since Eugenia had intruded into her life, she had been pushed aside; her parents, not to mention her suitors, had showered Eugenia with undeserved attention which should have belonged to Mildred. And she was quite simply beside herself with jealousy.

At least after tonight she no longer would be forced to endure Miss Eugenia Whalen's presence.

Mildred was heading back across the deck toward the dinghy when a soft whistle cut through the fog, which had begun to creep through the misty night air and engulf the schooner in its gray shroud.

Mildred dashed toward the dinghy, but Eugenia grabbed her hand before she could lower herself over the side and pulled her back behind a barrel.

"What do you think you are doing?" Mildred hissed in a strangled whisper, her eyes wide.

"I am not going to allow you to ruin this for

me." Eugenia could not let Cousin Mildred's panic expose their presence now.

A young, spindly sailor of no more than fifteen appeared through the fog like an apparition, then stopped not more than six feet from them. They waited for the wiry young man to move off, but he just stood there at the rail between them and the dinghy like an omen.

Mildred gritted her teeth and crossed her arms over her well-rounded chest to display her disdain. But she was not about to be responsible for disclosing Eugenia's presence and risk being saddled with such a social misfit back East at the exclusive school.

Wrapped up in their cloaks, the two remained hidden and vigilant for what seemed like hours, until their eyes grew heavy, and they drifted off into a sound sleep.

"Now, what be it I got me here?" Captain Derrick said in a deep voice.

Eugenia's eyes snapped open at the sound of the gruff, familiar voice, and she squinted against the bright sun silhouetting a wide-legged stance. Her heart sank when she noticed the still soundly sleeping Cousin Mildred. Her cousin rested peacefully with her head nestled against Eugenia's shoulder.

They had fallen asleep, and now her hastily crafted plan to stow away on her father's schooner was surely doomed to failure. Captain Derrick was sure to set her ashore, and there wasn't much she could do to combat it.

"Captain Derrick," Eugenia said in her most pleading tones, letting her eyes trail upward past legs which seemed as large as ship masts. His hands were clasped behind his back. Staring up at him, wide-eyed from her position on the deck, she meekly offered, "I can explain."

Meaty hands were brought from behind him and balled on his hips. "Sleep walkin', no doubt, Miss Eugenia?"

"We were sleep walking?" She nodded in accord with the man's bobbing head at what she took for a sympathetic prompt. "Sleep walking, yes, that's it."

"And in your sleep ye two somehow managed to end up on your father's schooner, right lass?"

Eugenia shrugged halfheartedly at the strange cue. "Daddy often used to lead me back to bed as a young girl," she fabricated.

"And your Aunt Iris had to lead Miss Mildred back to bed as well, I suppose."

"Cousin Mildred? Yes. That's it. That is the explanation," Eugenia said, bobbing her head in time with Captain Derrick's. Out of the corner of her eye she noticed that there was a pretty good wind adrift. Then her sight caught on the billowing sails, and she felt the roll of the ship beneath her.

They were underway.

Captain Derrick had not discovered them until after he had set sail.

She had successfully managed to stow away after all!

"Well, ye better be wakin' Miss Mildred so we can get this straightened out," Captain Derrick advised in a tone not devoid of the earlier hint of humor.

Eugenia's first inclination had been to jump to her feet and run to the rail. She so reveled in the feel of the wind tussling her hair, and the taste of the salty sea air, and the sight of soaring seagulls as they majestically followed the ship. And she was an excellent sailor. But she had not meant to place Cousin Mildred in such a precarious position. Her mind working furiously, Eugenia roused her cousin.

"Wake up, Cousin Mildred."

"W-what time is it?" Mildred said sleepily, sat up and rubbed her eyes. Then, as if she suddenly realized that she was not in her own bed, Mildred flew to her feet. "Holy Mother Mary," she cried, grabbing the small gold cross hanging around her neck. "We are at sea! I must get home!" A sudden wave of nausea hit her, and she doubled over, clasping a small hand over her mouth.

"Mates," Captain Derrick hailed two nearby seamen over, "help the young land lover to me cabin, and see to her needs before we chance losin' her. She's already turnin' a bit green around the gills."

Mildred let out an anguished wail, her greenish color deepening. She rushed to the rail just in time to lose the contents of her stomach over the side.

Keeping her face impassive, Eugenia shifted feet impatiently while the two men helped a whimpering Cousin Mildred away.

Eugenia waited until she stood alone with Captain Derrick before trying to convince him that he should allow them to remain until they reached the next port, and then send Cousin Mildred home on the first available ship bound for the harbor at Los Angeles.

She opened her mouth to plead her case, but the captain turned his back on her and strode to the edge of the deck. Determined, she followed the man who now stood with his back to her, his fingers out to his sides, strumming on the railing. She reached him and gazed out to sea, waiting for him to have his say so she could formulate a convincing defense.

"What am I goin' to be doin' with ye, Miss Eugenia, lass?" Carl Derrick finally shouted over the roar of the swells as the schooner smoothly cut through them.

He had just given her the opening she had hoped for.

"You can take me home so I can be of help to my father. He needs me; his letter said so."

"It did not say as much, lass," he said more softly.

"I know he needs me!"

His bushy gray brows lifted at the desperation in her voice. "And how do ye be knowin' that as fact?"

"Uncle Eduardo did not give Daddy the loan, did he?"

Carl Derrick hung his head before he returned his gaze to the young woman he had bounced on his knee since she was a year old. He could not spin tales to her.

"No, lass. Your uncle said he be through tossin' good money after bad." In the man's defense, Carl

24

added, "He be givin' your father money durin' the last three years."

Eugenia laid a hand over the captain's sun-burned, rough one. "I know. I am not upset with Uncle Eduardo. I do understand his position. I do. But I know oysters. It is a very profitable enter-prise, and I can help my father with whatever prob-lems he is having.

"Daddy may not have a head for finances, but the oyster business was making a tidy profit when he sent me to Aunt Iris, and now there are prob-lems. Don't you see? Daddy needs me. He needs me! I cannot—will not—go back to Aunt Iris's and simply abandon my father. I won't!"

"Aye." Captain Derrick thoughtfully nodded. "But those be some pretty strong words, lass."

The old dear was wavering; Eugenia could see it in his weathered face, hear it in the softening of his gruff voice. He always had a soft spot where she was concerned, and she intended to capitalize on it now.

"Captain Derrick, I promise you, once I am sat-isfied that Daddy is well and no longer needs my help, I shall go back East to that stuffy girls' school Aunt Iris intends to send me to and learn every-thing that can be taught."

"Aye, your Aunt Iris. The old shark's goin' to be wantin' our blood if I don't take Miss Mildred home. It—"

"But you can't!" Eugenia interrupted, fearing that she would not be allowed to accompany Cap-tain Derrick if Aunt Iris got her hands on her. She caught herself and offered more calmly, "I mean, isn't time of importance? Surely Aunt Iris will understand once she has the chance to think it over."

"I doubt that, lass. And what about Miss Mildred herself?" he reminded Eugenia.

Eugenia at first had thought the most expedient thing would be to send her cousin back on the first available ship sailing for Los Angeles after they put into port along the way. But Eugenia was worried about her father. She had to return home without the delay such arrangements would cause. She simply had to!

In a quick decision with little further thought, Eugenia said, "Cousin Mildred has often quietly inquired about my life in the wilds of Washington Territory. She said she would like to see it for herself someday, not to mention that a month or two away from Aunt Iris might be just what she needs."

"Ye ain't thinkin' what I think ye be, are ye, Miss Eugenia, lass?"

With an impish grin, Eugenia tilted her chin. "And if I am?"

Late spring rain had accompanied the schooner all the way to the entrance of Shoalwater Bay, north of the Columbia River, once it passed San Francisco. Eugenia had taken advantage of the inclement weather with its huge swells to demonstrate her skill as an able sailor when several of the untried hands who had hired on in Los Angeles had taken ill.

Mildred had not been able to keep a thing on her stomach since they had left Los Angeles, and

26

had been too weak to offer much resistance when Eugenia had made her announcement that Mildred was fortunate to accompany her to Oysterville. Eugenia had known that the captain's sea pie—crow cleaned, cut and served with dumplings, salt pork and onions—she had offered Mildred had helped to keep her resistance weak, since it was not one of the captain's more savory dishes.

Despite a positive attitude that everything would be fine once she returned home, Eugenia worried now that the ship had slipped over the Leadbetter Bar at the entrance of the bay and was anchored. As she was being rowed ashore to her beloved Oysterville, Eugenia could not quiet the deeply disturbing sensations from her mind that something was terribly, terribly wrong.

She motioned to the burly sailor to head toward the wharf built on pilings at the edge of the town. She sighted one of the familiar float houses that had once been set adrift by an extremely high tide. Excitement and anticipation rose in her breast. "Let me off over there instead."

The young sailor nodded and rowed to shore over the mudflats scarcely covered by the rising tide. Once she had thanked the man, Eugenia hurried in the direction of her father's house of redwood board and lathe. But catching sight of a throng of people milling near the town's center, Eugenia changed direction and headed along the bustling Front Street to join the crowd.

Curiosity drove Eugenia to push her way to the forefront of the clusters of people. On a raised platform in front of one of the saloons, an auctioneer was taking bids.

"Three thousand from the tall, dark stranger with the beard."

Eugenia's gaze shot to the stranger who towered over the men standing next to him. His black hair curled beneath the wide brim of his hat and over the collar of his duster in the raw mist hanging over the booming peninsula town. His shoulders were the broadest she had seen. He had a mysterious aura about him in the heavy duster, lending him a foreboding appearance which seemed to give the other people pause about bidding against him.

A murmur rose among her neighbors. She noticed one of her father's partners nearby. Rube Nelson had to stand out front or no one would notice him, he was such a quiet, mousey man. Pale, Nelson started to hoist his hand, but dropped it under the stranger's icy glare. Not another man raised an arm to up the ante, and Eugenia wondered what was on the auction block.

She then spied her father's other partner lingering in the background, craning his neck as if he were looking for someone. But before she could go over and question the man, the pounding gavel on the hastily erected podium drew her attention back to the slickered auctioneer.

In a scratchy voice, the man called out, "Going once . . . going twice . . . three times. Sold to the big feller. Step right on over to the table, and our town's banker Mr. Washer will be happy to make arrangements to take your money, stranger." Then the man announced to the general audience,

28

"Show's over, folks. Thank you all for coming out today."

Once the spectators began to disperse, Eugenia hurried to catch up with Len Sweeney, a rotund man of about fifty-five with close-set gray eyes and a thin ridge of salt and pepper hair that circled a bald pate hidden beneath an old hat.

"Mr. Sweeney?" Eugenia called out to her father's partner.

The man turned around, a surprised expression momentarily visible on his puffy face before he smiled widely and stretched out his hands in welcome. "Eugenia? Why I thought you were in California with relatives."

"I was, but I had to return when I heard that Daddy may need my help."

The man's face fell, and he ringed a hefty arm around her shoulders, pulling her into a protective embrace. "Oh dear Lord, Eugenia, you don't know?"

A frightening sensation shot cold through Eugenia, and she tensed. She had sensed something was wrong. Terribly wrong. And now that dread became acute. Eugenia took a deep breath and forced the lump of alarm clogging her throat out of the way far enough to ask, "Know what?"

"The business was so far in debt that in order to recoup some of the losses it was just sold at auction. And—"

"Oysters are Daddy's life; he would never do that!" She swung out of his embrace.

"Eugenia, your father's dead."

Three

The devastating news, delivered without regard or thoughtful preparation, slammed into Eugenia with such force that she did not make a sound when the trees and sky suddenly seemed to whirl about her head and a black void engulfed her. She slumped against Len Sweeney's barrel chest.

When Eugenia finally came to, she was lying on the Widow Garrett's patchwork, quilted bed. The elderly woman was swabbing Eugenia's forehead with a damp cloth, cooing soft words of comfort to her.

"What happened?" Eugenia mumbled, still in a mind-numbing fog.

"Len Sweeney brought you to me after you swooned. The crazy old fool told me how he had blurted out the news of your father's passin' on no more than a week ago, 'n' all. He should have known better. I am sorry, child."

It suddenly came flooding back to Eugenia—her father's death, his financial troubles, the business gone. She put her fingers to her temples to stave off the pounding in her head. Her mouth was abruptly dry, and she asked, "May I have a glass of water, please, Mrs. Garrett?"

" 'Course you can. Now you just hold this rag to your head and stay right where you are until I get back."

Eugenia held the cloth in place and watched the kindly, diminutive widow scurry from the room, only to return presently with a tumbler of water sloshing over her bony, gnarled hand. She offered the drink to Eugenia, and she took a few sips.

"Please, tell me what happened to my father?" Eugenia finally managed.

Ruth Garrett sat down on the bed next to Eugenia and placed a comforting hand over hers. Dark circles of unspoken grief were etched around the girl's hollow eyes. "We all loved your father; he was a good man, the best. It was a mighty shame he had to meet his Maker before his time, the way he did." She shook her white head with a mournful sigh. "Yes, a mighty big shame."

She squeezed Eugenia's hand in reassurance. It was ice cold. "The sheriff is looking into it, and I'm sure he'll catch whoever killed your father."

"Whoever killed him?" Through trembling lips, Eugenia barely mouthed the words, she was so stunned.

"Oh, my. I hate to be the bearer of such painful news, child. But I guess someone's got to tell you. Your father was murdered in his very own back yard, cowardly shot in the back. Len Sweeney and Rube Nelson found him lying near the fence. I am so sorry."

Eugenia fought a nearly overwhelming inclination to scream, and steeled herself. Later, she determined, after she had seen the murder solved, and the guilty party brought to justice, then she would allow herself to experience the anguish she fought to ward off. But not before.

There was nothing so sustaining as anger. Despite Eugenia's shock, her choler and desire for justice rose.

Eugenia gulped in big, buoying breaths, trying to stop her trembling, and determined not to cry. "Are there any suspects?"

Ruth Garrett had seen it before; Eugenia was in a state of shock over the dreadful news. When the full impact finally hit her, the poor young thing would be devastated, disconsolate. Ruth just hoped she would be nearby, since Eugenia had no kin in the territory.

"Sheriff Dollard has been nosing around, but he hasn't turned up much yet."

Ruth hesitated, wondering whether she should mention what else she had heard. Then she decided that Eugenia was going to hear it sooner or later anyway, so she might as well hear it from someone who cared about her. "There is something else I do think you should know."

Eugenia stiffened, preparing herself, although nothing could be any worse than losing her beloved father at the hand of a murderer.

"Now, before you go off half-cocked, I think you should know that it probably has absolutely nothing to do with your father's death."

"What are you trying to say?" Eugenia prompted,

growing impatient and more tense with the elderly woman's feeble efforts to pad the impact of whatever she was about to tell her.

"You know how Oysterville is divided between the saved and the damned; a magnet for the lawless—drinkers, gamblers and those birds of passage."

"What could loose dance hall women have to do with my father?"

"Outlaws always follow once those birds of passage come twittering into town," Ruth answered and took a breath.

"Anyway, the day after your father was killed, a mysterious stranger showed up in town asking folks all sorts of probing questions about the oyster business."

"And?" Eugenia interrupted, unable to stand the mounting suspense.

"And Len Sweeney told me that same stranger is the one who just bought your father's business at auction earlier today." Ruth noticed Eugenia blanch, so she added in a reassuring tone, "Your father's partners had no choice but to sell to pay off the debts owed, dear."

Eugenia's face went stark white, and Ruth feared the young woman might crumble under the weight of the burden just dumped on her. "Oh, my poor child, you didn't know about that either, did you?"

"Yes, Mr. Sweeney told me," Eugenia barely whispered at the sudden recollection, her mouth had gone so dry again. She had just learned she had been orphaned in the worst manner conceivable, and now the Widow Garrett had confirmed what Mr. Sweeney had told her earlier.

Eugenia hastily took another sip of water. An instant later she realized she should not have been so astounded by the news. Murders were often committed in relation to Man's greed.

"Are you all right? You are as pale as the bleakest days on this here peninsula."

"Mrs. Garrett, I shall not be all right, as you put it, until after I see my father's murderer hanging at the end of a rope."

"Oh, my." Ruth Garrett's hand flew to her lips at the strength of Eugenia's venom. Then she realized that the young woman needed something to hang onto if she were going to get through the terrible ordeal facing her. And she knew that there was little so fortifying as anger and the need for vengeance.

"Would you like me to accompany you out to the gravesite?" Ruth asked softly. That was the least she could do for Eugenia.

"No, but thank you for the offer."

"Are you sure?"

"I am not prepared to bid my father a final farewell yet."

The pain was too new, too deep, too raw. She needed time to absorb the horror of it all; time to find answers and the person responsible for taking her father from her so untimely; time to put such a senseless act into some kind of perspective. Only then could she say her final goodbye. She sniffled back tears. Only then would she weep at his grave. And only then in private.

Ruth was a little surprised that Eugenia did not ask exactly where her father was buried, but Ruth had known the heartache of losing her own husband and knew that each person had to grieve in her own way and time. "If you change your mind, you just let me know."

Eugenia stiffened and Ruth sought to change the subject. "I know this is little consolation, dear, but at least you will have the money from your father's portion of the business once the debts are settled to help cushion the shock."

Eugenia ignored the widow's mention of money. She had other things on her mind. She now had a pressing objective in life, a dark mission thrust upon her, a goal. And she was not going to rest until she saw it accomplished.

Eugenia set the damp cloth and tumbler on a nearby table and got off the bed to pace back and forth in front of the elderly widow. Three times she passed the widow before stopping.

"Tell me everything you know about this stranger you just mentioned, Mrs. Garrett."

A distant gleam sparked into the widow's watery hazel eyes. "He is a handsome devil, that one. Even with that thick beard." She gave a nervous titter. "Just like my dearly departed John was when we first married. Tall built, strong and sturdy to withstand the elements." She clasped her hands over her heart. "And all that curly black hair. Why, while I was at the mercantile the other day I saw it in the sun, and it had the bluest cast to it, it was so black, like a raven's wing.

"Must say, though, that beard he sports does

make him look like he's got something to hide, since it does such a good job shielding much of his face from curious eyes. And speaking of eyes, those steely blue eyes of his, serious and probing they are, make a body fondly remember standing on the ridge overlooking the weather beach and blue ocean beyond on the other side of the peninsula."

Ruth concluded with, "Other than that, nobody seems to know much about him."

Eugenia's green eyes narrowed, and Ruth Garrett began to worry that she had let her busy tongue run away with her mouth. "Now, Eugenia, just because the man is a stranger in town, asked a lot of questions about the oyster beds, and then bought your father's business, that doesn't prove him a murderer or even an outlaw, for that matter."

Recalling the auction earlier, Eugenia strode to the door but stopped to toss back over her shoulder, "Perhaps not, but it sure makes him a damned good suspect."

Ruth was shocked by the young woman's crudity. Ruth had known Eugenia since the family had come to Oysterville from Astoria when Eugenia was a young tike stealing Ruth's favorite rhododendron blooms from her garden. And she had never heard Eugenia Whalen curse before.

Eugenia thrust open the door just as Ruth was regaining her wits enough to ask, "Where are you going?"

"To see Mr. Washer and get some answers."

Eugenia walked out of the Widow Garrett's small salt-box house surrounded by a weathered picket fence. She hardly noticed the tidy yard filled with bursts of colorful rhododendrons, and the crunching of sparkling white paths made of crushed oyster shells beneath her feet, as she headed back toward town to learn more about this mysterious dark stranger.

An incredible wave of nostalgia washed over Eugenia when she reached her family home. Built with ballast from ships out of San Francisco, the two-story house with red gingerbread shutters and a welcoming porch complete with swing seemed to beckon her.

Unable to resist a short detour to spend a few moments reliving all the wonderful times she'd had in the family home before she set about her goal, Eugenia pushed open the rickety gate and crossed the stepping stones.

Eugenia went inside and was immediately struck by the warmth that surrounded her. Memories so strong, so overpowering with a bittersweet happiness filled her breast. She walked through the house, fingering all the well-known furnishings draped with crocheted doilies and knick-knacks that made a house a home.

Upstairs more personal childhood memories circled her. In her parents' bedroom, she touched the bedpost her father had altered so her mother could keep her valuables hidden in its hollow. It almost seemed like yesterday. And in her mind she could hear the echo of their laughter.

It was not until she returned to the top of the stairs that an incredible urge overtook her.

From the top of the stairs, she stood quietly staring at the polished banister, remembering how her father used to stand at the bottom with his arms outstretched, promising to catch her. It was such a fond memory of loving times past that Eugenia could not help herself.

She tied her skirts back and straddled the banister. The faded daguerreotype of her parents smiled out at her from the rose-papered wall nearby. Tears sprang to her eyes. She blinked them back. Not now. Not yet would she give in to the urge to break down.

She pressed a gentle kiss to her index and middle fingers, leaned over and reverently touched the image of her father. In a choked whisper, she murmured, "This is for you, Daddy."

Eugenia gave a shove with her toe and rode down the steep incline with record speed.

She was going so fast that she flew off the end of the banister right into the solid wall of a male chest.

With a winded "oaf" the pair was slammed to the braided rag rug covering the wooden floor.

The wind knocked out of her, Eugenia sat, momentarily stunned, on a male lap, encircled within strong muscled arms. Her skirt had ridden up, displaying shapely stockinged legs, disappearing into plain cotton underdrawers. Her hair had sprung free and corkscrewed over her shoulders, cascading over her face.

Eugenia closed her eyes and reveled in the warm embrace and musky, masculine scent for a moment, until she suddenly realized she wasn't merely daydreaming.

She actually was sitting on some strange man's lap, and he was holding her in his embrace!

A curious sense of dread sliding over her, Eugenia slowly swiveled around, parting her unruly mass of auburn curls so she could peek out between the thick, waving strands.

She swallowed hard as she came nose to beard with the mysterious, black-haired stranger.

Before she had given thought that she was alone in the house with the man who very well could have murdered her father, Eugenia blurted out, "Who are you, and what are you doing in my house?"

To her chagrin he did not remove his arms from around her person. Instead, he grinned, but it did not reach his piercing blue eyes. "Name's Zachary Kellogg. And you are?"

"I am?"

"Yes, you."

Mesmerized by those penetrating blue eyes, her heart pounding wildly between her ears, Eugenia barely managed to mouth, "Eugenia Huntley Whalen."

There was no gleam of recognition in those blue depths. When he made no effort to disengage himself from her person, Eugenia shook her head to clear it. Her senses returning, she pushed out of his embrace and righted her lavender skirts.

Still sitting on the floor, her skirt spread out in a circle around her, she demanded, "I asked you what are you doing in my house?"

One straight black brow shoved up, and Zach eas-

39

ily got to his feet. "I might ask you the same question."

Zach offered his hand to the pretty young lady, although she was acting rather bizarre. Ladies did not slide down banisters. He had it from a reliable source that the deceased's only daughter was in California.

When she finally decided to accept his outstretched hand, he helped her to her feet. Still holding her hand, he rubbed his thumb along the edge. It was not as smooth as warmed velvet like the women's he had known, and the unexpected difference threatened to rouse his senses.

"Ask me the same question?"

"Yes."

The warmth of his caressing fingers was causing a strange sensation to invade her chest. In an effort to stop the desire to respond, Eugenia ripped her hand from his and stepped back. She stood before the towering man rubbing her fingers in an effort to obliterate the lingering impressions. "I beg your pardon."

"As well you might since this is my house as of eleven o'clock this morning."

"Your house!" she practically shouted refusing to believe it.

His brows drew together, forming a line down his bronzed forehead. "You hard of hearing?"

"Hard of hearing? Most certainly not."

"Then why do you seem to find it necessary to repeat everything I say."

"Repeat everything *you* say?"

His brows and shoulders shot up into a shrug. "See? There you go again."

"There I go again," she repeated, then realized what she had done. "Oh . . ." she said in frustration.

Eugenia could feel her cheeks flame, she was so unnerved by the outlandish encounter. Yet she was not the least frightened that she might be standing in front of a murderer. His stance was not threatening; it was more questioning, probing.

In an effort to appear more formidable, she straightened up to her full five foot, six inch height. To her chagrin, it did not bring her eye to eye with the man; she still had to look up.

"I have been away in California and just returned . . ."

He nodded as he listened to her story, still questioning her identity. Although he was wavering, he could not be sure until he checked it out for himself that she was who she professed to be.

". . . This is my family home. I was raised in the bedroom at the top of the stairs"—she pointed—"and grew up sliding down that very banister."

"Then I can assume that you must still be growing, and have yet to reach your full maturity since you seem not to have given up the engaging habit."

Her father had been the only one in her life who had called it an "engaging habit." It caused Eugenia to flush at the mention of her untimely foray back in time a few moments ago. But her temper was rising because he did not seem to be taking her at all seriously.

"I shall have you know that I am a woman grown."

41

His eyes slid over her curvaceous figure, and a gleam of appreciation filled the sparkling blue depths. "Guess I shouldn't have tried to dispute such an apparent physical fact."

His blatant comment caught her off guard. In an effort to still a strange sensation in her breast, she moved to show him the door. He stepped in front of her to block her way. Her sensations transformed to dread and her mood sobered.

"What do you think you are you doing?" she asked cautiously.

That left brow shoved up again. "Think?"

"Perhaps you are the one who is hard of hearing," she blurted out before realizing the implications. If she were not careful, she could raise his ire, and only God knew what terrible things he was capable of.

She waited a moment, half-fearing, half-dreading Mr. Zachary Kellogg's response. When he merely stood his ground staring at her as if she were some silly, outlandish child, Eugenia raised her chin in a display of unfelt adult pique.

They seemed to be at an impasse, just staring at one another, neither willing to break the line of vision. In an effort to put a favorable end to the uncomfortable predicament, Eugenia dropped her fists on her hips.

"Now, I would be most appreciative if you, sir, would please step aside and allow me to open the door so you can leave my home before I am forced to seek out the sheriff and have you forcibly evicted."

Four

Eugenia could not have been more dumbfounded if Zachary Kellogg had uncharacteristically begged her forgiveness when he suddenly thrust open the door, bowed, and swooped out an arm with a practiced flourish.

"Please, *Miss Whalen*, be my honored guest. The world awaits you. Far be it for me to stand in your way. If you're of a mind to seek out the sheriff and save me the trouble, by all means do so with my blessing."

Each word was said tongue in cheek and left her astonished and reeling. He was either the coolest or most cunning murderer she had ever seen. Unsure quite how to proceed, Eugenia stomped to the door. She could not understand why a murderer would so nonchalantly invite her to summon the sheriff to his—or rather her—door.

She raised her chin a notch and stepped through the door. "I am going."

That same infernal brow shoved up. "So be it."

"I really am going to summon the sheriff."

43

"So you keep repeating."

"Well, I am," she finally said in a disgruntled voice. She had expected him to try to dissuade her, to offer some sort of excuse, or stop her if nothing else. But instead, the exasperating man was inviting her—no, egging her on—to have him arrested. "If nothing else, I am going to charge you with trespassing," she added in an effort to shake that calm exterior of his.

"Then trespassing it'll be. Now, are you going to step out of the way so I'm not forced to be rude and close the door while you're still standing on the threshold, or are you going to continue to remain, making threats until all the heat has been let from the house. I do prefer to keep my home toasty," he said with that disgusting smirk, leaning up against the door jamb.

Her determined glare faltered, causing him to add, "Look, I'm sorry about your situation, but this is my house now. I'm sure you have friends you can go to."

Eugenia ignored his shaded offer of condolence. She glanced past him, back inside at all the familiar treasures, then at the waiting man. An unsettling notion popped into her head. He was up to something! For some reason known only to him, he wanted her out of the house now. And in her mind she decided that he was simply too anxious to see her go.

She opened her mouth to accuse him of murdering her father, then thought better of it. If indeed he was a murderer, as she suspected, she could be putting herself in grave jeopardy. Then the notion struck her that he might want her out of the house so he could destroy some remaining piece of incriminating evidence.

She was not going to let him get away with covering up his guilt if she could help it!

She marched right past him and back inside the house. "You are welcome to close the door now."

That wiped the smirking grin right off his handsome face!

Zach slammed the door, rattling the hinges, and stood with his arms crossed over the enormous expanse of chest, glaring at her.

She ignored his dark frown and began stripping off her coat. In most unladylike fashion, her arm promptly stuck in the lining of the sleeve.

"You might quit staring at me and help me off with my coat," she said, struggling.

"I might. But, you understand, if I did, that would mean you're staying," he returned and made no move to play the gentlemanly role.

Eugenia had been grappling with the bulky coat and finally freed herself without his help. Carelessly tossing the wool garment to a nearby chair, she lifted her chin. "I am staying, thank you."

The young woman was proving to be more of a challenge than an annoyance. And while Zach had to admit to himself that he found her wit, if not her grit, quite refreshing, he had things to do which did not lend themselves to prying eyes.

It was time to put an end to the banter. Zach snatched the young woman's coat from the chair and held it out to her. "I'm afraid I'm not prepared to receive guests at this time, so I suggest

45

you go in search of your sheriff now before I'm forced to do the ungentlemanly thing and bodily remove you from this house."

Despite the drumming of her pulse, Eugenia stood her ground. "I am not leaving."

"Oh, but I'm afraid you are," he announced. In one fell swoop, Zach wrapped her coat around her shoulders, scooped her up, and deposited her out on to the porch.

Eugenia was too stunned by the speed of his actions to mount a retaliation before she heard the door slam and the lock click in her ears. But far from accepting defeat, Eugenia had only begun to fight!

She jammed her coat on to protect herself against the cool, moisture-laden weather and marched back to the door. She pounded against it to no avail. Zachary Kellogg did not intend to give her entrance to her own home. Well, she would just see about that!

Common sense would have sent Eugenia scurrying to the sheriff's office for assistance, but Eugenia had never been accused of using common sense when she was riled. Instead, she decided to do the unexpected. After all, she surmised, desperate situations called for desperate measures.

By the time Eugenia stepped off the covered porch, it was starting to rain. Her hair, already wild from her foray down the banister, was kinking up into wild curls. Eugenia ignored the growing number of drops and went around the house, trying the windows until she discovered one that judiciously had been left ajar.

She stepped up on the branch of an old hedge to get more leverage and promptly slipped off, her foot sinking into the swallowing mud. Not about to be daunted by a little brown goo, Eugenia slipped her foot from the delicate shoe, hoisted herself onto the window ledge, and heaved the window open.

Her efforts threw her off balance. She teetered for a precarious moment before she unceremoniously fell into the parlor with a thud.

When she smoothed her hair back and glanced up, Zachary Kellogg was standing over her, a pocket watch in his hand.

"Didn't even take you five minutes to break into my house this time. Figured it would've taken you longer than that. Am I to presume that you're accomplished at breaking and entering?"

"There was no breaking involved; the window had been left open. And as for entering, this is my home, and I shall enter it in any manner I choose."

"Pity," he said, ignoring her brazen justification. "I don't have anything to gauge your time against."

"I have no doubt you'll manage an adequate estimate."

"Spoken like one who intends to make a habit of improving upon her record."

"If I already had a record. Which I do not, I might add."

Lightning flashed, followed by a tremendous boom of thunder, before the sky ripped open and a deluge ensued. Eugenia scrambled to her feet and shut the window to keep the rain from coming in

47

and ruining her mother's favorite rag rug she had fashioned from Eugenia's baby clothes.

She turned to face her accuser. He was even more handsome now that he had removed his duster coat. He was dressed in dungarees and chambray shirt which gave him a decidedly masculine appeal she could not deny. But she was one female who was not going to fall victim to it!

"Since you have so ably set a baseline, why don't I take your watch and see if you can beat my record by vacating *my* home in less time."

Zach ignored her and dropped the watch back into his pocket. "I thought you were going for the sheriff."

"Well, I was."

"What stopped you then?"

Another crash of thunder gave her the idea she was groping for. "The rain. If you must know, it was the rain that stopped me." She stripped off her coat without difficulty this time and plopped down on the worn patterned sofa. To her unease, he plunked down next to her and draped his arm along the back of the sofa.

"And I suppose you were afraid you would melt?"

She raised her chin in defiance. "Sugar and spice, you know."

"No, frankly, from my experience with you, I didn't."

Except for the splattering of the rain against the house, everything was silent while each sat on one end of the sofa, glaring and waiting for the other to make the next move. Finally, Eugenia could endure the silence no longer.

Gaining her feet, she announced, "We should light the lamps before we end up sitting together in the dark."

He rose to his feet beside her. "That would be a shame," he said in a deep baritone, his eyes smiling into hers. "While you light the lamps, I'll add wood to the fire I started before you decided to throw yourself at me."

"Throw myself at you!"

He smiled that warm, enticing smile she was coming to detest. "Yes, from the top of the stairs."

A retort immediately came to Eugenia, but she swallowed it. She had not reentered her family home, putting herself at risk, to exchange barbs with the man. She had returned so he would not be able to destroy any remaining evidence of his crime.

Void of one of her shoes, Eugenia limped around the house, making short work of lighting the lamps, and returned to keep an eye on the man while he bent over, tossing logs into the fireplace. The flames popped and crackled, reminding her of how her father had imported the fireplace stones, since the material was not locally available. He had been so proud to be able to provide her mother with a fireplace since so few homes in the area sported one.

A bursting spark shot into the air like a flash from a gun barrel, redirecting her thoughts. Although she suspected him of killing her father, she had to admit that she did not possess any fear of the man. That in itself unsettled her, and she wondered if he had put her father at ease as well.

Zach laid one last log in the fire, then unfolded his big frame before her and looked around. "It looks real cozy in here now."

"It would be if you would simply leave," she said and took up a position by the window.

"Look, Miss Whalen, or whatever your name is, I don't know what it is you have on that pretty little mind of yours, but I've been patient long enough. What're you doing here?"

"What do you mean 'whatever my name is'?"

Tired of their banal conversation, he said, "Look, honey, I happen to know that the real Miss Eugenia Huntley Whalen is in California and will be on her way back East to some girls' school. So you better come clean. Who are you?"

Shock that he seemed to know so much about her did not impede Eugenia. She limped to the black-lacquered piano in the corner and grabbed a photo from the numerous ones adorning the spinet.

Holding the recent daguerreotype no more than three feet in front of his face, she said, "The indisputable evidence of my birth is plain enough from this photo, I believe. I am Eugenia Huntley Whalen. I was in California, as I informed you earlier, but just returned today to find that my father had been murdered, you—a total stranger who no one in town knows anything about—has bought my father's oyster beds, and seem to have taken up residence in my father's home. All without my knowledge or consent, I might add."

50

There was no longer disputing who she was. The likeness was unmistakable. She was Woodward Whalen's daughter.

For some quite engaging reason, he gazed at the likeness for a long moment. The tapping of her toe snapped his attention back to the problem at hand.

Zach realized what a shock the man's death must have been to his only child. It also explained the young woman's motives. But Zach was not about to let on what he was doing. Her unscheduled presence could put a crimp in his carefully laid plans, he inwardly grumbled.

He took the daguerreotype from her and returned it to its proper position. "So, you're who you say you are. I'm truly sorry about your pa, but it doesn't change the fact that I'm still the owner of his house now."

"You may have bought the oyster beds, but my family home did not come with them," she argued. For an instant, Eugenia thought she saw sympathy glint into his eyes. An instant later it was gone, and she decided it must have been wishful thinking on her part.

"Ah, but it did. I'm told it was sold to help pay off your pa's debts."

"I promise you, you will eat those scurrilous words on the half shell after we visit Mr. Washer. Although he runs the casket shop,"—her voice threatened to catch at the vision the word "casket" elicited but she kept it steady—"he is the town's only banker of sorts, Mr. Kellogg."

Zach suppressed a burst of laughter over her un-

51

canny choice of words concerning oysters and glanced at the clock. It was nearing early evening. "Pity his casket shop's probably closed, or I would take you over there and get this settled so I could have a little peace 'n' quiet in my own house."

"*My* house."

Zach's brow shoved up in consternation. She was one of the most exasperating females he ever had encountered in all his thirty-five years.

"Why don't I escort you wherever you plan to spend the night and then—"

"I am not leaving," she announced flatly.

A grin sparkled in his eyes. "You can't stay here with me."

"I do not intend to."

"Then, as I just so generously offered, I'll be happy to escort you wherever you'd like to go."

"I already told you, I am not leaving."

Zach scratched his head. He could scare her off; she was jumpy as a frog despite her determination. But an uncharacteristic sympathy for her newly orphaned status held him back.

"I gave up my room at the hotel this morning, and I'm not leaving either. So I guess it looks like until we get this impasse straightened out at Washer's, it's going to be you and me under this roof tonight." He grinned just to unsettle her further. "Just like newlyweds spending our first night together. Cozy, don't you think?"

"Hardly."

The rain increased and the wind howled through the trees with a gale force. It was not a night to be out and about.

"Why don't we go into the kitchen and see if there's anything in the house to eat," he suggested.

"Thank you, no. It has been an exhausting day, so I think I shall go to bed."

The grin crossing his lips was downright provocative. "Sounds like an excellent idea to me."

"Alone, Mr. Kellogg."

His brow shoved up. She was quick; he'd give her that much, he thought, surprised that his thinking had been quite so transparent. Without another word, he started for the front door.

"I see you have finally decided it wise to seek accommodations elsewhere," she said triumphantly.

"You can get those notions out of your mind, Miss Whalen. I'm merely going to retrieve the shoe which you seem to've left outside, so you won't have an excuse not to leave the house tomorrow morning."

Eugenia glanced down and wiggled her toes. She had forgotten all about the abandoned shoe. "You will find it stuck in the mud under the window outside the parlor."

"An apt place for a lady such as yourself to leave her slipper, no doubt," he said and left the house.

Abandoning the idea of attempting to lock him out of the house and barricade the door, Eugenia waited for him to return, then snatched the mud-encrusted footwear from his hand without a thank you. Lamp in hand, she mounted the stairs and stood staring down at him.

"What're you waiting for? For me to put out my

arms and catch you when you coming flying down the banister?"

Her lips tight, Eugenia said, "Thank you, no. I do not feel the urge at the moment."

"Any time you do—feel the urge that is—don't you hesitate to let me know. I'll be ready and more than willing to welcome you into my embrace at a moment's notice."

"I can only assure you that you need not hold your breath in anticipation," she said, aghast, and left him at the bottom of the stairs. She entered her old room.

An instant later she extinguished the lamp, crept from the room, and crouched low at the railing where she could keep a vigilant watch over Zachary Kellogg's movements.

Five

Eugenia watched through the stair posts until her eyes grew heavy. Zachary Kellogg had not proved cooperative at all. Either he had nothing to hide, or he was much more clever than she had given him credit. All the man had done was to open a tin from the kitchen, then settle into a chair before the fire, prop his feet up on her father's hassock, and devour the tin's contents with a fork.

Eugenia started to nod off until she heard the thud of his boots against the hardwood floor. Immediately she was wide awake. Zachary Kellogg had left the chair and was bent over her father's desk, rummaging through the drawers. Not long afterwards, he removed a sheaf of papers.

She got up to confront him, but when she saw him tuck the material into a loose stone in the hearth, she tiptoed back to her room. She must have interrupted an earlier search if he knew of the loose stone.

She felt a strange roiling sensation in the pit of her stomach. It was the heaviness of disappointment. He was indeed hiding something after all. For some reason, the proof of her suspicions did not give her satisfaction.

She stripped off her skirts and slipped into a plain cotton nightgown from the armoire. Then she cleared off the dolls cluttering her quilted spread. Remembering the knife she had used as a girl to whittle with her father, Eugenia got it out of a drawer and slipped it under her pillow before she climbed into bed. She felt more secure now that she had some protection.

She grabbed a book off the night table and leaned back against the pillows, fully intent on waiting until the man retired for the night before sneaking downstairs and retrieving the papers.

It seemed an eternity before Eugenia heard the creak of the stairs under his weight. She waited for the click of the bedroom door next to hers, then crept to the armoire, snatched out a wrapper and left her room.

She had not descended more than three steps when a deep baritone assaulted her.

"Anything I can get for you, Miss Whalen?" Zach asked, holding a lamp high overhead.

Eugenia pivoted around. Her breath caught at the sight of his brazen masculinity. He had removed his shirt; his bronzed chest displayed a curling forest thick with dark hairs tapering downward past a slender waist. His belt was unbuckled, the top button of his trousers undone, and he was barefoot.

She swallowed at the entrancing sight of raw maleness he represented and forced her attention back to his unsmiling face. "No. I am quite capable of taking care of myself." He just stood there, making her feel as if she owed him a fabricated explanation. "Since I missed supper tonight, I thought I would help myself to a midnight snack."

He joined her on the stair. "What kind of a host would I be if I forced you to go down these stairs in the dark. Why, who knows, you could fall and break your neck."

At the silken phrase, she shot him a troubled glance, then quickly recovered herself. Was that a veiled threat that she could end up like her father?

"I could just slide down the banister and save you the trouble." *Of breaking my neck,* she silently added.

"Nonsense. There's no one below to catch you, and I wouldn't want you to land on that hard floor and possibly injure yourself." His gaze momentarily shifted to her buttocks.

Eugenia rolled her eyes in dismay over his blatant perusal. But she was curious over the strange undertow to his words. And she cursed her earlier antics. "I shall take the lamp then."

He held it high out of reach. "I wouldn't think of it."

To her chagrin, Zachary Kellogg cradled her elbow. His hold was firm and warm. She steeled herself, wondering if he were going to give her a shove. But his fingers were strangely reassuring as he merely escorted her down the stairs and into the kitchen.

Eugenia grabbed some dried apples and quickly escaped back to her room. She sat propped against her pillows, munching on the leathery fruit, cursing Zachary Kellogg, and wondering about their strange encounter and the troubling feelings his touch had drawn from her.

For hours afterwards she imagined all sorts of noises; the wind blew the branches outside her window against the side of the house, and she jumped, imagining that since he'd missed his chance to push her down the stairs, he could be trying to get in through the window. The house creaked, and she was sure he was up prowling.

Feeling silly over such childish thoughts, since had he wanted her out of the way, he would have already seen to it, Eugenia finally threw the covers over her head and tried to get some sleep. There would be time in the morning to recover those papers.

Eugenia had not been asleep for more than an hour when she suddenly awoke. The hairs were standing straight up on the back of her neck. She sat up to the sudden bright flash of lightning only to find Zachary Kellogg silhouetted against the window, standing over her.

Shaking, but determined not to lose control, Eugenia carefully slipped her hand under the pillow and groped for the knife.

"What are you doing in my room?" she demanded, stretching under the pillow until her fingertips felt the cold, hard steel of the blade.

He lit the lamp and turned it up high until warm yellow light filled the room. "Here, let me help you."

He bent over, and Eugenia pulled the knife on

him. "Get back," she ordered, brandishing it at him.

He brought his palms up and stepped back. "That must have been some dream. Do you usually sleep with a knife under your pillow?"

"Only when there are strange men in my house. Now, what are you doing in here?"

"You cried out," he said softly, concern warming his eyes. "I only came in to see if you needed help." Eugenia looked down at the knife held in her hand and felt a trifle foolish. She was allowing her imagination to get the better of her.

She had been dreaming that she was trying to reach her father, calling out to him, but he just kept moving away from her. Tears threatened to fill her eyes, but she reminded herself that she would not allow herself to grieve until after her father's murderer was brought to justice—not before.

"I am fine now, so you can leave."

"You sure?"

"Yes."

"Good. Then you won't need this," he said, disarming her and taking charge of the knife before Eugenia could protest.

It amazed her how easily he had been able to render her defenseless. And she realized that a knife was of little protection.

Tomorrow she would take suitable action!

To her further surprise, he sat down on the edge of the bed and smoothed a spill of hair off her face. His fingers were warm, and his ministrations tender and nonthreatening, not at all as she would

59

expect a murderer's to be. Each stroke was strangely reassuring, and left a splendid liquid warmth glowing deep within her, which only served to further unsettle her.

She grabbed his hand to push it away before her resolve to learn what he was about weakened, and he closed his fingers around hers. His calloused grasp was firm, intimate, and stirring.

"Eugenia, trust me, I'm not your enemy," he said softly. "Get a good night's rest, and we'll resolve the house issue in the morning." Zach tucked the blanket up around her neck and touched her cheek with the back of his fingers. Then he further mystified her; he slipped the knife back under her pillow before he extinguished the lamp and left.

In the darkened room, Eugenia wiped at the tears threatening to puddle her eyes and murmured with a perplexed sigh, "Trust you? How can I? Nothing will ever be resolved until I see justice done."

Morning dawned cool and misty gray. The light of day reaffirmed Eugenia's weakening resolve of the night before. She was not going to waver toward Zachary Kellogg despite the tender way he had attempted to endear himself toward her. He was merely trying to throw her off balance with a facade, she determined.

She hurriedly dressed in a heavy woolen skirt and longsleeved blouse which buttoned up to her throat. Shoes in hand, she crept from her room, down the stairs, and into the parlor to find out what he was trying to hide.

There was little left but a few glowing embers from the fire when she plunked down on the hearth. She ran her fingers along the rough stones until she came to the one from which the mortar had been scratched away.

Just as she was about to remove the loose stone she heard a noise and glanced up. Zachary Kellogg entered the parlor, carrying an arm load of wood.

Eugenia had to keep herself from panicking. She took a deep breath. "Good morning," she said and quickly dropped her hands into her lap.

"Morning." Zach dumped the wood into the firebox. "Cold?"

"Ah . . . no, I am fine."

"Then why are you practically sitting on top of the fire?"

She tried to appear a little coy. "Actually, I was a little chilled," she said and rubbed her hands together as she slid into her shoes.

"In that case, if you'll allow me, I'll put more wood on the fire to get it going again."

She got up and moved away from the fireplace, disappointed that she had been foiled. "Shouldn't we be going to Mr. Washer's shop?"

"I made breakfast."

Eugenia's eyes trailed in the direction of the dining room. The table was set with her mother's favorite gold-rimmed china and silver. Eggs, bacon and potatoes adorned the plates, and cranberry juice glistened a rich wine-color in the crystal stemware Eugenia's mother had carefully brought around the Horn when her parents had left Massachusetts, ultimately to settle in Washington Territory.

"It seems you have gone to a great deal of trouble for nothing, Mr. Kellogg. I rarely indulge in breakfast."

Zach's smile was spare. "You look more like you're too frightened to eat. What's the matter, Miss Whalen, are you afraid I might be trying to poison you?"

Her eyes went wide at his comment, but she refused to fall victim to it. "Nonsense. I am merely anxious to get to Mr. Washer's and settle the issue of my family home."

"As you please. But since we've spent the night together, don't you think you could manage to refer to me as Zach?" The moment the words were out, Zach could have bitten his tongue. He needed the meddlesome young woman out of the way, and all he was doing was encouraging her.

Just to let her know that he knew what she had been up to when he entered carrying the firewood, Zach made a big display of taking the papers he had stashed behind the stone from his shirt pocket, brushing off a big piece of soot, and slipping them into his duster pocket.

Eugenia watched his blatant actions with dismay. He had made a capital production out of letting her know that he was aware that she had been after those papers. Well, if he thought he had defeated her, he was wrong!

She granted him a radiant smile. "I would be

delighted to call you Zach, but only if you will agree to refer to me as Eugenia."

Her brilliant smile created a strange roiling sensation in Zach's gut. Women rarely affected him one way or another anymore since his wife had run off with that visiting, wealthy Russian. He considered himself jaded where the fairer sex was concerned. And he was not going to let this particular well-endowed young woman, of all the females available, affect him! She would just get in his way.

"I'll get your coat."

"Since it is so muddy outside, why don't you hitch up the carriage while I clear the table?"

"Pity to let a hearty breakfast go to waste, but if you insist." Zach shrugged and left the house, muttering that he had not ridden in a damn carriage for years.

The moment Eugenia heard the door slam, she checked the fireplace to ascertain that the actual papers were in reality in his possession. He had made a grand production with the deliberation he'd displayed when he'd tucked them into his pocket, just to apprise her that he knew for what she had been searching.

As she cleared away the dishes, popping bits of savory bacon into her mouth as she went, she wondered why he had intentionally wanted her to know what he'd done.

She was still mulling everything over when he helped her into the carriage. "Where is Daddy's horse?"

"Heard it was sold."

She gave a wan nod. Her father's partners must

not have wasted a moment claiming anything of value. She forced herself to put the animal's loss from her mind when he climbed in next to her.

If she'd been in a different frame of mind, she would have laughed at the momentary surprised expression on his face when she snuggled up close to him.

"What is the matter, Zach, don't you share the warmth where you come from? We always have here on the peninsula."

Zach's brow shoved up. She was definitely up to something; he could see it in her green eyes. But, hell, who was he not to take advantage of what was offered him? He slipped an arm around her.

"I think I'm going to like your custom," he said and snapped the reins over the piebald's rump.

For all that she knew about Mr. Zachary Kellogg, she felt strangely secure and comfortable cosseted in his arms again as the carriage rocked over the rutted road leading east, crossing the short distance to the corner of Beach Road.

Trying to keep her mind on what she was about, and away from the sensations rippling through her, Eugenia chattered on at length about the history of the peninsula to help divert his attention while she clandestinely slipped her hand into his coat pocket.

"Oysterville was once a gathering place for Indians who dried the oysters here. Then only a little over twenty years ago two men—I.A. Clark and R. H. Espy—got lost in one of our famous fogs, and the Indians rescued them from the bay.

"At first they were partners in the piling business, but after camping on the peninsula, they found the oysters were profitable on this side of the bay and took out claims at Oysterville. They founded our town—"

"And the rest is history, right?" Zach supplied.

Fighting back a triumphant grin that she had managed to take possession of the papers so easily from him without his knowledge, Eugenia sat back and slipped them into her reticule. "Right, Zach. The rest is history."

By the time they reached the casket shop, Eugenia was sure he wouldn't stand a chance of swindling her out of her family home. They entered the spacious building, and she went directly toward Mr. Washer's desk, keeping her eyes purposely averted from the wooden boxes.

Cash in hand, Mrs. Garrett's eyes widened momentarily before she nodded in greeting and hurried from the shop. Eugenia watched the dear old widow for a moment, then returned her attention to Mr. Washer, with his fuzzy red hair. He looked like a scarecrow in a vest sitting stiffly behind his desk. The sheriff was standing nearby, talking to one of the craftsmen, and she hailed him over as well.

Once they had taken care of the greetings and introductions, and Eugenia accepted their condolences, she announced, "Mr. Washer, Sheriff Dollard, I am so glad you are both here. Mr. Kellogg is under the mistaken belief that he owns my family home . . ."

Zach clasped his arms over his chest and waited for Eugenia to finish with her story. Once this business had been taken care of, he could get on with doing what had to be done.

". . . so you see, I know there must be some dreadful mistake—"

"Miss Eugenia," Sheriff Dollard interrupted. "What's all this got to do with me?"

Eugenia turned a frown on the lanky sheriff. His reputation for inaction was legendary on the peninsula, and it was apparent he was going to continue the long-established tradition. "It concerns you because Mr. Kellogg is trying to hide something that may have to do with my father's murder."

All eyes flashed in Eugenia's direction, and she suddenly felt like a fish about to be filleted.

Sheriff Dollard cleared his throat as Zach seated himself in a chair in front of Washer's desk and complacently crossed his legs. Washer uneasily squirmed in his seat.

"Miss Eugenia, that's a mighty strong accusation. I hope you got something to back up them words," the sheriff blustered.

Eugenia's chin came up defiantly. "I most certainly do."

"Well then, young lady," interjected Morton Washer, who was now twirling the pen in the inkwell before him, "you had better present us with whatever you have, or Mr. Kellogg may not take so kindly toward you in the future. You have leveled a pretty serious charge against him."

It was a strange comment coming from the old family friend, but Eugenia was not about to be daunted. She snapped her reticule open and dipped her hand into the large carpet bag. When she did not immediately locate the filched papers, she looked up at the expectantly waiting men and forced a weak smile. "The evidence is in my bag."

"Then you had better produce whatever you're talking about because I have a business to run," Zach said in a bored voice, indicating his growing impatience.

Eugenia frowned at Zach and dumped the contents of the bag out onto the desk. She picked through the numerous items, growing desperate. "The papers were here. I put them in my reticule myself."

Zach grinned. "Well, they certainly don't seem to be here now."

"If they ever were," Washer supplied. Then he turned a condescending frown on Eugenia. "Eugenia, I know how upset you must have been to learn that Mr. Kellogg now owns your family's home and business. But you are going to have to accept that selling the home as part of the package was financially necessary in order to settle your father's accounts. I am afraid that after your father's debts were paid there wasn't any money left."

Shock and dismay registered on Eugenia's face before Washer continued. "I am sorry to be the bearer of such sorry news, Eugenia. But coming in here with some tall tale and trying to pull some underhanded trick is not going to salvage your father's depleted estate. So I suggest you offer your apologies to Mr. Kellogg and try to pick up the pieces of your life elsewhere."

Eugenia bit her lip and glared at Zach Kellogg. The disgusting man had outwitted her this time.

She must not have been as clever as she thought she had been. He must have been aware of her sleight of hand and stolen the papers back.

Nevertheless, she was not going to apologize, much less admit defeat!

Six

Eugenia stormed out of Mr. Washer's shop, she was so shocked, embarrassed and angry with herself. Somehow that man had managed to outsmart her. But she could hardly believe that Mr. Washer and the sheriff had taken Zachary Kellogg's side—a stranger—let alone sell her family home and even the horse. Ignoring the light rain that had begun to fall, she headed down the street toward Len Sweeney's house to confront him for selling the business in such haste without contacting her.

"Eugenia," Zach called out. He had to run to catch up with her. He almost had to laugh to himself. He had not run after any female, under any circumstances, since he was a schoolboy. In his life, the women did the running after.

Against her better judgment, Eugenia stopped in the doorway of the mercantile and waited for him. "What do you want?"

She looked so delicate, so fragile, so helpless, so vulnerable standing in the gray rain that Zach experienced a rare stab of guilt. "You should've known better, Eugenia," he said.

"About what? Those papers you stole from my father's desk?"

His expression never wavered when he said, "I don't know what you're talking about."

"Don't you? I took them from you in the carriage, and then somehow in turn you managed to take them back without my knowledge, making me look very foolish inside Mr. Washer's shop."

Zach's brow shoved up in mounting frustration. Damn meddling female. "Eugenia, you made yourself look foolish," he said, careful to avoid further mention of the papers.

"So you already said." Exasperation was threatening to get the better of Eugenia when three men holding umbrellas boldly stopped to listen to their conversation. "If you have nothing else to add, I shall take my leave. Now, if you will excuse me?"

She turned to leave, but Zach grabbed her arm. For some foolish reason he could not just let her walk away from him. "Eugenia, if you need any financial assistance until you can make other living arrangements—"

"Other living arrangements!" The outrage in her voice caused it to go up an octave. "You just took away everything my father and I ever worked for, and now you offer your financial aid?

"I do not know what you are trying to do, Mr. Zachary Kellogg, but my father's oyster business was highly profitable when I left for California last spring. Then suddenly my aunt receives a letter stating that my father is in financial trouble; I return to find him murdered, his business and home sold at auction, and I am left a penniless pauper.

"And on top of it all, some stranger—namely you—purchased the business, getting my family home in the bargain, for barely enough to cover what my father owed the creditors.

"Well, I will have you know I find that inconceivable, not to mention terribly suspicious. Highly. And I do not intend to stand meekly by and allow everything my father worked for go to some thieving—and God only knows what else—stranger."

He released her arm, and she stepped from under the cover of the store, but Zach kept pace with her. He used his duster as an umbrella to shelter them. "You're quite a spitfire. But you don't know what you're doing. Take my advice and just leave it be, Eugenia, before you get yourself hurt."

She stopped and turned flashing eyes on him, hissing, "Is that a threat?"

Zach took a deep breath and swallowed his frustration over her prying. "Suppose some might interpret it that way."

Eugenia did not retort. She merely started to move off again, Zach still at her side. They walked toward one of the saloons where the sailors off the schooners were known to haunt.

Eugenia stopped in front of the Salty Dog Tavern before she swung on him. "I shall remember your *advice.*"

"He botherin' you, Miss Eugenia?" the burly sailor who had rowed her from her father's schooner stopped and asked.

Eugenia raised her chin, silently daring Zach to

dispute what she was about to say. "The *gentleman* was just leaving, thank you."

Zach stared at the sailor, gauging his mettle. Hell, Zach could take on the entire navy, that woman got him so riled. But he was better off with her out of the way. He gave a curt nod.

"Just remember my offer and what I said, Eugenia." With that Zach turned on his heel and strode away.

"You okay?" the young sailor asked, concern mirrored in his eyes.

"I will be once you take me back to my father's ship."

The young sailor's hopeful face fell, and his brow drew into a troubled line. "Sorry, Miss Eugenia. I thought you knew. Captain Derrick and the rest of the crew's on their way back to California to return your cousin home before your aunt and uncle come after the both of you."

Eugenia's lips tightened in dismay. Another momentary defeat in what seemed to be a mounting number. Then she relaxed as she thought better of it. The schooner was the only asset left that all the town's vultures seemed to have overlooked. At least it was out of Zachary Kellogg's reach for the time being.

She thanked the young man, then made her way to Len Sweeney's fancy home, only to learn that he was across the bay at Bruceport on business.

Without funds or prospects, Eugenia went to the Widow Garrett's. But when the dear old widow answered the door, Eugenia could hear the joyous sounds of a roomful of children romping in the parlor. She could not visit her problems on the widow now.

Ruth's face froze for an instant before she seemed to catch herself. She clasped her hands in front of her and leaned forward expectantly. "This is an unexpected visit."

"I did not realize you had company."

"An entire houseful." She shot a quick glance behind her before moving out on to the porch. "My daughter and her children are visiting from Astoria. W-would you care to come inside? You must be chilled to the bone standing out here in this weather."

"No, no, I'm fine," Eugenia hedged. She could not intrude on the Widow Garrett's family. Since her son-in-law had moved his family to Astoria, Eugenia knew the old dear saw them too infrequently, and by the tone in her voice Eugenia was sure the widow was being polite.

Ruth crinkled a questioning brow. "Why did you come?"

"I seemed to have misplaced my gloves, and I was wondering if perchance I left them here yesterday," Eugenia improvised.

"I did not find anything. But I don't recall you wearing gloves when you were here."

"Well, thank you, Mrs. Garrett, I'll let you get back to your family."

Eugenia stepped off the porch. "Are you sure you won't come in and join us?"

Eugenia shook her head and walked back toward town, careful to avoid her family home.

Her whole world had fallen apart, and now, on

top of everything else, she had nowhere to go. As she briskly walked along the muddy road, she counted the few coins Captain Derrick had slipped into her bag. Enough for a couple night's lodging at the Stevens Hotel . . . or a gun.

She was still considering what she should do when she passed the mercantile and noticed the silver-plated pistol in the window.

Her mind made up, Eugenia entered the store.

The bell above the door jangled, and the aproned shopkeeper looked up from the potbellied stove where he was warming his hands.

"Miss Eugenia, ah . . . you're back," he said awkwardly, his handlebar mustache twitching.

"Yes, Mr. Buellen, I am back. I arrived yesterday."

"Ah, I'm sorry 'bout your pa and all. You must be full of misery. If there's anything the wife and I can do, you just give a holler."

"Thank you, Mr. Buellen. As a matter of fact, there is something you can do for me."

He wiped his hands on his apron and stepped behind the counter in preparation for getting her a few female items. "Name it, little lady."

"I want to see that gun you have for sale in the window."

"But, Miss Eugenia, you're a female lady," he sputtered, although he did not quite remember her in terms of being a lady. "Can't I show you something . . . ah, more to a lady's tastes?"

Eugenia raised her chin. "Mr. Buellen, if you cannot bring yourself to help me fill my order, I shall be forced to pay a visit to one of your competitors who will."

Buellen frowned, but he was first and foremost a businessman. He was not going to miss out on a sale to any of his competitors; it was not smart business. He retrieved the gun from the window and laid it on the counter. "Will you be needin' ammunition?"

"Yes. A box. And will you show me how to load it as well?"

Buellen's head snapped up in surprise, but he dutifully did what he had to do to make the sale. Shaking his head, he watched the young woman drop the gun in her reticule and leave his store. "Sorry state of affairs this world is comin' to when one of the fairer sex buys a gun," he said to himself and went into the back room.

Eugenia stepped from the store, only to come face to face with Zachary Kellogg. "What are you doing, following me?"

"Somebody's got to. What were you doing in there buying a gun, Eugenia?" She tried to move around him, but he blocked her exit. "You might as well tell me because I'm not going to let you go until you do."

"Oh, all right," she hissed out in exasperation. "I bought it so I could kill you."

He looked so stunned for a moment that Eugenia almost wanted to laugh out loud. At least he stepped aside and allowed her to pass. But to her further annoyance, he started walking along the boardwalk with her.

"What do you think you are doing now?" she demanded. "Testing fate?"

"If you plan to kill me, I might as well teach you how to shoot properly so you don't miss a vital organ and merely maim me or something."

She was not amused by his attempt at humor. But, she had to admit, he did have a point. "How do you know I don't know how to use it?"

"I've seen you wield a knife, remember?" He directed her to the waiting carriage and helped her in without resistance. "Sit back and enjoy the scenery. We'll head on out to the point in short order, then you can properly learn how to use your latest acquisition."

Patches of blue sky periodically peeked through the clouds by the time they were out of town, and for the rest of the afternoon Zach patiently set up targets while Eugenia shot everything from nearby branches to the hat from Zach's head.

"After that crazy stunt, I think that you've had enough practice," he said, plucking his aerated hat from the sandy beach strewn with silver driftwood.

"I think I know enough now," Eugenia crowed, amused with her efforts.

"Enough to kill some poor hapless soul, as long as he lays down on the ground." To her grunt he added, "Your aim's a little off."

"I got your hat, didn't I?"

He merely shook his head and pushed the ruined hat back on his forehead. He didn't have the heart to mention that she was supposed to be aiming at the rag he had tossed up on the above limb.

"Where to?" he asked once they were settled back in the carriage.

"What do you mean?"

"Where shall I drop you?" When she did not answer, he clarified, "Where're you staying?"

Eugenia looked over at the man. Although she was convinced that he was somehow mixed up in her father's death, her mind could not relinquish the thought that he seemed to keep coming to her rescue; that hardly seemed like something a murderer would do. She did not want to explore the feelings he had managed to so easily arouse within her.

Then a deflating thought struck her: She really did not have anywhere to go.

Captain Derrick had left with the schooner, Len Sweeney was out of town, the Widow Garrett had company, and she had spent all her money on the gun. She could not impose on any of the oystermen and their families, although they would undoubtedly welcome her. No. If she were going to fulfill her mission, there was only one logical place for her to stay, she decided.

"I am staying with you."

"Me!" He practically choked.

"Yes. You did offer your assistance, remember?"

His brow shoved up. "Only too well."

"Since you are responsible for putting me out of my own home, and I have nowhere else to go, the least you can do is put me up for a few days until I can make other more agreeable arrangements."

"Or until you can go through all my things, right?" he muttered. "And I was not responsible for you being homeless. I merely bought what was for sale."

Eugenia just cast him a benign smile and glanced out toward the ocean. The waves were angrily pounding the beach, and the wind threatened to topple the carriage by the time they reached the sanctuary of the huge cedar trees. And like the waves, she wished she could pound something.

Zach did not say a word for some time, he was so frustrated with himself. He had offered assistance, but he had never meant for that help to include living under the same roof with the young woman.

Finally, he turned his head toward her. She had an inviting profile. Deep-set green eyes surrounded by wispy long lashes, a tiny nose that turned up on the end, lips that were so full they begged to be kissed. He caught himself at that arousing thought.

Women were the cause of men making too many mistakes while engaged in dangerous pursuits. And the one at his side had "Extreme Danger—Keep Out" stenciled all over her.

"Eugenia, why don't I put you up at one of the hotels in town?"

So he definitely was hiding something at her family home. Why else would he offer to spend his own money when she could just as well sleep in the same room she had slept in last night?

"Thank you, but I would not think of it," she replied with sugared sweetness.

Her voice dripped with enough honey to stick some poor bee to a flower, he thought sourly. "I insist."

"And I must refuse. No."

"You'll be more comfortable at a hotel."

"How could I be more comfortable in a strange hotel than I would be in my own bed in the home where I grew up? Furthermore, I may never be able to repay you."

His brow shoved up again in growing frustration. "You don't have to repay me. I'll pay you to stay there." That should settle the matter, he concluded. Most women were greedy, willing to take a man's money.

"Certainly not!" Her voice was tinged with outrage. "I shall not be kept like some common . . . bird of passage."

"Bird of passage?"

Her spine stiffened. "That is what soiled doves are known as around here."

"Oh, for heaven sake, Eugenia. I wouldn't be keeping you like some whore."

"What would you call paying some female to live in a hotel? More to the point, what would the good citizens of Oysterville call it? No. It simply will not do. I am going to stay in my old family home."

"Well, what would you call living under the same roof with me, a suspicious stranger?" he shot back. A calculating grin spread across those disgustingly inviting full lips of hers, and Zach knew he was about to lose this round. And he was troubled that deep inside he subconsciously wanted to lose this one.

"You could go to the hotel. That way I would not be made to feel less than a lady being kept by some stranger, the good citizens of Oysterville would not have anything to gossip about, and you would not be living under the same roof with me."

Zach's hands tightened around the reins into a strangle hold, reaffirming his resolve. At that moment, if he weren't a territorial marshal working undercover on a case, the thought of wringing Miss Eugenia Whalen's beautiful long neck would be nearly impossible to resist.

Seven

The triumph that Eugenia felt for having bested Zach with reasoning he could not dispute was short-lived. He drew the carriage up to the gate outside her family home. He helped her alight from the carriage, and she bid him farewell, suggesting he try the Stevens Hotel. But he grinned and recommended that she make herself comfortable in the parlor; he would join her as soon as he saw to his horse and carriage.

Stewing over the nerve of his commanding attitude, Eugenia trudged into the house and stopped, slapping a hand over her mouth.

The house was in total disarray! In shock, she walked through the rooms. Drawers were open, their contents spilled onto the floor. Pillows were shredded, bedding and mattresses overturned. Pictures had been stripped from the walls and ripped from their frames. Even rugs had not escaped.

Valiantly holding back tears, Eugenia was bent over trying to piece back together her father's daguerreotype when Zach entered the house.

"What the hell!" he said, looking around at the mess. He sighted Eugenia at the top of the stairs and pounded up the steps. "Eugenia?"

Her fingers were trembling as she gathered up the torn photo. She glanced up at him, her haunted eyes filled with unspent grief. He had to hold himself back from gathering her into his arms and offering her comfort.

"Who could have done this?"

"Probably some no-account looking for anything of value to sell," he said in an offhanded manner. But silently he had his doubts. Looked more like someone had been searching for something.

"Or maybe it was someone who was trying to make a point."

His brow shoved up. "Such as?"

"That you would be better off in a hotel."

"Nice try. But I'm afraid it isn't going to work."

"You are not accusing me, are you?" she said, aghast at such an implication.

"No," he said softly. His heart started to go out to her again, but he quickly caught himself.

"But why did they have to destroy my father's photo?" she asked in a small, quivering voice.

"There's no accounting for the cruel whims of some folks, Eugenia." He bent down and began to help her retrieve the scattered pieces.

"I do not need your help," she said proudly, swallowing back the urge to cry. "This is my family home, and I shall tidy it up while you go report this dreadful incident to the sheriff."

"As you wish. But this doesn't change the little talk we're going to have when I return."

She glared up at him. "I shall be waiting with bated breath."

She was sitting, straight-backed, rigid, in her father's favorite striped chair, gazing out the window at the verdant scenery when he rejoined her. He plunked down on the sofa, put his feet up on the hassock and clasped his arms behind his neck. He looked much too comfortable and already settled in to Eugenia when she drew her gaze from the window to rest it on him.

"My dear Eugenia, I'm so glad to see you were able to perform the miracle of returning everything to its proper place in record time, and now you're seated and waiting for me."

"It is what you directed," she said with distaste. She never had been one to follow directives. Yet inside she experienced a strange prick when he used the term *dear* in addressing her. His voice was rich and full bodied, filled with an undefinable undercurrent.

"Ah, yes, so it is, just as I directed. Incidentally, the sheriff said he'd check around."

"No doubt he will make it his top priority," she said sarcastically, familiar with the sheriff's uncanny ability to hide his head in the sand. "Nothing appears to be missing."

"Glad to hear it."

She slid to the edge of her seat, growing impatiently curious with the apparent cat-and-mouse game he was playing at her expense. "Well, what it is you have to say?"

"On my way back from town, I gave our living arrangements a lot more thought and have reached a decision."

She raised her chin, not liking the gleam in his icy blue eyes. "An equitable one, I am sure."

"I'm sure," he echoed with silver-tongued efficiency. "I have no intention of spending my time in a hotel when I can be right at home here. And, besides, I couldn't possibly consider leaving you here alone now. That person or persons who broke in might return."

She stiffened, and his dark mood improved noticeably. She was not going to like what he was about to propose. But it should drive her to a hotel where she belonged.

"I offered to help you out, and God help me, I'll stick by my word. But I have absolutely no intention of giving up my creature comforts.

"And, since I certainly wouldn't want you to feel like some common kept woman, as you so eloquently put it earlier, I'm prepared to pay you to work for me as my housekeeper until you can afford to provide your own accommodations." He glanced around the room. "And from the excellent job you did straightening up, I won't even require references."

"References!" Incredulous, Eugenia's eyes rounded into huge white circles, and she slapped a beleaguered hand to her chest. "You expect *me* to keep house for *you*?"

"You would be paid the going rate, of course."

Her lips puckered in disdain. "Of course. How very generous you are."

He smiled at that. "It's the least I can do."

"The very least, naturally," she muttered.

"Of course, if you would rather go to a hotel, my offer to provide financial assistance is still open," he said, certain, she would run out of the house and get out of his hair so he could do his job.

"Your generosity is nearly overwhelming," she said sarcastically.

He was on a roll. It was apparent she was wavering in her insistence to remain in the house with him. She would be gone by nightfall, he thought with empty satisfaction. An idea to further assist her in making up her mind came to him.

"And to show you just how very generous I can be, I'm going to have you wear a uniform so you won't ruin any of your own clothes . . . considering how critical your financial state is."

"A uniform!" she choked, envisioning herself in some stiffly starched maid's habit.

"Black and white, I think would be nice, with one of those frilly little white caps to protect your hair, of course." Her forced grin almost showed her teeth, she was obviously so angry, and it served to make him take the conversation one step further.

"And just to show you how magnanimous I can be, rather than walking, you may use my horse and take the carriage into town first thing in the morning to make your purchases, so you will be properly attired without further delay."

She was not going to give him the satisfaction of watching her retreat in defeat so easily. "I do hope you will give me time to consider your *generous* proposition."

His brow shoved up the way she had come to anticipate during such exasperating discussions. "Proposition, an interesting selection of words, Eugenia," he said with a speculative smile. "Just to show you how charitable I can be, I'll give you 'til morning to give me your answer."

"No doubt you are known far and wide for your generosity," she spat through clenched teeth.

"Among other things." He grinned back with a wink.

All through the hasty supper she had furiously tossed together, and the remainder of the unpleasant evening, Eugenia silently fumed.

A maid. A house servant. Little more than a slave in her family's own home.

In order to remain in her own home and keep watch over Zachary Kellogg's movements, she would have to be a hireling to the very man who may well have murdered her father and stolen his business.

She thought about it a little longer, mulled it over in detail, then decided that perhaps playing the role of a domestic in order to expose Zachary Kellogg would not be too distasteful after all, as long as it served her purposes—except Eugenia never had been one to take the slightest interest in housework or any of the other banal domestic chores relegated to the female population in the guise of it being woman's work.

Other than enjoying cooking, she loved the great outdoors, the trees, the sea, working in the oyster beds, studying the marine life, sailing her father's schooner. Her mother even had teased her as a child, laughing that Eugenia should have been born a male, her interests were so far removed from the usual female pursuits. And now, here she was with little choice except to don some silly housemaid's costume.

When Eugenia came down the stairs in the morning, Zach was already up. He had spent the last two hours searching through Woodward Whalen's remaining papers, which had been locked away out of reach of whomever had rifled through the house, without turning up any additional intelligence.

When Whalen had written, requesting that a territorial marshall be sent to investigate the trouble he was having, he had not provided more than sketchy information.

Unfortunately, Zach had arrived the day after Whalen had been murdered. Whatever proof Whalen had stated in his letter that he had in his possession, he had hidden it away well because it had been apparent from the way the house had been torn apart that whoever had searched hadn't found what he had been looking for.

"I trust you did not find whatever you were looking for?" she said in much too cheery a voice.

Her nonchalant attitude made his fingers itch to encircle that beautiful creamy neck of hers and squeeze. The thought of placing his fingers on her flesh heightened the sensitivity in his fingertips and lent another response in his chest, a tightening. He ignored the heightening sensations. He was not going to let her get to him.

He casually leaned against the desk. "I was merely finishing the job of cleaning up and making room for my own things, if you must know."

She did not believe him for an instant. Someone had practically torn the house apart yesterday, and today she found Zach Kellogg going through her father's papers again. "I thought cleaning up was supposed to be my job."

Nonplussed, he grinned. "So you've decided to take me up on my offer?"

She returned the disgusting grin, although smiling at the handsome devil was the last thing on her mind. "I am going to be the best cook and most thorough housemaid you have ever employed."

His brow shoved up. "Undoubtedly."

They settled for the coffee Zach had perking on the stove for breakfast. Afterwards Zach hitched up his horse and drove her into town. He stopped outside the mercantile and handed her a lengthy list of supplies and errands he wanted accomplished, then turned over the reins.

"Where do you think you are going?" she queried and tucked the list into her skirt pocket without glancing at it. She did not want to let him out of her sight if she could help it.

"The weather looks like it's going to cooperate today, and I have an oyster business to get back on its feet, if you have forgotten, Eugenia. I'll be heading out to the oyster beds."

"I shall accompany you. I know all about the oyster business, and I can be of help."

"I know everything I need to about the oyster business. Furthermore, you have shopping to do before you start cleaning my house. Oh, and pick me up a new hat, same color, but one without bullet holes in it."

With his piece said, Zach gave her a wink, turned on his heel, and walked away before she could think up a retort or another harebrained excuse not to let him out of her sight. However, Zach could not stop himself from looking back over his shoulder.

Despite her frown, she looked most appealing even in that plain calico she was wearing. A moment of regret that he could not sweep her away for an afternoon alone on a deserted, windswept beach and feed her wild, fresh-picked raspberries assailed his mind in a most enticing vision.

Eugenia was not about to spend the day meekly hunting a similar hat and cleaning the house. Curious. He was heading inland, not toward the oyster beds. Without another moment's hesitation, she ignored convention, jumped from the carriage, lifted her skirts and hurried after him.

When she caught up with him, he grumbled, "What're you doing here? Didn't I give you enough to keep you busy today?"

As usual, she knew he had to be up to something, so she decided to ignore his rude remark and test him. "I was just wondering if you are heading toward the whack?"

His face went blank for an instant before it became hooded, and she knew she had him. She would bet her life that he was no oysterman. Just to reinforce her suspicion, she added, "Aren't you going to take the plunger?"

Scratch the fact that he'd thought she looked appealing in that calico. She would definitely look much better wearing a muzzle!

The meddlesome young woman had all the instincts of a resolute bloodhound. She knew he didn't have the foggiest notion what she was talking about, damn her!

"Eugenia, you take care of my home, and I'll take care of my business," he bluffed.

She narrowed her eyes. "I do not know why you bought my father's business, but you do not know the first thing about the oyster business. If you did, and were going where you said you were, you would be heading out into the bay, to your whack—the tract of ground where the oysters you own are."

His brow shoved up. "And the plunger?"

Triumph over her suspicions made her grin. "The plunger is a twenty-foot sailboat used for carrying loads of oysters."

"Thank you for the basic lesson on the oyster business. I have no doubt you're a variable wealth of information. But one does not have to know everything about a business to be interested in sharing in its profits, Eugenia.

"And as far as where I was headed, I need not account to my housekeeper for my every step. So, unless you plan to find yourself without a roof over your head or a job, I suggest you get busy and start making yourself useful before I no longer need you."

Feeling properly chastised by an obvious expert, not to mention stinging over being referred to as his housekeeper, Eugenia glared at Zach's back as he swung on his heel and strode down the street. Then she started to worry over what he had meant by "before I no longer need you." Could that be what had happened to her father?

Not one to remain daunted for long, she decided to follow him at a secure distance. It was much safer to spy on him without his knowledge than with it. And he would go about his business—as he called it—freely if he did not think he was being observed.

Eugenia followed Zach inland, past a swamp to a tall stand of pines about halfway between the weather beach and Oysterville on the bay side. He met a tall man wearing a hat slung low over his forehead and a duster. Pity he had his back to her, or she might have been able to get a better description.

She dared not try to move closer to overhear what they were saying. She could not take the chance of being discovered. Remaining hidden behind a tree, a strange sense of distress slumped her shoulders. For some nagging reason, deep down she had half hoped that she was wrong about Zachary Kellogg.

Steeling herself against an unfamiliar sensation of disappointment, Eugenia stood behind the huge pine tree and observed the two men a little longer. Zach exchanged the sheaf of papers he had taken from her father's desk for a brown envelope. When the two men shook hands, Eugenia left her position and quickly retraced her steps.

Eugenia went straight to the sheriff's office to

report what she had witnessed, but the man had tacked a poorly scribbled note to his door stating that he had business down in Ilwaco and would return late in the day or the next day.

Where was the law when she needed it? Sheriff Dollard never had been much use, the bungling idiot, she thought angrily. She would just have to proceed as she had been—without the sheriff's help.

Eugenia retrieved the hated list from her pocket that Zach had given her and read it. It would take her the remainder of the afternoon to accomplish everything he expected.

For hours Eugenia scurried around town angrily attending to everything Zach had on his list. It galled her that he expected her to be his nursemaid on top of house servant.

Why, on top of everything else she had to do, he had even included written instructions for her to make a barber's appointment for him so he would not have to spend his valuable time waiting in line to have his hair trimmed.

Residual memories of the coarse texture of his ebony hair against her touch momentarily haunted her until she stopped in front of the striped barber pole and peered through the window at the barber busily trimming Mr. Washer's red hair. In the chair next to him a man relaxed, his face covered by towels, and next to him another man sat in the chair evidently sleeping, a newspaper resting over his face.

Male camaraderie, she thought at the distinctly masculine scene. And Zachary Kellogg expected her to invade that hallowed male inner sanctum to make an appointment for him as if she were his personal errand boy.

An idea flashed into her mind in the form of an old cliche. She would dispose of two birds with one stone; she would teach Zachary Kellogg to send her on errands he should take care of himself! And she would teach him that she was not just another simpering female annoyance; she was someone to be reckoned with!

But even as Eugenia straightened her shoulders, put an innocent smile on her face and entered the shop, a nagging worry flickered in the back of her mind. God only knew how he would react once her plan was carried out.

Eight

By the time Eugenia had picked up the order from Mr. Buellen at the mercantile and located that disgusting hat and maid's uniform, it was almost suppertime. She would never have time to get a decent supper on the table. That was just too bad. She had agreed to be Zachary Kellogg's hireling, but she had not agreed to do everything on his time schedule.

"Eugenia, Eugenia child," Ruth Garrett called out from her yard as Eugenia drove past in the carriage.

Eugenia reined in the spirited horse and waited for the elderly widow to approach the carriage, seven rambunctious grandchildren tugging at her skirts. "Hello, Mrs. Garrett. You look as if you are in your glory with all those little children surrounding you."

"I am, child." Her wide smile faded. "But I am not so sure about you. Is what I heard true?" she asked, staring with troubled eyes at the carriage.

Eugenia suddenly wished that she had not

stopped. She took a deep breath and inquired, "And just what did you hear?"

"That you have moved back into your family home and are living under the same roof with that mysterious stranger I told you about the other day. Herbert Buellen's wife stopped by a little earlier to pass on the gossip that you bought a gun, and now are living with the man as his maid. Is that true?"

Eugenia detested having to defend herself, would not have felt the need to account to anyone else in town except the Widow Garrett. The kindly woman had always been her friend, and Eugenia could not simply inform the old dear that it was none of her concern.

"It is true. Now that I am alone in this world, I thought the gun would be good protection. And I am afraid I was left penniless, and Zach Kellogg offered me employment and a place to stay until I can make other arrangements."

Ruth put a hand to her cheek. "Oh dear, if you need a place to stay, you can always stay here with me and put a stop to all those wagging tongues."

"Thank you, Mrs. Garrett, but I shall be fine."

Ruth watched the flash of Eugenia's eyes and sensed the young woman was not telling her everything. Knowing Eugenia the way she did, she was sure of it. And knowing how hard-headed Eugenia could be when she made her mind up about something, Ruth knew better than to try further argument with her.

"I have a huge pot of moss fareen bubbling on the stove inside. Why don't I send over enough for you and your young man for supper tonight?"

Eugenia graciously accepted the widow's offer so as not to hurt her feelings. But waiting for the widow to return with her specialty, Eugenia could not help but wonder what Mrs. Garrett had meant by calling Zachary Kellogg Eugenia's young man. That was the farthest thing from truth, Eugenia thought. She was only living under the same roof with Zach so she could see justice done and nothing more.

But even while Eugenia accepted the warm pot and thanked the Widow Garrett, Eugenia could not get the vague sensations she had experienced over such outlandish observations out of her mind. And when she served the moss fareen to Zach, Eugenia found herself staring at him in a new and troubling light.

Zach took a spoonful of the lavender concoction, savored the flavor and looked up at Eugenia, still standing with the serving spoon in her hand. She looked appetizing and so domestic in that apron. "You have outdone yourself. This is delicious. What is it?"

"It is seaweed gathered at China Beach near Ilwaco." Eugenia was not going to admit that she did not have time to prepare the cream dish herself.

His gaze dropped to his spoon. "Seaweed?"

"Yes, locally it is known as moss fareen. Isn't it a lovely color? It is black when collected, you know."

He forced a weak smile. "No, I didn't."

"Oh yes, but after it is dried and then moistened, it turns pink, white or lavender. It is such a light shade of lavender because of the milk stirred into it."

"Why don't you sit down and join me?" he offered, trying to concentrate on the flavor and content of the food rather than how pink Eugenia's cheeks were and how silky smooth and salty her skin might taste.

"You mean you allow the hired help to sit at the same table?"

"On rare occasions," he returned, fighting for inner control of his thoughts toward her. He got up and pulled out a chair. She just stood there, like a statue. He had to take the spoon out of her hand. But when his hand closed around hers to seat her, Zach felt a hot spear shoot through him.

For some time Eugenia sat on the edge of her seat, her hand enclosed in Zach's warm one. Eugenia had never been interested in the opposite sex. When not at the oyster beds, she spent her time on the beach collecting sand dollars and studying marine life while other girls were wearing special hair ribbons and giggling over the local boys. She had not understood them then, but now she was beginning to.

Feeling awkward and strangely ill at ease, Eugenia pulled her hand from Zach's. She watched him take his seat before she served herself, dropped a napkin in her lap, and started to eat.

"Did you take care of all the errands I gave you to do today?"

Eugenia glanced up from her moss fareen and noticed the brown envelope sticking out of his jacket pocket. Her spirits fell. For an instant she had forgotten herself, allowed his touch momentarily to sway her.

Reaffirming her resolve to see justice done, she said, "I always follow through with what needs to be done. Even found a replacement hat; it is on the rack." She took a mouthful of the seaweed.

"Perhaps you'll work out after all," he said, pleased that he had been able to give her enough errands to keep her busy and out of his way.

"Perhaps. Oh, I made arrangements for you to have your hair trimmed first thing right after lunch tomorrow, since I know how full your days are with the oyster business. It was the only time the barber could promise that you would not have to wait if somebody arrived before you."

"Good, I can use a trim." He touched the back of his neck, and Eugenia could almost feel the coarse texture of the black curling strands. "Although with your many talents, perhaps you could give me a trim and save me the time."

Eugenia had often trimmed her father's hair, but she had already made special arrangements for Zachary Kellogg. "Ah no, no, I couldn't."

She seemed a little nervous, but Zach chocked it up to the quiver he had felt run through her when he held her hand. "Don't want to take the chance of snipping off too much, huh?"

Eugenia forced a weak smile. "Yes, that's right. I certainly would not want that."

In an effort to avoid him for the remainder of the evening, Eugenia busied herself in the kitchen. She did not want him to guess that she was up to something. But she kept an eye on Zach. She noticed that when he thought she was not looking, he tucked the brown envelope into her father's desk and locked the drawer, slipping the key into his pocket.

Zach stood up and stretched, then noticed Eugenia in the dining room setting the table for breakfast. He walked toward her. "You've had a busy day. Why don't you turn in?"

She looked up and gave him a half smile. "You mean you don't expect me to work twenty-four hours a day?"

He came around behind her and untied her apron. While he was still holding the ties, Eugenia suddenly swung around to face him. She glanced up into his eyes. He was staring down at her, and she could feel the warmth of his breath on her forehead, the strength of his arms around her, the pounding of his heart.

"I don't expect you to work twenty-four hours a day, Eugenia," he murmured.

His voice was such a soft whisper, a caress, that Eugenia's heart raced despite her determination not to forget what she suspected he may be guilty of. She brought her hands up to push against his chest and put more space between then, but he tightened his hold.

Her mind whirred with a legion of jumbled thoughts until she felt dizzy. Her knees started to buckle, and Zach increased his hold and helped her to a chair.

Concern filled his eyes. "Are you all right?"

Am I all right? How can I possibly be all right, let alone think clearly when you are holding me like this?

99

"Yes, I am fine now. I am a little tired though. I think I shall retire for the night."

"I'll finish cleaning up."

If Eugenia had not been firmly planted on her chair, she would have fallen to the floor, she was so astounded by his sudden generosity. She had never heard of husbands helping their wives in the kitchen, let alone employers doing their servants' chores.

Once they had said their goodnights and she was mounting the stairs, Eugenia glanced back down at Zach. He was busy at the table. A warm thought touched her until her hand brushed the smooth surface of the banister. It brought to mind her father and how she would never see him again, never hear his laughter at her antics, never stand at the bottom of the stairs to catch his grandchildren—her children.

Tears threatened to spring to Eugenia's eyes, and she remembered the brown envelope Zach had hidden in her father's desk. Firming her original intention, she told herself that Zach was merely helping out to confuse her, to throw her off his trail and make her abandon her quest.

Nothing was going to get in her way of solving her father's murder. She touched her arms where the feel of Zach's touch lingered. Nothing!

Eugenia waited in her bedroom until she heard soft snoring sounds issuing from Zach's room, then tiptoed from her room and into his. The room was filled with delicate silvery moonlight, gracing the sparsely furnished space, and she could clearly see Zach lying in the four-poster bed asleep—

He looked so peaceful lying on his stomach, and so incredibly manly with the sheet bunched just below firm buttocks. His well-turned, muscular legs, lightly dusted with hairs, stretched out to the end of the bed, and his toes curled over the edge.

So as not to awaken him, Eugenia knelt down and crawled on her hands and knees to his clothing draped over a chair near the window. With the stealth of a cat, she rifled through his pockets, found the key to her father's desk, and was out of the room without a sound.

The last time she had attempted to sneak downstairs, he had heard her, so she tied her skirt, straddled the banister and slid with accomplished ease to the bottom. She went right to the desk, unlocked it, and removed the brown envelope.

Eugenia's hand shook as she carefully worked the flap. Slowly she pulled the contents from the envelope and held it up to the moonlight.

Money. Lots of money!

"My God," Eugenia gasped, her heart pounding with dread. "Was my father's murder some kind of a conspiracy?"

Shaking, she stuffed the money back into the envelope and returned it to the drawer and relocked the desk. On unsteady legs she somehow managed to sneak back upstairs, return the key, and seek the sanctuary of her childhood room. She grabbed her favorite baby doll off the shelf, climbed into bed, and hugged it to her until she fell into an exhausted slumber.

Before dawn Eugenia was up. She slipped into the maid's costume she had purchased at the hotel yesterday and stood in front of the full-length mirror in the corner of her room.

She frowned at her likeness. The severe black dress with lace cuffs and collar was dreadful enough, but the white-ruffled apron and hat was just too much to bear.

"Well, Mr. Zach Kellogg, if you think I am meekly going to wear this atrocity you are about to be in for the shock of your life."

By the time Eugenia descended the stairs, she was feeling much better about her attire. And the thought of seeing the look on Zach's face was positively heart-warming.

His expression when he reached the bottom of the stairs some time later and saw Eugenia come out of the kitchen toting a tray was even better than she had imagined. His eyes rolled over her from head to toe as if he were looking at some type of abomination. His reaction made her smile.

"Good morning, Zach. Isn't it a simply lovely sunny day outside?" she said brightly.

He did not take his eyes from her when he answered darkly, "It may be a lovely day outside, but in here it looks as if I'm in charge of running the Lightning Express Stageline from Ilwaco to Oysterville, and you're one of the drivers in that getup."

"Why, whatever do you mean?" she asked innocently, knowing full well he was livid over the alterations she had affected to her maid's costume. "You are the one who specifically requested that I don a servant's uniform, are you not?"

His brow shoved up. Hell, he should have known

better than to think that Eugenia Whalen would do the traditional, expected thing. The exasperating young woman was anything but traditional or compliant.

"I thought white was traditional at breakfast, yellow at noon and black was reserved for supper. I've never seen a maid wearing black britches and shirt with a white bow-like tie hanging loosely at her throat before, not to mention the sailor's hat." He swung out an arm. "Have to admit that the cowboy boots and that apron over those britches are a nice touch though."

She pivoted around to give him a full view of her attire.

A glimpse of her nicely rounded bottom outlined by the hugging britches decidedly altered his foul mood. "Hmm, perhaps that isn't such a bad uniform after all. No, actually I think it has definite possibilities."

Eugenia's short-lived triumph drowned as sure as if she had gone swimming in the treacherous waves which crashed on the weather beach. She set the tray down so hard that the coffee sloshed out of the cups and a spoon clattered to the floor. When she bent down to retrieve the spoon, she noticed he was staring at her in a manner she would almost describe as lustful.

A surge of excitement mingled with her disgust and only served to further confuse her, for she could not understand how she could continuously experience these unprecedented feelings for such a man.

She glared at Zach as she set the spoon back on the tray and cleaned up the spilled coffee.

He merely shrugged. "I'm only human, Eugenia. And whether you know it or not, you're a most fetching young woman."

She felt suddenly awkward and dropped her eyes. No one had ever told she was fetching before. She had always been the tomboy; the pudgy girl who liked to work in the oyster beds; the one who went to school with a frog or banana slug in her pocket; the one who could climb the tallest tree and then got stuck; the one who enjoyed and envied all the things the boys in the schoolyard got to do.

She shifted from foot to foot before looking up at Zach. "I do not know what to say."

She was so endearing at that moment, and so guileless, so truly unaware of her appeal that it made Zach ache inside to take her into his arms. "I believe most females find it customary merely to say thank you," he said softly and forced himself to remain where he was.

"Thank you," she managed in a halting voice.

Eugenia immediately set about rearranging the place settings and clumsily dishing up the eggs and potatoes, he made her feel so foreign. And she wondered why her stomach seemed to be doing double somersaults all of a sudden.

In an effort to return to safer ground and get on with doing what had to be done to see her father's murderer brought to justice, she said, "I do not want you to miss your barber's appointment, so I am preparing a special dinner today."

"I look forward to it."

Shifting uneasily, she forced a halfhearted smile. "Yes, so do I."

Nine

Zach spent the morning at the courthouse poring over legal documents. Woodward Whalen had written that he was having unusual problems with his business, but Zach could find no evidence of wrongdoing or discrepancies. Whatever was going on and whoever was responsible had done a damn good job of trail-covering.

Certain he was not going to find anything, but being thorough, Zach finished going over the assessor's records, then replaced them in the tin box the commissioners had invested three dollars to buy.

One of the commissioners, a muscular man of about forty, shuffled in through the sawdust brought in deference to the tobacco chewers. "What you lookin' for? Maybe I can be of help. Been serving Oysterville for well on five years now."

Zach snapped the top of the tin box shut and set it aside. No one knew why he was in Oysterville, so he could not take the chance and ask questions which might start folks wondering. "Just interested in learning more about the business I bought at auction."

"Oh, you're that Zachary Kellogg fellow, the one who bought Woodward Whalen's holdings." A sly, suddenly uneasy twinkle flashed into the man's eyes. "And you're the one folks are talking about who's living in the same house together with Whalen's daughter."

Zach's brow rose. While he felt no need to explain himself to any man, Zach felt a sudden surge of protectiveness toward Eugenia; he did not want to cause Eugenia any trouble with her friends and neighbors.

"Miss Whalen and I are not living together," Zach said in a dark, warning voice. "She's merely working for me until she can make other arrangements . . . nothing more. Got it?"

The man seemed to shrink under Zach's icy glare. "Sure, Mr. Kellogg. Sure. I got it. No harm meant."

"Just be sure that none's done to the lady," Zach added with just the right amount of dire warning in his voice. He watched the man nod and back out of the room. Zach mentally noted the man's apparent unease after he had learned who Zach was, then he cursed himself. He probably had made things worse for Eugenia, but that man made Zach come close to losing his temper.

Thoughts of Eugenia reminded Zach that she was waiting dinner for him. He glanced at his watch. It was nearly noon. He returned the records box to the shelf and hurried back to the house.

"Ready for dinner?" Eugenia asked when he walked through the kitchen door.

The nervous look on her face should have alerted Zach that she was up to something again, but he had been running late. He washed his hands at the sink. "Only if it's served right away. I've got to get out to the oyster beds and round up some pickers so I can get my first shipment to market and start making money."

"What about your hair cut?" She set the dinner before him.

"I probably should forego it—"

"No!" Zach's head snapped up at the urgency in her voice, and Eugenia quickly had to amend it. "Ah . . . I mean, you cannot miss your haircut after I went to all the trouble to arrange it for you. After all, what would the barber think of the town's newest businessman if you started missing your appointments. You do want to make a good impression on Oysterville's biggest gossip, don't you?" she improvised.

His brow rose: the barber might inadvertently provide him with needed information. "No, I suppose not."

"Exactly."

She watched him polish off the bacon sandwich and drink the coffee that she had set before him, relieved that everything was going as planned. After he left, she did not waste any time washing the dishes before skinning off the apron and hat and hurrying after him.

Several of the town's ladies stopped to stare at Eugenia, but once she explained that she was wear-

108

ing the black outfit because she was in mourning for her father, they merely shook their heads over her less than traditional choice of dress and went about their business. Oysterville's female population took as much pride in their dress as they did in their gardens, and Eugenia knew she had always been considered an oddity to be pitied.

Eugenia often had worn britches since she worked in the oyster beds, although even she had to admit she looked like one of the peninsula's huge crows in the black shirt and pants.

She stopped just outside the barber's shop behind a watering trough and bent down, pretending to pull up the sock out of her boot. When she was sure no one was looking, she peeked over the trough and peered through the window.

Zach was sitting inside, yawning. She rubbed her hands together; it shouldn't be long now. She waited until he nodded off while the barber was trimming his hair, then went inside.

"Miss Eugenia," the young bushy-haired barber nodded in greeting. "What can I do for you, young lady?" He said the words *young lady* in a doubtful voice as his beady eyes roved over her attire, but Eugenia did not care. Everything was progressing according to plan.

"Just making sure that Mr. Kellogg gets everything that is coming to him."

Clem Ablehouse prided himself on the work he did and frowned at Woodward's only child. To think he once thought of asking for her hand in marriage. A man would be the laughingstock of the entire county to get saddled with a wife who would even consider dressing so outrageously in public.

"You needn't worry, Eugenia, I know my job. Can't understand why he's dropped off like he's done, but by the time he wakes up he'll be a new man."

Eugenia gave the barber her brightest smile. "Good." You do not have to understand, she thought. "Thank you. I shall leave Mr. Kellogg in your capable hands, Clem. Good day to you."

Clem puffed out his chest and felt far superior as he went about his business taking care of the soundly sleeping man. Zachary Kellogg was never going to make a go of the oyster business if he couldn't keep his eyes open during the day, Clem thought smugly.

Clem had waited on six other patrons by the time Kellogg finally roused from a sound sleep. "Mr. Kellogg, have a good rest?"

Zach felt as if he had been on a bender, his head pounded so hard. "Don't know what got into me. Don't usually fall asleep the way I did."

"Nothing to worry about, sir. I was able to give you the full treatment while you caught forty winks. You look like a new man now."

Zach's brow shoved up. "Full treatment?"

Clem Ablehouse fought to swallow the sudden lump of trepidation that was clogged in his throat. "Why, yes, Miss Eugenia had me specially rearrange my schedule so I would have plenty of time to devote to you. She was mighty specific in her instructions. Said you are an exacting gentleman.

That's why she only wanted me to work on you, Mr. Kellogg, sir."

Grabbing the mirror from the shelf to show off the unsurpassed quality of his work and placate the man's sudden black scowl, Clem went over to Kellogg and handed it to him.

"What in the hell!" Zach bellowed with outrage, rubbing his cleanly shaven chin.

That sneaky little spitfire had the barber shave off his beard!

"I only followed Miss Eugenia's instructions, Mr. Kellogg, sir. You were sleeping like a babe and couldn't be roused when she came in and reminded me what you wanted."

"I just bet I was," Kellogg said so darkly that Clem inched toward the door just in case he had to make a fast getaway if the man came after him.

Zach ignored the frightened barber, ripped the covering off his chest and stormed from the shop, leaving the barber gaping after him. If Eugenia's neck would have been within reach as Zach stomped back toward the house, he would have happily twisted it off and stuffed it down her pretty, scheming little mouth.

Zach had not calmed in the least by the time he slammed into the house and stomped through the kitchen to the parlor. Eugenia was sitting comfortably on the sofa with her feet up, reading a book.

Eugenia's head snapped up at the sound of the pounding boots. Zach was standing in the doorway, his clean-shaven, incredibly handsome face as black as a stormy night at sea. She had not realized how unbelievably handsome he would be without the beard.

"Hello," she said in her most welcoming voice. She suddenly knew what a cornered animal must feel like, for he looked like he was just waiting to pounce. Yet he was just standing there, glaring at her. Her heart pounding, she braced herself, ready to take flight if the opportunity presented itself.

She closed the book and set it aside. "You are home early. I thought you were going out to the oyster beds this afternoon, so I was not expecting you."

His brow shoved up. "Weren't you?"

"No. Why would I be?"

"Why, indeed, *Miss* Eugenia."

He was so calm, so deliberate, each word so deadly and delivered with such unhurried precision that he left no doubt in Eugenia's mind that she was in for big trouble.

Well, she was not going to broach the subject which burned plainly now that his handsome face was no longer hidden by a beard. Slowly, she edged off the sofa. She had done what needed doing so she could get a good look at his face. She was not sorry and would never say she was, regardless of what he did to her.

He took a step closer.

She moved toward the door.

He moved in between her and the door.

She glanced back over her shoulder at the open window.

"Don't even think about it, Eugenia. You'll never make it."

Eugenia did not move; she barely breathed. "I do not understand what you seem to be so upset about."

"Don't you?"

Oh, she hated this cat-and-mouse game. It would be easier if he just shouted at her and got it over with. But this cold, calculated delivery was nearly more than she could endure. She licked her lips, her eyes scanning the room for possible escape routes.

"Don't bother," he growled. "You aren't going anywhere."

She inched around the room until her father's favorite chair was standing like the last buttress of defense between them.

He rested his palms on the back of the chair, leaning toward her. "As a matter of fact, Eugenia, you won't be going anywhere where you have to sit down for a long, long while."

"Oh, yes, I will," she cried and darted toward the door.

Zach was quicker and blocked the door as Eugenia came to a screeching halt not more than three feet in front of him. He made a grab for her, but she bent low and managed to duck under his arms, dashing up the stairs.

"Why are you so upset? You look better without that bushy black beard," she screamed and ran into her room, slamming the door.

She had one leg out the window when Zach burst through the door and caught her.

"Zach, now be reasonable," she screeched as he dragged her back inside. "I merely wanted to know

113

what you truly look like. You can always grow another beard."

He flipped her over his knee. "I would not have to grow another one if you had kept your pretty little nose out of my business."

He brought his hand up to give her a whack, but she bit his leg. "Yeow! You little devil hellcat," he bellowed and dumped her on the floor as the pain caused him to shoot to his feet.

Eugenia scrambled to her feet and clambered out to the top of the stairs, but he caught her arm and whirled her around to face him.

Eugenia pushed at his chest to no avail. "You have caught me," she said in defiance, out of breath.

"Yes, I have," he crowed. Yet he made no move to carry out his threat.

"Are you going to punish me now?" Wide-eyed, unable to help herself, Eugenia reached up and stroked the baby smoothness of his cheek, tracing the angles of his square jaw and the high planes of his cheekbones.

The sensations were mind-altering and dangerously arousing. And the moment Zach looked into her green, silently beseeching eyes, all thoughts he had of teaching her to meddle in his business began fading.

"Yes," he answered in more of a murmur, his voice a whispered caress.

"What is my punishment?" Her fingers were alive with a sensitivity all their own as she continued to pet the smooth, velvety skin now denuded of the heavy black whiskers.

Zach swallowed, knowing he could not help himself. "At the moment I can think of only one appropriate punishment befitting the crime."

"Only one?" she whispered up at him.

"One," came out in a soft murmur.

Slowly, Zach pulled her up against his chest. Of her own volition, Eugenia lifted her face to his.

He kissed her.

It was a gentle kiss at first, but soon melted into a long, lingering kiss. His lips explored hers, soft, moist and searching, learning each contour, each luscious curve.

When he finally pulled back and looked into her questioning eyes, his anger had vanished, replaced with an equally strong emotion.

She did not say a word, did not try to pull away. Instead, she again reached up, running the back of her hand along his shaven cheek.

"I never really much liked the beard anyway," he admitted.

"You look much better without it. You have a strong chin." She stroked the square lines. "And high cheekbones." She ran her hand along the border where his beard had been. "A very handsome face as a matter of fact."

Eugenia was feeling mesmerized by Zach, and she was still experiencing the afterglow of their kiss. But when she lowered her hand, and it came into contact with the banister, her senses began to return.

"Zach?"

"Yes?"

"Why were you hiding behind that beard?"

115

She might as well have thrown scalding water in his face. Any self-recriminations he may have experienced for taking advantage of the moment dissolved. He had a job to do, and instead he had allowed her closeness to muddle his mind.

"I wasn't hiding. And you better consider yourself forewarned. The next time you pull a stunt like that—"

"Like what?" Eugenia jutted out her chin, the silken veil from his kiss still partially hanging over her mind. She did not recall that she had just admitted to her actions.

"Like what!" he snapped, incredulous, his ire returning. "Like slipping me some type of knockout drop in my dinner, which caused me to fall asleep in the barber's chair so the fool could follow the instructions you specifically left him."

"Since you have it all figured out for yourself, far be it for me to attempt to dispute your reasoning, if that is what you care to believe," she said to his booted feet.

She could not look him in the eye and deny what he already knew as truth. And she certainly was not going to inform him it was laudanum she had acquired from the doctor under the guise to help her sleep.

He was right after all. She'd never make a good liar. Guilt glowed bright red all over her face. She frustrated the hell out of him. She also intrigued the hell out of him. But he had a job to do, and he had better remember that or he could end up letting her get them both killed.

"Eugenia, quit playing detective. I'm a simple

businessman who saw money to be made by buying your pa's oyster business."

"If that is true, then why did you sneak off and meet that stranger outside of town. And why did you exchange those papers you found in my father's desk for an envelope full of money?"

Ten

Zach glared at Eugenia. How in the hell could she look so wide-eyed and innocent one moment and make him burn to kiss her, and then the next come right out and demonstrate just how underhanded and sneaky she could be? He would have to be more on his guard against her from now on.

"I don't know what you're talking about," he said in answer to her question about the money he thought he had safely locked away in the desk.

Apparently there weren't any lengths she wouldn't go to if she was after something. If he weren't more careful, she was going to ruin everything.

"Don't you?" She swung on her heel and stomped down the stairs.

How could she have forgotten herself and let that man, who could so easily lie to her, seduce her into kissing him just a moment ago?

Zach was right behind her. "Eugenia—"

She stopped on the bottom step and swung around. Her eyes registered hurt and confusion, along with another strong, hidden emotion which stopped Zach cold.

"No. Do not 'Eugenia' me. I am not a little girl, Zach. I followed you and saw you hand those papers over to that man. And I saw him give you that brown envelope with all the money in it."

"And how do you know this supposed envelope, which you say you saw, contains money?"

She was past caution, past caring whether he found out what she had done or not. "Because I stole the key from your pocket when you were asleep and looked."

Zach was stunned she had been able to breach his defenses, but he did not have the reputation as one of the best territorial marshals for no reason. He kept his features perfectly schooled. "As usual you're jumping to conclusions. There's a simple explanation."

A part of Eugenia wanted desperately to believe Zach was merely an astute businessman. But the skeptical portion of her nature refused to relinquish its hold.

"Then, by all means, let's hear this *simple explanation* of yours."

Zach had never explained himself to a woman since he was a little boy, and his mother caught him thieving a pie off the windowsill. Yet here he was about to offer an account, such as it would be, to a troublesome young woman who kept getting in the way of the job he had to do. The galling part of the whole situation was that he wasn't even sure he much liked her even though he was strongly attracted to her. She was proving to be an untimely hindrance to his investigation.

"First of all, next time I catch you meddling in my business, I'm going to toss your pretty shapely bottom out of here, home or no home to go to. Understand?" Eugenia gave a halfhearted nod. "Good. Now, for your information, that stranger you saw me with is my financial backer."

"Then why didn't you just meet him in town?" she blurted out before she could stop herself.

"Because the man prefers to remain anonymous. He's well-known in business circles, and if his name got out that he had an interest in the oyster business, it could start his business competitors looking at the peninsula long and hard, and he would prefer to keep the profitability of this venture confidential."

"Then why not send a messenger?"

She was the most indefatigable woman he had ever met. Most women would have simply accepted his fabricated explanation and been happy with it, but not Miss Eugenia Huntley Whalen, damn her.

"I told you, Eugenia. The man's widely known, and even using a messenger could bring more competitors here. Oysterville's one of the wealthiest towns in the West, paralleling the prosperity of any of the gold rush towns, and my backer intends to take full advantage of that.

"You know as well as I do that this town's so full of wealth that it's common to see men standing around town tossing twenty-dollar gold pieces at a line scratched in the sand, and the one with the best throw takes the pot."

Her features relaxed, and he could see in her face that she was finally starting to waver and buy his story. "Does that satisfy your over-active imagination?"

"For now." But she was already planning to head over to the jail first chance she got and check out the wanted posters.

Eugenia was pleasantly surprised and more than a little suspicious when Zach invited her to accompany him out to the southern arm of Shoalwater Bay. The shallows were home to her father's oyster beds, which were alternately enveloped by the sea's waters or exposed by the receding seven to eight foot tides.

"I did not think that a troublesome young woman such as myself could possibly teach a businessman of your acumen anything," she said before she went to get her coat.

Troublesome young woman, he thought ironically as he waited for her. Although he did not give voice to it, he was thinking that very thing among other troubling thoughts regarding her as they left the house.

The afternoon was pleasant, a gentle breeze whipping the water. They walked to the edge of the bay where Zach made arrangements for a rowboat so they could go out to the oyster beds.

"Miss Eugenia," old Doc Morris hollered with a wave from his buggy. "How are you getting on?"

Eugenia tried to ignore the white-haired doctor and trundle Zach down to the boat before the buggy reached them, but she was not quick enough.

The fatherly doctor caught up with them. Eugenia made a quick introduction and tugged on Zach's arm to leave.

"Miss Eugenia, how did that laudanum work I prescribed for you?"

"I'd say it worked just fine, Dr. Morris," Zach answered in a dark voice before Eugenia could open her mouth. Then his eyes shot to Eugenia. Guilty. Her face gave away guilt like Oysterville's fabled twenty-dollar gold pieces.

"Glad to hear it. Glad to hear it," the doctor repeated and scratched his head underneath the band of his hat. Gossip said there was something mighty peculiar between that pair. "Well, if you need any more laudanum to help you sleep, Miss Eugenia, you just stop by the office or the house again."

Zach took Eugenia's arm so she would not try to escape. "I don't think Miss Whalen'll have any further use for laudanum, Doctor."

"Yes, well . . ." The doctor's voice trailed off at the strange inflection in the man's tone. There was something going on between those two young people, and he had no intention of being caught in the middle of it. He said his farewells and spurred his old horse along the road.

Zach waited until the doctor was out of earshot before he turned his attention on Eugenia.

She gave a culpable shrug. "What can I say?"

"I'd say in your case, silence is a definite virtue."

He motioned for her to precede him. "Shall we go on out to the oyster beds?"

Eugenia nodded and strolled ahead of him toward the waiting boat, relieved and thankful that he did not resurrect her transgression further than the telling comments he had already made to the doctor.

They settled into the boat, and Zach dipped the oars into the icy waters of the bay.

Eugenia had to smile when his efforts with the oars splattered water in her lap.

"What're you grinning for?" he questioned through tight lips.

"The way you are rowing."

His brow shoved up. "And what's wrong with it?"

She kept her face impassive, although she almost had to laugh. Zach obviously was not as proficient with the oars as he was with other things. She blushed and touched her fingers to her lips when she thought of those *other* things.

"The way you are rowing reminds me of the men who started Oysterville."

"Able pioneers, I'm sure."

"Oh, they were. It is just that the men made arrangements to meet Chief Na-ko-ti to examine the oysters on the west side of the bay."

"What's the point of your story?" he asked with a sneaking suspicion it was not going to be particularly flattering.

"Well, they set out in a canoe they borrowed from the Indians and got lost in the fog. The Indians heard them paddling and beat on a drum to help

123

guide their way. Then the chief had to laugh once the men reached shore because they were making such a splash with the oars that the chief knew it was white men lost on the bay. No Indian made such noise when they paddled."

"I'll remember that if I ever get lost out here in a fog," he grumbled, less than enthusiastic over her story poking fun at his efforts. Hell, he'd take the back of a horse any day!

Zach rowed past the heavily forested, five thousand acre Long Island. "My parents and I used to have picnics with the deer, bears, elk and raccoons on that island when I was a little girl," Eugenia pointed out, fondly recalling a happy childhood.

Zach glanced at Eugenia. Her eyes were misty, and he quietly set an oar aside and took her hand. "Perhaps we'll make a day of it out there some time." Why the hell did he have to go and make such an offer? he silently grilled himself.

"Perhaps." In order to change the subject before the fond emotional memories got the better of her, Eugenia took her hand from Zach's and motioned toward the city on the north tip of Long Island. "That is Diamond City."

"Interesting name."

"When the sun sets, it shines on the banks of white oyster shells and they glitter like diamonds."

Zach nodded and noted the snapdragons and marigolds growing in the gardens along the shore and the oyster boats moored beyond the shallow water.

Eugenia fell silent after that until they reached

the northern tip of the whack of oysters which had belonged to her father.

"Here it is," she announced, rolling up her sleeves and leaning over the boat. She peered into the shallow water. "Aren't they magnificent?"

Although Zach had always had an inquisitive mind, he had to admit to himself that at the moment he was much more interested in Eugenia Whalen and the inviting, full-curving figure she cut leaning over the boat than the clusters of oysters in the Whalen whack.

"Magnificent," he answered, but he was thinking about Eugenia.

She glanced back over her shoulder at him. "Here, roll up your sleeves and lean over next to me; you can see better."

Zach inched over until they were shoulder to shoulder, bare arm touching bare arm. Her smooth skin made the hairs on his arms stand up on end, he was so in tuned to their nearness. She smelled of fresh soap and rose water. And her shiny auburn hair was threatening to escape the pins at the nape of her neck, a neck he would thoroughly enjoy nibbling at the moment.

He was beginning to burn for her until she reached over the side of the boat and plucked an oyster from the water.

"What do you think?" She plopped the dripping bivalve into his hand. "They are so near the surface that I do not have to use tongs to harvest them."

Zach looked down at the hard shell, then back at Eugenia. It was not at all what he had on his mind having in his hands at the moment. Without realizing it, she sure knew how to shrivel a man's desire.

But she was so excited over the mollusks that Zach couldn't help but get caught up in her enthusiasm. "Looks like a very profitable investment."

"Worth much more than you paid for it," she said and then caught herself. "Daddy and I were experimenting with returning the empty shells to the beds to serve as cultch for a new crop."

"Cultch?"

She frowned. "You really do not know anything about the oyster business, do you?"

"I already answered that question, if you'll remember, Eugenia."

"So you have." She was not going to trip him up with any more questions of that nature, she decided with a sigh. "Anyway, cultch is a phrase Daddy and I use to mean that shells scattered in the beds attract a set of young oysters after the mollusks spawn, and they attach themselves to solid objects such as mature shells. Oysters are born as free-swimming, nearly invisible fish. They are called spat after they develop a carapace and affix themselves to the handiest object."

"Sounds interesting."

"You really think so? The other oystermen laugh at Daddy and me and our efforts. But if something is not done to replenish the supply of oysters taken out of the bay, someday there won't be any oysters left, just like what happened in San Francisco harbor."

"Sounds like you are ahead of your time."

"I enjoy studying marine life. Oysters were my life before Daddy died," she said with a sad smile.

He patted her hand with his free one. It was not as soft as some of the hands of the women he had known. But those women led frivolous lives. They did not engage in any useful endeavors such as Eugenia did. The very thought caused him to gain a grudging respect for her before he said, "A budding scientist?" to lighten the mood.

Eugenia gave him a grateful smile, plucked the shell from his hand, and dropped her eyes before she returned the oyster to the bed. Zachary Kellogg was such an enigma. He was different from the local men who had laughed at her and told her father she should get back into the kitchen where a woman belonged. Yet she knew Zach was hiding something, and she did not completely trust him, despite the fact that at times he was so supportive and protective that he threw her quite off balance.

She forced her mind from the confusing thoughts back to her beloved oysters. Somehow, some way, she was going to return to the oyster beds, she silently vowed—in spite of this latest impasse in which the beds were sold right out from underneath her.

She suddenly seemed shy and awkward after Zach had complimented her. It was so uncharacteristic of Eugenia, and Zach found himself drawn further to the unconventional young woman.

"How do oysters from y-your own beds sound for supper tonight?" Eugenia stammered over the portion of her sentence involving ownership.

The sound of her voice had broken into Zach's reverie and he glanced up at her face. Her cheeks

127

bore the kiss of the afternoon sun, and Zach silently wished that they bore his kiss instead.

"Zach?"

"Oh, yeah, my own oysters for supper. Sounds delicious."

He merely sat there until Eugenia said, "Don't you want to be the one to pick your first oyster supper from your own beds?"

My life's desire, he thought. "Guess that would be fitting."

"Absolutely!"

He watched her fresh face glow with excitement as she proceeded to demonstrate how to harvest the bivalves. But he was paying more attention to the movements of her desirable ripe body as she reached and stretched over the side of the boat. The motions brought her bottom up and beneath her shirt he could just make out the outline of her full breasts pressing against the fabric.

At that moment the last thing Zach Kellogg wanted to close his hands around were oyster shells!

Eleven

Zach popped the last bite of oysters on the half shell into his mouth and smiled. It brought to mind how Eugenia had threatened to make him eat his scurrilous words on the half shell when they'd first met.

"What are you smiling about?" Eugenia questioned as she set her fork down on her plate.

"I was just wondering if you had captured any of my words to cook tonight."

"I beg your pardon?" she questioned, but knew full well that to which he was referring.

"As ingredients for your oysters on the half shell." Partial truth was better than a lie, he decided. He was not about to remind her of her dubious promise to him.

"Delicious, aren't they?" She consciously ignored his remark, deeming not to begin another round of sparring banter this evening.

"You're quite a cook," he said and meant it. No one, not even his mother, ever cooked like that.

Eugenia was pleased that he appreciated her

cooking. She had always prided herself on her skill with oysters, whether it was cooking them or working in the beds. She grabbed both their coffee cups and started to rise.

"Why don't you sit back down? The least I can do is get the coffee."

"Thank you." She settled back into the chair, surprised and secretly pleased at Zach's willingness to share the work by getting the coffee from the kitchen.

He took the cups and returned a few moments later with two steaming cups of coffee. Zach took his seat, sipped the rich brown liquid and looked up at Eugenia.

"Why haven't you married?"

Eugenia glanced up through the steam rising from her cup. It was an unusual question coming from Zach Kellogg. Folks in town had quit asking several years ago, assuming that she would probably end up a spinster. An assumption she herself had come to accept as fact.

"I was betrothed about four years ago when I was eighteen," she said honestly, after thinking about whether she should answer his question or not.

For some reason Zach did not receive the news with his usual indifference. He wondered about the type of man who could have attracted Eugenia's heart.

"I can see by the expression on your face that you are wondering what happened."

"Don't want to pry."

"You wouldn't be. It is common knowledge around town."

"And?" He took a sip from his cup, keeping his eyes watchful for her reactions. For what, he wasn't sure. She wasn't nervous or anxious that he had asked. And the thought that she was comfortable with her present marital status caused him to relax. He decided that it was because he was not in the market for a wife, and she did not seem to be on the lookout for a husband.

"Len Sweeney's son, Gale, and I became engaged shortly after my father took Len Sweeney and Rube Nelson on as partners."

Zach's brow shoved up. That tidbit concerning Eugenia's father and the oyster beds pricked Zach's professional interest, not that it necessarily had anything to do with his investigation. But it always paid to be thorough.

"Gale?"

"He was born during a particularly bad storm in Astoria."

"Almost a native, huh?"

"Other than the Indians, about as close as someone our age could get. Anyway, Gale and I shared a common interest in the oyster beds at first. He had a lot of commercial ideas to increase the beds' profitability, and we were drawn together by our interests in oysters."

Eugenia shrugged and decided not to relate the entire story of how his greed had caused a irreparable schism in their relationship. "Gale and I finally realized that our interests in the oyster beds were not so mutual after all, and I broke off the engagement shortly thereafter. We rarely even see each other any longer."

Mention of Gale Sweeney's interest in the oyster beds got Zach's attention, and he made a mental note to check out this Gale Sweeney.

"Why don't I help you with the dishes?" Zach suggested and picked up his plate before she could answer.

It was the second time he had surprised her tonight, and as Eugenia cleared the table, she was beginning to wonder if she could have been wrong about Zach all along. She grabbed her more functional cotton apron off the hook on the back door.

"Here," he reached out, "I'll tie it for you." She handed Zach the apron and stood with her back toward him while he knotted it into a bow.

It took a great deal of self-restraint for Zach to keep his hands on the apron ties and off Eugenia's nicely flaring hips, she was so close. Her hair fell in a mass of shiny curls down her back and smelled of fresh soap. He quickly finished the bow and stepped back.

"Thank you." Eugenia poured water into a pot, put it on the stove, and stacked the dishes in the dishpan while she waited for the water to heat.

Zach was pouring the hot water in the pan for her when a wave of dizziness struck her.

"You okay?" He set the pot aside.

"I am not sure," she said, her fingers at her temples. "I suddenly felt a little dizzy."

"Too much sun this afternoon perhaps." He dragged a chair from the corner of the room.

Eugenia gratefully accepted this latest bit of consideration on Zach's part and sat down.

"You're not trying to get out of doing the dishes tonight, are you?"

She tried to laugh at his humor, but her head was suddenly starting to spin. She got back up and tried to focus on him as she said, "If you will excuse me, I think I should go upstairs and lie down . . ."

Zach listened to her voice fade, and she slowly started to crumple to the floor. He caught her and lifted her limp body into his arms. He held her close. Her lush body was warm against his chest, and again he had to force himself to remember why he was in Oysterville.

Starting for the stairs, he said with a flicker of remorse to an unconscious Eugenia, "Guess you'll be doing dishes by your lonesome self tomorrow morning after you sleep it off, Genie."

He took the stairs easily despite the added burden of her weight. "Turnabout's only fair."

In her room, he laid her on the bed and covered her with the quilt before gently kissing her forehead. The moment his lips touched her skin, given a blush from the afternoon's sun, Zach got such another strong hankering for her that he was almost tempted to lie down beside her.

Maybe he'd better take himself across the Columbia River to Astoria for a spell and seek out a willing woman in the business to ease the heightening need he seemed to be experiencing as of late.

It had been some time since he had bedded a woman. He wondered if he ought to chalk it up to spending too much time with Eugenia, or if there really was something to the old adage that oysters were an aphrodisiac.

Hell, if that was true, he'd better stay away from those tasty morsels until he solved this case.

He stroked Eugenia's cheek, a flicker of guilt glowing in his mind. "Sweet dreams."

Zach stopped to turn out the oil lamp burning on her dressing table and took one last look at Eugenia before he left.

She was out cold.

"That should keep you from trying to follow me this time."

Zach went to his room and changed into an old pair of dungarees, shirt and work boots. He grabbed his heavier coat and left the house, not feeling quite so proud as usual of his efforts to cover his tracks. A man in his line of work did what had to be done. And he had to keep Eugenia from following him this time.

The moon was partially hidden by clouds by the time he met Cliff Granger at the designated meeting place.

"What kept you?" Cliff asked, leaning against a tall tree, smoking a cigarette. "You're later 'n a skunk caught out at noon."

Zach set the lantern down on a fallen log. "I had something to take care of first."

A telling grin split Granger's long, thin face. "As in skinnin' off that pelt from your chin for a certain Miss Eugenia Whalen?"

"Decided it was time for a change, is all." Zach chafed over his partner's remark, but he was not going to give Granger cause for a good laugh.

134

"Quite a change. Ain't seen your ugly face in years. That Whalen woman manage to get past your prickly whiskers to pierce that thick hide of yours?"

Again Granger grinned as he took one last drag and crushed out his cigarette. This time Zach's fist itched to punch it off his face. Instead, Zach ignored him. He was not inclined to share anything concerning Eugenia with Granger or anyone else.

Cliff could not suppress the urge; he tossed back his head and laughed at Kellogg's scowl. "Don't tell me I'm right as rain hittin' a roof? Why maybe I ought to mosey on into town and get myself a looksee at this woman."

Zach's brow shoved up. "And maybe you ought not."

" 'Fraid of a little competition, old friend?"

Zach was coming close to losing his usual exterior calm. He took a breath and said, "Nothing to compete over. Now, shall we get on with business?"

"Sure, Kellogg. Sure."

The two men settled onto the log, and Cliff rolled another cigarette and put it between his teeth. He struck a match and sucked in a good drag. Letting it out, he asked, "Whaddya got?"

"Forgot to tell you, somebody broke into the house, apparently searching for the information Whalen said in his letter he had. The place was torn apart. Other than that, a whole helluva lot of nothing. But one thing is for sure, this case doesn't seem to be a simple open-and-shut murder investigation. Whalen was right in being afraid to go to

135

the local authorities. The man didn't know who he could trust—"

"Evidently the poor bastard got himself killed trustin' the wrong person." Cliff took another drag.

"The more I nose around, the more I'm sure that this thing's more complicated than we anticipated. Nobody knows anything, at least anything they're willing to tell. It's almost as if it's some kind of cover-up."

"Conspiracy maybe?"

"Maybe. Or a pretty clever murderer. Don't rightly know yet."

"It's strange though," Zach continued. "Because everyone in town speaks real highly of Whalen. Everyone seemed to like him—"

"Not everyone."

"Yeah." Zach pushed his hat back from his forehead. "I'm right about one thing. There's money involved."

"Isn't there usually?" Cliff smirked. "That or a good lookin' woman. Right, friend?"

Zach's brow shoved up at his partner's candid remark, but he sagely ignored it. He was not going to bring Eugenia into this conversation again.

The two remained silent for a moment until Cliff said, "All right, if I gotta drag it out of you, what's money got to do with it?"

"Well, Whalen was supposedly going bankrupt. I found out he had even asked his brother-in-law for a loan and was turned down. But when I rowed out to the whack and surveyed the oyster beds, they were teeming with good-sized oysters. Not at all what one would expect someone's business that was about to go under to look like."

That same knowing smirk that Zach had seen all too often in the past flashed across Granger's face. "And how would you know so much about oysters and jargon associated with them all of a sudden?"

Damn Granger. "Because you know as well as I do that I'm posing as a businessman involved in the trade."

"Sure, friend, it's your call. Speakin' 'bout business, there wasn't nothin' in those papers you handed me that'd link anyone to the murder. Just a bunch of receipts 'n' such. What about that money you had me get for you? You know that's government money."

"And well spent, too. I bought Whalen's business at auction and plan to use the cash to pay for it." Then Zach mumbled, "That is, if it's still where I put it."

"Whaddya mean, if it's still where you put it? You know how the government is, like a grizzly when riled," Cliff reminded Kellogg.

"I just had a little problem with the key, is all. I'm sure the money's safe."

"Can you stall payin' for the beds until the case is solved? You're really stickin' your neck out on this one, buyin' that there business without prior approval."

"No," Zach answered a little too quickly, a little too vehemently. If he held title then no one else could buy Eugenia's precious oyster beds out from under her nose once the case was solved, and perhaps there was still a chance she could reclaim them. They meant too much to her to go to anybody else.

Zach looked Granger straight in the eyes. "I'm going to need more time with this one."

"There somethin' you ain't telling me, friend?"

"Would I keep anything from you?" Zach answered vaguely.

The two territorial marshals grinned at each other, both knowing the answer to that one.

Eugenia's head pounded when she awoke, and she felt dreadful—as if she had been sampling her father's spirits. That was absurd since she did not drink. Then she remembered Zach's eagerness to get the coffee last night, and how he had remained at her side, offering to help with the dishes. At the time she had thought he was considerate; now she wasn't so sure.

She got up, stripped off the wrinkled clothes she still wore from last night, tossed on a wrapper, and searched the house for Zach.

He was nowhere in the house to be found.

On a sinking hunch Eugenia went back into the kitchen. The dirty dishes remained in the pan. So he'd help her with the dishes, would he? She picked up her coffee cup from the night before. A strange residue ringed the bottom along with the dried coffee stains.

"You bastard," she hissed at the cup and tossed it into the dishpan to soak.

Zachary Kellogg had drugged her!

Storming upstairs to dress, she continued to

138

curse Zach Kellogg. "How could I have believed for a moment that my first impression of that man was wrong," she muttered to herself as she slid her legs into her work britches. "How!"

She angrily donned an old shirt, grabbed a lightweight jacket and determined to search the town until she found him. She was going to give him a piece of her mind!

She reached the front door, swung it open, and stopped dead, startled. Gale Sweeney, in all his blond splendor, was standing on the porch, his hand raised, about to knock on her door.

Twelve

"Gale?" Eugenia said, startled to see the handsome blond man to whom she had once been betrothed. He was decked out in the same way she remembered him—in his usual tailored suit and stiff white shirt.

He doffed his bowler, holding it under his arm in the same jaunty manner that used to annoy her to no end.

"Eugenia, my God, how are you? I came as soon as I returned to town and heard. Is there anything I can do?" Gale glanced at her black work pants. The time she'd spent in California hadn't changed her. She still didn't know how to act like a proper lady.

"Do?" She was not prepared for his sudden display of concern.

His lips tightened, and his pale brows drew together. "To ease your bereavement, of course."

"No, but thank you for your kind offer, Gale," she said stiffly. She was not going to let him see how mention of her grief affected her.

He craned his neck to look past her. "Aren't you going to invite a dear old friend in?"

Although she could not understand his concern for her welfare, since their last parting had been anything but cordial, Eugenia stepped back. "Of course, do come in, won't you?"

He stood in the vestibule, his gaze wandering about the house while Eugenia closed the door.

When Eugenia turned back toward Gale, she noted that his attention was not settled on her. He seemed to be looking around, awfully curious about something. "How may I help you?"

"Eugenia, I am surprised at you. Aren't you going to take my hat and ask me into the parlor?"

Suspicious of his motives, she hung the hated hat on the rack in the vestibule and showed him into the parlor. She took a chair across from Gale, who settled onto the sofa and crossed his legs. For some time they remained stiffly silent, Gale continually looking over his shoulder until Eugenia could tolerate it no longer.

"Gale, what is it I can do for you?"

"I simply do not understand you—"

"You never did, Gale." She gave him an insincere smile she hoped he understood, since her impatience with him was growing. Gale had never done anything simply out of concern for his fellow man since they were children. He always expected to reap some benefit.

"What is it you want, Gale?"

He looked wounded. "How can you think that at a time such as this I have come for any reason other than to render my assistance?"

"Because we grew up together and were betrothed once, if you will recall."

"Oh, Eugenia . . ." His voice trailed off with a long, sorrowful sigh. He leaned over and reached out to take her hand.

She moved it out of his reach, uneasily clearing her throat. "Please, Gale, can't we dispense with this charade of concern?"

Eugenia watched his pretty, sympathetic face undergo a metamorphosis, his true cunning nature emerging as his gray eyes narrowed and his lips thinned. It was an expression she recognized all too clearly—the real Gale Sweeney.

"Since you have come to offer your condolences and have so ably done so, I might add, I shan't keep you any longer. I know such an industrious businessman such as yourself must have a very busy schedule."

"Never too busy for you, Eugenia," he persisted.

Eugenia let out a frustrated sigh. "Gale, surely your father must have informed you that the oyster beds were sold at auction to settle my father's accounts. No doubt your family has received the monies that were legally due them."

"Eugenia, I am stunned at you. What makes you think that I have come here today to talk about the oyster business?"

"If you aren't here to discuss oysters, then exactly what did you come here for?" Zach asked in a less than civil tone from the doorway.

Eugenia had been sitting with her back to the door, but immediately swung around at the sound of Zach's voice. He was casually leaning his shoulder up against the doorjamb, his arms crossed over his chest. His face did not give away his feelings, but he had not been able to keep the annoyance from his voice.

"Zach," she said, then amended with a glare, "I mean, Mr. Kellogg." His eyes flashed in her direction for an instant before he settled his frigid gaze on Gale. "What are you doing home?"

"Home? Zach?" Gale registered with surprise.

Eugenia took secret delight in the daggers that the two men exchanged. "Gale, allow me to introduce Mr. Zachary Kellogg, the new owner of my father's oyster business and this house. Mr. Zachary Kellogg, this is Mr. Gale Sweeney, the gentleman I told you about."

"All good, I hope." Gale suddenly found the need to straighten his tie. He forced his most pleasant businessman smile and rose to offer his hand.

Zach glanced at the long, manicured fingers and ignored them. Zach was of no mind to exchange pleasantries with the snake. At the moment he would have liked nothing better than to take the fancy *gentleman* by his stiff collar and toss him out of the house. Instead, Zach plunked down on the chair near the window and crossed his arms over his chest.

"Gale stopped by to offer his condolences," Eugenia said in an effort to put an end to the tension. "He was just leaving."

"Actually not," Gale interceded and gingerly settled back on the sofa.

Zach's brow shoved up. "Just what *actually* then?"

"I came to check on Eugenia's welfare now that

she no longer is surrounded by relations. And to render my financial assistance, since she does not have any prospects in the foreseeable future. After all, we did grow up together and share mutual interests."

"I understand that's not all you shared," Zach said, unimpressed with the man. How could Eugenia ever have been interested in the likes of that?

"We did share business interests in the past," Gale said, selecting his words carefully.

Zach's brow shoved up. "Ah, yes, business interests. She told me."

"Yes, well, Eugenia had many unique business ideas. And since I was involved with the business, if I can be of service to you now or in the future, please, do not hesitate to call upon me."

"I'll keep that in mind, if and when I have any questions for you," Zach said, his features a benign study of indifference masking his anger at finding the man with Eugenia. "Of course, Eugenia's now in my employ, so I'm sure she'll be able to offer suggestions . . . if asked." Eugenia's eyes flashed at Zach over the unmistakable innuendo.

"Your employ?" Gale had heard the rumors circulating around town about their living arrangements. For a moment Gale's male pride was pricked over such impropriety. But, of course, the only thing Eugenia had been interested in when they were engaged was the oyster beds. Gale concluded that if Eugenia had not fallen into his own bed, much less had not allowed him even so much a kiss, surely she could not possibly have allowed the likes of Kellogg to lay a hand on her.

"She's my housekeeper."

Stupefaction raised Gale's thin blond eyebrows. "Eugenia?"

"Eugenia."

If Eugenia hadn't been so angry at Zach for drugging her, she might have enjoyed watching him put Gale in his proper place as the two parried words. It was obvious that Zach was more skilled than Gale. But at the moment, Eugenia was feeling quite put out by both men.

They were discussing her as if she weren't even there!

She glanced from man to man. Both were up to something. She'd bet on it. And she had the distinct feeling that it had something to do with the oyster beds. But at the moment the main thing she was interested in was putting an end to this tiresome interview.

She stood up and settled an annoyed frown on each man in turn. "I am so gratified that you have paid me this call, Gale. Your kindness is duly noted. But as Mr. Kellogg just informed you, I am merely the housekeeper here. I should not have taken the liberty to entertain my guests in the parlor. Therefore, if you care to continue this interview, we must retire to the kitchen and leave Mr. Kellogg to the enjoyment of his home."

Gale took out his fob watch and glanced at the time as he stood in concert with Eugenia. "I really must be leaving now. I have an appointment. But I would very much like to return and continue our visit at another time. We have a lot to catch up on, Eugenia."

Zach got to his feet and began ushering Gale to the door before Eugenia could respond. "She'll have to inform you of her schedule after her working hours have been established."

"Of course." For the second time Gale stretched out his hand, confident that Zachary Kellogg would not hesitate this time. "As I said, if I can be of any assistance, please do not hesitate to call upon me."

And for the second time Zach let those long fingers remain in the air, unclaimed. Rather, Zach snatched the man's hat off the rack and plopped it in his hand.

Gale looked at the crude indentations Kellogg's fingers had left in his hat with an expression of impotent irritation and confusion on his face.

Eugenia barely managed to keep a straight face. Remembrances of how she used to long to flatten that infernal hat materialized in her mind.

"Yes, well, thank you for allowing me to visit Eugenia in your home," Gale said awkwardly. He smoothed the dents from his hat and set it on his head.

His dislike for Zachary Kellogg was given birth. Kellogg had not only just rejected his generous offer of assistance with the oyster beds, the man had rejected his offer of friendship, as well as deliberately manhandling his hat.

Gale said his goodbyes to Eugenia, but his thoughts were silently focused on Kellogg. The man had rebuked him without cause, in front of Eugenia no less. Well, Kellogg would soon learn that he had made the biggest mistake of his life!

Zach returned to the parlor and propped his feet up, waiting patiently until Eugenia saw Sweeney out, waved farewell from the porch, and returned to the house.

When the door slammed, Zach's brow shoved up. "What's the matter, Eugenia? Did my untimely return ruin your happy reunion?"

"Why, whatever do you mean?" She wasn't going to volunteer anything.

"Gale Sweeney. He's the one you were once betrothed to, isn't he?"

She raised her chin. "And if he was? Aren't I allowed to entertain guests outside the kitchen?"

"You suggested that, not me. But as long as we're talking about guests, I noticed that you found it necessary to refer to me as *Mr.* Kellogg. What happened to Zach?"

It seemed to grate on him. Good. "You are my employer, after all. Isn't that the way you referred to my station in your home . . . as your housekeeper?"

He gave her a sheepish grin coupled with a shrug. "There aren't any other positions within my home open at the moment, but if one becomes available, you'll certainly be the first to know."

Eugenia had had to fetch her father from the Salty Dog Tavern often enough after her mother died not to understand clearly his lascivious inference. "There isn't another position within your household that could ever hold my interest."

Touché, he thought. He deserved that. But there was another position he had in mind for her, one he had been thinking about quite a bit lately; one

147

that heading over to Astoria should hopefully satisfy. He blinked to get such thoughts of Eugenia and his needs out of his mind.

"Eugenia, in all seriousness, I doubt that Gale Sweeney came calling merely to pay you a social visit."

"And why wouldn't he merely stop by to visit me? What other reason could Gale possibly have?" She kept her own suspicions to herself. Zach had put her in the position of having to defend Gale. Furthermore, she did not trust Zach either.

"Why, Gale even was kind enough to offer you his assistance. And now that we are talking seriously, as you put it, you were rude to him."

"A man's home is his castle, and this is my house." *At least until my superiors have my hide for buying it with government money.* "You're not in a position to demand an explanation, and I'm not in a position to have to offer one."

"No, you most certainly don't, and neither do I."

"Need I remind you that this is no longer your home?"

She shrugged. "A mere detail."

He ignored the indifference of her remark, despite the inclination to forbid her to have anything further to do with the man. She was one determined, pigheaded female. "I didn't treat Sweeney any way he didn't deserve."

Eugenia almost wanted to smile at his explanation, since he had made it plain a moment ago that he did not owe her one. Instead, she kept her expression sober.

Zach was not used to such a flagrant refusal to follow his directives, and it galled him. "Just stay away from the man, Eugenia."

She had intended to. Of course, now, after such a rude attempt to control who she could or could not see, she planned to do just the opposite.

Zach did not like the lengthy pause; it did not bode well. Yet he had not truly expected her to be readily compliant. "Listen to me. I know what I'm talking about," he said in exasperation.

"No doubt you always do."

Zach recognized female sarcasm, pure and simple, when he heard it.

Just to prove to her that he could be reasonable, he said, "No, I don't. But at least I'm willing to admit when I know I'm wrong."

There was the drone of male falsehood in his smooth delivery, and the word *know* would have elicited a proper response until he said, "How 'bout I make a pot of coffee while you prepare the fresh-plucked chicken I bought from a family just outside of town."

Eugenia's line of thought shifted, and she immediately tried to figure out all the places on the peninsula where he could have bought a chicken. It might give her a clue as to where he had been.

Then suddenly the word *coffee* registered in her mind, and a storm-warning flag waved before her eyes.

"I might have considered your generous offer except the dirty coffee cups are still in the dishpan." She gave him an icy smile cold enough to freeze a lesser man. "As I have no doubt that you are aware."

"Why would I be so inclined?"

"Do not try to pretend you do not remember what happened last night."

"If I remember correctly, you weren't feeling well last night."

Eugenia crossed her arms underneath her bosom and drummed her fingers along her forearms. "I am certain that the manner in which I was suddenly stricken last night remains quite clear in your memory."

He smiled, shrugged, undaunted by her telling sarcasm. "Actually," he grinned, "I've heard that what you were suffering from is going around."

"Yes, in a circle," she muttered. Then added caustically, "And if I'm not mistaken, I caught it from you."

She knew exactly what he'd done!

Turnabout was fair play, he thought as he had last night. "Guess it's been known to happen. When one gets ill, it isn't long after that that the one nearby often experiences the same symptoms. I think it's called sympathy pain or the such." That should teach her not to try something like that on him again!

"Even when sympathy does not exist?" she asked too sweetly.

"Oh, it's there, Eugenia, even if you don't know it yet."

Eugenia stared at him, unsure how to interpret his last remark. But one thing she knew for sure—there was a growing tension between them.

"Well, why don't I help you with supper, and afterwards, we'll do the dishes together," he suggested after a long moment of silence had stretched between them.

"Only as long as I am the one who gets the coffee."

Thirteen

After a tenuous truce, Eugenia ended up cooking chicken and potatoes for supper while Zach made the coffee under her watchful eye. They ate in the kitchen and after supper lingered at the kitchen table. Zach quizzed her about the oyster beds and asked a whole passel of questions pertaining to the town's more prominent citizenry.

Eugenia almost had begun to let down her guard until Zach brought up the subject of a ship on which to send the oysters to market in San Francisco.

"How did your father ship the oysters to market?" he asked out of the blue.

Eugenia stiffened, her adrenaline pumping. She struggled to calm herself before she answered. But as she dropped her eyes to her lap, all that came to mind was, "The same way all oystermen do, by sea, of course."

At first Zach thought she was being flip, but then he noticed her uneasiness, and made a mental note to add shipping to his list to check out. "Was there a specific ship he employed, or did he have a contract with a particular company?"

Eugenia breathed a silent sigh of relief. He did not know about her father's schooner. She hoped to keep it that way, since it seemed to be the only asset left in the estate and everyone seemed to have forgotten about it. She did not meekly intend to give that up. Thank goodness Captain Derrick had seen fit to return Cousin Mildred to California. It gave Eugenia the time to protect her interests in the ship.

"Eugenia?"

Her head snapped up. "Oh, sorry," she said a little sheepishly. "My mind was elsewhere."

Zach frowned and his lips tightened. "With Gale Sweeney?"

Why would she be thinking about Gale Sweeney of all people? Then she noticed the jealousy in those drawing blue eyes of his. The thought that Zach could be jealous caused her heart to begin to beat a little faster and her palms to suddenly become damp.

"I was not thinking of Gale at the moment."

Her response annoyed him. It was too measured. "At the moment?"

"If you actually want to know, I was mentally making a list of shipping companies for us to visit in the morning."

Zach let Gale Sweeney slip from his mind. She was trying to intrude further into his investigation. "Us?"

"Of course. It makes sense. Most oystermen ship

153

out of Bruceport, but I know the local owners and can procure the best deal . . ."

And I'll make sure that no one mentions the schooner either, she thought as she prattled on about shipping rates and the most expedient method to pack oysters for shipment to San Francisco.

Again, as in the other times that Eugenia started talking about her precious oyster beds, Zach noticed her green eyes twinkle with the joy of life. She became animated, gesturing with an excitement that drew him like a hapless fish to a baited hook.

"Why don't we finish our discussion in the parlor?" he suggested when she finally stopped to take a breath. Outside the rain had started to pound against the roof. "I'll build a fire, and we can sit on the sofa with our feet up."

Eugenia glanced into his eyes, and for the first time she thought she caught a glimpse of Zach, the man. It was an unsettling sensation she had not anticipated. They were locked into battles on so many fronts, at opposite ends of the spectrum on so many things, that she had not been prepared for the usually carefully covered emotion she saw there.

"You know, when I was a little girl my parents and I used to sit before the fire on rainy nights; Mother would make hot chocolate while Daddy read to me."

"Then hot chocolate and reading it will be," he announced.

To Eugenia's amazement, Zach popped out of his chair, grabbed her hands and led her into the parlor. He plumped two needlepoint pillows and settled her against them.

"Just make yourself comfortable while I build a fire."

Eugenia was speechless as he donned a slicker hanging on the rack in the vestibule and headed outside to fetch wood from the woodpile.

She may have been speechless, but she was not helpless. Eugenia waited until he had closed the door behind him before she went into the kitchen, added enough wood to the stove to heat the milk and put the chocolate on to warm.

By the time Zach had the fire started in the fireplace, Eugenia was returning with two steaming cups of chocolate.

Still kneeling before the fire, he looked up at Eugenia. "I thought I told you to get comfortable."

"I am not helpless, and I will not be treated as if I am some defenseless china doll, Zach Kellogg," she said, even as she noticed the blazing firelight flame in his eyes and the golden highlights in his coal-black hair.

He got up and took the cups from her, setting them on a nearby table. "Eugenia, I've never thought of you as either helpless or defenseless."

Their fingers had met when he took the cups, and Eugenia had to wonder whether the heat climbing her cheeks was from the flames or his touch. When she watched him bend over and toss the pillows from the sofa onto the floor, she could not help but notice how his powerful thighs rippled underneath his trousers.

She had never given much thought to men in the

way she now was with Zach, and it confused and excited her at the same time.

He folded his big frame onto the floor and patted the pillow next to him, reaching out a hand for her. For an instant his outstretched hand reminded her of Gale's earlier in the day. But Zach's hand was more powerful, his fingers blunt and strong. It was a hand that belonged to a physically powerful man used to taking charge and brooking no dissent.

She could never be a meek and obedient female, and she was troubled over the urge to place her hand in his. Zach put an abrupt end to it; he reached up and grabbed her hand, pulling her down beside him before she could react.

"Make yourself comfortable," he said and adjusted the pillows. Then he leaned over and snatched the chocolates from the table and put one in Eugenia's hand. Settling against a pillow, he leaned his head back and looked over at her, announcing, "There, that's more like it."

Reading was now the farthest thing from her mind, and Eugenia fought for control of these strange awakening impulses inside her. But sitting next to Zach on the floor before the fire seemed so natural, so suddenly enchanting, that she gave in to the urges and leaned her head back against the pillows only inches from his.

He stared into the cup but did not attempt to take a drink.

"You needn't worry, it is not drugged." To allay his suspicion, Eugenia drank from the cup. "See? I am fine."

"Yes, you most certainly are without a doubt," he said softly.

Zach took a sip of the chocolate and wished it had a kick to it. He was going to need some type of fortification to help him keep his wits about him . . . and his hands off Eugenia. She was so near, so enticing.

Eugenia followed his lead and took a big glug of the chocolate. It was as sweet as the memories. She set the cup aside as Zach had done.

"You have chocolate on the edges of your mouth."

Eugenia's hand came up, but Zach took it in his. With the thumb of his other hand, he wiped the chocolate from her lips.

His fingers gently lingered on her mouth, outlining her lips. His eyes were smoldering. Her tongue came out and tentatively touched his fingertips, sending sparks through his body.

"Zach?"

He didn't answer; he did not want to talk.

Possibly she had spoken too softly. Eugenia was rarely at a loss for words, but at the moment she did not know the appropriate thing to do or say. The back of his hand smoothed down her cheek and snaked around behind her head. She stared into his heated gaze as his fingers slid the pins from her hair.

Her glorious auburn tresses tumbled down her back in disarray.

Zach splayed his fingers through the thick auburn locks. They were so wild and free, so untamed, so much like Eugenia. Unable to stop himself, Zach cupped the back of her head and drew her to him.

He dipped his head and kissed her.

It was a gentle, probing kiss, meant as a prelude.

Her response surprised Zach. He had not been sure what her reaction would be after the last time he had kissed her. She had seemed more curious last time, more inquisitive. This time she drew back and silently gazed deeply into his eyes. And for a moment Zach wondered if she were looking deep inside him. He wondered if she could see how much he wanted her.

"Are you planning to make love to me tonight?"

There it was—*the question*. It had been burning, unexplored, in the back of his mind for some time now. If he answered her, a moment of raw truth would lie bare between them. Thus far their relationship had been built on an ocean of lies.

"What if I told you I was?" he probed.

Lying back against the pillows, their faces were mere inches apart. Eugenia could feel the flow of Zach's moist breath on her cheeks quicken. She knew what the answer should be, knew what society dictated. But she was here, all alone with Zach and her awakening desires.

She shifted her gaze, staring into the fire. She did not answer. With the crook of his index finger under her chin, Zach turned her face toward him.

"Eugenia?"

There was only one answer if she were honest with herself. But could she be honest with Zach when she knew that somehow their relationship was built on falsehoods and the shifting sands of suspicion? She thought of dropping her eyes, but could not take them from Zach's. His deepening blue eyes reflected the growing intensity of the moment, pinning her gaze to his.

She reached up tentatively to touch his face, but put her hand in her lap. "I do not know how to answer you."

"Then don't," he murmured thickly.

He took her hand and placed it on his cheek. It was warmed by the fire. He nuzzled his cheek against her palm, his lids half-closed at the sensations. Her hand still clasped in his, he brought it to his lips and suckled each finger.

"Let yourself feel," he whispered.

He took her face between his hands and kissed her. She closed her eyes. Her lips clung to his, and he boldly slipped his tongue into her sweet cavern. She did not attempt to pull away, emboldening Zach.

Without breaking the kiss, he lay her down, his elbows against the floor, his fingers wrapped in her hair.

Eugenia felt fragile, her determination liquefying under the weight of heightening passion. A building need was encapsulating her, encircling her in mystical moments where no outside world existed with its barriers to stand between them.

In response to their deepening kiss, her arms hooked over his shoulders, feeling the bunched muscular contours. She moaned against his lips as lush eddies rippled throughout her flaming body. Building. Building. All rational awareness fled under a tidal wave of wildly coursing hunger, and she eagerly followed his lead.

Zach was losing control. If he didn't stop now, he was not going to be able to stop. He could have her, totally possess her without protest; he was certain of it. But something held him back. From out of nowhere some sudden moral concern for her feelings in the bright light of day was stopping him.

God, he ached, he wanted her so badly!

Damn her eager innocence!

Damn honor!

Damn her!

With a sigh, he eased his lips from hers. "Once you've made up your mind, you don't waste time, do you?"

Eugenia's lashes fluttered open, and she stared up at Zach. He was watching her.

"W-what did you say?" she asked, confused and feeling strangely frustrated at the sudden interruption.

He toyed with a long auburn curl, dragging it along the side of her face. "I'm sure you usually get what you go after."

She leaned up on an elbow, disbelief heightening her color. "Did I hear you correctly? Were you implying that I set out to seduce you?"

Zach raised a knee in a display of indolent smugness he did not feel. Why the hell did a sudden wave of conscience have to hit him? "Isn't that what your story about hot chocolate before a fire was all about?"

Her dander was replacing the unschooled passion of a moment ago. "If you will remember correctly, it was your suggestion to retire from the kitchen to the parlor before a roaring fire."

"And finish out the evening reading after concluding the discussion we were having about the oyster beds."

"Then surely you will recall placing me up against the pillows," she said.

"But you, my dear, did not remain where I put you. You hurried into the kitchen to get the drinks."

"Hot chocolate! You make it sound as if I had brought hard liquor in those"—she swung out an arm indicating the chocolates—"two cups."

"Yes, and I seem to recall you returning with the chocolate and informing me that you were neither helpless nor defenseless. What did you expect me to do after such an open invitation?"

She sat up stiffly. "It was hardly an open invitation. And I can tell you exactly what I did not expect you to do!"

"Oh?"

"I did not expect you to toss the pillows on the floor and pull me down beside you."

"Didn't you?" His brow shoved up. She was safer kept at arm's distance. It was easier to remain on safe ground with her. He knew what to expect when they were at each other's throats. He could even deal with her unexpected antics. He had a job to do, and he did not need any romantic complications with a woman muddling up his mind at this stage of the investigation. Although in the back of his mind, he was genuinely disappointed that the evening had to end thus.

"No, I did not!"

"And I suppose you did not expect me to kiss you either?"

She tilted her chin up in defiance. "It was the furthest thing from my mind."

"For being the furthest thing from your mind, you sure didn't make any effort to dissuade me, darlin'."

That stung because it was true. She hadn't tried to dissuade him. And even as she glared at him, she feared that if truth were known and she found herself within his embrace again, she still wouldn't make any effort to dissuade him.

Fourteen

Eugenia had lain in bed for hours, unable to sleep after making her grand exit speech to Zach last night. It had been meant to save face, but no doubt had just the opposite effect.

She turned over and punched the pillow, chiding herself for asserting that if they could not agree on whether she had made an effort to dissuade him from kissing her or not, they should refrain from further discussion or action on the subject henceforth. All he had done was give her a wolfish grin in response. It had been such a silly statement that it continued to haunt Eugenia far into the wee hours of the morning.

Unable to get to sleep, Eugenia finally conceded that she might as well go down to the kitchen and get the drudgery of her daily chores out of the way early. Abandoning any further effort to dress in anything resembling a uniform, she dressed in an old pair of baggy britches and a plain blue work shirt, a piece of rope tied around her waist to hold the ensemble together. Not attempting to silence her exit, she pounded down the stairs and built a fire in the stove. Then she began tidying up the house.

After several hours, she forced herself to go into the parlor. She immediately came up short. Embers still smoldered among the ashes in the fireplace.

"How fitting," she muttered as she gathered up the half drunk cups of chocolate.

Her life was in ashes around her. But like the fireplace before her, there smoldered the embers of something she dared not acknowledge, dared not consider.

"Good morning," came an all-too-familiar voice from behind her. "Sleep well?"

The essence of her problem was up!

Eugenia swung around, wondering if Zach knew she had been unable to sleep. She tilted her chin up. "Perfectly, thank you."

"Dark circles become you," he observed, but his eyes had been focused on those lush, inviting lips.

She touched her fingers to the discolored skin beneath her eyes. "I notice you certainly are up earlier than you normally rise. Guilt keep you awake?"

"It's not one of the qualities I possess."

"Pity."

"Isn't it a little early for you as well?" he said, ignoring her corrosiveness and wondering if she had been snooping around the desk again.

"I work here, in case you have forgotten."

"No, Eugenia, I haven't forgotten," he said softly. I never should have allowed you to remain under the same roof with me, he reflected with a sigh.

"If you will excuse me, I shall get your breakfast."

"Just coffee, black and strong. And you can serve it in the parlor." He sat down at the desk.

"I would like to serve it in your lap," she muttered under her breath.

She watched him remove the key from his pocket and unlock the drawer. Without any effort to hide the envelope from her Zach moved the money and set it on the top of the desk. Then, as if he suddenly recalled that she had not left the room, he glanced up.

She noted that infernal brow of his slant up. "The coffee, remember?"

"I could reheat the chocolate," she suggested and could have bitten her tongue.

Eugenia could have sworn that his damnable brow reached new heights. There was the strangest glimmer in his eyes, but its meaning was unreadable.

"Perhaps another time. I've had my fill of chocolate for awhile. Just coffee."

"Really? Too sweet for you?"

He looked her directly in her snapping green eyes, then his gaze shifted to her lips. With a beleaguered sigh, he said, "I'm afraid so this time."

"Some things are truly better off discarded," she tossed at him.

As Eugenia went to the kitchen, she could not understand the peculiar tone in his voice, although she had been aware of the symbolism of their exchange. When she returned to the parlor, Zach took only two sips of the strong coffee she prepared and set it aside.

"Strong enough for you?" she said through her teeth, managing a complacent grin.

"Strong enough to put hair on your chest. I wouldn't advise you to drink any of it if I were you."

"I wouldn't think of it. I made it specially for you this morning."

"No doubt." The unpredictable spitfire, he thought. For an instant, concern that she had again attempted to drug him entered his mind. But he maintained his indifferent composure despite the unsettling thought.

Pleased she had made it strong enough to cut with a knife, she set about her work. She spent an inordinate time dusting the parlor, trying as nonchalantly as possible to peek over his shoulder until he set the pen aside.

"Eugenia, if you polish that table behind me any longer, you're going to wear away the finish."

"Nonsense," she argued lamely, taking the feather duster from her back pocket and moving to a lamp near the window. "I always do a thorough job. But if you would prefer a dirty house, I shall—"

"Yes, right now I would. And I'd like some solitude to finish these figures."

"Figures? I am good with figures."

He let his gaze roll down her from head to toe. "I have no doubt you are—especially in those tight britches you wear."

"Can't you ever take me seriously? I can be of help."

"I don't need your kind of help," he said and returned to his figures.

"My kind of help?" she demanded.

Help that muddles a man's mind, sets his insides on fire, and keeps him from doing the job he was sent here to do, he reminded himself.

"Oh, all right," she said in defeat when he made no reply; she left the parlor.

She worked in the vestibule where she kept a curious eye on him while he added up column after column. She'd sure like to get a look at whatever he was working on, but after the fiasco when she admitted taking the key, she dared not try that again.

"I'll be going out," he announced, locking the desk.

"Will you be back for dinner?"

"No, but I'm sure you have plenty to keep you busy right here" was all he answered as he slid his arms into a slicker and left the house.

She stood at the window and watched him head toward town. He had jammed his hands in his pockets and was whistling as if he hadn't a care in the world. But she knew better!

If he thought she was going to remain at the house and clean all day, while he engaged in whatever intrigue he was up to, he had another think coming.

Eugenia tossed on a slicker and hurried so she would not lose sight of Zach. The rain from the night before had left the ground strewn with puddles, and every now and then a bird would alight on a tree branch above and send a shower of raindrops spewing over her.

She was not surprised when he went straight to Washer's casket shop. It was just opening. His timing was impeccable. She drew the hood up over her head and walked into the shop with her head down, remaining behind a hefty woman garbed in black.

Eugenia was grateful for the small table Mr. Washer had installed for his customers, and she made a beeline for it. Hunching over the table in an effort to look busy, she craned to listen to what Zach was saying to the man.

"Mr. Washer, I've brought the cash to settle the final arrangements for the oyster beds," Zach announced, shaking the man's bony hand.

"Ah . . . ah, yes, of course you have, Mr. Kellogg. Please, do sit down."

Morton Washer uneasily settled behind his counter, and Kellogg sat down across from him, took a stack of bills from his vest pocket and laid them on the counter. Washer's gaze shifted to Rube Nelson, who was standing nearby at a stack of pine wood. The two men exchanged quick glances before Washer focused his attention back on Kellogg.

Washer set a pair of wire-rimmed glasses on the end of his nose, and shuffled through a batch of papers before he located the ones he was looking for. "Here are your papers, Mr. Kellogg," Washer said and shot a quick glimpse over Kellogg's shoulder.

"Good. Let's get this transaction over with, so I can get on with the business of making money."

"Yes." Washer's smile was forced. "You know, of course, that those oysters are worth their weight in gold in San Francisco."

"Of course," Zach said dryly, waiting for the man to hurry up and conclude the deal. His superiors were not going to be happy that Zach did not get prior approval, and he wanted to get this over with before he thought better of it and changed his mind.

"Why, I hear tell around town that they are selling for seven dollars a bushel," Washer continued. "Seems that no evening of pleasure is complete without them."

Zach smiled, his mind replaying the oysters he'd had with Eugenia. "I've heard that a time or two myself, Mr. Washer. I can honestly say they certainly have enhanced mine on occasion."

A short distance from Zach, Eugenia nearly choked when she heard his ribald comment to the town's self-appointed banker, the smug, insufferable male!

"They are simply delicious in stew, soup, pie, sauce, stuffing. Served broiled, fried, scalloped or raw. Of course, they are considered an aphrodisiac, you know, Mr. Kellogg," Morton Washer added.

"Yes, I've heard of their seductive powers," Zach returned, wondering about the authoritative information the man was spewing forth. He kept the smile from his lips when he thought of Eugenia and the innocent manner in which she unknowingly had wielded her own power of seduction.

"One look at you, sir, and one can easily believe

169

it." Washer grinned at Zach in a way Eugenia could only describe as male-understood lechery.

Eugenia blanched and colored over the implied powers of oysters. For an instant, she wondered what would have happened that night she had fixed oysters if he had not drugged her. She wished she could see Zach's face, but he was seated with his back toward her.

"Why, I have heard oysters are also used for—"

"Thanks for the dissertation on the product, Mr. Washer," Zach interrupted, growing bored with the man's excess gift with the spoken word. "My time this morning is limited."

"Mr. Kellogg, it isn't necessary for you to complete the transaction at this time. I know a busy man such as yourself must have many engagements. Besides, I am certain you have better uses for your money at the moment. After all, you are just getting started in a new business venture." Washer tried to hand back the money Kellogg had placed on the counter. To his chagrin, Kellogg did not take it.

"No doubt your capital could be put to better use elsewhere, Mr. Kellogg. Naturally, I shall be more than willing to extend the time on your note."

Zach's brow shoved up. There was something mighty curious about a banker, even a self-appointed one, who did not want to take a customer's money. And the man was starting to sweat. Mentally, Zach added Washer to his list of suspects.

"I insist, Mr. Washer. I always pay my debts when owed."

"I am sure we can work out an equitable schedule when you have more time, Mr. Kellogg." Washer waved the money like a carrot before the man.

Zach was closely watching the man's eyes. A man often gave himself away through his eyes regardless of how well his face may be schooled. Morton Washer was no exception. The man definitely was hiding something.

Throughout their conversation Washer had kept glancing over Zach's left shoulder. Under the guise of a racking cough, Zach twisted from Washer to find out what the man had been looking at. From behind his handkerchief, Zach noticed the nondescript, medium-height man from the auction immediately turn his back on him and face toward the caskets.

Zach also noticed a familiar figure loitering nearby. Eugenia, the little sneak!

Washer got up, ordered a glass of water be brought immediately, and went around his counter. He patted Zach on the back, obstructing Zach's view of Eugenia for a moment. When Zach stopped coughing and looked up, she was gone.

"Are you all right, Mr. Kellogg?"

A carpenter handed Zach a tumbler and returned to his work. Zach took a sip. "Fine. Shall we conclude this business? It seems something more pressing has just come to mind."

"I would not want to detain you. Why don't we conclude this another time?" Morton pressed, his eyes shifting over Kellogg's shoulder.

Zach leaned forward. "Is there a problem you wish to discuss with me, Washer?"

Washer retrieved his gaze and nervously settled it on Kellogg. "Why no, no, of course not, Mr. Kellogg."

Zach pushed the money lying on the counter toward the scrawny man, his urbane congeniality of a few moments ago gone. "Then take the money and get me a receipt. I'll sign the papers while the receipt's being made out."

Washer swallowed hard, his Adam's apple bobbing like a gill net float out on the bay. Zach watched with interest as Washer's hand reluctantly slid across the counter and reclaimed the money as if it were on fire, and he was about to get burned.

By the time Zach left the shop, he was slipping the deed of ownership into his coat pocket. He kept his eyes peeled for Eugenia, sure that interfering little spitfire was still lurking about nearby.

He wasn't disappointed.

He spotted her lingering in the alleyway directly across the street. Pretending not to see her, he leaned against the building and removed the papers from his pocket. Under the guise of studying the documents, Zach bent his head and waited for the nondescript man he had noticed inside the shop.

Zach did not have long to wait.

Not five minutes later, the man, accompanied by Morton Washer, came out of the shop and headed south. Zach tucked the papers away and strolled along the boardwalk, careful to keep a safe distance between himself and the two men.

The pair were acting awfully nervous. They stepped up their pace, and Washer kept looking around. Washer glanced back over his shoulder, and Zach barely had enough time to duck into the doorway of a tavern.

The two men quickly rounded a corner, and Zach had to move fast before he lost them. With the fleet grace of a hunting cat, he sprinted from the doorway. With long strides he was closing the distance between himself and the corner of a two-storied building when all of a sudden pounding footfalls vibrated the boardwalk beneath his feet.

"Zachary Kellogg, what the devil do you think you are doing, following Mr. Washer?"

Fifteen

Zach ignored the familiar feminine voice chasing him and continued after the two men. But by the time he finally rounded the corner, the pair had disappeared. Slowly he pivoted around and waited for Eugenia to catch up with him.

At the moment his fingers itched to wring that long, slender, interfering neck of hers, and he realized that she had a way of making him feel the uncharacteristic urge quite often.

Eugenia was panting from her exertions by the time she reached Zach. Out of breath, she pressed her hand against the stitch in her side. He was standing with his hands on his hips, glaring at her.

"What were you doing following Morton Washer and Rube Nelson?" she demanded, dropping her hands on her hips in concert with his.

"I might ask you the same question." Although previous thoughts of wringing her neck were sounding better and better, she had inadvertently supplied him with the name of the other man. He added yet another name to his mental list in this case.

"Oh for heavens' sake, I was following you," she said without guile. Her forehead wrinkled. "But what were you doing following them?"

Zach thought fast. She certainly was forcing him to stay on his toes. He could not say that about any of the women he had known.

"Trying to catch up with Washer." She did not look convinced. "If you must know, I needed clarification on the papers you watched me sign inside the shop a few moments ago."

She ignored his telling remark. So what if he had seen her. It was too late to worry about that mere detail. "Then why didn't you just call out to the man?"

Chrissake, she was making his job impossible!

"Why did you follow me?" he asked in an effort to throw her off the track.

"Why?" she echoed. She had to buy time to come up with a plausible explanation. She couldn't merely blurt out that she suspected him of having something to do with her father's murder.

"Eugenia, quit stalling." He clamped a hand around her upper arm and began walking back in the direction from which they had come. "You've been following me around since I bought the oyster beds, and I think it's about time you tell me exactly why."

The boardwalk was beginning to teem with citizens going about their business in the thriving bay side town. Eugenia felt a spectacle being guided along by Zach and his strongarm tactics as if she were a criminal under arrest.

All he was lacking were handcuffs!

"The way you are acting, one would think that you are a lawman rather than a businessman," she blurted out angrily.

A gentle breeze could have blown Zach over at the moment, he was so stunned by her unknowingly astute observation.

"Why would you say a thing like that?" He immediately released her arm before he caught himself and divulged more information than was wise.

Eugenia rubbed her arm where he'd had hold of her. She stepped forward and peeked inside his slicker at the breast pocket on his shirt. A hidden badge was not pinned there, but touching him caused her heart to race. "Because you are acting like you think you have the authority to treat me as if I am some criminal under investigation."

She had done the unexpected again. For as jaded as Zach considered himself to be after working in law enforcement for over fifteen years, the little spitfire had managed to amaze him with her unwitting perception. She had guessed the truth; he wondered if she had guessed the truth about how her being so close made him feel, let alone the vein in which his thoughts swerved.

In order to throw her off the track and get his mind back on it, he tossed his head back and laughed. "Eugenia, if I were some kind of lawman, let me assure you that right now you would be sitting in a cell for obstruction of justice. And for good measure I might just throw away the key."

She frowned, but she had not missed the ease with which he used the terms. She began to worry. What if he really was more familiar with the law than she had considered? What if he were some type of criminal? She had put visiting Sheriff Dollard at the jail out of her mind after Zach had kissed her, but now she had best not put it off any longer.

After a long pause, Zach said, "Are you going to tell me why you've been following me?"

Two oystermen passed them on the boardwalk and nodded, which gave Eugenia the excuse she had been groping for. "If you must know, I have no intention of merely stepping away from the business my father and I built. I care about the oyster beds. And I thought that if I knew what you were planning for the business, perhaps I could make you an offer which would interest you."

"Of that I've no doubt."

His infernal brow shoved up over a disgusting grin. Although she remained silent, she knew his reply had nothing to do with oysters, nor had he believed her excuse. There was no use trying another one on him. He could accept it or not.

"Eugenia, how could you ever hope to buy me out?"

"The same way you said that you bought the oyster beds—with a financial backer."

"You with a financial backer?" He chuckled, which heightened her anger and also served to fortify her determination.

"And what makes you think that I am not capable of getting a backer?"

"Eugenia, I have no doubt you are most capable

of a lot of things. But a backer to throw good money after a young woman in a cutthroat business . . . you must be jesting."

She pursed her lips and decided not to reply. But her mind was working overtime. It originally had been an excuse, but why couldn't she locate a backer? The answer in her mind was resoundingly simple: She could. And at the moment it did not matter to her what she had to do to get one—even if it meant suffering Gale Sweeney's unwelcome attentions.

"If you're done tailing me, I must go make arrangements to hire pickers and secure services of a schooner to deliver the oysters to market. So, since you now have my agenda for the remainder of the morning, why don't you go back to the house and start working in a capacity you are capable of succeeding at."

He might as well have chopped a hole in the hull of a ship at sea, she was so agitated over such a male-driven comment. It only served to fortify her will to succeed. What better way to do just that than to drive the price of the business down and have a backer waiting?

Once she managed to implicate him in whatever was going on, the price would drop. But that might take longer than she wanted to wait. No. She would have to think of another way. She glanced at Zach before her eyes drifted toward the bay.

Inside, she found herself hoping that Zach was not involved in her father's death. And she wondered if a price manipulation could have had something to do with her father's financial troubles.

Zach started to walk away, but she was not at his side. He turned to find her staring off into space.

What the devil was she plotting this time? he thought and went back to fetch her.

"Eugenia, are you going to stand in the middle of the boardwalk, blocking folks' way all morning?"

"What? Oh, no, no, I am going to accompany you on your visit to the shipping companies." Her chin tilted up, defying him to try and stop her.

"I suppose there would be no harm in it," he relented. Better to keep her at his side this morning than at his back, he quietly surmised. A sensual shift in his thinking caused his lips to curve up; better to keep her on her back beneath him than at her side.

"Even though you think I am only capable of cleaning houses, I just might surprise you."

He took her arm, and they started walking. Dryly, he said, "There was a time when I would have said that nothing you could do would surprise me, but I'm no longer so inclined toward that vein of thought."

Eugenia grinned and kept to her silence. She definitely had a few surprises in store for Mr. Zachary Kellogg!

"Where to first?" Zach said, sure that she had some definite place in mind.

"Holm's Boatworks."

"I want to contract with a company to ship my oysters, not make arrangements to have a ship built."

"The boatworks is run by a Finnish family with a long history in fishing and ties with the sea. Peter

179

Holm does a little of everything. Who better to talk to than him?"

"I suppose you're right," he said. But inside he wondered what she could be up to this time, and a small voice that had guided him as a lawman warned that he would be wise to seek another company.

Hell, his boss should have sent a marshal who knew something about the damned oyster business! Particularly because, despite knowing better, her reasoning was making sense.

Eugenia steered him straight to Holm's Boatworks at the north end of a row of false-fronted businesses. They stopped outside the shop, and he glanced down at Eugenia. She was intently staring at the schooners gently bobbing out in the bay.

"Shall we go inside, or do you plan to stare at the boats?"

Boats, humph! Definitely a land lover, she thought.

She smiled up at him, and he could have sworn he saw devils dancing in those green eyes. "I was just making sure that they have adequate ships available."

It was a curious comment since she had already said that Holm's Boatworks was the best. Zach held the door open, and they entered to find the place full of nautical equipment. Zach didn't have the vaguest idea what most of the paraphernalia was, so he kept his peace until Eugenia had made introductions.

"So you are the one who bought Woodward Whalen's oyster beds?" Peter Holm commented, shaking Zach's hand. "Folks have been wondering about you and our Eugenia."

Zach scowled at the red-cheeked man with silver-brown hair. "There's nothing to wonder about."

He looked unconvinced. "Of course not, forgive me. What can I do for you folks today?"

"I'm here to hire one of your schooners to make the first delivery of my oysters to San Francisco."

He dipped fingers into his thinning hair. "I don't rightly understand. What about—"

"It is all right, Mr. Holm," Eugenia interceded before her father's longtime friend could ruin everything with mention of her father's schooner. "I know you and my father usually did business, and I was telling Mr. Kellogg that you would give him the best deal."

"You did do business with Whalen, didn't you?" Zach was suspicious of Eugenia and the man's sudden unease.

"Well, yes, of course we did, but—"

"It is all right to do business with Mr. Kellogg, Mr. Holm," Eugenia interrupted again. If she were not careful, Peter Holm was going to blurt out that her father, unlike so many of the other oystermen, had his own ship and then she would be sunk.

Peter Holm settled a confused expression on Eugenia's earnest one. He fidgeted with his graying mustache before he finally said, "I am not sure I can be of assistance to you at this time, Mr. Kellogg. My ships are all in service."

"They are not!" Eugenia blurted out. "There are two out in the bay at this very moment riding high in the water, no doubt just waiting for a cargo."

Peter Holm was awfully nervous about something, and Zach now had another name to add to his rapidly growing list of people to check out.

"Eugenia, you don't know what you're talking about," Holm said.

She slapped her hands on her hips. She had her own reasons for needing one of Peter Holm's schooners, and she was not going to be put off. "If I do not know what I am talking about than I am sure you can enlighten me. Who has commissioned the two ships presently out in the bay?"

Peter Holm picked at the dirt under his fingernails. "Well, they aren't exactly lent yet. But I have a tentative offer from Mr. Sweeney."

"In that case, it's settled," Zach said before Eugenia could work the man over any more. "Whatever the man offered you, I'll double it."

Peter Holm nervously toyed with his mustache. "That isn't very good business on your part, Mr. Kellogg."

"But it is on yours." Zach stuck out his hand to seal the deal.

Peter Holm wiped his hands on the denim apron he wore and hesitated. He walked to the window in the front of the store and tensely glanced out before returning his attention to the pair.

"Folks might just start thinking that you have something to hide if you pass this offer up," Eugenia said, perturbed at the man's reticence.

"Well, Holm?" Zach prodded.

"I don't rightly know," Peter Holm hedged in a voice scared of defeat. "The *Gull Berry* won't be ready to take out at least until after the Fourth of July regatta at the end of Court Week."

"That's perfect," Eugenia set forth before Zach could answer. Again his fingers itched to encircle that lovely neck of hers. He'd never let a woman talk for him before.

Although Zach was irritated with Eugenia, he did not miss the man's tight lips. Peter Holm sure wasn't very happy over the idea of making such a good deal. Zach decided that the man needed to be moved up a notch on his list of suspects.

Peter Holm kept glancing toward the window, and Zach nonchalantly strolled over to the window and glanced out in the same direction Holm had been looking. Zach caught a glimpse of a shadowy figure disappearing in between two buildings down the street. The thought crossed his mind to chase after whomever it was, but it would be futile—particularly with Eugenia hot on his tail.

"Do we have a deal?" Zach inquired with an authority to his voice that brooked no quarter.

"Mr. Kellogg—"

"I'll have an attorney draw up a contract," Zach cut the man off as he returned from the window.

Holm sighed in defeat, seemingly unable to present another excuse. "That won't be necessary. Folks 'round these parts do business on a handshake."

"I'm not from around these parts. I'll have a contract to you as soon as possible," Zach said, hoping that the case would be concluded before he had to explain this to his superiors; they'd never agree to provide such a contract.

A rather subdued, slumped-shouldered Peter Holm and Zach exchanged farewells, and Zach and Eugenia left the boatworks behind.

Walking back toward the center of town, Eugenia said, "That sure was not like Mr. Holm. I simply do not understand his strange behavior. He usually is quite jovial and much more agreeable."

Zach's brow shoved up. "Is he?"

"Yes. It must be you."

"Me?"

"Of course. Everywhere you go, you seem to have the same effect on people."

She continued to chatter as they neared their next stop, but Zach was only half-listening. Eugenia had been correct. Everywhere he went and everyone he talked to were acting mighty strange. Zach wondered how they would react if they knew he was a marshal inquiring into Whalen's murder.

One thing was for certain: this case was not going to proceed without a major hitch.

The trouble was that he was not sure whether the hitch was going to be with the complexity of the murder investigation or Eugenia.

Sixteen

They stopped to make arrangements for Indian pickers to harvest the oysters, and then went to the post office to dispatch Zach's letter. Zach had insisted on paying a courtesy call on Len Sweeney, much to Eugenia's chagrin. Eugenia hoped to enlist Gale to her cause; the last thing she needed was for Zach and Gale's father to form some type of alliance. Luckily, Len Sweeney was still in Bruceport.

"Will you be home for supper tonight?" Eugenia asked outside Sweeney's offices.

"Don't tell me you aren't planning to accompany me the remainder of the afternoon?"

"All right, I won't," she said and sauntered off; she had plans of her own this afternoon. She half-expected Zach's hand to clamp on her shoulder and stop her. But to her surprise when she glanced back, Zach was already headed in the other direction.

A curious sense of disappointment overcame her. She had a mission, a goal in life to bring her father's murderer to justice, yet the thought that Zach was somehow mixed up in it distressed her more and more.

Setting aside such disturbing female emotions, Eugenia entered the modiste's shop three doors down from the mercantile and awkwardly went over to the ready-made dress rack.

Gertrude Englestrom swept back the curtain separating her workroom from her shop. "Good afternoon, how may I help you?" Startled when she glanced up, Gertrude stopped and clasped her hands in front of her. "Oh, Eugenia, what may I do for you?"

Eugenia frowned at the buxom, dark blonde-haired woman in her middle thirties, attired in a fashionable black striped frock. "What do you usually do for ladies when they enter your shop?"

Gertrude's eyes roved over the young woman wearing men's britches. "When *ladies* enter my shop, they are interested in purchasing fine wearing apparel." A sly grin barely turned up the corners of her thin lips. "But how may I be of service to you, my dear?"

If there had been another shop of Gertrude Englestrom's caliber in town, Eugenia would not have come in here. It was no secret that Eugenia had never approved of her father's relationship with the greedy, conniving divorcee.

From the moment she had come to town, that Englestrom woman had set her sights on Eugenia's father. It had not taken her long to hook the lonely widower. Every Saturday night for over four years,

Gertrude had made supper for her father, and he did not return until time for church on Sunday.

"I need a special dress," Eugenia stated flatly. With any luck, Gertrude Englestrom would not inquire further.

"Whatever for?" Gertrude asked, which threatened to deflate Eugenia. "The only time I have seen you wear a decent dress is to church. And then you usually wore the same outmoded fashion."

"I did not come here to discuss my fashion sense. I came here for a dress. If you cannot help me, I shall take the stage to the next town."

Gertrude pulled three pleasant dresses off the rack. After all, she was a businesswoman despite her personal feelings toward Woodward's interfering daughter. She tilted her chin a trifle higher than it already had been. "Of course, I can help even you. I could have helped you with Gale Sweeney if you would have allowed me."

Eugenia held up the dresses in front of her and discarded each selection. "I did not need your help."

Gertrude looked down her nose. "I needn't remind you that you did lose him, my dear."

"Funny, I seem to recall the circumstances differently. But, as an outsider, it truly was no concern of yours anyway."

With a condescending sigh Gertrude handed Eugenia a special frilly confection of mint green lace. "Eugenia, I cared for your father and he for me. I may very well have become your stepmother had he not passed on. I am truly sorry—"

"Murdered," Eugenia corrected, ignoring the woman's offer of sympathy. "My father was murdered. He did not just 'pass on.' Furthermore, you were only after his money."

Gertrude could no longer endure the impudent young woman's blatant accusations. She had suffered Eugenia's rudeness for expediency's sake, but since Woodward was dead, she did not have to suffer it any longer. Gertrude marched into her workroom and returned a moment later with two pieces of paper, which she flung at Eugenia.

Eugenia caught the sheets against her chest with one hand. "What are these?"

"Look for yourself." Gertrude snatched the dress from Eugenia's hand and waited while she read the contents.

Once Eugenia had finished perusing the papers, she looked up, a bewildered expression on her face. "I do not understand."

"Don't you?" Gertrude answered sarcastically. "If you can read, as you profess you can, I think they are clear enough. I loaned your father sizable sums of money on two separate occasions over the last three years." Gertrude's chin gave an even haughtier tilt. "Now, is that finally proof enough for you that I was not after your father's money?"

"It would not seem so," Eugenia said, at a loss for a more appropriate phrase. She could hardly believe she had been wrong about the modiste's motives. For several moments Eugenia stared at Gertrude, neither breaking eye contact until Eugenia finally relented and broke the silence with, "I'll take the green one."

Laden with packages, Eugenia wondered if she had made so many purchases because of the sudden guilt and shame she'd experienced. She had disliked Gertrude Englestrom for so long, only to discover that the woman had quietly lent her father money to rescue his business. How terribly wrong she had been about the woman.

Gertrude even had been kind enough to open an account at her shop for Eugenia. Only trouble was Eugenia did not have the foggiest notion how she was going to pay for all the fancy garments she had purchased.

Eugenia rearranged the wrapped bundles more comfortably and headed toward the jail. She would worry about paying the bill later.

At the moment she had to find out if Zach Kellogg was a wanted criminal.

Eugenia tried the door to the jailhouse, but all her packages made it impossible to turn the handle. She attempted to shift the packages so she would have a free hand to open the door. But the packages tumbled out of her arms. Awkwardly, she bent down and gathered up the bundles, leaning against the door.

Before Eugenia could react, the door opened and she fell inside, coming face to pant leg with Sheriff Dollard.

Sitting on the rough wooden floor, Eugenia glanced up at the lanky sheriff. He looked to be ten feet tall from her position at his booted feet.

She forced a weak smile. "Sheriff Dollard, thought I would drop in on you."

"Looks like you have too, Miss Eugenia." He helped her to her feet and picked up her packages and set them on the nearby cluttered desk. "What can I do for you?"

Eugenia strolled about the room which was jammed with paperwork, guns and an old battered desk. "Actually, I dropped in to have a look at your wanted posters."

"Miss Eugenia, if you're still stickin' your nose in the investigation into your pa's murder, it ain't gonna do you no good. I already done told you last time you was nosin' around that I'm doin' everythin' that needs doin'."

"I am sure you are, Sheriff. But I would like to have a look, if it is all the same to you."

Bob Dollard did not like folks nosing around in his business; they often tried to interfere with the job he had to do. And he sure enough did not need some oyster-harvesting female who wore britches sticking her nose where it wasn't wanted.

"I was just headin' out."

Eugenia smiled brightly at him. "You go right on ahead about your business, Sheriff. I will not disturb anything."

"Then how you proposin' to get a looksee at my wanted posters?"

"I will leave everything in the same order in which I found it. I promise, Sheriff."

Argumentative, contrary female! If he had a say over her, he'd keep her naked and in bed. "All right, Miss Eugenia,"—he plunked down in a chair next to the door and crossed his arms over his chest—"have your own way. You can go through the posters, but I ain't leavin'. So you had best make it quick, or I'll down right arrest you for gettin' in the way of a lawman tryin' to carry out his duty."

Eugenia set about going through the posters, but her mind kept replaying the sheriff's comment; it had a vague familiarity to it. It was strangely similar to what Zach had said. Eugenia put the unusual coincidence from her mind as she went through the posters, only to come up empty-handed.

For a moment she did not know whether she was relieved or disappointed. But she did know that something did not ring true about Zachary Kellogg. And despite the undeniable draw she had for him, she was going to find out what!

All the machinations she'd had to go through to get a good look at Zach's face had not netted the desired results. Or had it? Zach was not a wanted man trying to hide behind that thick beard. She smiled to herself. Secretly she was glad Zach was now clean-shaven. He was a most handsome man. And inside, truth be known, she was relieved he was not a fugitive.

"You gonna sit there daydreamin' 'bout somethin' or you gonna gather your packages up off my desk so I can get on with what I got to do," Sheriff Dollard said in a grudging voice.

"Are you trying to get me out of the way, Sheriff?"

"Miss Eugenia, if I wanted to get you outta the way, as you put it, I'd simply lock you up and toss away the key."

"What did you say?" she puzzled.

"I said I might just as soon lock you up and toss away the key if you don't get a move on you."

"That is what I thought you said." Eugenia furrowed her brows and cocked her head in contemplation over the remark the sheriff had just made. Curious. It was almost uncanny. Zach had said nearly the same thing verbatim, word for eerie word.

Eugenia picked up her packages and was strolling toward her family home, troubling over the similarity of the comments made by Zach and the sheriff when she sighted Len Sweeney disembarking from a ship making a return run from Bruceport.

Waving and trying not to drop her burden at the same time, Eugenia hurried to catch up with the barrel-chested man who had been her father's partner. "Mr. Sweeney, Mr. Sweeney, may I speak with you?"

Sweeney stopped and waited for the young woman to catch up with him. "Eugenia, how are you? I am so sorry I had to be the one to break the news about your father."

"Yes, I know, Mr. Sweeney. You could not have known that I was unaware of the events." Eugenia's voice caught, but she was not going to allow an exhibition of her inner emotions to be displayed now. She took a deep, cleansing breath. "What I need right now is your advice."

Sweeney's lips tightened; he was constantly sought after for advice. "What can I do for you?"

"You were at the auction when my father's oyster beds were sold."

Sweeney shifted feet uneasily. "I was merely passing by. I did not stop, and I was not engaged in the bidding."

It was a strange comment. "But I saw you standing in the rear of the crowd during the sale."

"Of course you did. What is it you need?" he asked with a sharp edge to his voice that had not been there before.

"I am afraid that the man—Zachary Kellogg—who bought my father's beds, is somehow implicated in his murder, and I need your advice to help me prove it."

Sweeney leaned forward, a look of relief on his bloated face. "My dear Eugenia, that is a pretty serious accusation. How can you be certain?"

"I just am. But I need to get enough hard evidence to see justice done."

"Don't you think you should let the law handle evidence gathering, Eugenia?"

"If I wait until Sheriff Dollard gets around to doing anything about it, no one will be brought to justice. No. I cannot rest until I have seen justice done, and I need your advice."

His demeanor returned to smug self-aggrandizement, Sweeney directed her toward his office building. They stopped in front of his tidy plank offices, and he opened the door. Once they were inside and seated in the plush room, decorated in heavy mahogany furniture and plaques attesting to his leadership role in the community, Len Sweeney settled behind his desk, clasped his hands together and leaned forward.

"Before I agree to advise you, Eugenia, I think you had better tell me exactly what makes you think that this man—Zachary Kellogg—may be guilty."

Eugenia had not meant to divulge particulars, but she had no one else to turn to, and she desperately needed counsel. Despite her resolve, she was developing feelings for Zach, and she had to do something before they got out of hand.

For nearly a half hour Eugenia poured out her story. She described how Zachary Kellogg—a stranger with no one bidding against him—suddenly showed up in town the day after her father was murdered and then purchased the oyster beds.

She went on to relate how she had been spying on Zach, detailing the incident in the woods where Zach had met a man who gave him an envelope which she later discovered was filled with money. Eugenia told Sweeney how Zach had followed the town's self-appointed banker, his lack of knowledge concerning the business he had purchased, and all about the questions he had been asking the local people.

She was careful to delete a few of her more colorful antics which had ultimately backfired. And she certainly was not going to share the drugging incidents, or the kiss they had shared before the fire, or the helplessness she was experiencing over the growing strength of her feelings for Zach.

Sweeney tented fat fingers in front of his face, drumming them together. "Very interesting. Very interesting indeed, my dear. His actions certainly can be considered suspect," he said for her benefit; he did not put any true credence to her tale.

Eugenia moved to the edge of her chair. She was convinced that she had found an ally in Mr. Sweeney. "So you understand, Mr. Sweeney, why I believe that Mr. Zachary Kellogg is not merely a businessman with a good eye for profit as he professes to be. I am certain that he is up to something, but thus far every time I have attempted to catch him, he is one step ahead of me.

"I have to do something before he can send the oysters to market, take the remaining profits out of the business, bleeding it dry and then possibly disappear. Please, Mr. Sweeney, I need advice."

"Well, of course, I can't say for certain that Mr. Kellogg is guilty of anything. But from what you have been telling me, I definitely think that you were brave to remain under the same roof with him so you can keep an eye on his activities."

"That is becoming increasingly difficult because I believe that he is suspicious of me." That was an understatement!

"Then what you need to do is to put him at ease; throw him off guard. Maintain your vigilance while you gain his confidence until he is willing to confide in you without thinking what the consequences of an unguarded tongue may be." She looked somewhat confused at his suggestion, which would keep her occupied. "In other words, my dear Eugenia, you want him to talk freely to you."

Eugenia toyed with an errant auburn curl, attempting to digest his advice into some semblance of reason as she pondered what Len Sweeney had suggested. But achieving such a triumph seemed beyond her. Finally, still in a quandary, she asked, "How do you propose I accomplish that feat?"

Seventeen

Len Sweeney searched Eugenia's face. She looked so earnest, so innocent, so damned naive that he finally had to believe what his son had been telling him for some time: Eugenia Whalen was totally unaware of the potency of her feminine wiles. My gawd, the Whalen girl really had spent too much time out at the oyster beds!

"You mean to tell me that you have no idea how to make this Zachary Kellogg talk freely to you?"

"You mean confide in me?"

Eugenia watched the man's heavy lips as he said, "Yes, confide, as I said. Make him your confidant." He scanned her face to ascertain whether she understood that the European interpretation of the word meant lover.

"Befriend him?"

His lips tightened. She was not a woman of the world. "In a manner of speaking. To really *befriend* a gentleman so you can get him to . . . shall we say . . . cooperate without realizing it . . . you may need to give him the impression that you are—that you find him a particularly . . . interesting . . . ah, I mean a fascinating gentleman who holds you well . . . in thrall."

Eugenia shrugged. "Actually, Mr. Sweeney, Zach Kellogg is interesting. And I must admit that I really do find him rather enthralling, as it were."

Sweeney took a breath. Semantics. He was not getting through to her. From what she'd said, she did not truly understand what he meant at all.

"Eugenia, often a clever lady will show a gentleman that she finds him particularly captivating by displaying a certain amount of fascination with the gentleman. Make the gentleman feel that he has special significance in the lady's life."

Eugenia was beginning to comprehend all too clearly. She placed her hand to her chest, although if truth were known the notion did not particularly upset her. "Are you suggesting that I encourage Zachary Kellogg's attentions with the pretense of personal attraction?"

When Eugenia returned to her family home, Zach was not there. She scurried about the kitchen, getting supper started, then went upstairs and laid all the clothing she had purchased across the bed. She had bought the items with the specific purpose of using them to convince Gale to back her efforts to buy out Zach. But the thought of dressing up in such finery to attract Zach Kellogg instead caused her heart to pound.

Nerves, she told herself. She had never done anything like she was about to do. That's why her heart was pounding. No other reason. Just nerves.

By the time Eugenia heard the slam of the door, she was outfitted from her bare skin outward in the finest that Gertrude Englestrom had to offer. To Eugenia's surprise, Gertrude had included a generous bottle of sweet-smelling toilette water.

Eugenia uncapped the bottle and took a whiff. It smelled like the orange blossoms Eugenia recalled from her aunt's orchard in California. She splashed herself with half the bottle. After all, she figured she needed all the help she could get with what she set out to accomplish tonight.

Holding out the billowing pale green skirt, Eugenia glanced at herself in the mirror. She hardly recognized the pretty young woman staring back at her. It was amazing what a fancy dress and a few ribbons could do.

If only her feet did not ache from the high heels she had donned. Why the devil did women wear the fashionable torture chambers? It was hard enough to stand in the leather shoes without trying to walk in them!

She grabbed a fan she had brought from her aunt's and somehow managed to make it to the top of the stairs, prepared to make a grand entrance.

Zach was standing at the bottom of the stairs, his hand on the banister as if he were about to mount the steps.

"Good evening, Mr. Kellogg," Eugenia said with a beckoning smile and snapped open the fan.

"Good evening to you, Miss Whalen." Zach watched her descend the stairs.

From the appreciative expression on Zach's face, Eugenia knew she looked her feminine best, but inside she felt awkward and ungainly.

With slow, precise steps she managed each stair, maintaining a white-knuckled death grip on the banister. As she neared Zach she took her hand from the banister and stretched it out toward him, so he could escort her properly. But the moment her fingers left the steadying force of the banister, her ankle twisted and she found herself propelled forward.

She landed against his chest.

Zach closed his arms around Eugenia, catching her. He barely managed to brace himself in time to stay their fall. Instead they rocked precariously, and Eugenia was left locked within Zach's embrace.

Eugenia pulled back from his encircling arms, and shifted the bodice of her dress back into place. Looking up into those laughing blue eyes, she announced, "Guess I managed pretty well to catch your attention tonight."

"I'd say that I'm the one who made the catch," he answered and offered his arm. "You look lovely this evening."

"Th-thank you," she said shyly, recalling an earlier conversation they'd had concerning compliments.

"Going out alone?"

"No. You are my escort."

"Incidentally, where is it I'm to escort you?"

Eugenia took Zach's arm and glanced up into his grinning face. She batted her long lashes at him. "Into supper, of course."

Zach did not take a step. He dropped her arm, took out his handkerchief, lifted her chin with his finger and asked, "Which eye's bothering you?"

"What?"

"You were blinking a moment ago as if you had something in your eye. Which eye's bothering you, so I can help you get whatever it is out?"

"My eyes were merely filled with the sight of you," she said with a baleful sigh.

Not about to give up yet, Eugenia took the hankie from him and coyly stuffed it back into his pocket. She took his arm once again and tried to walk like a lady as they headed toward the dining room. Her ankles were not cooperating.

"Never made a woman blink at the sight of me like that before."

Eugenia was silently chagrined. Either he had not realized that she was attempting to flirt with him, or he was playing games.

He seated her at the dining room table and took a place across from her. The glow of the candles flickered golden-red highlights to her auburn curls.

A mere setback, Eugenia thought, continuing to mull over his comment about never making a woman blink at him before. She smiled brightly. "Everything has a first."

"Yes, so it does. No doubt one of yours is wearing high heels."

Eugenia had already kicked off the offending shoes, and his remark caused her to wiggle her toes. Although she wanted to add that wearing high heels would be a last as far as she was concerned, she merely said, "Nonsense, I have often worn heels while attending numerous soirees at my aunt's home in California."

Eugenia fanned herself to hide the look of falsehood she was sure shone on her face.

"If you're warm, I can open a window," he offered in gentlemanly fashion.

"I am fine, thank you." She snapped the fan shut and set it aside. Obviously, the pleated bit of lace only worked on the men in California.

They sat there, neither saying a word for several moments until Zach finally picked up his linen napkin and polished a fork. "The table looks real nice."

"Thank you." She glanced at the table set with the family's best china and crystal. "I want supper to be very special tonight."

"Did you hire someone else to serve?"

Zach's eyes went to the kitchen door, and Eugenia's followed. Of course, there was no one else in the house to serve!

His comment reminded her of a detail she had forgotten about. She was the hired help.

"What makes you think that I may have hired someone else to serve you?" she asked in an effort to stall. She had kicked off her shoes. Blindly she made a valiant attempt to locate the constricting leather.

"You are seated at the table."

She gave a guilty shrug. "So I am, aren't I?"

"Yes. You are."

Eugenia squirmed in her chair as she stretched out her leg in frantic search for the shoes. The damned shoes seemed to have disappeared from under the table!

"Eugenia, if there's a problem, perhaps I can be of assistance." Talk about squirming in one's seat! Eugenia was practically doing a jig!

She forced a smile. "No. No problem. If you will excuse me?"

Zach nodded, suspicious yet amused over her apparent unease. But Zach was not prepared when the little spitfire lifted up the corner of the fine linen tablecloth and suddenly ducked underneath it.

Determined to find out what she was up to, Zach grabbed the tablecloth and ducked his head under it as well. "Eugenia—"

He ceased his question the moment his eyes came to rest on her. She was bent over, stretching for one of her shoes, which lay just out of reach.

"Fancy seeing you under here," she said with a forced smile.

"Imagine that," he answered and stifled a grin. He grabbed up her shoe and tossed it to her while she managed to reach the other one.

Eugenia slipped into the shoes and in her haste bumped her head on the tabletop as she righted herself in her chair. Holding her head, she watched Zach return to an upright position in his seat.

"The shoes got away from me," she offered coyly.

"Walked right off your feet, no doubt."

"One would think they had feet of their own," she said with a weak grin. She got up and hurried

203

into the kitchen before the conversation could take on a more ludicrous twist than it already had.

Once in the sanctity of the kitchen, Eugenia leaned against the cupboard and sent the shoes spinning into a far corner. She did not need an uncomfortable pair of shoes to loosen the man's tongue.

Much more relaxed in her stocking feet, Eugenia removed a succulent baked Chinook salmon from the oven and lined the serving platter with vegetables. The fragrant aroma wafted from the fish. She smiled when she thought how residents told of being able to open their windows and whistle, and the fish would fly into the house on their own, they were so abundant.

Her confidence restored, Eugenia held the platter high as she returned to the dining room. Her poise returned as well as she watched him enjoy the meal she had hastily prepared. Surely courting a man's attentions was no more difficult than a meal well staged.

Zach took one last bite and pushed back from the table. "You're an excellent cook, Eugenia. My compliments."

"Where are you going?" she asked when he stood up.

"After such a meal I need to walk."

"Wait!" she said much too fast. "I shall accompany you."

Eugenia got up and realized that she could not accompany Zach outside. She was not wearing those damned shoes. Thinking fast, she took his arm. "Why don't we go into the parlor instead?"

Zach glanced down at her. She was noticeably shorter than she had been when they'd gone into supper, and he had to smile to himself. No shoes. Eugenia would not become a stuffy matron, overly concerned with appearances and regally presiding over her parlor.

They adjourned to the parlor, and Eugenia settled on the sofa next to Zach. She felt a trifle bold, sitting so close to him. But he did not seem to mind. At least he did not scoot over to escape her.

She stretched her arm along the back of the sofa in a further display of cheek. Still he made no effort to move.

"It certainly is bright in here," she said.

He did not answer. He merely sat next to her with that brow of his lifted, intently watching her. That had to be a sign that he was receptive to her.

She leaned over the back of the sofa and reached for the lamp she had lit earlier, extinguishing it. The room was now bathed in a pale glow from a single dim lamp, burning softly in the far corner of the room.

"There, that is better, don't you think?"

His eyes appeared bathed in a blue incandescence. "Much."

She had not had time to build a fire, but the way her cheeks flamed, Eugenia did not think that a fire was necessary. She took Zach's handkerchief from his pocket and swabbed her forehead.

"Warm?" he asked.

"You?"

"It's definitely heating up in here," he observed.

Eugenia leaned over and placed her hands on

his shoulders. "In that case, let me help you off with your jacket." Zach did not try to stop her.

To alleviate the sudden surge of nerves, Eugenia chattered while she removed his jacket. "A man should be comfortable in his own home, don't you agree?"

His eyes seemed to have transformed into two glowing blue flames. "Always," he murmured.

"Shall I loosen your string tie?"

She said the words in no more than a strained whisper, and Zach found himself beginning to squirm. But his unease was from his growing desire, and he had to wonder if she realized what she was doing to him. The lawman in him thought to question her about what she was up to, but the man that he was held his curiosity and hunger in check as he waited for her to make the next move.

"By all means. Be my guest."

Eugenia's fingers trembled as she untied the braided fabric and draped it over the arm of the sofa. "Would you like me to loosen your collar? It appears to be a little snug."

"Please do. Loosen whatever you wish."

Her fingers spread fire across the skin at the base of his neck, and sent flaming gooseflesh down his arms. Whatever she was about, Zach was not certain he could resist if she asked something of him at the moment, he was becoming so mesmerized by her.

She sat back and stared. Zach looked incredible in his white shirt, open at the neck with just a hint of dark hair peeking from the open collar. The sensitivity heightened in her fingertips, and she longed to sneak her fingers inside his shirt.

"Thank you."

"It was my pleasure." The pupils of her eyes were dilated, her lids heavy with the sensuousness of the moment, sending a silent indication of her readiness to respond to him.

"Let's make it mutual," he whispered.

Eugenia did not attempt to stop him when he reached up and pulled an end of the ribbon holding her curls in place. She remained still, watching him as if she were in a trance as he slid the ribbon from her hair and the curls flowed down her back.

But her mind was busy warning her of the similarity with what had happened the last time they had sat together in the parlor. She was rapidly losing control of the situation. If she did not do something—fast—she was in imminent danger of becoming the seduced, rather than the seducer!

Eighteen

Zach's hand slipped underneath Eugenia's hair to the sensitive spot on the back of her neck. His fingers were magical, massaging, numbing her senses to all thoughts of protest, willing her to accept the fiery sensations she was experiencing.

This cannot be happening, she frantically thought of the overpowering forces she had unwittingly unleashed between them. She had meant to engage his attentions so she could convince him to talk freely. Instead he was engaging passions she had never known she possessed.

"Mmm." She nuzzled his palm with her cheek, unable to control herself.

"Here, turn around," he murmured. "Your muscles are knotted in your neck."

She complied without objection, dropping her head while he continued to work his magic on her. "I thought I was the one making you more comfortable."

"You'll get your chance," he quietly replied, inhaling her fresh fragrance of orange blossoms. He thoroughly massaged her neck and shoulders with an expertise Eugenia hadn't known possible before his fingers slipped away. "Now it's your turn."

Eugenia had expected him to face away from her, as she had done, but instead he remained facing her, his mouth set in a serious line, his eyes burning into hers, mesmerizing her and setting her on fire.

Tentatively, Eugenia began working her fingers along his shoulders. As the blazing heat of the moment overtook her, a boldness overcame her, and she slid her hands inside his shirt to glide her palms over the smooth fiery skin beneath the fabric.

"Do you like what you feel?" Zach's baritone was coaxing, drawing. He was gently urging her, pressing her forward.

"Mmm" was her only response.

"Would you like to explore further?"

"Mmm" came again.

He glanced into her face to find that her eyes were closed, a broad, sensuous smile on her slightly parted lips. Without further hesitation Zach shed his shirt in an easy, fluid motion and guided her delicate hands through the hairs foresting his chest toward his slender waist.

Zach waited for Eugenia to pull back at the sudden intimacy. Instead she dipped her fingers beneath his belt, causing his stomach muscles to contract at the sudden surge of excitement coursing through him.

He was in danger of losing control again. He was considered one of the most controlled, deliberate lawmen out of Vancouver, and he wanted Eugenia so bad that he was starting to ache.

"Eugenia, I want to show you exactly the way you're making me feel."

"Mmmm," she answered again and did not stop gliding her fingers over his muscled torso. She experienced his words as a silken caress, which only served to heighten the sensations racing through her body.

Zach made deft work of the top of her dress, unhooking the bodice with one hand. Her satiny smooth skin was heated, and he leaned over and kissed the milk-white flesh of her shoulder. She pressed herself against his lips, emboldening him to slip the bodice and her camisole off her shoulders, letting it drop to the floor.

Her breasts were freed to his hungry sight, causing his sex to press for release against his trousers. Her hand skimmed over the bulge, and Zach took in a sharp breath.

"I hope you realize what you're doing to me, Eugenia," he groaned in the agony of desire.

"Mmm, I want to learn," she mumbled and partially opened her heavy-lidded eyes.

His face was a mere heartbeat from hers, his smile disarming. His magic fingers glided over her.

"Are you a good student?"

"The best," she said with the tremor of desire in her voice.

He shifted his weight and gently lay her back. Her cheeks were flushed, heated with a fervor.

"You are not leaving, are you?" she asked in a

small, husky voice, threaded with barely masked alarm.

"Not unless you want me to." His husky tone was provocative, tempting. `

"No, I don't," she murmured, past considering proper convention or the consequences of what they were doing. Her hand drifted up behind her head, and she let her lashes flutter closed again in an expectant fashion.

She seemed to be adrift in a sensuous world of her own, and Zach wanted her to realize who she was with, who was about to intimately possess her.

Far some reason, he wanted her to be fully aware, fully cognizant of what she was doing and with whom. She seemed to be growing in importance in his life, and he did not want her to think he was merely bedding another female in the heat of the moment. He needed her to see him—as a man who'd desired her as a woman.

"Open your eyes, Eugenia, and look at me. I want you to see what you're doing to me. I want you to see who I am and what I want and need from you. I want you to know who you are with. And I want you to be aware of what you are about to give."

Dreamily, Eugenia complied with the extraordinary directive, although she did not exactly understand its full import. He was sitting beside her on the sofa, staring intensely down at her. She gazed into those blue delving eyes; they had deepened to the color of the ocean just after sunset, and she had an inkling that she was engaging in a very dangerous game.

But at the moment it made no difference. She

had already relinquished control to her senses. And her senses cried out to be sated.

"I know whom I am with," she whispered and reached up to stroke his cheek.

"Do you know, what's going to happen if we remain here together like this?"

He curved his fingers over her hand and brought it to her side. Then he stroked her cheek before his hand shifted to outline her breasts. The centers rose into peaked questing buds in response to his feathered touch.

"Yes, and with whom." Her voice was filled with promise.

Eugenia did not take her eyes from his. She could see what she was doing to him, see the fire in his eyes, the flaring passion, the flaming desire. For an instant she attempted to consider what he was doing to her.

Her senses were aflame, screaming for her to toss caution to the wind and pursue the heightening pleasure, give in to the recklessness of the moment.

"Heaven help me," he breathed against her lips.

It seemed like a strange epitaph until his lips met hers and all rational thought fled.

His kiss was hungry and raw, devoid of the gentleness he had displayed when he had kissed her earlier. He was ravenous and devoured her lips, his tongue exploring hers, his teeth nipping in response to hers.

His lips left hers to take a breath, and he moved lower to fasten his ravenous mouth on a breast. Hungrily, he suckled, his tongue swirling around the straining nipple. His hand kneaded the other breast.

"You're very good." Her breathing was becoming labored as she melted against him from the heat of the wild sensations pulsing through her.

He lifted his head to respond. "Only very good?"

"Considering my vast experience, I would say that it is a compliment," she managed to breathe out.

"And am I to presume that you're a woman of vast experience?" He kissed her navel.

"I've had a wide range of experiences," she murmured with subtle inference of challenge.

Zach only smiled, thinking that nothing she had done in the short time he had known her indicated that she was versed in life's sensual pleasures. But he was beyond holding himself back. The atmosphere around them was charged with unrestrained passions.

"When are you going to demonstrate how very good you are?" Her voice was tentative, inquisitive, seeking. But she was no longer able to stop herself and withdraw from the room. She had already relinquished her will, leaving to him the possession of her body the foregone culmination to their passions.

"Now, if you want."

"I want," she answered with a beckoning sigh, having given herself up to the honeyed sensations.

Zach reacted by divesting himself of his remaining clothing. He smiled when he lifted her skirts to find she had indeed already shed her shoes.

"Let me help you," she offered, sat up and begun unhooking the skirt band of the dress.

Zach was pleasantly surprised that Eugenia did not intend to prove to be stiff and still as a plank while he undressed her as many of the women he had known had insisted was proper.

It did not take long until both were nude. But Zach was not inclined to prolong the moment this time. His need was too urgent, too overpowering, too great. He spread her thighs and dipped a finger into her. She was hot and ready, wet and waiting to welcome him. Caressing her a moment longer, he then moved to lie on top of her, supporting his weight with his elbows as he entered her slowly. To his pleasant surprise, he encountered the barrier of her *experience*.

He started to withdraw when she clamped her hands on his shoulders and thrust herself against him. He breached the barrier, becoming totally encased in her velvet fire. For intense seconds he lay still until overwhelming urges took control. Slowly, sliding strokes at first, then faster and harder they moved.

Following his lead, she ground her hips against him in circling motions, emitting small moans of pleasure. Her fervor, unleashed, grew wild and uninhibited. Zach responded with an ardor in concert with hers, expertly building the intensity until she cried out in climax. Only then did Zach allow himself to find release.

They lay, quietly joined together, until Eugenia reached up and smoothed a stray curl behind

Zach's ear. "Mmm, you were most definitely very good."

"You think so, huh?" He gazed tenderly down at her face, flushed from their spent passion.

"Yes, I do. And I certainly think I would enjoy doing this again."

Zach smiled down at her, but did not comment. She never ceased to amaze him. He had let passion override his control, and had just taken her virginity. He had not been able to stop himself, although he'd discovered that the vast experience she had alluded to had not included bedding with a man. And instead of being distraught, as one would expect, she was complimenting him on his performance.

Zach withdrew and moved to the edge of the sofa. Eugenia sat up unhurriedly, making no attempt to hide her nudity. He reveled in the view of her supple breasts, the indentation of her waist and the rounded curve of her hips. But sense was returning. So he retrieved her clothing, and helped her back on with the blouse top of the dress, allowing his fingers to linger on her skin.

"I had not planned to dress yet. Furthermore, I think that the experience is definitely something worth repeating."

He shook his head at the brash honesty of her remark. "Oh, you do, do you?"

"Yes, I do."

"Eugenia, you don't have any idea what you're saying," he advised, further astounded by her nonchalance. He deliberately picked up his clothes and began dressing.

Eugenia dropped her eyes for a moment before lifting them to stare directly into his. "Yes, Zach, I do know what I am saying."

Eugenia watched each of his movements, the outlines of his muscles, the lift of the veins in his arms as he pulled his trousers up strong thighs and slender hips. Her gaze shifted to the maleness of him, and she longed to reach out and touch him.

"I am not sorry," she said quietly with deliberation.

Leaving his shirt unbuttoned, Zach took up a position next to her on the sofa and draped an arm across the back of it. Against his better judgment, he pulled her into the crook of his arm.

"Eugenia," he began in a serious voice, "what you and I just did is not something a young woman such as yourself should be considering doing again . . ."

All the while Zach lectured her on the necessity of future abstinence, he was wondering if he had totally lost his mind. He had never hesitated to take advantage of a willing woman before, and now here he was advising one of the most desirable young women he had ever been with to stay away from him and all men in the future until the proper time.

Eugenia laid her head on his shoulder, her fingers snaking across his bare chest. She toyed with the hairs, wondering what other glorious discoveries could be made between a man and a woman.

"Why shouldn't a young woman such as myself consider making love with you again?"

"Love?" The word "love" stuck in his throat like

a fish bone. That word and all it entailed made him uneasy, but he kept his face void of the tumultuous feelings such a word elicited. He had no intention of being wounded by love again.

"The word 'love' was a poor choice," she explained, feeling an unsettling sense that she had overstepped some invisible boundary. "But it was a very pleasurable experience. Had I realized how pleasurable, I might not have resisted Gale so vehemently," she offered in an attempt to disarm what had become a tenuous conversation.

Zach sighed and removed his arm from her shoulders. He did not like hearing Gale Sweeney's name on her lips; it piqued his male ego. And with one simple four-letter word, she was suddenly making it very difficult for him. He clamped his hands on her shoulders and turned her to face him directly.

"You can't just fall into bed with any man because you found what just happened between you and me pleasurable, you hear me?"

"I cannot help but hear you." She was beginning to get annoyed. "Furthermore, I have no intention of falling into bed, as you put it, with just any man. I said the experience was worth repeating; I did not say I intended to repeat it with just anyone."

His lips tight, Zach said, "I suppose I should be relieved?"

Eugenia shrugged. Then in a matter-of-fact voice, "Since you are the one I intend to repeat it with, I would say, yes, you should be."

Zach threw up his hands in a mixture of frustration and elation. Although she was wearing his patience thin, she at least had not brought up Sweeney's name again. He could not deny that she was a refreshing change from the women he had known. She was not trying to hide her feelings among a tangled web of feminine games. So why did that four-letter word refuse to quit haunting his mind?

"You're making it sound rather calculated," he finally said, after mulling her comment over.

"Well . . . it was and is, I suppose."

"Darlin', I hate to disappoint you, but seducing you was not the first thing on my mind when I walked through the front door."

"I never meant to imply that you were the one who planned to seduce me." She stared directly into those probing blue eyes. "Actually, it was my idea."

His brow shoved up and slanted into a suspicious line. "What're you saying?"

"I thought I made myself perfectly clear. If you will recall, you accused me of that very thing the other night before the fire. You put the thought in my head," she improvised. "It was my idea to se—"

"I heard what you said; you don't have to repeat yourself." Disbelief captured his expression.

"Then why are you staring at me as if you are in some type of quandary?"

She certainly had a way with words! She had captured his emotions with precision. He usually was aware when females were deliberately offering themselves to him for a clandestine purpose, regardless of how subtle or resourceful they were.

He got up and paced back and forth in front of

the fireplace, his hands clasped behind his back. She was constantly throwing him off balance—especially with that word "love." Finally, as if he had been overlooking the obvious, the answer occurred to him.

He stopped before her, his arms crossed over his chest, his feet planted wide apart, his face set.

"Exactly what are you up to this time that would cause you to go to such extreme and forbidden lengths, Eugenia?"

Nineteen

Eugenia stared into Zach's darkening face. She had just had one of the most exciting experiences of her life, and now he was ruining it! Before she could respond, he leaned over and placed a hand on either side of her on the sofa cushions.

Practically nose to nose, he demanded, "You're up to something, and this time you're going to tell me exactly what it is."

She could not simply blurt out her suspicions concerning her father's murder, although in her heart she did not want to believe any longer that he had anything to do with it. She could not believe it. Not after giving herself to him. Her mind whirred with options.

"Eugenia, I'm not going to wait much longer."

She ducked under his arm and scooted to the end of the sofa. "Oh, all right. But sit down first. I do not want you standing when I say what I have to say."

Zach took up a stiff position on the opposite end of the sofa so he would not be tempted either to take her again or strangle her.

"Okay, Eugenia, I'm sitting. Now, out with it."

"I wanted to engage your attentions, seduce you, if you prefer, so you would be more amenable to selling the oyster beds." Part of what she said was true, but she would never admit to her discussion with Len Sweeney. Never.

He opened his mouth to comment on such an astounding piece of information, but she brought up her hand.

"No, let me finish. I did want to make you more agreeable to selling, but I had not meant for it to go quite as far as it did."

Again he opened his mouth, and again her hand came up.

She stood. "But I am not sorry in the least that it did."

He shot to his feet beside her and took her into his arms. Resting his chin on the top of her head, he took a deep breath. His first inclination had been to give her a good tongue lashing, but she was so genuine that all he could do was say, "I'm not sorry either."

Then he kissed her.

After a long, lingering kiss, Eugenia pulled out of his embrace and gazed directly into his eyes. "Then you will consider returning the oyster beds to me?"

"No." He answer was firm, final. His ardor cooled by the force of her misguided convictions. "If you think you can use that luscious body of yours to get me to let you have the oyster beds, you've wasted your time, Eugenia."

He might as well have doused her with a bucket

of the icy waters from Shoalwater Bay. The remark stung that much. She had freely given herself during the heat of passion without conscious consideration of the oyster beds or anything else for that matter. She had been carried away, but she would never admit it to him. Never! She stood there, before him, her cheeks flaming.

"I did not waste my time, and I do not think that I wasted yours either," she announced, turned on the ball of her bare foot and marched upstairs, leaving him staring after her.

Zach plunked back down on the sofa and shook his head, raking his fingers through his mussed hair. Since his ex-wife, he had not let a woman get to him, but Eugenia seemed to be doing just that.

He had accused her of using her body to get what she wanted in order to keep her at arms' length. Inside, Zach did not believe it for a moment. Her responses to him had been too real, too unrehearsed. What they had shared had been special, and if he were willing to admit it, he had just found himself to be quite infatuated—possibly more than that—with her.

Eugenia slammed the bedroom door for good measure, but it did not satisfy her. She was filled with the humiliation of her unbridled desire and troubled by his accusations. She had not meant to use her body, nor had she expected to be in such turmoil. She needed help to sort out the unexpected feelings barraging her, and there was only one person alive who could provide it.

She changed into a plain tan muslin shirt and split skirt, donned a sturdy pair of boots, tied her unruly hair back and sat down in the middle of her bed cross-legged to wait until she heard Zach's door close. Then she snuck from her room, slid down the banister so he would not hear the creak of the stairs, slid into her heavy coat, and slipped from the house.

A light rain was falling as Eugenia hurried toward the Widow Garrett's house. Eugenia crossed the widow's yard. For an instant she thought she saw a shadow move. A breeze waved the tree limbs, and she relaxed. It was merely her raw nerves.

The warm, inviting light spilling from the lace-curtained windows drew her attention. Eugenia was thankful that the dear old soul was still up. As she knocked on the door, a whiff of freshly baked apple pie met her.

Ruth Garrett was wearing a thick quilted robe and nightcap when she answered the door. Her hand grasping her robe closed at her neck, she startled, "Eugenia? What are you doing here?"

"May I come in?"

"How thoughtless of me." Ruth relaxed. "Of course, come in, child."

"Thank you. I am not intruding on you or your visit with your family, am I?"

Ruth stepped back with a wan smile. "No. I am all alone again."

Eugenia stepped inside and was momentarily shocked at the austere setting which greeted her. The widow's house was once filled with treasures. Ruth took her coat. "What brings you out at this late hour? Are you all right, child?"

"Yes—No . . . I mean, I need your advice, Mrs. Garrett."

There was a troubled expression on Eugenia's face, and Ruth directed her toward the kitchen. Eugenia sat at a small table in the center of the cheery room hung with brightly flowered curtains. Ruth fixed two cups of warm milk.

"How about a big slice of the apple pie I just took out of the oven?"

Food was the last thing on Eugenia's mind at the moment. "No, thank you, Mrs. Garrett."

Ruth Garrett set the cups on the table and sat across from Eugenia, watching Eugenia's trembling fingers circle the china. Ruth leaned forward.

Patting Eugenia's hand, Ruth said, "It is that terribly handsome gentleman who bought your father's oyster beds, isn't it?"

Eugenia hung her head before she lifted her eyes to the meet the widow's. "How did you know?"

Ruth took a sip from her cup and set it down. "Because I know people. And from your face I can see that you've got it bad. Furthermore, folks've been talking. While I don't pay no mind over wagging tongues, I had a sneaking suspicion that that living arrangement you two got was going to bring you much more than answers about your father."

"Oh, Mrs. Garrett, I am so confused. I do not want to—I cannot—believe that Zach had anything to do with my father's murder, but there is so much evidence that forces me to believe that he is up to something.

"Mr. Sweeney advised me to court Zach's attentions as a way to get him to tell me what is going

MORE PASSION AND ADVENTURE AWAIT... YOUR TRIP TO A BIG ADVENTUROUS WORLD BEGINS WHEN YOU ACCEPT YOUR FIRST 4 NOVELS ABSOLUTELY *FREE* (AN $18.00 VALUE)

Accept your Free gift and start to experience more of the passion and adventure you like in a historical romance novel. Each Zebra novel is filled with proud men, spirited women and tempestuous love that you'll remember long after you turn the last page.

Zebra Historical Romances are the finest novels of their kind. They are written by authors who really know how to weave tales of romance and adventure in the historical settings you love. You'll feel like you've actually gone back in time with the thrilling stories that each Zebra novel offers.

GET YOUR FREE GIFT WITH THE START OF YOUR HOME SUBSCRIPTION

Our readers tell us that these books sell out very fast in book stores and often they miss the newest titles. So Zebra has made arrangements for you to receive the four newest novels published each month.

You'll be guaranteed that you'll never miss a title, and home delivery is so convenient. And to show you just how easy it is to get Zebra Historical Romances, we'll send you your first 4 books absolutely FREE! Our gift to you just for trying our home subscription service.

BIG SAVINGS AND FREE HOME DELIVERY

Each month, you'll receive the four newest titles as soon as they are published. You'll probably receive them even before the bookstores do. What's more, you may preview these exciting novels free for 10 days. If you like them as much as we think you will, just pay the low preferred subscriber's price of just $3.75 each. *You'll save $3.00 each month off the publisher's price.* AND, your savings are even greater because there are never any shipping, handling or other hidden charges—FREE Home Delivery. Of course you can return any shipment within 10 days for full credit, no questions asked. There is no minimum number of books you must buy.

4 FREE BOOKS

TO GET YOUR 4 FREE BOOKS WORTH $18.00 — MAIL IN THE FREE BOOK CERTIFICATE T O D A Y

Fill in the Free Book Certificate below, and we'll send your FREE BOOKS to you as soon as we receive it.

If the certificate is missing below, write to: Zebra Home Subscription Service, Inc., P.O. Box 5214, 120 Brighton Road, Clifton, New Jersey 07015-5214.

FREE BOOK CERTIFICATE

4 FREE BOOKS

ZEBRA HOME SUBSCRIPTION SERVICE, INC.

YES! Please start my subscription to Zebra Historical Romances and send me my first 4 books absolutely FREE. I understand that each month I may preview four new Zebra Historical Romances free for 10 days. If I'm not satisfied with them, I may return the four books within 10 days and owe nothing. Otherwise, I will pay the low preferred subscriber's price of just $3.75 each; a total of $15.00, *a savings off the publisher's price of $3.00.* I may return any shipment and I may cancel this subscription at any time. There is no obligation to buy any shipment and there are no shipping, handling or other hidden charges. Regardless of what I decide, the four free books are mine to keep.

NAME

ADDRESS _____ APT

CITY _____ STATE _____ ZIP

(   )
TELEPHONE

SIGNATURE _____ (if under 18, parent or guardian must sign)

Terms, offer and prices subject to change without notice. Subscription subject to acceptance by Zebra Books. Zebra Books reserves the right to reject any order or cancel any subscription.

ZB0194

on, but when I did that, it-it . . ." Eugenia's voice trailed off, and she lowered her eyes.

Ruth let out a troubled sigh and relaxed. She got up and pulled a chair next to Eugenia. She ringed a comforting arm around Eugenia's shoulders. "It got out of hand, didn't it?"

"Well, yes, sort of," Eugenia forced herself to admit.

"How out of hand did it get?" Ruth probed, fearing the answer. She could see in Eugenia's eyes that the girl was smitten. And she knew firsthand what happened between a man and woman when that special spark ignited.

"Completely."

"I see," Ruth said, careful to keep her voice evenly modulated. She remembered all too well what it was like to be young and in love, even when you did not admit it to yourself. And Eugenia had all the symptoms. "And now you don't know what to do about it, right?"

"I know what I want to do; I know what I should do; but I am all mixed up."

"Of course you are, child. Of course you are," Ruth said softly and waited for Eugenia to talk.

"I am not sorry over what happened between Zach and me, although convention dictates that I should be. With my suspicions I do not even know how or why I put myself in that position. It just happened. Although I no longer truly believe that Zach murdered my father." Eugenia had not looked the Widow Garrett directly in the eyes as she spoke, but now she lifted her gaze. The elderly woman's face was pinched. "Does that brand me some kind of—"

"Absolutely not," Ruth broke in, silently wishing her John were still alive. "It makes you human and nothing more. And in your heart you know that your young man had nothing to do with your father's sad passing.

"If folks were honest, you'd be surprised how many followed their hearts prior to getting a piece of paper making it legal. So, you got nothing to be ashamed of. Now, why don't you spend the night with me so you can tell me more about your young man?"

"I really should be getting back," Eugenia hedged, silently praying that what the widow said was true. Everyone in town knew that the Garretts had had a very special marriage before John Garrett had died three years ago in an oyster boat accident while working for Eugenia's father.

Somehow simply talking to the Widow Garrett relieved Eugenia's mind, but she did not want to dredge up more painful memories for the widow. She could see a troubled sadness in the widow's eyes.

"Zach does not know I am gone."

"You stay here with me tonight. It will give him something to think about when he discovers you are not there. It is the wise woman who keeps a man a little off balance and guessing. Keeps him from taking you for granted. That is what I did before my wedding to my John," she reminisced wistfully. "It worked out just fine for us. Married forty-seven years, we were."

"Really?"

"My marriage was as solid and good as they come. Not that we didn't have our little tiffs now and then, as well as a few major battles, because all marriages have those."

"I am not interested in marrying Zach Kellogg," Eugenia protested.

"No, of course you aren't," Ruth soothed to humor the girl. Eugenia did not know what she wanted. Ruth silently wished she could help Eugenia resolve her concerns, but she didn't dare.

"The most important thing in my life is to fulfill Daddy's dream for the oyster beds."

"Of course it is." Ruth forced a smile. "Now, you come along with me. I'll loan you a nightdress so you can get some rest. In the morning after we talk, I'll send along some of the tea cakes and apple pie I baked earlier. Your young man will enjoy them. I always say that good food takes a direct route to a man's heart."

Eugenia followed the widow's lead, but she attempted to explain that Zach was a means to an end; theirs was merely a flirtation, possibly a bit of an accidental infatuation which had gotten out of hand, nothing as strong as the feelings that lead to a lifetime commitment.

The widow merely bobbed her white head and remained silent while Eugenia poured out a detailed account from the time she left California to the present. Talking about it did little to alleviate the feelings starting to churn inside Eugenia again by the time she crawled in between the cool, smooth cotton sheets and extinguished the lamp. Even when she closed her eyes, her mind visualized Zach.

Zach leaned against a tall cedar across the road from the house he had followed Eugenia to. He made a mental note to check out the house's inhabitants, and waited until the house was dark before he left to keep a scheduled appointment with Cliff Granger.

"Ballin' bears, what kept you this time?" Cliff groused and tossed his cigarette aside when Zach joined him. "I've been waitin' for hours, and it ain't exactly dry out here in the woods."

"Had something to take care of first," Zach responded with unconcerned dismissal. He had heard Eugenia on the banister and followed her. And tomorrow he would check out who she had gone to see.

"Bet you did." Kellogg's lips tightened, warning Cliff that this case came with more than the usual dangers. "You any closer to solving the murder?"

"The more I dig, the more suspects I keep turning up." Zach went on to fill his contact in on what had transpired with Washer and Nelson, Gale Sweeney, the shipbuilder, the shadowy figure lurking across from the building, and all the uneasy responses he continued to receive when he broached the subject of Woodward Whalen's demise. Then Zach told Granger about the letter he'd sent requesting a contract and his plans to actually begin shipping oysters.

"Jumpin' croaker legs, Kellogg! Our superiors

expect you to wrap up this case soon and return the government's money. I had to do some pretty fancy footwork over that deal you pulled with the money to keep you out of trouble. If you ain't careful, you could lose your shirt over this case."

"Well, you tell our superiors for me that I'm staying with this case until it's solved, shirt or no shirt." Zach wasn't as worried about losing his proverbial shirt as he was a certain organ inside his chest. "Hell, I've never let them down before. They can quit worrying; they'll get the damn money back."

"Whatever you say," Cliff answered in response to Kellogg's sharp tone. Sagely, Cliff decided not to inform Kellogg that he had been commissioned to keep a closer eye on the unorthodox behavior of his long-time partner.

Cliff was worried that Kellogg was beginning to lose his perspective, and when a lawman let himself get personally involved, as Cliff's gut told him Kellogg was doing, he left himself open to make dangerous mistakes.

Mistakes were what got a man killed.

The two men parted, and Cliff waited until Kellogg was out of sight before he left his position. But this time instead of heading southwest toward the next town, he headed east.

Captain Derrick stood just inside the grand entrance to the sprawling adobe house outside of Los Angeles, withstanding the gale-force tongue lashing he was receiving from the old albatross.

"What could you possibly have been thinking to

allow Eugenia to talk you into taking her and my precious Mildred to Oysterville after I specifically had forbid it . . . !"

Captain Derrick hung his head under the weight of such a chastisement. Iris was an expert, and he was not going to make matters worse by trying to justify his actions to the unreasonable woman. But he was not sorry either.

". . . Whatever could have possessed you to leave Eugenia there?"

"The lass's father was murdered—"

Iris's talon-like fingers went to her throat. "Woodward murdered? When? How? Why?"

"I wasn't there long enough to get details. My gut convinced me that I should return Mildred home." *Before you came after her and intruded on Eugenia,* he added silently. "So, since I be done with me duty, I'll be settin' sail for Washington with the tide. I be sure Miss Eugenia will be needing me."

"Needing you!" Iris huffed, incredulous at such a preposterous notion. "Why, the poor girl will be needing family now."

Eduardo had been listening from the dining room and joined his wife. Ringing a meaty arm around his wife's waist, the obese Spaniard raised his double chin. "Eugenia will be requiring expert business advice now that her *padre* is gone."

Captain Derrick's lips tightened as he watched the albatross settle her glasses on her prow. He did not much like the conniving pair, and the man's heartless comment only served to reinforce his feelings. They weren't interested in Eugenia's welfare;

they were interested in Woodward Whalen's estate and how it could benefit them.

"I be sure I can offer the lass proper guidance, me sailing for the family for well over twenty years."

Iris looked down her nose in her most impervious manner. "No doubt you are an able sailor, Captain Derrick. But Eugenia will require someone with expert business acumen, which my dear husband possesses, to help the girl make the most expedient decisions regarding the welfare of her business interests.

"I am certain you realize that you simply are not qualified to advise Eugenia. Therefore, Eduardo and I shall be sailing for Washington with you, Captain."

Mildred, who had been standing quietly in the background, stepped forward. "What about me? I think I should accompany you as well. After all, dear Cousin Eugenia and I are close relatives."

Iris was not totally blind to her daughter's secret wishes for independence, nor the tension between the two young women. But she was aware of the sway Mildred often had over Eugenia and decided that Mildred might prove useful if necessary. "Yes, Mildred, you are right. It is the least all of us can do for my poor dead sister's child.

"Once we reach our destination and are reunited with Eugenia, we shall take over responsibility for putting her business affairs in order. And, of course, I am certain she will finally welcome my personal guidance so she can become a proper young maiden, and, if nothing more, I shall be

231

able to interview any eligible young swains whom I deem worthy to make Eugenia a proper husband.

"Only after we are satisfied that the estate has been settled in accordance with the wishes of all involved, and Eugenia properly wed to one of the town's upstanding citizens, could we even consider returning to our own humble lives."

After Captain Derrick had been summarily dismissed and was on his way back to prepare the ship for sailing, he wondered how the lass would react when her aunt and uncle, the scurvy pair, arrived and verily announced their detailed plans for her future.

Twenty

Zach was fumbling around the kitchen, putting the coffeepot on the stove when the door slammed. Before he glanced up, he sensed Eugenia's presence, smelled her fresh scent. He felt a tightening surge in his groin.

Eugenia was standing just inside the door. Streams of morning light splashed in through the panes of glass and illuminated her tousled hair, lending it a glowing reddish cast. His senses honed from years as a lawman, he noted the subtle change in her demeanor. Her stance was stiff, almost ill at ease.

He fought an inner battle to suppress the urge to go to her, and instead went about getting the cups from the cupboard, pretending not to have noticed Eugenia's absence last night.

But he was most cognizant of every detail about Eugenia Whalen. She was pale, making the dark circles under her eyes stand out. Zach wanted to kick himself for losing control. As a seasoned lawman with a reputation for hardened self-control in the most difficult situations, he should have known better. God only knew who she had run to last night after he had made love to her . . . and why.

The word "love" caused a further tightening in his chest, and he quickly transferred his thoughts to safer territory before his urges got totally out of control. He ought to question her about that untimely little foray, but he knew better than that; she would only deny it, and he did not want her alerting the occupants of the house she had gone to before he checked them out.

"Sleep well?" she inquired, breaking into his jumbled thoughts as she set aside the covered platter she held.

"Of course."

"Like a man without a conscience, no doubt," she mumbled, annoyed and downright put out by his seeming lack of concern in the gray morning light.

"Like a man pleasantly exhausted." He grinned, fondly remembering the silken touch of her skin. "And you?"

"Me?" she said nervously and turned her head away, attempting to hide a yawn behind her hand.

"You sleep well?"

Not a moment, she screamed inside. "The instant my head touched the pillow. I always slumber without the least difficulty."

His brow shoved up. So, she was a better liar than he had suspected. The tilt of her chin defied him to contradict her claim. But those snapping green eyes, wary yet determined, gave her away; she was up to something again, and right after breakfast he

234

was going to find out exactly what she had been doing last night.

"Glad to hear it. Coffee?"

Despite his impatience, Zach waited until Eugenia had changed and informed him that she was going into town to purchase groceries. Once he had watched her until she was out of sight, he left the house and made his way to the tidy house he had followed Eugenia to the night before.

"Yes?" Ruth Garrett answered the door and looked up into the man's face.

Zach's lips split into a big grin of relief. He had not known what he was expecting, but it hadn't been an elderly white-haired woman with a dishrag in her hands. He tipped his hat. "Sorry, I must be at the wrong house."

"I don't think so, Mr. Kellogg." She opened the door, her keen eyes boring into him. "Come in. I think you knew exactly which house you were coming to."

After receiving less than she had hoped for in the way of further advice from the elder Sweeney, Eugenia had gone to Gale's office inside his father's building. Soon, though, Eugenia stormed from Gale's office, stinging over his lack of interest in backing her on a strictly financial basis.

Gale had had the unmitigated gall to suggest a more personal arrangement in which he'd agree to put up the money in exchange for certain . . . mutually pleasurable pastimes. After all, he had argued, "You are living with that stranger. Why should such a *little arrangement* with me, someone whom you've known most your life, upset you?"

She stomped down the boardwalk but glanced back over her shoulder at the sound of Gale's aggrieved voice attempting to hail her back.

"Oh!" she cried and collided with a male chest. "I beg your pardon."

Cliff Granger never was one to pass up a ready opportunity with an attractive young woman, especially one with generous curves in all the right places. He stepped back and tipped his hat. "Think nothin' of it, miss. Name's Clifford Granger."

There was something strangely familiar about the lanky man dressed in a stiff suit, as if it weren't his usual attire. And when he turned his back to her and bent to retrieve the bundle she had inadvertently knocked out of his hands, Eugenia recognized him.

He was the man Zach had met in the woods, Zach's financial backer. An idea flashed into her mind.

Ignoring Gale until he gave up and slammed back inside the building, she put a welcoming smile on her face and offered her hand. "Eugenia Whalen. It is a pleasure to meet you, Mr. Granger."

"Miss Whalen, the pleasure's purely all mine." Cliff brought her hand up and kissed it. So this was Kellogg's Eugenia Whalen, Cliff thought. No wonder Kellogg was not so anxious to solve the case and move on.

To Cliff's stunned surprise, she said through

smiling teeth, "Although I already know what you and Zach Kellogg are about, I am surprised to see you since I thought you did not want anyone to know of your involvement."

Dumbfounded, he nonetheless grinned at her. "That was the general idea. Kellogg actually told you all about it, did he?"

"He had no choice, truly. He could not deny it after I confronted him over the money I saw you hand him during one of your clandestine meetings in the woods. He had to take me into his confidence. You are his financial backer and partner."

Cliff measurably relaxed. Kellogg had not blown his cover after all. Actually, he thought, as they began to walk together along the boardwalk, Miss Eugenia Whalen's thinking that he was bankrolling Kellogg might just prove the best entrance into the Oysterville business community he could get.

"And you must be the lovely daughter. Kellogg told me about your father; I'm mighty sorry," he offered out of genuine concern and sympathy.

"Thank you." Her eyes threatened to fill with unspent tears. She swallowed the urge. She had vowed to hold all grief at bay until her father's murderer had been brought to justice.

"I'm not sure where Kellogg is staying in town. But since my plans've changed, and I've decided to get more openly involved, possibly you might see your way clear to direct me?"

"I can do more than that. I shall be happy to take you."

By the time they reached a pleasant two-story house just outside of town, Cliff understood Kellogg's fancy for the little lady. She was everything most young women weren't. Eugenia Whalen was daring, the way she had just suggested he back her rather than Kellogg. She had not accepted a simple no; he'd had to be firm. She was unconventional in those britches. And she seemed both resourceful and guileless.

Once they were settled in the parlor, Eugenia barely had time to offer Mr. Granger tea, prepare it, and serve him a cup when Zach returned.

"What the devil're you doing here?"

"Miss Whalen invited me." Cliff gave Kellogg a full-toothed grin and leaned back in his chair, watching Kellogg closely. "Wasn't it downright social of her?"

Zach's brow shoved up and his jaw bunched. "Yeah, downright social."

Eugenia also noticed Zach's less than subtle irritation and sought to capitalize on what the Widow Garrett had told her. *It is a wise woman who keeps a man a little off balance and guessing.* If she were indeed wise, she might be able to keep Zach Kellogg more than a little off balance and guessing. But she was not sure it was so she could regain her rightful oyster beds or. . . .

"I just thought that since you two are partners, you would want Mr. Granger to stay here with us," she said with a twinkle in her eyes.

"Call me Cliff, please, Eugenia, if I may call you that."

"Of course."

Zach did not miss Eugenia's electrifying smile directed toward Granger. The beckoning turn of

238

her full, lush lips settled on his partner ate at Zach's gut as much as her words did.

"It would be the most expedient place of operations to have Cliff stay here with us, don't you think?" Eugenia added.

"I sure do," chimed in Cliff pleasantly. "It'd be the perfect answer to serve our immediate business interests in the most useful manner." He sent Eugenia a brilliant smile. "You're very wise to suggest such an arrangement, my dear. Must admit I've always found hotel accommodations most dreary."

Kellogg's dark scowl was clearly unmistakable for a hard-cut lawman with a normally unreadable face. Cliff smirked, wondering if Kellogg himself was aware of how much the little lady affected him.

Zach opened his mouth to suggest that Granger would be smart to seek accommodations elsewhere before Zach was tempted to rearrange his grinning face, but a resounding knock at the door stopped him.

"Please, remain seated, gentlemen," Eugenia said when both men started to rise. "Since I am merely the household help, it is only fitting that I meet your visitors before you receive them."

Cliff shot Kellogg a startled look as Eugenia left the parlor. "Hoppin' horn toads, household help, huh? Pretty clever way to keep the little lady nearby, Kellogg."

"She gave me no choice," Zach muttered. "It was the only way to keep an eye on her since she keeps interfering with the investigation."

"I just bet it was." Cliff raised his eyebrows in mocking disbelief.

"What the hell're you doing here?"

"We're partners. Thought you might need a little help. Though now that I'm here, I'd say I might have arrived just a mite too late. 'Course, nobody knows the future." Without further comment, he turned to focus his attention on the vestibule.

Zach ignored his partner's telling remark and also turned toward the vestibule. But inside he burned. Zach knew Granger's love 'em and leave 'em reputation, and since the man had arrived, his interest in Eugenia was as transparent as a window pane fresh washed.

Eugenia opened the door and was astonished to find Gale standing on the welcome mat for a second time after years of absence. Despite her still simmering anger toward his lewd proposition, she kept her face schooled.

"Gale, what can I do for you?" Eugenia asked in a distinctly chilly voice.

He brought a huge bouquet of dahlias, marigolds and chrysanthemums from behind his back and held it out to her. "I came to humbly offer my deepest apologies for my inexcusable behavior earlier. I do hope you can find it in your heart to forgive me. I don't know what got into me, Eugenia. I truly am sorry, deeply."

The urge to slam the door shut in his pretty face was near overwhelming, but then she would have to explain her actions to Zach and Cliff—something she was not prepared to do. Reluctantly, she accepted Gale's peace offering, although she had not forgiven his earlier overture and was not certain she ever would.

"Ah-ah-ah chew!" Eugenia sneezed when the pollen from the bouquet tickled her nostrils. She held the flowers at arm's length with one hand and with the other put her index finger beneath her nose.

"Gazoon-tite. Do invite Mr. Sweeney in, Eugenia," she heard Zach's deep voice echo coldly from the parlor.

Reluctantly, Eugenia stepped aside, and against her better judgment allowed Gale to enter past her. Zach and Cliff had left their seats and were now standing in the archway.

To Eugenia's dismay, Zach made the introductions while she hurriedly excused herself under the pretext that she needed to put the colorful, fragrant flowers in water. She set the bouquet aside before it caused her to sneeze again and grabbed a vase from the dining room sideboard.

While she was drawing water into the fine cut glass container, another knock sounded at the front door. By the time she carried the bouquet toward the parlor, the elder Sweeney, accompanied by Morton Washer and Rube Nelson, were standing inside the door involved with introductions.

"Eugenia, would you bring more teacups while I show these gentlemen into the parlor," Zach suggested, mentally making a note of the latest arrivals' nervous stances.

"It seems as if we suddenly have more guests than anticipated," he remarked, as he noticed out of the corner of his eye more people heading toward the house. "And unless I'm wrong, two more're on the way."

Fighting another urge to sneeze, Eugenia set the vase down and parted the patterned lace curtains hung on either side of the door, peering through the long, rectangular window on the left. Her brows drew together. Gertrude Englestrom and Sheriff Dollard strolled together toward the yard.

Unable to comprehend why such a seemingly incompatible assemblage of people were gathering in the parlor all of a sudden, Eugenia scurried back to the cupboard and loaded a tray with cups and the tea cakes the Widow Garrett had given her.

Without a word, Cliff seemed to take some silent cue and dragged several of the straight-back dining room chairs into the parlor. "Gentlemen," he said and swung out an arm, indicating the empty chairs, "I'm Cliff Granger, Zach Kellogg's business partner. Set yourselves down until the two headed this way get here."

Zach opened the door as the buxom blonde clad in salmon silk and the lanky sheriff climbed the steps. The question on their faces caused him to say, "Noticed you from the window. Right this way. You both can join the others already convened in the parlor."

Gertrude gave a hesitant nod and hastily introduced herself as Woodward Whalen's dear woman friend. Her voracious eyes appreciatively rolled over her host. The stranger who bought Woodward's oyster beds was one of the best-looking masculine specimens she had seen in these parts since she moved into the territory.

She let out a disappointed sigh and shook her head slowly. Pity. Real pity the circumstances weren't different, she thought as she joined the others already in the parlor. Then she and Bob Dollard were introduced to another rugged stranger. This one didn't have the draw that Zach Kellogg had, but he was more man than most, she deemed and took up a prominent position in the middle of the cramped parlor, keeping her eyes averted from the younger Sweeney.

Eugenia had returned with additional cups and a platter of tea cakes. Despite the hundred and one questions searing the tip of her tongue, she quietly and efficiently served everyone. She shot Zach a questioning glance, but he only shrugged.

Strange, Eugenia mused. The only sounds filling the crowded room were the clank of china cups against plates and silver spoons swirling sugar into the brewed tea. No one was exchanging pleasantries.

"Is everyone here now, or are there other uninvited guests any of you may anticipate arriving?" Zach asked in a firm voice, breaking into the bizarre, energy-charged silence.

Zach waited expectantly as the others glanced at each other as if waiting for one among them to take the lead. Finally, Len Sweeney set his cup aside, cleared his throat and stood up.

"Mr. Kellogg, I do hope you will forgive us for barging into your home uninvited, but—"

Another loud knock at the door stopped Sweeney in mid-sentence. All eyes swung toward the door as Eugenia went to answer it.

Eugenia's eyes rounded in bewilderment. "Mrs. Garrett, to what do we owe the pleasure of your visit?"

A covered platter in her hands, Ruth Garrett stepped past Eugenia and peeked into the crowded parlor. All eyes were silently staring at her.

"From my window I saw all those folks heading your way, child, and I thought I'd better hurry right on over and see what's wrong."

Twenty-one

The house was virtually charged with an energy that reminded Eugenia of years past when her father had held meetings filled with heated debate and lively discussion at the family home. But this time a foreboding anticipation filled that place in her breast where before there had always been an interested curiosity.

"Eugenia, it really isn't polite to stand before a guest with your mouth open," Zach said from her side as he stepped up to greet the widow.

"Mrs. Garrett, it's nice to see you again so soon." He took the platter from her hands and handed it to Eugenia, then took the widow's arm to escort her past a gaping Eugenia. "You needn't worry, Mrs. Garrett. Nothing's wrong."

"I wouldn't be so sure about that, if I were you, Kellogg," the younger Sweeney announced in a dire voice filled with a sense of upcoming doom.

Zach's brow shoved up. "Why don't you wait until we're all seated before you say whatever it is you came to say," Zach stated flatly.

245

Daunted, Gale slumped back in his chair and shot a support-seeking glance from Gertrude to his father.

Cliff noted that the others did not attempt to come to the man's aid. He grinned to himself. The sly weasel of a man was not so tough.

Eugenia set the widow's offering on the small table in the vestibule next to the flowers and followed Zach and Mrs. Garrett into the parlor. Her heart was drumming against her chest. She did not know that Zach knew the widow and feared more what he had gleaned from the old dear about Eugenia's feelings toward him than whatever all the others combined could've possibly come to say.

The only places left to sit were either next to a smirking Zach on the edge of the crowded sofa or next to the Widow Garrett on the hassock. Despite a sudden longing to feel his hard thigh against hers, Eugenia gingerly took up a position next to Mrs. Garrett.

Zach crossed his massive arms over his chest, noting with uncanny interest that all except Gertrude Englestrom and the sheriff were already suspects in the case he was working on. Silently, he added their names to the people to be investigated.

"All right, Sweeney, spit out what you've got to say. My business associate and I have a lot to do," Zach demanded when no one spoke.

Gale looked to his father for direction, and the older man cleared his throat. "Mr. Kellogg, as I am sure you well know Woodward Whalen was held in the highest esteem in Oysterville. When he passed on, Oysterville lost a valued leader, and . . ." He scrutinized the other's expressions.

Every mien was solemn.

"And?" Zach prompted, bored with the apparently self-appointed committee; he'd seen their ilk in other towns. Self-important, self-serving, pious do-gooders.

". . . and shortly after church Sunday it was suggested that a concerned body of Whalen's friends pay you a visit regarding your, ah, scandalous living arrangements with his daughter."

Ruth folded Eugenia's hand in hers and squeezed for support. Eugenia would have none of it. He was discussing her as if she were not even present. Well, if there was any chastising to do, she was going to have a say!

"Scandalous!" Eugenia cried before she could stop herself. "Why, all you come-again-gone-again sinners, where was my scandalous behavior discussed? At the bar across from church where the majority of you go right after services to toast the Lord?

"And you call yourselves my father's friends. Where were all of you fine, upstanding citizens of Oysterville when my father was alive and truly needed your help?"

Gale ignored what he deemed Eugenia's hysterical outburst and looked to Kellogg. "Mr. Kellogg, I am sure you must agree that this arrangement is not to the lady's, shall we say, advantage."

Furious, Eugenia shot to her feet. "And what is to my advantage, becoming your own personal bird of passage as you suggested this morning, Gale?" she demanded to horrified gasps from the others.

Zach's narrowed glare could have frozen the bay, it was so cold. "That true, Sweeney?"

"Of course it's true," Eugenia cried.

Ruth Garrett pulled her back down to the hassock and circled a comforting arm around Eugenia's shoulders.

"I don't doubt your word, Eugenia," Zach said in a low, dangerous voice. "I want to hear what Sweeney has to say for himself before I show him just how appreciated his concern for your welfare is."

Gale was starting to sweat despite the cool weather. Nervously, he removed a hankie from his pocket and dabbed his forehead. "Although I would never accuse Eugenia of telling falsehoods, I am certain she must somehow have misunderstood my intentions." He pressed splayed fingers to his chest in a gesture of personal distress.

"I would never suggest such a thing to Eugenia." Gale turned to face Eugenia directly, his anger carefully hidden behind a disheartened mask. "Eugenia, I am deeply sorry and distressed if I somehow have offended you, but I never . . . never meant for my humble offer of assistance to be misconstrued in such an utterly unthinkable manner."

Gertrude stiffened her spine. "Since we all know Gale would never intentionally make such an outrageous proposition, let's not lose sight of the reason we've come. Eugenia, we simply, in good conscience, cannot allow you to continue to live under this roof alone with Mr. Kellogg, no matter how innocent it may be."

The others took up the argument where Gertrude left off. Their convoluted reasoning faded from Eugenia's mind when she considered just exactly how *innocent* her living arrangement with Zach truly was.

She vividly recalled the hot, molten fire of his touch on her bare flesh. Each igniting stroke of his heated fingers. Every hypnotically murmured phrase. All the glorious moments she had spent in his arms, her body wedded to his. Her own cries as he brought her to the brink of ecstasy.

"Eugenia, Gertrude offered you a place to stay. The least you can do is respond to her kind overture," Morton Washer was saying as Eugenia's thoughts were rudely ripped back to the present.

"My wife said you are welcome to live with us until you can return to your relatives in California," Rube Nelson set forth.

Eugenia felt Mrs. Garrett suddenly stiffen. The widow had invited Eugenia to live with her, but Eugenia had no intention of going anywhere. "Since I am the one under discussion, you all might as well know before you so graciously attempt to control my future that I am not going anywhere."

To another round of aggrieved gasps, Eugenia added, "And since what seems to have precipitated your duly noted concern is my living alone under this roof with Zach Kellogg, you can all rest in peace now."

To gaping poses, Eugenia announced, "Mr. Granger will also be residing here, and since I am employed as the housekeeper in this house, there no longer is anything for you fine, upstanding citizens of Oysterville to concern yourselves with."

"Well, I never!" Gertrude snapped with indignation.

"Might be it's time you did," Cliff returned with a beguiling grin that made Gertrude blush and demurely drop her eyes to her lap.

Zach was not in the least amused, although he had to admire Eugenia's spunk. She sure didn't buckle under at the first sign of trouble. However, he knew those self-righteous busybodies would no doubt spend little time before spreading word of their encounter.

Having had his fill for one day, Zach said, "Guess that's settled. We wouldn't think of detaining you folks any longer."

Ruth Garrett remained seated next to Eugenia while Zach none-too-politely showed the bemused group the door.

"Eugenia, child, there was another reason I think you should be aware of that brought me directly over rather than waiting until those nosy meddlers left."

Ruth patted Eugenia's hand and leaned over close to her ear so no one else would hear what she had to say. "While I was in town, I noticed your father's schooner sailing toward the wharf. Won't remain any longer myself, but thought you ought to know. And don't worry, I didn't let on a thing to Zach Kellogg when he came to visit me earlier."

The implications of what Mrs. Garrett said hit Eugenia full force. Thus far she had been successful at keeping the schooner, her only asset, hidden. Now Zach would find out about it unless she moved fast. And why had Zach gone to visit the widow?

Eugenia saw the widow to the door, then turned to grab a wrap.

"Just where do you think you're going?" Zach asked in a dark voice from behind her.

She swung around to face him, and her gaze shifted to Cliff Granger, who was standing behind Zach. Then silently she glared at Zach. What gave him the right to start treating her like she was some type of possession all of a sudden?

Cliff scratched his ear. "I think this is my cue to go in search of one of them guest rooms 'n' get myself settled in."

"Third door to the right up the stairs," Zach said without taking his eyes off Eugenia.

Cliff grabbed his bundle, gave Eugenia a sympathetic wink, and made a quick exit, his heavy boots pounding up the stairs.

Seething from Zach's sudden take-charge attitude, Eugenia crossed her arms over her chest and stood stiffly before him, refusing to give him the simple courtesy of an answer.

To her chagrin, he did not do the gentlemanly thing; rather, he clamped a steely hand around her upper arm and escorted her back into the parlor.

"You might just as well make yourself comfortable because you're not going anywhere until you tell me exactly what that was all about."

Eugenia plunked down on the sofa, but her expression did not change. She was mad as hell at Zach for questioning her as if she were some sort of suspect. Strange, there it was again—he was acting like a lawman.

"Well?"

She looked at him in a different light. "I do not know what that was about. This town has been divided between the damned and the saved for some years. I suppose in their eyes I have just switched sides, is all."

Zach had to fight to keep from smiling. She'd have to do a helluva lot worse ever to be considered one of the damned as far as he was concerned.

"That group often appoint themselves as moral judge and jury in this town?"

There it was another time—a reference to the law sliding off his tongue as easy as everyday language. "They are a strange assemblage of people, actually. Never saw them band together as a group quite like that before."

In a single, unwitting sentence she had confirmed his suspicions about that lot. "What about Gale Sweeney's proposition?"

"What about it?" she said through clenched teeth. "He made it and I turned him down. Those flowers he brought were a peace offering."

"If he ever dares to come near you again, for any reason, I want to know about it," Zach said in a deadly voice, his hands balling into tight fists.

"I think he got the message." She stood up, her chin jutted out. "If that is all, I had best be heading back to town." She put a distant, dreamy smile on her face. "We shall be needing more supplies since Cliff will be staying here with us."

Hearing Granger's given name float like a cloud

on Eugenia's lips grated on Zach. And he didn't like the expression on her face either. His partner was a real ladies' man, and the last thing Zach needed was Granger's magnetic presence. He watched her leave, then headed upstairs to find out exactly what Granger was up to, openly making his presence in town known.

Zach also intended to set the man straight about a few things!

Eugenia did not waste another precious moment. She immediately headed toward the wharf. Off shore, beneath a sky feathered with wisps of clouds, she could see a dinghy from the schooner bobbing in her direction.

The tide was out, so the schooner had laid anchor a good distance from shore beyond the sand flats. Eugenia paced back and forth impatiently, fearing that someone would recognize the vessel and word would get around that her father's estate had not been stripped of every asset.

"Ahoy, Eugenia, lass!" Captain Derrick waved from the schooner's dinghy, gliding toward her.

Eugenia waved back, but could not help but notice the grave expression on the usually jovial captain's face. Despite the scraggly beard, his weathered face was set in harsh angles, and his mouth was a mere straight slash.

When he stepped ashore, he hugged her tightly to him. It was as if he were trying to protect her within his massive embrace.

"Oh, lass, I be so sorry to be the one to bring

ye a more distressin' cargo than ye be already carryin'."

Eugenia stiffened in his embrace and drew back to search the old sea dog's face. "They did not seize the schooner already, did they?"

Captain Derrick wore a puzzled frown until Eugenia brought him up to date with everything that had happened since her return. She fought to keep her shaky voice steady as she told about her father's murder and her efforts to find justice after his estate had been liquidated. She described Zach and her suspicions, although she no longer believed him capable of cold-blooded murder—not when she recalled his gentle touch.

"Me poor little lass, and now I be returning only to add more barnacles to the already heavy anchor ye got weighing ye down."

Despite the dread in her stomach, her face looked hopeful. "But if no one has seized the schooner, everything can be put to right. You can weigh anchor until I can return, so we can talk leisurely. While you were gone, I have been thinking, and I believe I have come up with the perfect solution to help get my father's oyster beds back."

"Aye, if only it be that simple, lass."

Eugenia frowned at the captain. "But I have not even told you yet. Why shouldn't it be simple?"

"Because, sad it be for me to say, I've got aboard one of the most troublesome cargoes I ever be havin' the misfortune to haul aboard her."

Eugenia shrugged, unable to understand what could be so distressing. "Well, then simply unload

254

it as swiftly as possible, then you can sail over to Bruceport, out of sight, and wait for me."

"I could very well unload it, and without much time taken. But I fear that would no doubt waylay your plans, whatever they be, lass. For it be an evil wind which filled the schooner's sails northward this trip. Ye see, lass, I have the dire misfortune to be carrying your blood kin aboard the schooner."

Eugenia suddenly felt faint, and her stomach churned, threatening to empty its contents. "You mean Aunt Iris and Uncle Eduardo? Here?"

"Aye, and your very own cousin, Mildred, too."

Twenty-two

It had taken nearly half an hour for Eugenia to convince Captain Derrick to take her aunt and uncle over to Bruceport and make arrangements for them to travel overland via Ilwaco to Oysterville. After all, she reasoned, they would be none the wiser, and it would buy her valuable time if Captain Derrick bribed the right people.

Eugenia breathed a sigh of relief as she watched the schooner up anchor and grow smaller against the high-reaching pines on the distant shore across the bay. Captain Derrick had reluctantly agreed to return and hear out her plan after unloading his "cargo."

Court Week, when the territorial judges traveled from Spokane and Vancouver, and attorneys came from Portland and Astoria, accompanied by jurors and witnesses, descended on Oysterville, was still two weeks away, and already the accommodations in town were nearly booked up. If she could keep Aunt Iris and Uncle Eduardo away long enough, they would have nowhere to stay and no choice but to return to California and leave her to her own life.

She stood and watched the schooner until it disappeared. Then she turned back toward town to wait until the captain returned so they could work out the details of the plan that had been churning in her mind since visiting Holm's Boatworks. Confident that Captain Derrick would agree to help her out, all she needed was to come up with something to distract Zach long enough so she could put her plan into motion.

"Look, it's your life, pard," Cliff said, lying across the bed, his hands behind his head. The guest room was a bright, cheery room, decorated in pale green ruffles and lace, and filled with the loving personal touches of a woman who had obviously cared for her family very deeply.

"Humpin' horses, you 'n' me been partners for well on six years, and I never seed you risk your badge the way you done." He grinned at Kellogg, who was standing stiffly near the lace-curtained window with his arms crossed over his chest. "Got to admit, though, that little lady's got enough spunk to tame a bear—even one of your ilk."

Zach's lips tightened ever so slightly, but he was not about to let on how near to the truth his partner was.

"And she ain't bad looking, neither," Cliff continued, determined to get a rise out of Kellogg. "Matter a' fact, she's so down right purty that it's no wonder the sun don't peek its face out on this here peninsula more oftener; it can't outshine that little lady's smile and knows it. It sure enough does."

"If you're through singing Eugenia's praises, let's get down to business," Zach grumbled. "What the hell're you doing here?"

Cliff grinned. Kellogg's open irritation spoke for itself. "Already answered that back in the parlor. Furthermore, weren't through yet with the topic of the little lady, actually. I'd like to know what your intentions are toward her."

Zach's frown deepened into a dark scowl. "What's Eugenia got to do with the case?"

"It was her papa who was murdered. And other than your usin' government money without prior approval to buy her papa's oyster beds, and then keepin' the lady under the same roof with you and quite possibly ruinin' her reputation, maybe nothin'."

Hell, he had come into Granger's room to set him straight about Eugenia, and Granger was doing all the talking. "Then make your point so we can get on with the business of solving this case."

Cliff got off the bed and walked over to a rocker near the window. He leaned his big hands on the back of it and stared directly into Kellogg's cold blue eyes.

"My point, friend, is that if you ain't got no personal interest in the little lady, I might. She's got a fire that could get a man so damned hot he'd burn right up to have her."

For an instant, Zach visualized how Eugenia had set him on fire, searing him like no other. He shook his head to shake the memories. "She's not your type, Granger," Zach said darkly.

"Friend, any female with half her curves in a skirt's my type."

"Eugenia rarely wears skirts," Zach blurted out, his anger getting the better of his usually cool demeanor.

"That's part of the lady in question's particular charm, friend."

Zach was coming as close to losing his temper as he ever had. "Then let me give you some sage advice, *friend*. Stay away from Eugenia Whalen."

Cliff threw back his head and laughed. "Clappin' clams, I thought as much. You got an itch for that spunky little lady as wide as the Columbia River. And you got it pretty damned bad." Then his face grew serious. "Just don't let it cause you to make a slip."

"No woman's going to get in the way of my doing what I'm here to do," Zach grated out.

"Well, we'd best get busy and solve this case soon then. Court Week's comin' up in a coupla weeks. With all them judges and lawyers pourin' into town, one of them's bound to recognize you."

"Then what're we standing here for? Let's get going. We got investigating to do."

"Whaddya got in mind?"

"Another look at the county records. Somehow I've got a nagging feeling I've overlooked the obvious. After we have a little talk with Holm at the boatworks I'm going to begin shipping oysters. The way I figure it, the only thing that makes sense is that Whalen's murder had something to do with them. Might just force the murderer's hand and flush him out into the open.

"Then I thought we'd head on over to the nearest saloon with a billiard table. No telling what bits for information we can pick up over a friendly game."

But even as Zach and Granger headed into town to delve further into the county records, and anyone who might be remotely connected with the oyster beds, Zach was hard pressed to deny Granger's observation. Zach had a growing hankering for Eugenia Whalen.

Eugenia was whistling by the time she got through presenting her plan to Captain Derrick. He had made arrangements in Bruceport to force her aunt and uncle to travel the long way around to Oysterville, and he had agreed, although reluctantly, to go along with her plan.

Just as she passed the Barnacle Tavern, Eugenia spotted Zach and his business associate through the swinging doors. She peered inside the darkened room crowded with tables and rough-looking men. Zach was leaning over a large green felt table, a long stick in his hands. That in itself was not what had drawn her through the doors to stand quietly in the back of the dimly lit saloon; it had been the remark she had just overheard about his beginning oyster shipments right away.

"You can't be in here, Miss Eugenia," the huge proprietor said, coming around the bar to confront her as he wiped his hands on his apron.

260

"There is no law against it, is there?" she retorted. She knew that wives often entered these dens of iniquity to drag wayward husbands home, often leaving smashed liquor bottles and shattered glasses in their wake.

"Not exactly, no, but ladies aren't—"

"Then I am staying."

Zach dropped the last two balls into the side pocket. "Guess I win again. I'll expect the pickers out at the beds bright and early," Zach announced to the frowning man he'd just beaten.

Sid Simpson threw his pool cue down. "Shoulda knowed you was one of them ringers the first time I talked to you when you was with the Whalen girl. But you won the services of my men fair 'n' square. We'll be there tomorrow mornin'. You have made arrangements to have them shipped, haven't you?"

"Of course he has," Eugenia said and stepped forward.

"Just start picking according to our agreement," Zach reiterated. "The ship will be waiting."

"Women," grumbled Simpson as he slugged down the rest of his drink to leave. "Next thing you know, they'll be steppin' up to the bar and demandin' to be served just like a man, as if it is their God-given right."

Zach pulled Eugenia out of earshot of the other patrons sitting at nearby tables, then swung on her. "What the hell're you doing in here?" Although he shouldn't be surprised to see her; she had an uncanny habit of showing up at the oddest times.

"The same thing it seems that you are; looking to make arrangements to have the oysters shipped to market ahead of schedule. I talked Mr. Holm into releasing one of his schooners. We will not have to wait any longer."

Zach's eyes narrowed at her continual meddling. "We?"

"You cannot believe, after I told you my intentions, that I am simply going to sit back and not help keep the business going until I can regain ownership. Mr. Holm was very cooperative this time."

"I'm a step ahead of you. I already had made arrangements with Holm. Go back to the house, Eugenia."

He turned from her, but she grabbed his arm. "I will not!"

His brow shoved up. He had to ignore the arousing warmth that her silken touch wrought through his groin. "Yes, you will."

Keeping a grin off his face, Cliff stepped forward, a pool cue in his hand. "Looks like you two got yourselves a mite little impasse on your hands."

"Not at all," Eugenia said, her chin jutting out. "I have a perfectly equitable business solution."

"The only solution is for you to go back to the house and do the job I hired you for, and nothing more," Zach insisted, tempted to bodily carry her back to the house and up to his bed.

Eugenia shot the stubborn man a frown. "You just played Sid Simpson for the use of his crew."

"So?"

"So, I am willing to play you for the right to be

a part of a business that should legitimately belong to me."

"Don't be ridiculous, Eugenia. Women don't play billiards."

"Are you afraid you will lose to a *mere* female?"

Insult to injury. That little spitfire needed a husband to take control of her, Zach ruminated, with more than a little disturbance at the very notion of marriage and Eugenia combined in the same thought.

Zach's face was set in rock. "There isn't going to be a game."

"What's the matter, Kellogg? Don't you think you can beat the little lady?" Cliff said with a goading smirk.

"It wouldn't even be a contest."

"Then you got nothin' to lose and everythin' to gain, to my way a' thinkin."

"Play her so she'll leave us in peace," one man shouted from his hunched position on a bar stool.

"Yeah, send her away with her tail atween her legs. Maybe then womenfolk won't be so dad-blamed anxious to show their faces in here again," another seconded.

The proprietor wiped a glass and set it on the clean stack. "Go ahead, get it over with before she runs off all my paying customers."

"Looks like it's settled," Cliff crowed to a round of snickers and jeers.

Zach's scowl deepened. The last thing he wanted to do was beat the pants off Eugenia in front of her deceased pa's friends and neighbors. Although in a more secluded setting, he wouldn't mind slipping those pants down her silken thighs and coaxing cries of passion from her.

Eugenia's heart raced over her impetuous display of bravado. She hadn't the foggiest notion how to play the game of billiards. And she had just impetuously bet her future on it!

"All right," Zach said begrudgingly. "I'll play you. The stakes are that if I win, you go back to the house and keep your nose out of my business."

"And if I win, you will let me help with the oyster beds, and give me a chance to buy you both out."

Zach's lips tightened, and his gaze shot to Granger. "Sounds fair enough to me," Cliff said to another round of jeers and snickers from the men watching.

Zach's last chance to put a stop to the trouncing Eugenia was going to take had just been dashed. And by his own partner!

"All right, Eugenia. But I'm warning you now that I play to win. So don't try to pull some typical female tears on me afterwards, blubbering that you weren't properly warned."

She licked her lips and raised her chin. "I do not blubber, as you put it. But I would not be so smug, if I were you. You have not won yet."

Zach definitely had met his match. Maybe not with billiards. But the little lady was the perfect answer to make his hardened partner forget all about that greedy ex-wife of his and how she'd run off with another man, Cliff thought with secret delight and heightened interest.

"Before she takes you on, I'll just give her a few pointers." Cliff ignored Kellogg's scowl, handed

Eugenia his cue, and curled an arm around her shoulders. "You just come on over to the table with me, little lady, and I'll show you some basic moves."

Cliff spanned his hands around Eugenia's waist. "Just lean over the table and rest your hand on the edge . . . that's right." He leaned over behind her and closed his hand over hers. "Take hold of the cue stick like this . . . good. Now let the cue slide back and forth between your fingers real smooth, just like makin' love." He glanced back at Kellogg and gave his scowling partner a sly wink.

"That's enough, Granger," Zach warned, clamping a steely grip around Cliff's arm.

"Sure, Kellogg, sure. If you say so." Cliff recognized the murder in his partner's eyes and backed off without further argument. "I'll rack 'em up."

While Eugenia watched Cliff set up the balls, she wondered about the warning tone she'd heard in Zach's voice. It was almost possessive. Well, she did not belong to anyone!

"You want to break?" Zach asked, intruding into her thoughts.

Break? Eugenia swung out an arm, then leaned on the end of her cue stick. "I would not think of taking the advantage simply because I am a *mere* female." Zach stepped up to the table and set up the balls. She closely watched him until she got the idea.

Before he could send the white ball spinning toward the triangle, she broke in with, "We shall flip for it."

She looked at all the men crowding around the

table, their faces expectant. A short oysterman dressed in muddy dungarees dug into his pocket and spun a twenty-dollar gold piece in the air.

"Call it," Zach advised.

"Heads."

The coin clattered onto the table. "Heads it is." Cliff laughed and shot Kellogg a smirk. "Always preferred tails myself," he remarked, letting his grinning gaze linger on Eugenia's nicely rounded bottom.

Eugenia chewed on her lip and moved over to the table. Keeping in mind Cliff's instructions, she leaned over, closed one eye, took aim, and rammed the cue stick between her fingers. She missed her target and slammed the cue into the triangle of balls, ripping the green cloth covering in the process, and wildly sending several of the balls scattering off the table.

"Whew-eee!" hollered an oysterman as the men scrambled to get out of the way of the flying balls. "She sure packs a wallop, and she ruint the table to boot."

Four balls sailed off the table, one crashing into Zach's wrist. It caused him to grunt in pain.

"Needle and thread anyone?" Eugenia moaned over the surrounding bursts of laughter and grumbling that she had destroyed their table and effectively put a temporary end to their game.

"You don't win by ruining the playing table or disabling your opponent," Zach grumbled and rubbed his throbbing wrist. If she weren't so troublesome, he would have laughed with the rest of the men.

"No, by outwitting him," she mumbled, her mind whirring with all the possibilities to regain the oyster beds since her father's schooner had returned.

When the ribald remarks and snickers did not die down, Zach felt a sudden need to protect her. "That's enough!" Zach said in a harsh voice.

A mere fifteen minutes later, once the cloth had been hastily patched, Zach dropped the eight-ball with ease into the side pocket. He looked up at her. Disappointment shadowed her face. For an instant, he felt remorse that he had not given her one opportunity to try her luck at dropping a couple of balls.

"Looks like you're done helping," Zach said softly.

Eugenia bit her lip against the snickers echoing around the room. She expected to see Zach gloating. But his expression showed no signs of outward triumph. For an instant he looked almost as if he was sorry she had lost.

Eugenia felt awkward and out of place for the first time since she had left her Aunt Iris's. She set the cue down, raised her chin, and in an effort to maintain what little dignity she still retained, despite the male chuckles assaulting her ears, walked proudly from the tavern.

She no longer could openly insist on participating in the decisions concerning the business. It had been foolish as a novice to bet something so important to her, let alone attempting to win at a man's game.

But she was far from defeated yet!

Twenty-three

Eugenia had just tied off the last stitch on the outfit she'd been sewing when she heard the thudding of footfalls on the front porch. She quickly stuffed her handiwork behind a pillow on the sofa, and stashed the sewing basket on the floor.

"You're back," Eugenia said in an overly bright, startled voice.

Zach filled the arch leading into the parlor, his hands grasping the molding around the edges. "Had you hoped I wouldn't return?" When she did not answer, he continued. "About the billiard game—"

"You won," she said through tight lips. "There is nothing more to say about it. Can I interest you in a late supper? Or would you prefer to wait for Cliff?"

"Granger's otherwise engaged this evening," Zach said, thinking about his partner's wink when he remarked that he intended to pay a social call on the buxom blonde, Gertrude Englestrom.

Eugenia rose and started to walk past Zach. "Hungry?" she asked in a cool voice.

Zach dropped a gentle hand on her shoulder. "Eugenia, I've told you I'm sorry about your pa, and I even understand your desire to reclaim the oyster beds. But—"

"But what?" she snapped, unable to stop herself. "You show up—a total stranger—in town right after my father was murdered and then buy the beds for barely enough to cover the outstanding debts. It is a little too coincidental, don't you think?"

Her eyes were filled with angry, unspent tears and her chin quivered. Zach ached for the proud young woman. "Eugenia, believe me, I didn't have anything to do with your pa's murder. I just happened to be in the right place at the right time," he lied, hating the necessity of maintaining his cover.

His hands hooked over her shoulders so he could gaze directly into her face. "You do believe me, don't you?"

"I do not know what to believe anymore," she said with a ragged sob.

"Oh, God, Eugenia," he soothed and gathered her into his arms. His heart ached for her pain. "Believe that I would never harm you."

Zach took her cheeks between his palms and with the pads of his little fingers wiped away the tears pooling on her lower lids.

Her resolve weakened under the caring he displayed. "Oh, Zach, before Daddy sent me to California for a formal education, he and I had such a good life. He was such a good man, so kind and understanding. He never tried to mold me into what others thought I should be. He said I should be myself and follow my heart."

He searched her face. "And you should."

"But he is gone now." She sniffled back the tears to keep from totally breaking down. She had promised herself not to cry until she'd seen justice done, and somehow she'd manage to keep that promise.

Her shoulders were trembling despite a valiant effort to maintain her composure. His heart went out to her, and he enfolded her into his embrace, cradling the back of her head against his chest.

"Trust me, Eugenia. Trust me."

She felt so secure wrapped in his strong arms. The strong beat of his heart against her ear was so reassuring, so calming, that her arms snaked around his waist of their own volition.

Although she had not answered his entreaty, Zach was roused as she held him, and he gathered her in tighter against his chest. She finally seemed to trust him. Was not trying to pull away. That knowledge caused a dam to threaten to burst inside of him.

"Oh God, Eugenia," he groaned in a quiet voice. "Heaven help me, but I want you." He held her at arm's distance. "I don't usually make a habit of saying things like that to a woman." No. When the need had presented itself in the past, he had merely acted on it.

The simplicity of his unexpected declaration caught her completely off guard. The first thing that came to mind was, "You don't?"

Her fingers crept up to stroke his cheek, and she smoothed back an errant black curl.

"Never."

"Any woman ever tell you she was falling in love with you?" she whispered hoarsely.

Painful memories of his former wife who had run away with that rich Russian flashed before his eyes. Those words had dripped off her tongue like a river of honey, nearly destroying him when she'd left. He steeled himself.

"You aiming to be one of those women?"

"If you are wondering if I am planning to get in line, you can quit worrying," she murmured in self-defense, sensing his unease. "My only love is the oysters."

"Ah yes, oysters. But you can't lie in the arms of an oyster in its bed," he said, catching her off guard.

He folded her hand in his and pressed it against his chest as he leaned over and kissed her. His lips were hot, yet tender and seeking. She eagerly responded to his invitation to deepen the kiss. It did not take much persuasion for Zach to draw his tongue along her lower lip and slip it inside the sweetness of her mouth.

Eugenia experienced a rapid thudding of his heart against her palm, and felt that potent male portion of him press hard against her. Passions heightening, their lips and mouths demanded, tasted and reveled.

His hands roamed over her back and down the ridge of her spine as a hot pressure continued to build in his groin. An urgent desire burst forth deep inside him, and his chest rose and fell at a rapid pace.

"Oh, Eugenia, my sweet Genie, I want to show you what you do to me. I want and need you in my bed," he groaned against her lips, their breaths mingling.

"There is no other bed on my mind right now." She nibbled on his lower lip.

Lost in the riptide of delicious sensation, Eugenia wrapped her arms around his neck and dropped pressing kisses to his throat as he lifted her into his arms.

Zach took the stairs easily and gently laid her on his bed. His hungry eyes devoured the white silken sight of her all the while his deft fingers peeled layer after layer of clothing from her body. She reached up to caress his face, but he captured her hand and kissed the tender inside of her wrist.

"I vowed to myself to stay away from you."

"And I promised myself to keep you at arm's length." Eugenia's fingers were now urgently working the buttons on his shirt.

"Some vows and promises are meant to be broken."

Zach shed his shirt. A tremor shook him when she ran a fingernail down the center of his bare chest to the waistband of his trousers. Her finger dipped beneath his belt, and his stomach muscles contracted at the wild sensations.

"Take off your pants and join me," she whispered, her lids heavy.

Zach's body was sleek perfection, muscles corded in his powerful thighs, arms and across his chest, all dusted with fine curling black hairs. Her gaze shifted to his groin. He stood erect, proud, ready for her. With tentative fingers, she reached out and touched the satiny smooth length of his male core rising from an ebony nest of black curls. It jerked and she drew her hand back.

"See what you do to me?" He folded his large frame next to her. Taking her hand, he guided her back to his most sensitive, potent flesh. "I want you to know all of me, my sweet Genie."

Her breathing accelerated into tiny gasps when he bent his head and fastened his hot, hungry mouth on an eager nipple. Waves of pure sensation washed over her. She felt a moist tingling heat between her thighs, and her grip tightened around his pulsing shaft.

His bronzed hands roamed over her white flesh, his palms circling the swollen rosy buds of her breasts. Memorizing every curve with his probing touch, he stroked the silken texture of her flesh. With his tongue he traced a path toward her womanly curls.

She squirmed, causing him to lift his head and murmur, "Are you ready for me?"

"Mmm," issued from deep within her throat. She was so heated she thought she would lose her mind if he did not claim her soon.

"Then open your thighs to me," he commanded between scorching kisses. He was in danger of losing control, he was so aroused.

Eugenia spread her legs, and his eyes devoured the beauty of her woman's center. "That's right, my sweet Genie, open yourself to me. Open all the way. I need to lose myself inside you."

His gaze consumed the vision of her woman's cleft, lightly furred with auburn curls. "You are so beautiful," he murmured, stroking her there. "So very beautiful."

Zach then leaned over, and his tongue slid between the folds to touch that most sensitive of spots. The slippery skin had stiffened into a hardened peak. Her pungent and spicy fragrance increased his excitement.

After he had savored her, he lifted his head to gaze into her green eyes, heavily dilated with passion. "So ready. So unbelievably ready."

Eugenia moaned as his hand slid between her legs, and he dipped two fingers into her molten core. She cried out his name and began to move against his delving hand. Her entire being was incredibly sensitized to the bombarding stimulation.

"Oh Lord, Zach," she breathed in shallow, rapid pants. Her hips worked, bucking against him. "Oh, Zach."

She was so hot and wet with liquid fire within the soft folds. Her woman's muscles tightened around his fingers, and he increased the friction, encouraging her toward an abandoned frenzy.

Wild, fevered flames threatened to engulf Zach's groin as she rode his hand until she suddenly cried out, squeezing her thighs together and straining against him. Unable to hold himself back much longer, he withdrew his fingers. With his lips he smothered her protests, mounted, and plunged deep inside her.

"Move with me," he said in a dissolving murmur.

"I'll follow," came her muffled moan.

She fastened her mouth on his neck as they began to move. Slowly at first, then Zach increased the pace, his erection sliding in and out setting the rhythm, pumping. She matched his thrusts with her own. As the momentum built, Zach captured her mouth, simulating their mating cadence with his tongue.

The tension soared within Eugenia, a frenzied force building, building until it burst into spasm after wild spasm. She pressed against him, crying out his name. Her body convulsed, raising goose-flesh on her drenched skin. Only then did Zach bury his face in the curve of her neck and release his life-giving seed in pulse after throbbing pulse.

Slowly the crest subsided, and he lifted himself up on his elbows to smile down at her. She reached up and tucked a drenched strand of hair behind his ear.

"I wish we could remain like this forever," she whispered through lips swollen from their lovemaking.

"Nothing would suit me more."

"I am so glad we know how we both feel about each other," she began dreamily. But cautiousness was returning, and she was careful not to use the words of love again. Her feelings for Zach were too dear, too fragile, too new to hazard stripping bare her entire inner self again so soon.

He kissed the tip of her nose. "Why's that?"

"Because this changes everything between us. We

do not have to be at odds over the oyster beds any longer. Now we can work together."

Zach stiffened and reluctantly moved to her side. Running a finger down her chest between her breasts to rest his palm on her flat belly, he gazed into her wide, trusting eyes and hated himself.

"Eugenia, the oyster beds have nothing to do with you and me."

A troubled light flickered into her eyes, replacing the openness of a moment ago. "What do you mean? Of course they do."

"No, Eugenia, they don't. The oyster beds are a business venture. What's between you and me is personal."

A sinking feeling settling heavily in the pit of her stomach, Eugenia scooted up and wrapped the sheet over her breasts. "The two cannot be separated, Zach. They are intertwined. I told you what my father's oyster beds mean to me. You know how I feel about them. Furthermore, with my practical experience, I can help you make them highly profitable again."

"No, Eugenia, you can't."

She tensed. Suddenly every nerve ending was raw. "Exactly what do you mean that I can't?"

He could see the icy curtain drop over her face, and the flicker of emotion in her eyes dimmed. She was withdrawing from him. She was not going to make what he had to do easy.

In order to solve her father's murder, he was going to have to speed things up, and take risks he did not want her involved with. He dragged his fingers through his mussed hair. Hell, he could not put her in jeopardy. And he could not take the chance of taking her into his confidence. With her unbridled enthusiasm, she could very well unwittingly ruin the little progress he had made in the case.

"Are you going to answer me?" she demanded.

"You're not to go near the oyster beds."

"No!" she cried, jumped from the bed and angrily began dressing without regard to the alluring figure she presented.

"You lost the game of billiards fair 'n' square, Eugenia," he gently reminded her.

Her face a furious red, she spat, "What happened to 'my sweet Genie, I want to give you the world'? Was that merely part of the seduction? A lie?"

"I expect you to keep to your word," he said, his voice a soft warning. Her accusation stung him deeply, but being a marshal had always meant tough choices. And he had to look out for that beautiful, soft sunburned neck of hers.

Half-dressed, her underclothes pressed against her chest, Eugenia slammed from the room with, "Just for your information, I lied too. The only thing I feel toward you is hatred!"

Buck naked, Zach ran from the room after her, only to come face to face with Granger, who was coming up the stairs, carrying his shoes. Her bedroom door slammed in Zach's ears.

Cliff's face slid into an amused smirk. "Well, well, well. Here I am, shoes in hand so as not to wake you, partner, and you ain't been sleepin'."

He grunted and shook his head. "I warned you that you could lose your shirt over this case, but your pants too? Naked notions, I never meant it quite so literally."

"Go to hell, Granger." Zach swung around on his heel and stomped back into his room, Granger right behind him.

"I may very well end up there, but that Gertrude Englestrom was pure heaven on earth," Cliff said with a lascivious grin while Kellogg angrily jabbed his legs into his pants. "She knows what a man needs and exactly how to give it. What an appetite!"

"Don't want to hear about another one of your conquests," Zach grated.

"Since I'm sure not gonna hear about yours with your little housekeeper, I—"

Cliff did not see the fist before it slammed into his jaw, knocking him flat to the floor. Rubbing his throbbing chin, Cliff looked up at his long-time partner. "You son of a bitch, what was that for?"

"Don't you ever mention my *little housekeeper* in that regard again."

Kellogg's voice was deadly cold. Colder than Cliff had ever witnessed it, even when Kellogg had come up against some of the West's meanest gunslingers.

"Sure, friend. No offense meant. But since you're so damned sensitive 'bout the topic, I gotta tell you that you'd best wear a neckerchief till that roarin' suckled mark on your neck fades, if you don't want the whole town to know what you been up to. You get my drift?"

Kellogg's face did not soften, nor did he respond

to Cliff's advice, so Cliff quickly sought to change the subject before Kellogg's feelings for the little lady blasted the whole case to hell. "When do you plan to start shippin' oysters?"

Zach eyed Granger with disgust, but he said, "You were with me when we twisted Holm's arm. The man gave in without much persuasion and swore he'd have the *Gull Berry* ready before the end of the day, so I'm going to start picking the oysters tomorrow morning for shipment."

Eugenia stepped away from Zach's door where she had crept back to listen. She had heard enough. *Little housekeeper,* was she? Her heart hardened. She had been a fool. But no more. Somehow she would block out the memories of his touch, of his body, of his lies. She silently vowed to see justice done and get the oyster beds back.

She tiptoed downstairs to retrieve her sewing basket and the outfit she had been stitching before Zach returned earlier. Once safely back inside her own room with the door locked, she held up the garment before her.

"Well, Mr. Zachary Kellogg," she let out a wistful sigh, "if you think you can seduce me into agreeing to abandon my rightful heritage, you are in for one of the biggest surprises of your life!"

Twenty-four

It had taken nearly all night, one of her favorite shirts, and her mother's best white linen tablecloth. But Eugenia was finally pleased with her efforts. She held her handiwork up in front of her.

"There. This will make it official," she said to the rectangular strip of fabric hanging from her fingertips, as if its mere existence somehow lent credence to her plan.

Eugenia dressed in the outfit she had fashioned and bundled up the strip of fabric. After donning a long coat, she crept downstairs to put breakfast on the table for her employer and his guest before she left.

Her employer. An employer who had taken advantage of her. That was how she was forcing herself to think of Zach Kellogg after last night. She quickly scribbled a note to cover her absence and slipped out the back door into the misty, predawn darkness.

Captain Derrick was waiting for her at the end of the wharf. "Ahoy, lass."

"Let's hurry out to the schooner," she said, not bothering with the usual niceties. "I do not want anyone to see us."

"No one's goin' to sight ye, all bundled up the way ye be, lass."

Once aboard the schooner, Captain Derrick assembled the crew on deck after reassuring Eugenia that there wasn't a man with a disloyal bone among them.

"For those of ye salty dogs who don't know, this lass be the owner of this ship." Murmurs rose among a few of the men until Captain Derrick raised a hand. "If there be any among ye who can't or won't follow the lass, then abandon ship now, or ye'll find yerselves tossed overboard right where we float."

Quiet immediately descended over the crew, lending an eerie aura to the fog-enshrouded schooner gently bobbing in the bay. Eugenia searched the crew's weathered faces. Each bore a solemn countenance.

"As you all may know," she began, "my father was murdered and his oyster beds sold without my knowledge or consent. You all have made a good living from the oyster beds, and I do not intend to stand meekly aside and allow some stranger to take that away."

Shouts of support rose until Eugenia motioned for silence. She was heartened at their endorsement. "And to meet that end, I have come up with the perfect plan, and with your assistance we shall regain ownership."

While the men waited expectantly, Eugenia flung

off her coat in a dramatic move, revealing a puffed sleeve blouse top, heavy belt with saber dangling along purple satin trousers disappearing into heavy boots. She bent over and removed the rectangular strip from her bundle.

"With this we are going to beat Mr. Zachary Kellogg at his own game." Proudly, she unfurled a flag sporting a skull and crossbones that she had fashioned.

Her arms akimbo, she announced, "I am going to become the Pacific Raider, oyster pirate par excellence. And all of you will be my crew of cutthroats."

To her bemused annoyance, she did not receive the response she had anticipated. The men fought to stifle chuckles behind their hands. And even Captain Derrick made a sudden study of his battered boots.

Eugenia's balled fists dropped on her hips. "What is the matter with all of you? It is the perfect solution."

The men just looked to one another, dumbfounded and not at all convinced. Finally Captain Derrick stepped forward and cleared his throat. "Miss Eugenia, other than your, ah, colorful outfit, lass, it be obvious that ye ain't had much experience flying the Jolly Roger."

Eugenia looked at the flag she had painstakingly fashioned. "What is wrong with it?"

"Yer flag, lass, it be a white background with a black skull. Every sailor who's encountered the scourge of the seas knows that the background be black and the skull be white. Ye've done your best handiwork backwards."

"A mere detail," she said through tight lips, dismissing the error as a minor annoyance. A smile split her lips. "This flag is . . . unique. It will be our personal insignia!"

"Unique." Captain Derrick shook his head at her reasoning. "That it be, lass."

"Excuse me, miss," an awkward young sailor said, hat in hands. "But pirates get a swift swing at the end of a rope from the yardarm if caught. Most of us got families. We ain't pirates."

"We will not get caught," she insisted, excitement for her plan building in her breast. "Furthermore, it is not as if we are truly going to be pirates. We are only going to get back what rightfully should belong to me. We shall only take the oysters from Zachary Kellogg's shipments. So it is not as if we are actually engaging in piracy. And every one of your families will benefit from the money we make."

It took Eugenia, along with Captain Derrick's support, nearly an hour to sway the reluctant men to her cause. She laid out her strategy to lie in wait until Kellogg's ship left Shoalwater Bay before stopping the schooner and relieving it of its cargo. Then they would sail to Astoria and transfer the oysters to another ship sailing for San Francisco.

"Beggin' your pardon, Miss Eugenia," a one-eyed sailor grinned, "when do we begin?"

"The oysters are being harvested as we speak. As soon as Kellogg's hired schooner leaves the bay, we will attack." She settled on the deck with her legs crossed and motioned for the men to crowd around her. "Sit down and I will map out exactly how we are going to proceed . . ."

Zach and Cliff stood aboard the plunger watching the oystering. Booted men used tongs to pluck the oysters from beneath eel grass where the water was too deep to handpick the mollusks. They loaded their haul aboard the fast, narrow twenty-foot sloop for transportation to the schooner Zach had arranged.

"Looks like it's gonna be a pretty good haul," Cliff remarked as the receptacles containing salt water to keep the oysters fresh filled rapidly. "The government's gonna want a detailed report on the profit."

"Well, the government can just piss into the wind this time. Since there aren't any banks in Oysterville, I'm going to hitch a ride on the schooner to Astoria and deposit the profits into a bank account in Eugenia's name."

Noticing the neckerchief tied at Kellogg's throat, Cliff had been waiting for him to bring up the topic of the little lady since they'd left the house. "Moundin' moles, hope she's worth your badge, friend. You've been takin' a awful risk stickin' your neck out"—he hesitated, but Kellogg ignored the reference, so he continued—"and gettin' so personally mixed up with the little lady. And now you're plannin' to divert government funds."

"To my way of thinking, I'm not diverting anything," Zach shot back. "The government isn't going to lose anything. The profits from this shipment rightfully belong to Eugenia; the helpless young woman has been orphaned, her pa's business sold right out from under her, and she desperately needs the money. And as far as my personal involvement with Eugenia Whalen, it's none of your damned business."

"Hogtied hamhocks, I don't dispute that the little lady may be desperate, but I seriously doubt that she's as helpless as you seem to think."

Zach ignored his partner's remark and turned his attention to the oyster harvesting. He knew that Eugenia was not as helpless as he had made her out to be to Granger; she had proved that often enough. But he was the only hope she had of reclaiming those precious oyster beds she loved so dearly.

For the remainder of the day, Zach and Cliff oversaw the loading. Oystermen picked until the schooner's hold was brimming with the bivalves worth their weight in gold. Zach made arrangements to sail with the morning tide, then he and Cliff parted. Cliff was heading back to Gertrude Englestrom's, and Zach to face Eugenia.

Eugenia's spies had kept her abreast of Zach's progress during the day. So by the time he reached the house, her feet were curled beneath her on the corner of the sofa in the parlor, thumbing through a family album. She was grasping a crumbled hankie. Her nose was red, and her lashes were wet, sticking together as if she had been crying.

"Eugenia," he said softly.

Startled, she glanced up and snapped the album shut. After setting out her strategy with her crew, she had spent the remainder of the day trying to find a financial backer and quizzing Sheriff Dollard, only to come away disheartened.

The sheriff had made no progress in coming up with a suspect in her father's murder and had hinted that as far as he was concerned, the case would be closed as unsolved. And not one person she had approached was willing to take a chance on the business acumen of a young female.

The only course left to her was to sell the pirated oysters and raise the money herself.

She got off the sofa. "I will fetch your supper."

"Wait." He put a staying hand on her arm.

"You would not want me to neglect my duties, would you?" she said in a cold voice, recalling his housekeeper comment to Cliff the night before. Then she recalled the neckerchief remark from Cliff and how Zach had come to wear it, and she had to fight down a blush of embarrassment.

"Trust me, Eugenia," he said, hating himself for not being able to confide his mission.

She ignored his plea. "Trust is something earned," she said.

His gut tightened. Her response was not what he'd hoped for, but at least she was talking to him.

"There is a regatta during the Fourth of July celebration at the end of Court Week that Daddy always participated in. I expect as owner of my father's business, you will want to carry on the tradition."

"I wouldn't think of breaking with tradition. But only if you'll agree to teach me how to sail."

"You mean you do not know how to sail either?"

"I'm a quick learner."

And a good teacher, too, she thought of how he had made her body sail past the heavens last night. "All right," she agreed reluctantly. "We can start first thing in the morning."

"It'll have to wait until after the first load of oysters are shipped with the tide. Then I'm all yours."

All mine. The words rang hollow in her heart. All hers as long as she agreed to become one of the typical Oysterville ladies who tended their gardens. Well, she wanted more to do with oysters than making paths of the crushed shells and sprinkling salt water from the bay on them to keep the weeds and pests down.

If everything worked out according to plan, she would regain her rightful inheritance, then she could pay a private investigator to solve her father's murder. At least Zach had just given her the information about the oyster shipment without having to ask.

"I have baked oysters in the shell with cheese and bacon for supper."

"You didn't sneak out to the beds, did you?" he questioned at the mention of oysters.

"You specifically forbade me to go anywhere near them, if you will recall." She let out a belabored sigh. "I spent my day collecting moss from rotting logs so I can arrange it into a pine cone-framed picture for the wall like the good ladies of the town do. I may even take up the art of fashioning my own hair into decorations."

Frustration shoved up his brow. "Eugenia, you don't have to try to fit into some traditional mold you may think is expected of you."

She glared at him. "Don't I? Everyone has made it perfectly clear that my true interests are not acceptable. What choice do I have?"

Hell, how could he answer that? For at the moment, she had no other choice until he solved the case. However, there was the glint of the devil dancing in those green eyes that warned Zach that she was not as defeated as she made out.

"Why don't we have a picnic before the fire tonight. Granger's otherwise engaged again this evening, so it'll be just the two of us."

"Just the two of us, how convenient," she muttered. But even as she wondered if it had been prearranged, her heart was beginning to increase its pulse beats. Despite her anger, she could not deny that she was helplessly drawn to Zach Kellogg as the waves were to the beach, and she wondered why her heart was betraying her mind.

While Eugenia was in the kitchen loading a tray with their supper, Zach laid out a fire and spread a blanket before the flames. He met her half way to the parlor and took the heavy tray from her hands.

"We'll pretend we're on a picnic on Long Island, just like the picnics you used to have with your family."

He remembered. And despite herself, it caused her heart to soften. Zach seemed to have a way of recalling the little details that were such a cherished part of her life. Damn him. Why did he have a way about him that could so easily pierce her armor and disarm her?

They sat on the floor, the fire crackling and lending its warmth to Eugenia's already heated cheeks. Trying to avoid eye contact, she picked up her fork.

Zach's rough hand folded around hers. Despite her resolve, an electrifying sensation shot through her.

"Allow me," he said in a husky voice.

He was melting her resistance, seducing her with such subtle expertise that she was unable to combat the very essence of his latest sensual assault.

Silently she watched as he scooped the oyster from the shell and slowly fed it to her. The blending of flavors was a sensuous encounter of its own and heightened the building tension.

Zach took a bite and savored the piquancy. "Eating oysters is a true sensual experience, don't you agree?" he said and offered her another.

Eugenia ate quietly, unsure how to respond. She should hate him, stay as far away from him as was humanly possible. But instead she was seated next to him of her own free will, willingly partaking and engaging in this delicate prelude to passion.

He was silently undressing her, savoring her with his eyes. Inviting her to participate in her own capitulation.

"Berry?"

She glanced at the fingers holding one of the salmon berries she had picked earlier. Feeling awkward, she blurted out, "Salmon berries grow wild on the peninsula. They got their name from an Indian custom of catching spring salmon and putting the berries in the salmon's mouth, then pointing its head upstream."

"Very interesting. Open your mouth for me, Eugenia, so you can savor its flavor."

Zach dropped the berry into her mouth, then withdrew his fingers to his own lips. "Hmm, very sweet."

In an effort to break the tension, Eugenia said cutely, "Do you plan to point my head upstream now?"

Zach's smile was seductive. "Never let it be said that I broke custom."

He leaned over, took her face between his hands and kissed her. The instant his tongue penetrated her mouth, Eugenia knew she was lost. He gathered her into his arms as he leisurely took possession of her mouth. Eugenia trembled from the intensity of emotion he evoked in her.

"Zach," she murmured into his mouth, but continued to nibble on his lips. "We should not be here like this."

"Why not?" he said between drugging kisses.

"Because I hate you." She breathed heavily, returning his kiss for heated kiss.

"Hate's a strong emotion akin to love. Just keep hating me like you are now." His hands explored her supple breasts, all the while he rained kisses over her face and neck.

A sense of urgent intensity was overtaking them, and in an intimate frenzy each plucked at the other's clothing, racing toward the ultimate culmination.

The last conscious thought to enter Eugenia's mind before she totally surrendered herself to the flaming sensations was tomorrow.

Tomorrow she would do what had to be done.

Twenty-five

Dressed in the pirate's outfit, her auburn curls tucked up under a ridiculous plumed hat, her face hidden behind a silk scarf in which she had snipped eye holes, Eugenia stood on the bow of the schooner waiting for her prey. Last night her body had succumbed to Zach Kellogg's persuasive urgings. But the cold light of morning had a way of jolting one's senses back to reality.

Today his precious shipment would succumb to a little persuasion of her own.

"Thar she be," hollered a sailor on watch.

Her adrenaline pumping, Eugenia watched her motley crew scramble to man their positions. Each man carried a rifle or pistol, the extent of the firepower on board. She waited until their target sailed closer, unaware. Then she ran to the main mast and raised the flag.

Determined to be in the forefront, Eugenia grabbed a rifle and pulled the trigger. The blast knocked her off her feet, her hat falling over her eyes. She shoved the hat back and fought to get her unruly hair tucked away.

A battle of errors had begun.

Captain Derrick maneuvered the schooner to within six feet of their mark. The schooners furled their sails. And the men on each schooner exchanged verbal harangues.

Eugenia clambered to her feet and, waving her saber, ordered, "Board her, men!"

When the men just stood their positions, Eugenia took the lead. She grabbed a length of rope she'd had readied for just such a purpose. Taking a running start, her feet left the deck. She swung toward the other schooner, but did not release her hold in time; she helplessly swung back to her own ship.

She was so intent on carrying out her plan that she pushed off again. Only this time she lost her hold and plunged into the sea.

While Captain Derrick fished her out of the ocean, the rest of the crew scrambled to board the other schooner and had taken possession of the ship without a fight. Soggy and dripping, Eugenia climbed over the side from the dinghy Captain Derrick had lowered to rescue her.

"Good work, men," she said and swaggered toward the captain of the captured ship as she hiked up her heavy belt. Her boots were filled with water and she was soaked, her clothing clinging to her like gills on a fish.

"What is the meaning of this?" the middle-aged captain demanded, his expression displaying more confused annoyance than fear.

"Didn't you notice the flag we fly?" Eugenia motioned toward the pirate insignia, fluttering in the wind.

The captain broke into a smile, then a hearty belly laugh. "Is this some sort of joke the fellers out of Bruceport are playing? That is the most pathetic excuse for the Jolly Roger I've ever seen in all my fifteen years at sea."

Eugenia did not appreciate not being taken seriously one bit! "If you consider the Pacific Raider relieving you of your cargo humorous, then you are welcome to go ahead and continue laughing."

The man sobered. "This is unheard of! I have no intention of relinquishing my cargo to the scrawny likes of you and that ragtag bunch you got with you, Pacific Raider."

"Maybe you would rather walk the plank?"

"Pst. Pst. Raider," a nearby sailor hailed after hearing her threat. "Pst."

Eugenia rolled her eyes and turned to the persistent sailor who was determined to interrupt her. "What is it?" she hissed.

"We ain't got no plank."

Eugenia frowned at the sudden dilemma. Being resourceful, the solution immediately came to her. "Well, then we'll merely toss him over the side without benefit of a plank."

"On guard . . . *Pacific Raider!*"

Eugenia swung around at the shout of the sinkingly familiar baritone voice, tinged with the merest hint of amusement.

Zach was standing before her, a saber held in his hand. He stood in a ready position to take up the battle, his ebony hair blowing in the wind. Even in dungarees with that neckerchief at his throat, he cut such a dashing figure that he could be the one considered a pirate. And his face was anchored in stone.

Sinking pirate ships! she thought miserably. She was going to end up being the one walking the plank. At least she was already wet. Her gaze shifted to his sword. She hadn't the foggiest notion how to use one of those long blades. Her pride keeping her from unmasking herself right then and there, Eugenia struggled to get her father's saber out of its scabbard.

Zach fought to keep a straight face as he waited for his masked adversary to engage him. He took out his watch and noted the time.

Zach had been fighting a queasy stomach, lounging in the cabin on the way to Astoria, when he witnessed the awkward takeover attempt. At first he had drawn his gun, prepared to defend the ship until he caught sight of the curvaceous masked pirate's comical efforts to board the ship. He breathed a sigh of relief and waited until the *pirate* managed to climb onto the deck, then burst out laughing.

"Shall I assist you?" Zach asked the struggling masked pirate. "I'm sure you must have other ships on your agenda to waylay today, and I'd hate to hold you up for an undue length of time over such a trifle inconvenience. Or perhaps we could locate a spare sword for you on board somewhere. It is only fitting, seeing as how I am your host."

Eugenia glanced up and frowned. Such a thoughtful host, indeed! "No. We'll settle this just as soon as I can get this stubborn sword out of its scabbard."

Zach leaned on a water cask and crossed his legs at the ankles. He set his saber aside and tented his fingers in front of his mouth. "Whenever you're ready, you will let me know, of course."

"Of course. You will be the first," she grated out in frustration.

The crews from both schooners forgot their adversarial positions and were now milling around, watching the strange interaction in disbelief and more than a little befuddled amusement.

"Perhaps we can settle this in another manner," Zach suggested.

"Hand to hand combat is part of being a pirate," Eugenia snapped.

"Umm, hand to hand, you say. Now, that sounds rather promising."

"With swords!" she spat, envisioning his bronzed hands caressing her white flesh.

Zach got up, towering over his *pirate* adversary. In his most platonic voice, he said, "I'm sure there are no hard and fast rules in the pirate's handbook."

"Truly?"

"Cross my heart." He drew an "x" across his heart. Hell, his heart was pounding just gazing at the fetching figure the little spitfire cut in those wet, clinging clothes.

"Do you have an alternative in mind?" she queried, still unable to disengage the saber.

His brow shoved up, and a wide, seductive smile

spread his lips. "There's definitely a few I think we could pursue in private."

He was being so damn congenial, to the point of being ludicrous considering the circumstances, that Eugenia wanted to scream. And to top it off he was timing her!

If she weren't masked, and he didn't know she was the pirate leader, she'd almost think he was attempting to seduce her. Nothing was working out the way she had so carefully planned. Nothing! Somehow she had to salvage this muddle without Zach finding out who she was. But how?

A sudden idea flashed into her mind.

Rather than cross swords with the man, which she'd had every intention of avoiding at all costs anyway, she would order him bound with the rest of the crew. It was so simple. Why hadn't she thought of that in the first place!

"Seize him, men," she suddenly ordered.

The men cautiously moved forward, and Zach raised his sword. They stopped cold in their tracks, not one prepared to take on the big man. Zach shook his head in feigned disgust and settled his gaze on the leader.

"I do apologize if your men are inconvenienced, but I must insist on dealing directly with you."

"Why?" she asked, exasperated.

"Well, this is my cargo you're pirating. Therefore, I believe it's only proper protocol that the two leaders settle any dispute. Anything less would damage your reputation as the Pacific Raider. Furthermore, no self-respecting pirate would want such gossip to get around."

Eugenia finally managed to win the release of her saber, nearly losing her balance for her efforts.

"Ten minutes. I would suspect it's not your best time."

Holding the heavy sword with both hands as she pointed it at Zach's chest, she ignored his reference to the amount of time it had taken to unsheath her sword. "Lead the way to your cabin unless you'd rather force me to run you through in front of your crew. And I can assure you it will not take me ten minutes to accomplish that feat."

"I certainly wouldn't want to be a bloody spectacle, or for that matter create additional work for the poor wretch left to swab the deck." With that he kept his face straight and went directly to the cabin, the earlier flip-flopping of his stomach forgotten.

Once Eugenia closed the door behind her, Zach easily disarmed her. Pinioning her arms behind her back, her breasts held tight against his chest. "I've always had a secret hankering to bed a pirate."

"It is not natural." Eugenia struggled against him, causing his shaft to harden and press at her belly.

"Oh, I don't know." He toyed with an escaping auburn tendril. "I've heard that some find it quite pleasurable during long sea voyages when no others are available."

"No!" She broke free and backed against the door. "You try anything unsavory, and my crew will slit your throat."

He took a step toward her, his eyes devouring

her. "Speaking of throats, yours looks mighty inviting to a man starved for *companionship*."

They had just bedded last night! "You are not starved for companionship," she snapped, her vision caught on that damned neckerchief.

"Oh, but I am." His voice was a mere whisper. "Yours."

Before she could react, he lunged forward and ripped the silken mask from her face. "Eugenia."

"You knew all along, didn't you?" she charged. "Is that why you were timing me?"

He gave a shrug. "Of course."

"How did you guess?"

"Maybe you've forgotten, but I know every delicious inch of your body, wet or dry. And wet, there isn't an alluring curve left to the imagination in that outfit."

Her anger replacing any guilt she had momentarily felt, Eugenia jabbed a finger into his chest. "Then why did you allow me to struggle with my sword on deck before both crews?"

"Wanted to see if you could better your time."

"I was not breaking into a house," she spat. "How can you compare?"

"I'll take an average."

She glared at him in silent fury, at a loss for a properly stinging retort.

"I would stick with breaking into houses if I were you. You made much better time climbing through my window."

"You enjoyed making a fool out of me, didn't you?"

His warm fingers encircled her finger. "Eugenia,

if I had wanted to make a fool out of you, I would have taken you over my knee on deck before both crews. Now I suggest you sit down and tell me why you deemed it necessary to become the Pacific Raider and try 'n' hijack my first shipment of oysters."

"Because they rightfully belong to me. Someone wanted my father out of the way bad enough to murder him. Then you come along and buy the beds for a mere fraction of their value. The beds should be mine, but not one person in town was willing to back me financially so I could buy them back from you. This is the only way I could think of to raise the money to get them back."

"You mean you planned to steal the oysters from me, sell them, and buy back the beds with my own money?"

"Yes, if you must know." Eugenia crossed her arms over her chest, effectively cutting off Zach's view of the merest hint of breast through the wet, white fabric.

"Resourceful. I'll give you that . . ."

"Kind gentleman that you are," she finished for him in a mocking voice.

"Believe me, if I weren't I'd run the lot of you in."

There it was again, a reference to the law in the vernacular. Eugenia furrowed her brow, but did not comment.

"And I suppose you know piracy's against the law?"

"Taking back what should rightfully be mine is not piracy," she insisted.

Zach grabbed her upper arm and sat her down on his narrow bed. She glared at him. "Although I've got to admit you've got a creative flair for the dramatic to your way of thinking, you don't know how damn lucky you are that I was aboard."

Lucky? he thought as an ocean swell rocked the ship, causing his stomach to lurch; he fought to ignore it. He would not have been aboard if he hadn't wanted to make sure she reaped the profits from the sale.

Eugenia rolled her eyes. "Oh, yes, damn lucky."

Leaning over her, his lips a tight line, Zach grasped both her arms. "Damn lucky indeed, you little fool. My crew might very well have imprisoned you, and you would've found yourself sitting in the Oysterville jail awaiting trial during Court Week."

"Or I might have gotten away with the oysters and made a tidy profit," she shot back, feeling the need to defend herself.

"Get this through your beautiful head, Eugenia. Your pa's case isn't going to be solved and the oyster beds returned to you through such silly antics!" She opened her mouth to reply, but Zach cut her off with, "I'm going to forget what you tried to do . . . this time. But do not, I repeat, do not *ever* try anything so outrageously stupid again."

She shivered and he snatched a blanket from the bunk and wrapped it around her.

"There are dry clothes on the hook. You can change while I go up on deck, dismiss your crew, and explain to mine that it was no more than a harmless joke engineered by my prankster partner.

"Then after the oysters have been transferred to another ship at Astoria, you will return to Oysterville with me as if nothing happened, and we'll resume our lives. And you will allow the law to do its job without your interference."

"The law! Sheriff Dollard is threatening to close the case and let it go unsolved," she cried.

Zach's anger lessened over the anguish in her voice. And he silently wished he could confide in her. But at the moment that was out of the question. She would insist on helping, which was the last thing he needed to further muddle an already complicated case riddled with more suspects than he cared to consider.

"Right now," he advised, "what you need to concern yourself with is keeping your job."

"My job?" she spat. "You mean keeping you in freshly laundered neckerchiefs?"

Zach grinned at that and touched the fabric that hid the evidence of her ardor. "Only until the scar from your kisses fades. Although I have to admit, under similar circumstances, I wouldn't mind making them a permanent part of my attire."

"If that is the case, I would not start growing fond of them if I were you," she snipped.

"Afraid it's too late, I already have."

Eugenia turned her head away and refused to look at Zach, let alone give him the satisfaction of further response. Hot tears of angry frustration pooled in her eyes, but she was not going to let him see the humiliation of her momentary defeat.

Nor was she going to allow him to dictate that she cease trying to seek justice!

Twenty-six

For a week after their return from Astoria, Eugenia was forced to endure guffaws over her aborted escapade, as the townsfolk referred to her disastrous expedition. Eugenia kept her chin held high in spite of them.

Yet while few truly seemed to believe that Kellogg's partner had indeed engineered the piracy attempt as a prank, not one was willing to reap Kellogg's wrath by openly voicing their opinions to the contrary.

Eugenia did not know what to think of Captain Derrick, for the man had taken to Zach as if he were his long-lost son. The captain had even gone so far as to suggest that Zach take the helm of a plunger and represent the whack during the Fourth of July regatta. The only good to come out of the entire incident was that Zach had not tried to claim title to the schooner when he learned that she owned it.

Captain Derrick had even arranged for Zach to

become a member of the Shoalwater Bay Yacht Club, which had been organized by the oystermen.

Life settled into a routine, but Eugenia secretly refused to give up. She could not control her body's response to Zach, but she could control her efforts to seek justice. She made a list of everyone with something to gain from her father's death, and whenever she was in town, she set about doing her own checking.

"Eugenia, I want to speak with you," Gertrude said, poking her head out of her shop as Eugenia walked by.

Eugenia stopped but did not approach the woman clad in ruffled rose. Regardless that the woman had produced proof that she had helped Eugenia's father, there was something about Gertrude Englestrom that Eugenia just could not like no matter how she tried.

"Won't you come into the shop?" Gertrude's pleasant voice turned cold after several shoppers left her establishment and she stood alone with Eugenia. "We have business."

"If it is about the account you opened for me, I do not have the money to repay you."

"From the look of you, you do not have the good taste to wear the lovely dresses either." Her eyes took in the young woman's worn beige skirt with disdain.

Eugenia ignored Gertrude's rudeness and started to turn away.

"If you know what's good for you, you will come in and listen," snapped Gertrude.

Trepidation filling Eugenia's breast, she hesitantly followed Gertrude into her shop.

"Sit down."

Eugenia settled onto the edge of the chair near the door and remained tight-lipped. "Say whatever it is you have to say that is so important that you would insist I listen to you."

"It's about the money I lent your father. I want it back."

Straight-backed, Eugenia said, "As I just told you, I do not have the money to repay the loan, and you know it."

"I heard that you still own the schooner. Sell it. I am sure Gale will give you a fair price."

Stunned at the woman's audacity and that she was in possession of such knowledge, Eugenia's mind reeled as she rose to her feet. She had been right about the woman's greed all along. Eugenia hesitated only a moment to regain her composure before she headed for the door, tossing back over her shoulder, "No."

It was the strangest thing. For the remainder of the day while Eugenia ran errands, she was approached by Len Sweeney, Peter Holm, Morton Washer and even Rube Nelson about selling the schooner. She was exhausted from refusing by the time she walked past the Widow Garrett's handcrafted picket fence.

"Eugenia, child." Ruth waved from her porch and came forward, wiping her hands on a dishtowel. "I'm so glad to see you. I have been giving your tragic dilemma a lot of consideration, and I believe I have come up with a reasonable solution."

She clasped her gnarled hands. "You have been like my own daughter, and I do so want to help you, dear."

"Thank you, Mrs. Garrett, but I shall manage."

"Nonsense. I have set aside a little money, and—"

"I would not think of taking your money," Eugenia protested, aghast at the very thought that she would even consider taking advantage of the widow's charitable offer.

"Then why not sell me your schooner, if it would make you feel better?"

Shocked, Eugenia blurted out, "What would you do with a ship?"

Ruth took a hopeful breath. "With a ship to provide my son-in-law work, maybe my daughter's family could move back from Astoria. I do so miss having them close to me. And the money would be a help to you as well."

Eugenia's heart went out to the widow, for she knew that the widow's daughter's husband was a no-account who had not been able to keep a job. "I am sorry that Daddy was forced to fire your son-in-law, and he then moved his family away. I wish I could help you, but I cannot sell the schooner."

By the time Eugenia reached the house, she was feeling troubled. She had left a trail of disappointed people when she had turned down offer after offer. There was too much interest in her schooner.

Zach was sitting in her father's favorite chair, his feet resting on the hassock, when she passed by the parlor. He looked so natural, so comfortable. He fit here, and it gave her a twinge.

"Eugenia," he called out, causing her to enter the parlor. "Finish your errands?"

"For the time being."

"You'll be happy to know that since you put my sailing lessons in Captain Derrick's capable hands, the man says I've mastered the skill and will be ready to participate in the upcoming regatta."

He kept his face impassive, although in the back of his mind he was thinking that it had taken more determination to master his roiling stomach's reaction to the rolling motion of the ship than to master sailing.

"You have taken to it like a gull to the mast of a ship, I am sure." A strange feeling at the domestic picture he presented disturbed her. "But you may have been exerting yourself for nothing, though."

His brow shoved up. "Oh?"

"Fact is I am thinking of selling my last tie to the oyster business. Practically everyone in town but Sheriff Dollard has expressed an interest in buying the schooner. And since it is my only asset, I may be forced to consider selling it."

Zach got up and went to her. He dropped a hand on her shoulder. "Eugenia, you don't have to sell it. We'll work something out."

It was a curious remark, that for an instant settled in the core of her heart, along with the warmth from his touch. *We'll work something out,* as if they were a couple. As if her troubles were his. But, of course, they weren't. He owned her family home and business. She had been reduced to working for him as a domestic, until, now that the ship had returned, it could turn a profit. The only thing they truly shared were their bodies. Lust. Carnality.

"How? By offering to buy the schooner as well? You are the only one connected with my father who has not tried to buy it. That entire pious contingent who came to protest our living arrangement tried to buy the ship. Even Mrs. Garrett, who has little left of her treasures, made an offer."

Zach threw up his hands, but Eugenia thought for an instant that she noticed the slightest glint of interest in his eyes. "Eugenia, how many times do I have to tell you I have no connection with your father."

Eugenia and Zach stood staring at each other. Eugenia wanted to believe him. Wanted to believe that they could work something out. Zach wanted to protect her and take care of her. He wanted to lose himself in her arms.

Cliff bounded into the house, effectively breaking the moment. Without glancing up, he said, "Been doin' some nosin' around and heard that there's a meetin' at Washer's casket shop tonight that ought to be mighty interestin' . . ." His voice trailed off when he walked into the parlor and noticed Eugenia. "Oh, hello, Eugenia. I didn't realize you were here."

"A meeting?" she questioned, her interest captured.

Cliff's glance shot from Eugenia to Kellogg and back to Eugenia. He grabbed a half-smoked cigarette from his shirt pocket and lit it. Taking a long drag, he blew a smoke ring into the air, and said, "It's nothin' that would concern you, little lady."

"You mean as a lowly housekeeper I should keep my attention directed toward mops and buckets?"

"As long as you don't use the mop to swab the deck of a ship after you have filled your bucket with oysters," Zach muttered.

"You know very well what I was referring to," she retorted. "Furthermore—"

"Eugenia," Zach interceded, "no doubt the meeting Granger's talking about has to do with oystering."

"Oh yes, and since I have been banned from the oyster beds, there is no reason for me to be privy to any of the future plans the oystermen have. Is that correct, *gentlemen?*"

"Eugenia, we've been over 'n' over this."

"If you two'll excuse me, I got a willin' woman waitin' for me as soon I get shaved," Cliff announced and made a quick exit. Whenever the fairer sex was involved in a case, it only complicated matters. And that pair lent complications all their own to it.

Eugenia waited until Cliff had left. "I want to attend that meeting, Zach. And I want to know what Cliff meant that he has been nosing around. I have felt it from the start; you two are up to something, aren't you?"

"For heavens sake, Eugenia. I don't know what you're getting at. Businessmen often try to find out what the competitors are doing in order to keep ahead of them. Working with your pa, you ought to be aware of that."

"I do not believe you."

"Believe what you will."

"I intend to."

"Just don't go getting any harebrained ideas about sneaking out to that meeting tonight," he warned. "Because I'll be there to see to it that your beautiful butt is removed before you can create any havoc."

Zach could see the inner workings of her mind spinning. And he did not like what he saw.

"Promise me you won't try to sneak into that meeting tonight, Eugenia. Promise me."

His eyes were boring into her, silently demanding that she not attempt to interfere.

Eugenia forced a half-smile. "I promise that I will not sneak out to that meeting tonight. There. Does that satisfy you?"

There were those same dancing devils he had seen before when she was not telling the whole truth that warned him that she had every intention of meddling. The thought of making love to her until she was too exhausted to interfere crossed his mind as an attractive alternative. But he had to get into town and get himself into that meeting tonight.

Cliff joined Kellogg in the alley near the casket shop as twilight was descending over the town. Lights from ships out on the bay glimmered on the darkening waters, winking back at clusters of stars beginning to make an appearance in the velvet sky.

"Anythin' to report?" Cliff questioned and crushed the butt of his smoke out with his boot heel.

311

"I've been watching the shop for over an hour."

Cliff grinned. "Any sign of that little lady of yours?"

Zach ignored his partner's referral to Eugenia as his little lady, although the thought of it was more persistently plaguing his mind as of late. "Eugenia promised to stay away tonight."

"I just bet she did. If I hadn't checked out the area on my way here, I'd be given to think that she was lurkin' about somewhere nearby, the way she keeps gettin' in the middle of thin's. Got to admire her dogged determination though."

"Yeah, got to," Zach grudgingly agreed. "What makes you think that this meeting tonight could have something to do with the case?"

Cliff gave a wily grin. "You know I've been keepin' real close 'n' personal company with a certain Miss Gertrude Englestrom."

"So?"

"So, she's a pretty good poke." Cliff grinned. "But I don't usually make it a habit to mix business an' pure downright pleasure unless it's got a use. And you know, friend, there ain't nothin' like a willin' woman's loose tongue while she's got a buckin' stud buried deep inside 'er. That one's so horny that she'd beg to tell me 'er rightful age if I asked while I'm layin' my tongue to her."

Zach overlooked Granger's bragging about his male prowess. "And?"

"And she let slip that each of those fine citizens who're meetin' tonight tried to buy out Whalen's business, and were none too happy when he refused. Were even less happy when their man was 'fraid to bid against you at the auction. Interestin'?"

"Especially when Whalen's beds were supposed to be in such trouble. Could just be a coincidence. You sure this isn't a wild goose chase?"

"We ain't turned nothin' else up. I'd say it can't hurt to check it out."

"Those folks did seem a mite overly interested in me as the oyster beds' new owner. And it was that same group who came to the house to nose into Eugenia's relationship with the owner. Eugenia told me that today they tried to buy her schooner."

"You think it's a conspiracy with all of 'em, like we talked about before I came to town?"

"I'd say that it seems near all the puzzle pieces must be on the table now," Zach reflected. "We just have to put them together."

"And come up with enough hard evidence to make the case stick."

Zach's watchful gaze shot past his partner toward the casket shop. Two of the men were nearing the front door. "Looks like the party's getting ready to begin. They're starting to gather now."

"Let's go around back." A self-satisfied grin came to Cliff's face. "I paid a little visit to the shop earlier to do some reconnoiterin' and just happened to leave the back door open a crack."

Zach and Cliff snuck into the rear of the shop and took up positions behind a stack of unfinished caskets to eavesdrop, once all the participants were assembled.

A nervous Morton Washer was seated next to

Rube Nelson, who kept his hands clamped tight in his lap; to Nelson's right, Gertrude Englestrom sat a trifle close to Gale Sweeney, leaning into him.

Cliff's face appeared puzzled when his gaze took in Gertrude's behavior with the younger Sweeney.

"Looks like Gertrude didn't get around to telling you that she was going to be here tonight."

"Prob'ly 'cuz she was too busy screamin' in ecstasy," Cliff returned and rubbed his jaw.

Zach frowned at Granger and shook his head at his partner's boasting before directing his attention back to the attendees.

Len Sweeney was standing near the door and kept glancing out into the street as if he were expecting another participant. Moments later he checked his watch, shut the door, pulled down the shade, and cleared his throat.

"The wife's waiting supper, so we had better get right down to business," Len Sweeney advised, a disapproving frown lifting his brow when his gaze shifted to his son and that Englestrom woman.

"Eugenia's pious contingent," Zach mused. He intently watched their body movements for anything out of the ordinary as they spoke about their attempts to secure Eugenia's schooner to increase their profit margin.

Out of the corner of his eye, Zach's attention suddenly caught on an expensive redwood casket sitting directly behind the participants. The flower-covered top of the casket was slowly creaking open.

An instant later Cliff elbowed Kellogg and said in a whisper "Bobbin' bodies, unless one of

Washer's clients decided to come back from the beyond, I'd say we ain't the only ones spyin' on this here meetin' tonight."

Zach watched as four long, slender fingers curved over the edge of the casket. From the mute lighting he could just make out the hint of curious green eyes peering out.

Hell, he should have known.

Eugenia!

Twenty-seven

Lying cramped in the casket for hours, Eugenia had to fight to suppress the near-overwhelming urge to leap out of the satin-lined box. A myriad of troubling emotions circled her, and she screamed inside.

Remembered visions of her mother in such a box revisited her, and she imagined her father in a similar coffin. Her heart hammered in her breast, and sweat trickled down her face. But she refused to give in to the frantic force building within her.

Swallowing her fears, she inched the lid open a little further to get a better view. The mingling fragrance of dahlias, marigolds and chrysanthemums that Mr. Washer had set atop the casket just before she heard Mr. Sweeney's voice moments ago assaulted her nostrils.

As an argument continued to ensue among the participants over purchasing Eugenia's schooner, and missing out on the auction of Whalen's oyster beds due to Nelson's lack of action, Zach watched the casket lid begin to quiver.

The impetuous little fool was about to give away her position!

Several of the flowers slipped over the edge of the lid, hanging near where Eugenia peeked out. She could feel the tickling sensation begin to build behind her eyes and tickle down the inside of her nose. She slapped a finger under her nostrils to suppress the urge to sniffle.

Too late.

She sneezed.

"Ah-choo!" Zach honked into a handkerchief and started to rise up from his hidden position in order to protect her. In swift reaction, Granger grabbed Zach's arm and popped up instead, slamming the coffin lid down as he jauntily sauntered forward, toward the heads swiveled in his direction. Angry, confused faces stared at him. He stopped and nonchalantly leaned an elbow on the casket lid.

"What the hell are you doing here?" Gale demanded.

Cliff gave them an easy grin. But behind those full grinning lips, he had to press his full weight against the lid of the casket to keep Eugenia from exposing her position; the little hellion was pushing from within.

"Heard tell there was a business meetin' here tonight, and since I was out takin' in the air this evenin' and noticed the back door open, I decided why not join you fine folks. After all, I'm one of the newest businessmen come to reap the hearty profits from the oyster business, and we all got the same interests."

"Who told you about us?" the elder Sweeney demanded.

Cliff's calculating gaze swung to Gertrude. He gave her a sly wink. "A nameless little song bird."

Gertrude shifted uneasily in her seat, but remained silent, her pouting lips pinched together. One of the men muttered "a bird of passage" as they looked at each other, assuming guilt.

Len Sweeney, his barrel chest puffed out, stepped forward to take control of the situation before it got completely out of hand, and they ended up fighting among themselves. "We thank you for your interest, Mr. Granger, but this is a private gathering of the shareholders in a business venture rivaling your own. Therefore, I am certain you no doubt will understand that we cannot invite you to join us."

Cliff ignored the man's pompous blustering, lit a smoke and sent two smoke rings drifting toward the ceiling. "Since I've already interrupted this private shindig, why don't I buy you all a round at the Pacific House?" He shrugged. "Just to show there ain't no hard feelin's and to prove we can keep the competition friendly."

The participants looked to each other. It was apparent from their expressions that there would be no productive discussion after such an untimely interruption.

"Why not?" Len spoke for the others. "Perhaps we can discuss the benefits of you selling to a heretofore established and successful private group of investors."

"Perhaps," Cliff said offhandedly and offered his arm to Gertrude Englestrom.

"Not to toot our own horns, Mr. Granger, but we already quietly command a growing percentage of the oyster business on the peninsula," Len Sweeney bragged.

Silently, Cliff noted the subtle admission that they secretly seemed to be attempting to expand control of the oyster industry into a monopoly as he directed Gertrude toward the door.

Zach also noted the conversation with keen interest, wondering why Whalen's whack had even gone to auction, especially since Sweeney and Nelson had been Whalen's partners.

Zach waited until Granger boldly led them from the casket shop with his usual panache. Once alone in the room with Eugenia, Zach leapt up and flipped open the casket lid. His lips tight, he yanked Eugenia out of her cramped hiding place.

She came out sneezing and stumbled. Zach caught her up in his arms. She leaned over and rubbed her cramping calf muscles. "A few more minutes in there, and I may never have been able to stand again."

"You wouldn't've lasted a few more minutes in there. If Granger and I hadn't covered your pretty little ass, it probably would've been Sweeney who would've pulled you out of there. Although I have to admit, it might've been interesting to hear your explanation."

Why the hell did she have to feel so good in his arms? And why did the glimpse of leg make his insides ache?

319

She mutinously looked up at him. "I could have talked my way out of it. Besides, there would not have been a need, at any rate. I was doing just fine without your help."

"Yeah, and oysters have legs. What the hell did you hope to prove by breaking your promise with that dumb stunt?" he demanded, holding her at arms length.

Despite his anger, Eugenia could denote the concern in his voice and the worry mirrored in his usually unreadable blue eyes. "I did not break my promise. I promised not to sneak out of the house *tonight*. I have been here for hours."

Zach rolled his eyes. She was forcing him to weigh each word he said to her.

"Furthermore, it was not a dumb stunt," she continued. "And now I know that they are all in it together."

He sighed in frustration. "In what, Eugenia?"

"You heard Len Sweeney, my father's so-called partner and friend," she said with dripping sarcasm. "Don't you see? He was my father's partner, and my father was in dire financial trouble. Yet Sweeney seems to head up a secret group of investors who are trying to further their own interests by increasing their holdings in the oyster industry . . ."

Zach forced himself to listen patiently to Eugenia's argument. Despite her crazy stunt, what she said made sense. "Eugenia, even if what you're saying is valid, then why didn't they attempt to keep your pa's beds by buying his share?"

Her brows furrowed. "I do not have the answer to that yet. But I shall."

"You should know better than trying to take the law into your own hands, let alone sneaking in here. You could get yourself killed," he lectured, although, by the defiant set of her lips, he should know better than to waste his breath; nothing he said was going to stop her. "Get smart and let the law handle this."

"Sheriff Dollard? The only thing he is any good for is collecting his paycheck." Jerking out of Zach's arms, she glared at him. "Why, he has never even bothered to make the slightest effort to find out who broke into my family home."

"Justice will be served. Take my word for it, Eugenia. Trust me." It was becoming very important to Zach that she put her faith in him.

Eugenia's brows drew together. There it was again. Zach had just made another all-too-familiar reference to the law.

"I did not see you in attendance earlier," she remarked, continuing to mull over his assertion concerning justice.

"How could you see much of anything from inside a casket?"

She ignored his evasive commentary. "Well?"

"I was here."

"Hiding?"

When Zach did not answer, a troubled expression wrinkled her forehead. She searched his face. It gave nothing away. All his previous comments about arrests, jail and justice suddenly seemed to make perfect sense.

321

He very well could have had brushes with the law, and now he might be engaged in some type of scheme!

She stepped back, away from him so his nearness would not perplex the conclusion she'd just reached. She had to keep her thinking clear. "My God, you are not just a businessman, are you?"

"Of course I am. My partner and I bought your pa's business, didn't we?" he bluffed. But he did not like the suspicious expression on her face. She was no longer buying it.

Eugenia crossed her arms over her chest. "Two men who do not know a thing about oysters, and who are more interested in questioning townspeople? Oh yes, I have heard all about the questions you have been asking. But until now, I foolishly dismissed it. It has been right there, before my eyes all along, and I overlooked it. Why, you even questioned Mrs. Garrett."

"Eugenia." Zach reached out and curled his fingers around her arm, but she flung it back.

"No!" she cried. "I am not going to allow you to fill my head with any further lies."

" 'Lies' is a pretty strong word," he said in a soft, calming voice.

"What would you call it, Zach? You are not who you have been professing to be. I am beginning to see it. I feel it inside. I know it in my heart. What are you up to? What are both of you doing here in Oysterville? I want the truth. And I want it now!"

I know it in my heart. For an instant he longed to learn what else she knew in her heart; what else she felt; what else she saw. Her eyes snapped fire, causing Zach's groin to tighten. She was filled with such spirit, such unbridled passion that he sorely burned to whisk her into his arms and carry her away to find out exactly what was in her heart. But years of tightly reined self-control kept him rooted where he stood.

When he did not answer, disappointment squeezed her heart. She swung on her heel and tossed back over her shoulder, "If you refuse to tell me, I am sure that if I prod Sheriff Dollard hard enough, he will be able to do some checking that will."

Lightning fast, Zach caught up with her at the door, slamming it shut as she pulled it open.

"The only place you're going is back to the house with me."

"What are you going to do? Keep me a prisoner? You cannot stop me forever from talking to Sheriff Dollard," she spat stubbornly.

"Christ! You're more troublesome than a bungling pirate of the feminine persuasion," he gritted out with the faintest grin.

Eugenia bit her lower lip to keep from commenting at the comparison and did not try to fight Zach when he clamped a steely hand around her arm and escorted her, none too politely, out the rear door and back to the house.

Zach stomped into the parlor, dragging Eugenia behind him. "Sit down."

She remained standing stiffly, her chin in a defiant tilt. "I would prefer to stand, thank you."

"And I'll thank you to sit," he snarled. "Or so help me, Eugenia . . ."

The serious glitter in his eyes warned her that he meant business. She plunked down on the sofa, but maintained a obstinate slash to her mouth.

Zach paced back and forth in front of her, rubbing the back of his neck. She was a hair's breath away from guessing the truth. She would keep at it until she knew. She was not going to make it easy for him, she was so tenacious. Then, again, she had never helped to make this case easy. She had constantly complicated the investigation. But hell, despite her interference, he had to admit to himself that he wouldn't want to change her even if he could, knowing full well that would be a hopeless effort.

When he finally stopped to face her, a dire expression shadowed his face, and his brow was lifted. Eugenia inwardly questioned the sagacity of her impetuous demands, fearing what she would hear.

"All right, Eugenia," he sighed, "you want to know the truth?"

"Yes," she said quietly. But her heart was riveted with apprehension and anxiety over what she was about to attend. She moved to the edge of the sofa.

"Before your pa was murdered, he wrote to Vancouver requesting help—"

A light suddenly brightened, glowing in her mind. She suddenly recalled many of his phrases which had plagued her: *Justice will be served. Evidence. Obstruction of justice. Moral judge and jury. Run the lot of you in.*

"You're a lawman?"

"What did you think I was?" he asked at the pure relief in her voice, relaxing his features.

"I thought you might be involved in some scheme," she said without hesitation. "But a sheriff?"

"A territorial marshal sent in response to your pa's plea for help. But I arrived too late. He had already been murdered."

"And Cliff Granger?"

"My partner."

Trying to assimilate the implications of Zach's astounding confession, Eugenia softly questioned, "Why didn't you tell me?"

There was no use trying to hold anything back from her any longer. Zach folded his big frame next to her. He took her hand, but she pulled it back and laid it in her lap, stiffly silent. Zach's brow shoved up again. He had expected appreciation, not her withdrawal.

"I couldn't take the chance of anyone finding out and unknowingly alerting the murderer."

A sinking thought entered her head when visions of the time they'd spent together rose up in her mind's eye. "W-was I part of your cover, too?"

"Eugenia, your arrival wasn't exactly anticipated."

That was not what she had hoped to hear. "But you made the best of it. Used it to your advantage."

A little smile curled the corner of his lips when he recalled her antics. "I'd say your presence has probably helped keep the murderer off balance."

Inside Eugenia screamed, *You were the one who was supposed to be kept off balance when all along you were using me to keep the murderer off balance. Using me.* Suddenly she wanted to flee from the room and throw the bolt on her door, locking him out of her life.

Before she could stop herself, she asked, "Do you often use available females to solve your cases?"

"No."

"What about the oyster beds?" she questioned, changing the subject. She was awash in a mix of raw, clawing emotions, but now was not the time to explore what was weighing so heavily on her heart.

Later. After she had sorted all this out in her mind. Later. When what she wanted was clear. Later. When the confusion and hurt were not so new. Until then she'd tuck those feelings safely inside . . . for later.

"What better cover?" he said and decided it was time to let her in on the rest of the events surrounding the case.

Her heart pounded as she listened to the details of his investigation. He had questioned more than half the townsfolk, followed every lead to a dead end. And when nothing turned up, he decided to start shipping oysters in an effort to force the guilty party's hand. Yet his explanation did not include her part in it, only serving to add to her confusion.

"But I interceded," she said, concerned that she was responsible for botching his plan as well as needing to clarify her role.

"You've a tendency to get a little over exuberant at times. It's an endearing quality, though. But now that you know Granger and I are investigating the case, I expect you to back off and stay out of the way so we can finish the job we set out to do without further *assistance*."

Was he done with her? Had she and her body served his purpose? Could she have been no more than a diversion?

"You consider me someone who has been underfoot?" she blurted out.

"No. You've helped out in the house with the cooking and cleaning. And you led me to Holm, as well as saving me time with gathering other bits of information." They were discussing the case now; anything else between them was personal. That discussion would wait until he sorted out all his own feelings.

Disappointment in her breast, she asked, "The oyster beds? What will happen to them now?" *When the case is solved, what will happen to us?*

"Since they were purchased with government money, they may have to be sold at auction to the highest bidder." At the devastated look on her face, Zach covered her hand with his. This time she did not pull away, but her hand was cold. "I'm sorry, Eugenia. I know how much they mean to you."

At first when he gazed into her eyes, he thought he glimpsed a new sadness, troubling questions she had not asked. Quickly those familiar devils turning the wheels in her mind took over, which almost made him want to groan out loud.

"What if I could come up with the money to pay the government back?" A portion of her face was suddenly glowing with excitement, although Zach still detected that she was holding something back.

"Then the beds would not have to go on the auction block, would they?"

"I might be able to convince the powers that be to forego an auction." Always the pragmatist, he added, "But, Eugenia, you don't have the money, and you weren't able to locate a financial backer when you thought to buy them from me."

Secretly, Zach wished he had the money to give her. But he had quit trying to save for the future a long time ago after his wife had run off. Had quit even thinking in terms of a future. He had learned the hard way to live minute by minute, a day at a time. Now, for the first time in years, Zach had begun to think in terms of the future.

She frowned. "That is because those *investors*, who probably are responsible for my father's death, want the beds for themselves."

"Sorry to splash cold water on your hot theory, little lady," Cliff hiccupped from the doorway. He was unsteady on his feet, and his eyes were bloodshot. He staggered into the parlor and sank onto the chair by the window.

"Surprisin' how a little whiskey can set even the tightest tongue to waggin'." He chuckled over some private thought and wagged his tongue in a lewd fashion.

"Put your tongue back in your mouth, and let us in on what you found out," Zach instructed, unamused by his partner's attempts at levity.

Cliff's bleary eyes settled on Eugenia. "What about the little lady?"

"It's okay, Granger, Eugenia knows everything. You can talk in front of her."

His head seemed to waver on the edge of his neck. "Everything?" he slurred out.

Eugenia stiffened, but managed to maintain her silence despite the desire to grill him.

"Everything. Now, out with it. What did you learn?"

Twenty-eight

Cliff studied his reflection in the window, pulling his bottom eyelids down. "Ugly, drunken son of a bitch," he mumbled.

He turned back to his partner seated next to the little lady. The thought that flashed through his hazy mind was that it was a crying-ass pity he wasn't the one sitting next to her.

"Let me see, what're we talkin' 'bout?"

"You're about to tell us what transpired with that group of investors?" Eugenia urged.

"A bit a drinkin', darlin'." A lopsided grin tilted his lips. "Quite a bit, I'm afraid. And a mighty interestin' proposition from a certain . . . *lady.*"

"We're not interested in your personal life, Granger," Zach warned.

Undaunted, Cliff winked. "Likkored louts, leastways I got one."

For a moment, Eugenia feared that Zach was going to reveal their private relationship. But a quick glance in his direction showed a face that did not give away anything. Inwardly, she sighed in relief, and it gave her something else to consider. Zach had not shared their private moments with his partner, who was all too blatantly flaunting his.

"It's getting late, and I'm sure you want to get back to your *personal life,* so get on with it."

"Sure. Sure." Cliff sobered when his longtime partner did not rise to his efforts to rib him. He wondered if Kellogg realized what it meant. Kellogg had never cut him off quite so sharply in front of another before. "Those investors ain't involved in no murder conspiracy."

"How do you know?" Eugenia demanded.

" 'Cuz there's too much arguin' among themselves how to go 'bout doin' the simplest thin's. Too much blusterin', and accusin' each other of missin' opportunities. Too many wanna be in charge. Hell, that group couldn't decide on what'd be a fair price to offer me for the oyster beds. Spent most of the good drinkin' time debatin', leavin' me to drink with that captain and his crew off the schooner. No, it ain't no conspiracy among 'em. I'd bet my badge on it. If the guilty party was in that casket shop tonight, he acted alone."

"Or she," Eugenia put in sharply.

A slow grin grew on Cliff's face. "Little lady, the only way Gertie Englestrom woulda kilt your papa woulda been by wearin' him plumb out, devourin' him with that insatiable appetite she's got. If a body's got to go, I gotta say, there ain't no better way known to man."

Eugenia blushed, causing Zach to snap, "I think we get the picture." Then Zach got serious. "You sure about that group?"

"Sure as all my years of experience. Said I'd bet my badge, didn't I? And you know what it means to me. It's the only thin' either of us has cared about for years."

Cliff paused to cast a telling glance in Eugenia's direction before he turned back to Kellogg. Her face had stiffened. "They didn't act together. Now, I ain't sayin' that one of 'em couldn't a done it. But it weren't no conspiracy, like we was thinkin'. I'd stake my reputation, whatever that is, on it." He chuckled. "Now, if you'll excuse me, I do got personal business."

Just as Cliff stood up on wavering legs, a bullet shattered the glass, whizzing past his head.

Zach reacted lightning fast. He grabbed Eugenia, slamming her to the floor, and covering her with his body as he blew out the lamp.

The sound of gravel crunching beneath heels hurrying away from the house spiked through the broken windowpane, then nothing. Silence. Cliff crashed through the remaining shards of glass to chase after the assailant, but his reactions had been slowed by the alcohol. By the time he got to the end of the yard, the only sounds were of the night creatures. Not even a leaf rustled in either direction.

When he returned to the house and lit a lamp, Zach was still lying the length of Eugenia, shielding her head with his arms.

Embarrassed to be in such an intimate position with Zach in front of a smirking Cliff, Eugenia shoved at Zach's chest.

"Friend, you can let the little lady up now, if you

got a mind to, that is. There ain't nobody out there no more." He scratched his head. "Strange how the son of a bitch managed to disappear so quick without a trace. Guess we're lucky he's better at disappearin' than aimin'."

Zach inhaled the fresh smell of soap and reluctantly moved off Eugenia, helping her to her feet. "Are you all right?"

She nodded, unable to speak.

Zach went to examine where the bullet had slammed into the wall, careful to keep his back to them since the evidence of his arousal was all too apparent. Using his pocket knife, he dug out a small caliber bullet.

"Interesting," Zach said, holding the bullet between his fingers as he gauged the angle from which it had entered.

Cliff took the bullet. "See what you mean."

"What are you two standing there so calmly for? Someone tried to kill you, my God!" Eugenia cried when she finally found her voice.

Cliff glanced at Eugenia, then offered, "I'll go see to some planks to board up that there window. Then, since Kellogg's got everythin' so well in hand,"—he winked—"I'll be headin' out."

Disturbed by the evening's events, Eugenia nonetheless settled back onto the sofa and watched quietly while the two men hammered the planks in place.

Once Cliff had left, she stood. "I do not understand. Could Cliff have overheard something he does not recall at the moment to give one of those

333

investors a reason to try to kill him? Maybe you should call him back and question him further."

"You might as well know, from the angle of the bullet, it's not at all certain that Granger was the target."

"What are you trying to say?" she questioned, confused and further disturbed by his comment.

"That you very well could have been the mark."

She shook her head in disbelief. "Me! Why? Who?"

"When we solve your pa's murder, we'll undoubtedly have the answer to that."

"But you were seated next to me. You could have been the target," she said in a frantic effort to deny Zach's supposition.

"True," he said, but there was a doubtful glint in his eyes.

The events of the day were nearly overwhelming, and Eugenia needed time to think and sort through it all. She pressed her fingers to her aching temples.

"It has been a very long day. I think I need to get some rest." Almost as if she were in a daze, Eugenia lit a lamp and began to mount the stairs, her hand grasping the rail to steady her progress.

Zach's hand covered hers, and he steadied her. "Eugenia, do you still have that gun you bought?"

She swiveled around on the stair, coming face to face with Zach, who was standing on the step below her. "You mean the one I bought to kill you with?"

He smiled into her troubled green eyes. "I'm glad you haven't completely lost your sense of humor, because as we get closer to solving this case, I have the distinct feeling you're going to need it."

Eugenia gave him a weak smile, unsure exactly how to interpret such a remark. But even while she had been stunned by the evening's events and his revelations, she could feel the heat from his calloused palm on her hand. And he smelled of wood and leather.

"Zach, what if whoever fired that shot is still lurking outside somewhere, waiting? My bedroom window opens on to the street."

He squeezed her hand, silently wanting more. "Pull the shades. Then put the gun under your pillow. And I'll keep my ears open."

"Will you check out my bedroom first, just to make sure no one is hiding under the bed?" she requested. Suddenly surrounding her were childhood memories of how her father used to drop to his hands and knees and look under the bed to reassure her that there were no sea monsters before she would climb into bed each night.

The mention of her bed brought visions other than of someone concealed under it to Zach's mind. His thoughts ran more along the lines of the two of them entwined on top of it.

"Don't worry, Eugenia, I'm not going to let anyone or anything harm you."

"Daddy used to say that to me," she said, bringing her mind back to Zach.

As they ascended the stairs, Eugenia could not help but wonder if her heart were more in danger of being "harmed" by Zach then her person by some unknown assailant.

Her mind was churning with thoughts from their earlier conversation when Zach took the lamp, opened her door, and began checking her bedroom. She watched from the doorway as he pulled the shades and looked into the armoire.

"Do not forget to check under the bed."

She watched Zach get down on hands and knees and lift the quilted spread. A tremor shook her all the way to the foundation of her soul. Moments before she was fondly remembering how her father had done the very same thing in the very same fashion.

"No one lurking under here," he announced and pulled a pair of lace panties from underneath the bed with a grin.

Eugenia blushed at the contrast of tanned fingers against white lace satin. Rough against smooth. Hard against soft. She sat down on the bed and snatched them from his hand, stuffing them into her skirt pocket. Forcing the comparison from her mind, she said, "I wondered where those had gotten to. Thank you. I think I shall be fine now."

"The gun, Eugenia?"

"Huh? Oh, yes, the gun." She grabbed it out of the nightstand drawer and slipped it under her pillow.

"Good night. Sleep well," he said and reluctantly walked to the door.

"Zach?" Her voice halted him, and he swung around. "Will you stay with me tonight?" At his slow, sensual smile, she quickly amended, "I am not asking in a Biblical sense, I mean."

"Genie, I wouldn't mind if you were."

Eugenia's cheeks flamed. While she had to admit she had been a more than willing participant in their bedding, she would not come right out and ask him to bed her. She could not. Not after their earlier conversation had left her with so many questions.

"I mean in the line of duty as a lawman. Just as a precaution."

His smile faded, but there was a gleam in his eyes. "The line of duty. Sure. Just as a precaution."

He unbuckled his gun belt and hung it over the chair. Then he plunked down on the bed and removed his boots. Lying back against the pillow with his arms behind his head, he watched Eugenia slip from her shoes, extinguish the lamp, and gingerly lie next to him, stiff as one of the planks he had used to board up the parlor window.

Frustration wasn't the least of his feelings. His body was hard, hot, and ready for her soft one. He could hear her breathing, inhale her fragrance of orange blossoms. And here he was lying in bed next to the most desirable young woman he had ever known, fully dressed, staring up at the darkened ceiling.

Eugenia was also experiencing feelings of a similar nature. She ran a hand over her chest. Her breasts were peaked against the cotton fabric, and at the apex of her thighs, an uncontrollable throbbing was causing her heart to race. Unable to wait any longer to explore the raw emotions their earlier discussion had aroused, she turned her head toward him.

"Zach, are you asleep?"

He could feel her warm breath caress his cheek. "No."

"Zach, earlier I asked you if you used me as part of your cover. D-did you . . . did we . . . uh . . . do you often bed females as part of your cover?"

"I already answered that. No, I don't. I don't use women, Eugenia."

"Oh."

His every nerve ending sensitized. He reached over, took her hand and placed it on his cheek. "Do you feel my skin?"

It was heated beneath the beginning growth of stubble since morning. "Yes," she troubled. She could not understand what it had to do with her question.

"It's clean shaven."

He dropped her hand to his chest. "Can you feel my heart beating?"

"Yes."

"It's racing."

"Yes. But I do not understand."

"Eugenia, years ago I was married. My wife ran away because I couldn't give her the things she needed and wanted on a marshal's salary. He could. After that I grew a beard and buried myself in my work."

Eugenia took his hand and held it tightly pressed in hers as she listened. "You mean you used the beard and your badge as some sort of shield from the world?"

"Never thought of it that way before. The beard was my cover." Without letting go of her hand, he leaned up on his elbow, squinting into the darkness in an effort to see her face and gauge her reactions, but there was not enough light. "But then you literally crashed into my life."

She smiled up at his silhouette. "Down the banister."

"Eugenia, when you tricked that barber into shaving off my beard, you did more than have a few whiskers removed. When I looked in the mirror, I took a real good look at myself for the first time in years. It started me thinking.

"When you didn't run, and we started living together under the same roof, and you made supper and talked so lovingly about your home and family, it did something to my insides. Sparked something inside me that I thought had died long ago. And I knew I wanted you. You. Not to use you to help me catch your pa's murderer, Eugenia. I wanted you.

"I'm not perfect, Eugenia. I've bedded more than my share, I guess. Men have appetites, even ones who don't want a good woman. But you are a good woman. A little unconventional and headstrong. But not the kind of woman a man uses to sate his body, and then discards when he moves on.

"Look, I'm not real eloquent with words, never have been, but I hope I got my meaning across. I didn't just use you."

Eugenia's heart swelled and words failed her, she was so filled with pride and love. He had just answered her questions, opened his heart and bared his soul. Tears of joy spilled from her eyes.

Dread encircled Zach when she did not respond to his awkward declaration. He felt the first real stab of paralyzing fear he had experienced since he was a boy. He had just shared his soul. Taken a big risk and opened himself up. Afraid she may be repelled by such a confession and no longer want his touch, he nonetheless forced himself to reach out and tentatively run the back of his hand down her cheek.

It was wet.

Hell, he was a hardened lawman used to handling the toughest situation, the toughest outlaws. And here he had professed his feelings with merely the slightest prompting. Suddenly her tears made him feel helpless; it was a completely foreign sensation he did not know how to handle.

He sat up. "I'll sleep in the chair," he stated flatly, the emotion gone from his voice, replaced by a renewed hardness.

Eugenia caught his arm. "Please. I want you to stay with me."

God, how he wished he could see the expression on her face! But he could feel the tension in her firm grip. "Are you asking me to remain near you for protection or . . . ?"

The pressure of a moment ago was fading, replaced with a spirit of playfulness grounded in a new understanding.

A short while ago she was pondering that very same question. Would never have asked him to sleep with her. She smiled into the darkness, wishing Zach could see her warm glow.

"In the Biblical sense," she answered after a moment's hesitation.

Zach lit the lamp so he could read her face, then

bounded across the bed and embraced Eugenia with a smacking kiss. "Well then, woman, let's shed these clothes so we can lend our own interpretation to the Bible."

"I was thinking about the need you are going to have for a fresh supply of neckerchiefs."

"A recent special favorite of mine."

Eugenia giggled as they undressed. But in the back of her mind, she wondered if his scars were so deep that they would prevent him from ever saying the three most important words she now longed to hear.

Twenty-nine

Zach lifted Eugenia into his arms. Her naked body soft against his hard one. Her arms wound around his neck, and he felt the hairs on the back of his nape come alive. She nestled her mouth against his chest, licking and swirling the hairs around her tongue. Then her lips fastened against his throat.

"You're trying to drive me mad with desire, aren't you?" he groaned and lay her against the cool sheets.

"Absolutely." Her nails raked down his sides, and she pulled him down beside her.

A sensual grin curved his full lips. "You will be gentle with me, won't you?"

Emboldened by the passion mirrored in his eyes, she mounted him, all inhibitions gone. "I am not looking for a gentle ride on an old nag." She scraped her nails down his chest and pinched his flank. "Good solid flanks, I would say." She leaned over and nibbled at his neck. "Strong neck. Able to go the distance."

"Well then, my sweet Genie, what are you waiting for? Grab the pommel and hop into the saddle."

"Gentlemen always help a lady mount," she advised. She was jubilant, her senses still spinning toward the heavens over his honesty.

"And ladies ride side saddle."

She lifted her hips to move to the side of him, but he grabbed her by the waist. "You may be a lady, but, darlin', I'm no gentleman. In order not to get bucked off, you're going to have to ride astride."

He took her hand and closed it around his erection. He was hot and throbbed against her fingers. Guiding her, he brought himself to the opening of her female core, then removed his hand and gripped her waist, slowly impaling her. Her tight liquid warmth encased him, took his entire length and held him.

His fingers slid up her sides to cup her breasts. Gently, he squeezed the luscious mounds in rhythm with each slow stroke.

Her smile melded into his, joined as were their bodies. Their eyes locked in unspoken emotion as potent as the physically erotic sensations of pleasure possessing them. She gyrated her hips against him, controlling the tempo, reveling in the growing friction. Back and forth. Rocking. In and out.

Eugenia could not believe such sensitivity could come from him. She felt her life being altered irretrievably. Out of the tragedy that brought Zach Kellogg into her life, a new person was emerging. No longer were the oyster beds her entire life. New meaning was adding definition, forming a changed entity; a woman with a woman's hunger, a woman's needs, a woman's love.

"When I'm inside you, you make me forget there's an outside world," he breathed, his hips reaching up to imbed himself in her heat.

Her head rolled backward, and she was vaguely aware that her tongue was simulating her fervor. Her nails dug into his chest. She increased the pace.

"Look at me, Eugenia," he murmured. "See what you're doing to me."

Her eyes partially glazed, she leaned her hands on his shoulders. There was an expression of the sweetest pain, the agony of passion's torment across his face. It urged her every nerve ending forward into a tempestuous frenzy.

In. Out.

Rocking. Rocking.

Grinding.

Back. Forth.

"Slow down, Genie. I don't want this to end for us yet," he panted, lifting his hips and meeting her stroke for pounding stroke.

"I can't."

The pulsating force building inside her was greater than any control she possessed. Her hips ground against him in an exquisite, excruciating need to seek sweet release.

Zach knew she was on the edge of climax. Another time they would spend hours exploring and delighting in each other's bodies. Another time. Wanting at that moment to give her the world, he gripped her hips and penetrated her again in a crushing motion.

The words, *I love you,* stood on the edge of his tongue, and he grasped her tighter to him. He opened his mouth to release the long pent-up phrase. Before the utterance could leave him totally open and vulnerable for the first time in his life, Eugenia's hungry mouth devoured his.

He thrust forward, unchecking the male force within him until Eugenia threw her head back and cried out in unbridled ecstasy, straining against him as wave after delicious pulsating wave consumed her.

Mere seconds passed before Zach joined her behind ecstasy's door.

"Hello," she whispered, once the spasms had subsided. Her chest still heaved from their exertions, and she cradled his drenched face between her palms.

"Hello, yourself." He held her burning body to him and rolled with her until he was gazing down on the incredible young woman.

He had come so close to uttering those words of love. So close to proclaiming himself lost. As he smoothed a wet auburn curl from her face, he was amix with emotions, not sure yet relieved that the moment had passed without declaration. Their lives were too far apart, their missions in life too different, too incompatible.

For the first time realization hit him that when he looked into her green eyes he could see the ocean reflected there. His gaze shifted to the bronze of his arms that held her. They were colored by the hot summer sun of the inland valleys. Darkened toward the hue of newly tilled earth.

Land and sea. They came together, one washed by the other. Both engaged in an unrelenting battle, pitted against the other for eternity, not mellowed by time.

The moisture of her breath on his skin reminded him of the sea. And she tasted of the ocean's salt. While the dirt ground into the callouses of his work-hardened hands was reminiscent of the land.

Reminders. Even as he attempted to block them out, the reminders were there. Would always be there.

In an effort to drive their insurmountable differences from his mind, he pinioned her arms above her head. She grasped the brass of the headboard. "Do you have a hankering to ride a filly?" she teased, in an attempt to bring him out of the dark mood he seemed to have fallen into.

The intensity of his chain of thoughts broken by her unfettered responsiveness, he grinned down at her. "Like never before."

Zach could hardly believe he was hard again so soon. To escape from the merciless reality of their differences, he totally unleashed his driving thrusts, penetrating her with pounding force.

Eugenia met his hips with a crushing force of her own. She took all of him, wanting more, needing more. Her nails pressed into his back, and as her climax neared, she sank her teeth into the firm flesh of his shoulder, tasting the sweetness of his blood.

Zach experienced the savagery of her release in

spasm after spasm, her female muscles squeezing and straining, pressuring him until he burst forth in surge after surge with one of the most powerful orgasms ever to grip him.

"Zach, I am going to burn up," she whispered in breathless gasps.

"We'll burn together."

Moments passed before he reluctantly disengaged himself and slid to her side. He pulled the sheet up over them, cradling her nicely rounded body to him. She was curled next to him, so trusting that Zach squeezed his eyes shut at the painful knowledge that this would have to end when the case was solved.

Land and sea.

Eugenia's breathing soon grew shallow and even. She had fallen into an exhausted slumber. Zach was still staring at the ceiling, agonizing over his feelings when he heard the rear door creak open.

His senses instantly alert, he grabbed Eugenia's gun from beneath the pillow and slipped from the bed. Gun in hand, he quickly managed to jam his legs into his denims. Not wasting time to button them, he silently tiptoed from Eugenia's bedroom.

In the darkness, Zach crept down the stairs. A sliver of light glowed from beneath the door to the kitchen. The dark silhouette of a man's boots mixed shadows with the light. Zach moved to the edge of the door, his finger on the trigger of the silver-plated gun.

The shadow shifted to the other side of the door, and Zach reacted.

He burst through the door, knocking the man

on the other side from his feet in a shower of arms and legs.

"Jesus Christ, Granger, what the hell're you doing back here tonight," Zach said, the gun pointed at his partner's heart. "I could've killed you."

Cliff lay sprawled on the floor, the fixings for a late night sandwich spilled around him. "I'd say you still could if you were holdin' your own gun on me. When did you start totin' a toy pistol?"

Awakened by the ruckus downstairs, Eugenia frantically wrapped the sheet around herself. She searched beneath the pillow. No gun. Recalling Zach's gun hanging from the chair, she grabbed it. Fear that the would-be killer had returned to finish the job and that Zach was in trouble, she rushed down the stairs without regard for her own safety.

"Put your hands up, or I'll shoot!" she shouted from the other side of the door.

Her hands trembled when the door slowly creaked open. She was shaking so badly that when the silhouette of a man suddenly appeared framed in the door, she instinctively pulled the trigger.

Zach made a leap for the six-shooter as a blast issued from the barrel.

The shot went wild, shattering a jar of preserves. She shook over the near disaster. "I could have killed you."

"It's all right. No one got hurt." Zach slipped an arm around her trembling shoulders and disarmed her.

His easy humor returning at the little scene before him, Cliff climbed to his feet and wiped at the tomato preserves staining his shirt. At Eugenia's horrified expression, Cliff announced, "Just a good midnight snack gone to waste. It ain't blood, little lady."

"What're you doing back here tonight?" Zach demanded. "Thought you had a date with a certain waiting lady."

Cliff scratched his head. "So did I. Hell, she was all hot for me, beggin' she'd be naked and waitin' in bed. But when I got back there, she was gone. No note. Nothin'. It was the strangest thin'."

"Maybe you're losing your appeal."

"Not to brag, but that ain't likely to happen 'til after I done took my last livin' breath."

"Then where do you think she ran off to?" Eugenia asked.

"Good question. Wherever she went, she was in a mighty big hurry 'cuz her perfumed bed was left all turned back and welcomin'."

Zach's brow rose. "Rather late for her to be out, don't you think?"

Cliff nodded. "I think." A wry grin curved his lips when he noticed the fresh teeth marks in Kellogg's shoulder and another purple brand on his neck. "I also think it interestin' that the little lady standin' quietly at your side was totin' your own gun, partner." He smirked. "And Miss Eugenia, nice nightie you got on."

Eugenia, suddenly made aware of the sheet barely covering her breasts, let out a mortified squeal and fled back upstairs, slamming the door behind her. An instant later curiosity overtook her. She had to find out if male camaraderie superseded what she and Zach had just shared. She opened the door, tiptoeing to the top of the banister to eavesdrop.

Cliff chuckled and untied the neckerchief he was wearing. "Looks like you're gonna need this again. And you'd best put somethin' on that love-bite you got on your shoulder, you sly dog, you," he said to Kellogg. "If I'd've known, I would've left you to savor that delicious little piece's charms without the likes of me interferin'."

Cliff did not expect the fury of the fist that smashed into his mouth, knocking him off his feet for the second time tonight.

"What the hell you do that for?" Cliff grumbled, holding his aching, bleeding mouth. "Losin' loons, I think you loosed two of my teeth this time."

"You still haven't learned, have you?" The glint in Zach's icy blue eyes was deadly; his muscles tensed and ready to kill as he stood over Granger, glaring down at the man. "I'll do more than that if you ever even so much as whisper that way about Eugenia again, hear?"

Cliff climbed back to his feet, suddenly recalling the last reference and its consequences. He took out a handkerchief and dabbed at his mouth. "I more'n heared. You got the message across mighty clear this time. Sorry, friend. I won't forget myself again. Didn't mean nothin' by it though. Truly. I didn't realize you was so smitten with the little lady." He thrust out his hand. "No hard feelin's?"

Zach stared down at the outstretched hand, but made no move to clasp it. Zach's mouth set in cold granite, he snarled, "Whatever's between Eugenia

350

and me is just that . . . between her and me. Nobody else. It's real personal, and if you want to keep the rest of your teeth, you'll mind your mouth about Eugenia from now on."

Eugenia lingered at the top of the stairs a few more moments, listening, before she returned to her bedroom and quietly shut the door. She climbed into bed and hugged the pillow to her. Closing her eyes, she buried her face in the downy softness.

Zach's manly scent still clung to the pillowcase. A mixture of hope and joy that Zach had defended her against the ribald remarks of his longtime friend and partner mingled inside her breast with disappointment that once again he had not declared himself.

Thirty

Eugenia had fallen asleep still hugging the pillow to her breast when a persistent rap at the front door jarred her from her slumber. Streams of light flowed in around the edges of the shade at the window.

"It is morning already. I must have been dreaming." She rubbed her eyes and stretched, thinking how in her dream Zach had spoken the words of love. She smoothed her hand over the rumpled place in the bed where she and Zach had made love last night.

She smiled, remembering his passion until the pounding resumed and the thudding of boots heading down the stairs shook her out of her lethargy.

By the time Eugenia had tossed on a simple patterned calico dress, tied her unruly hair back and hurried into the parlor, Zach and Cliff were seated across from Captain Derrick.

"Good morning." She beamed, settling a bright, impish smile on Zach's neckerchief. The seriousness of his expression caused her smile to fade. "Is something wrong?"

"Sit down, Eugenia," Zach directed. "I'm afraid Captain Derrick's visit affects you, too."

Her brows drew together into a troubled frown, but she took a seat next to the captain on the sofa. "Lass, it be so sorry I am. I should've known better. Can ye ever forgive an old fool?"

"For what?" she asked, confusion and dread circling her like gulls following a fishing boat.

"Eugenia," Zach took over. "Last night while the captain and crew were ashore, someone snuck aboard the schooner and ransacked it."

Captain Derrick hung his white head. "I be so sorry, lass. I should've left someone aboard on watch, but the bay was so calm, not a ripple, that I thought a little grog would suit . . . oh, may I be sent to Neptune's watery hell, I didn't think."

She patted the old sea dog's hand. "You could not have known."

Eugenia listened quietly while Zach and Cliff brought the captain up to date, letting him in on who they were and their mission. The three men discussed the latest incident in relation to the events which had occurred since Whalen's death. Cliff remarked how he had been at the Pacific House with the investors at the same time the captain and crew were there, so anyone of them would have known the ship had been left unguarded.

"Do you think that whoever broke into the house could be the same person who ransacked the schooner?" Eugenia troubled.

"It's a good possibility," Zach answered, angry

353

at himself for not considering that Whalen might have hidden the evidence he had written about on board his schooner. "I think we better go check it out," Zach suggested, his stomach already protesting the thought of boarding another ship.

"I am going, too," Eugenia announced, rising in concert with the men.

"Ye sure ye want to see what some bastard done to the schooner, lass?" Captain Derrick said.

"I shall get my coat."

Eugenia was uncharacteristically quiet while they were being rowed back to shore after inspecting the schooner.

Cliff hopped from the dinghy the instant it reached the marshy shore. "I'll catch up with you later," he said with a sly grin. "Got a few hunches I wanna check out."

Eugenia stood up to leave the boat, but before she could lift her skirts and step over the edge, Zach was there, lifting her into his arms.

"What do you think you are doing?" she squealed, flushing at the young sailor's gaze.

Zach held her close and trudged across the marsh. "Don't want you to get your dress wet . . . it's so seldom you wear one."

Eugenia leaned away from his chest. "Is that a subtle hint?"

"I like you in a dress." A sensuous grin curved his lips. "Actually, I like you better out of your dress."

Zach's remark silenced a retort poised on the tip

of her tongue. Visions of the time they had spent together last night rose up in her mind, and her breasts peaked against her camisole. "We have reached dry land. I think you can put me down now."

"What if I told you I wasn't ready to?" he said in a low, thick voice.

She could feel the heat of his arms on the back of her thighs through the thin fabric. "You want folks to start talking again?"

His face was only inches from hers. "Maybe it'll throw the murderer off. Then maybe the man—"

"Or woman."

"Or woman . . . might get sloppy."

"I thought you did not use females as part of your investigations," she said in a hoarse voice.

"Not when we're alone, I don't," he murmured. "I told you how I feel when we're alone."

Off in the distance, Zach noticed a stream of carriages heading their way. Reluctantly, he lowered her down the hard length of his body until she was standing on her feet.

Eugenia's heart was racing, and she tried to swallow the words she longed to say. Her hands were still on his shoulders, looking up into his face. "What if I tell you how I feel?" She did not wait for him to answer; she forged ahead. "What would you say if I told you I think I am in danger of—"

"Eugenia, it's my job to keep you out of danger," he broke in, taking her by the elbow and escorting her toward the boatworks.

She increased her pace, unsure whether she was relieved or disappointed that he had stopped her from declaring her feelings. "Since it is your job to keep me out of danger, let's hurry up and get this case solved, so I will not be in danger any longer."

As they headed toward Holm's Boatworks, Eugenia couldn't help but think that she was in more danger of losing her heart to Zach than she was from whomever had murdered her father. No. That wasn't true. She was not in danger of losing her heart. If she were honest with herself, she would admit that she already had lost it.

When they first entered Peter Holm's shop, he insisted to Eugenia that he could not possibly spare the time to repair the sail damaged by the person who had ransacked the schooner. But once Zach had stepped forward and taken over, his commanding presence seemed to cow the reluctant man.

Eugenia was amazed at the ease with which he handled the situation, then realized that it was Zach, the marshal, who had dealt with Holm this time. He no longer was forced in her presence to be Zach, the businessman.

As they left the shop for the sheriff's office to report the trouble with the schooner, Eugenia could not help but keep thinking about him. "You are very good at your job, aren't you?"

"Yes, Eugenia, I am."

Zach easily threaded them through the throngs of people who had swarmed into town for Court Week. As they strolled past the plate-glass window of the mercantile, Eugenia noticed their reflections. They were a very handsome couple. "Zach, have you ever thought of doing anything else for a living—"

The question, seemingly out of nowhere, caused Zach to glance down in her direction. She was gazing up at him as they walked, and her face was so earnest that he wished he could give her a different answer.

"No, I haven't. My grandpa and my pa were lawmen back in Kansas where I grew up. Guess it's a tradition in my family. I wanted to be a lawman from the time I got to trail after my pa to the jail."

That was not the answer she had hoped to hear. "Kansas?" she said in an effort to mask her disappointment.

"My folks and my younger brothers died in a fire outside of Dodge. After I caught the bastard who set it and saw him hang, I no longer had any reason to stay. So I came west. Been a lawman ever since. It's what I do best. Guess you could say, it's in my blood; it's the only thing I know."

"No, it isn't," she insisted. "Since you have been on this case, you have learned all about oysters. I watched you drive a hard bargain and get a very profitable price in Astoria. You make a good businessman. And Captain Derrick taught you how to sail. You are even a member of the yacht club."

Zach's brow shoved up. By her enthusiasm, he had the distinct feeling that she was doing more than listing his experiences since he arrived in Oysterville. They stepped off the boardwalk and started across the alley.

Zach suddenly pulled her into the alley, out of sight of the crowds, townsfolk and visitors. Her back against the side of the building, Zach leaned a calloused hand on either side of her.

Eugenia stared into eyes that warned her that she was not going to like what he was about to say. "Eugenia, this is a hell of a place to have this conversation, but—"

"You are right." She pushed his arm aside. She rushed from the alley and continued past the casket shop, forcing Zach to catch up with her.

"You are here to solve my father's murder," she said in a strained voice over her shoulder. "So let's not waste time on other matters right now. We have a sheriff to visit."

"We'll visit the sheriff. Then we're going back to the house and have that talk," he called out darkly.

As Zach had rushed to reach Eugenia, he had noticed Washer and Nelson with their heads together inside the casket shop. They continued past Gertrude Englestrom's shop. She was inside obviously arguing with Gale Sweeney. Zach tried to keep his mind on his job and sort out what the pairings might mean, but all he could think of was Eugenia.

Even as they weaved their way across the street to the sheriff's office, Zach's mind was busy trying to formulate the best way to say what he had attempted to say to Eugenia in the alley. But all that kept coming to mind was: Land and sea.

"Sheriff Dollard," Eugenia said, entering the building, "I am so happy to see you are at work for a change."

"I do my job." Dollard leered back at her.

Bob Dollard's expression shrank, he took his lanky legs off his desk, and sat up straight in his chair when he noticed the town's newest businessman follow that female troublemaker into his office.

"If you do your job, why isn't my father's murder solved?"

The sheriff glanced at Kellogg before returning his attention to the Whalen pest. Kellogg was standing silently against the door, his arms crossed over his chest, his face solemn.

Dollard got out of his chair and offered his hand in greeting to Kellogg, but the taller man ignored his courtesy and stood before him as if he were that interfering troublemaker's guard.

"Look, Miss Eugenia, Oysterville's full of fellers passin' through. And since there ain't been no clues turned up, the way I figure it is that your daddy probably took one of 'em home and got hisself killed for it. You know how he was always hirin' on no-accounts."

"My father believed in giving people a chance," she shot back in defense of her father.

"Yeah, just like he done for the Widow Garrett's son-in-law. The whole damned town knows how that turned out."

"No, it doesn't," Zach said in a low growl. "Why don't you enlighten me?"

Bob Dollard swallowed hard. He did not like Kellogg. The stranger spelled trouble. "Look here, Kellogg, I ain't got no quarrel with you."

"And unless I'm mistaken, *you ain't got no quarrel* with Miss Whalen either." The sheriff's Adam's apple bobbed in his throat. "So why don't you tell us your version of what happened between Whalen and the Widow Garrett's son-in-law."

"Sure. Sure. It ain't no secret. Everybody knows that out of pity Whalen gave Gerard Hamlett a job after no one else in town would hire him. Then the son of a bitch was caught in Bruceport tryin' to sell baskets of oysters stole from Whalen. The old man fired him, but not until after he'd threatened Whalen with revenge for firing him and causing John Garrett's death. Shortly after that, he uprooted his family and moved to Astoria. Nobody's seen hide nor hair of him since."

Zach's gaze shot to Eugenia.

"Gerard was drunk at the time he threatened Daddy," she cried. Eugenia's mind suddenly flashed back to a visit she had paid the widow shortly after she had returned from California. She dismissed it. It was merely a coincidence, not worth mentioning.

"Everyone knows Gerard is harmless," she continued. "And, furthermore, John Garrett's death that stormy night out at the oyster beds was an accident. No one held my father responsible for that."

"What about the widow?" Zach questioned. "Did she think your pa was responsible?"

"No!" Eugenia vehemently shook her head. "She knew it was a dreadful accident. Daddy was with John Garrett and nearly drowned himself trying to save him after their boat capsized."

Growing impatient to get out of the office and over to the saloon to fleece some of those visiting lawyers at the pool hall, Bob Dollard stepped toward the door.

"If why you come was to ask about your daddy's murder, and since I ain't got no new information, I'll show you out. With Court Week on us, I got to get out about town and tend to sheriffin'."

Zach stepped in front of Dollard, blocking him from opening the door. "You can tend to *sheriffin'* right here. Miss Whalen isn't through yet."

After relating the incident on the schooner to the sheriff, who grudgingly took the report, Eugenia stepped out into the sunshine.

"The only thing Sheriff Dollard is good for is taking bribes," she said to Zach.

Zach did not comment, but out of the corner of his eye he watched the man lock up the office and scurry toward the saloon.

"He is worthless," Eugenia was adding when Zach took her arm and began strolling in the same direction the sheriff had headed.

His brow shoved up. "I'm sure the man has his redeeming qualities."

"To whom?"

Zach rubbed his chin. "Interesting question."

"Where are we going?" she asked, breaking into his thoughts.

He stopped and gripped Eugenia's shoulders. Staring straight into her eyes, he said with authority, "*We* aren't going anywhere. You're going to go back to the house and do whatever it is that housekeepers do. When I get there, we're going to have that talk."

She frowned, worried about *that talk* as Zach

turned her around and gave her a gentle shove in the direction of the house. She had not gone half a block when one of the young lawyers, a family friend, greeted her.

An idea flashed into her mind. *Keep him off balance.* She took the man's arm and chattered amicably while they strolled in the direction of her family home. She glanced back over her shoulder in Zach's direction. He was watching her, a scowl on his handsome face. Although she had cause to fear *that talk,* at least she had given him something to think about in the meantime.

While she half-listened to the self-important lawyer drone on about himself and his many accomplishments, another idea dawned on her. There was something she could do to be prepared for *that talk.*

She would go back to the house as ordered, but Zach did not say anything about going directly there.

Thirty-one

Eugenia strolled alongside the lawyer, pretending to be held enrapt by what he was saying until they rounded the corner, then she politely dismissed him and changed direction back to Territory Road on her way toward the wharf. It was the beginning of Court Week, and many of the oystermen spent their time ashore attending the many trials that took place in the county seat.

She removed her shoes and trudged across the sandflats, her toes sinking in the wet sand. She had padded across this way many times before and never experienced anything like she was now. It was a sensual sensation, and caused her to think of Zach and his lovemaking.

Forcing herself to keep her mind on the task at hand, she spied a line of plungers ahead, bobbing in the shallow waters. Eugenia lifted her skirts and waded to the nearest boat. Climbing aboard, she quickly tossed off the line and set the sail toward the Whalen whack.

Fortune smiled on her.

No one was at work anywhere near her destination.

She anchored the boat, grabbed a basket and tongs and began harvesting oysters. She had been out about an hour when a familiar voice assailed her.

"You take on a new job, little lady?"

Startled, her head snapped up. Cliff Granger was sitting in a rowboat alongside the plunger, grinning up at her.

She was caught!

Caught oyster-handed, she grimaced and glanced down at the sea delicacy in her palm.

"Cliff, what are you doing out here?" She dropped the oyster she held into a basket.

He shoved his Stetson back on his head and took a long drag on the cigarette he had just lit. Blowing a smoke ring, he said, "Might ask you the same question."

"I-I am working." In a bold move, she grabbed the tongs and plucked another oyster from the bay.

He took one last drag and flicked the butt over the side. After tying the boat to the plunger, he climbed aboard. "Talked to Kellogg in town. Told me you had some scrawny, fancy-dressed dude in tow when you left him." Cliff winked. "Shouldn't be tellin' you this, but it didn't set real well with Kellogg."

Eugenia did not try to fight a smile; the information secretly warmed her heart and spurred her determination to keep working the beds.

"Kellogg said you were goin' back to the house." What Cliff didn't let on was that Kellogg had directed him to check on her, and if the man had accompanied her to the house, Cliff was to hang around and keep her out of trouble. "Saw you strugglin' with this here big boat, and thought I ought to have me a little looksee."

"Now that you have, I will not detain you any longer." She leaned against the six-foot tongs in an attempt to hide the number of oysters she had already reaped. Despite his easy-going manner, the man's lips were quirked into a suspicious line, causing her mind to grope for a reasonable excuse.

"Just exactly what're you up to, little lady?"

"If you must know, I am gathering supper." She stopped to take a breath as her tale gained momentum. "It is a surprise for Zach, so I would appreciate it if you would not say anything about this to him."

Cliff's keen eyes scanned the area, and he scratched his nose. Her story just didn't have the smell of truth to it. "Hungry hunters, I know how Kellogg can eat, but a dozen starved men couldn't pack away that many oysters, little lady. So, unless you've invited all the visitin' judges and lawyers in town to the supper table, and you don't want me spillin' my gut to Kellogg, you had best can the fish story and start talkin' true."

Eugenia's lower lip began to tremble while she frantically considered what to do. It was obvious Cliff Granger was an intelligent lawman with a keen sense for sniffing out the truth; he was not going to be fooled with another swiftly concocted tale.

Cliff stretched his neck and wiggled his Adam's

apple. "Unless you hurry up and make up your pretty mind, little lady, I got to get goin' and start tunin' up my singin' pipes so they'll be in fine hummin' order for Kellogg." He turned and started for the rowboat.

"No! Wait! Please. Come back."

He pivoted back around to face her and noted her shoulders slumped in defeat. If Kellogg hadn't already more or less staked a claim and properly warned him off, Cliff wouldn't stop to think twice about pursuing the resourceful, eager young woman himself. She sure was singular among the female population.

"All right." She sighed and squared her shoulders. "I am going to sell the oysters."

Surprise crossed his face. "Like in thievin'?"

She frowned. She had to make sure it was kept in proper perspective. "No. Not exactly. I am not taking them from anyone else's beds. I only planned to pick enough oysters to reimburse the government so I can get the beds back."

"Flyin' fish, didn't you pull that crazy piratin' stunt for the same reason?"

"Not exactly."

"What exactly?"

At his skeptical expression, she burst out, "It is not as if I merely wanted the beds back for myself this time. I need them so Zach will have a reason to stay on the peninsula and not have to leave after my father's case is solved."

Cliff picked up on a glimpse of desperation, sincere hopefulness, coupled with another strong emotion in her eyes at the reference to Kellogg's remaining on the peninsula with her. He also noted the dark shadow of barely restrained sorrow when she mentioned her papa.

"Holy hot jumpin' salmon spawnin' upstream, you've really come down with a bad case when it comes to Kellogg, ain't you?"

Her heart buoyed with hope that he had not immediately threatened to arrest her. She opened her mouth to speak.

"No use denyin' it. You're plumb loco crazy in love with the lucky son of a bitch."

Hearing Zach's partner give voice to the true feelings which had been churning inside her for some time now caused Eugenia to turn her back on Cliff so he would not see the sudden tears springing to her eyes. She stared up at the sky dotted with large puffy clouds, taking in big gulps of air.

Oh, Daddy. I wish you were here to advise me like you did while I was growing up, she silently wept inside.

The sun, which had dipped behind a cloud, peeked through, caressing her cheek with its warmth, like her father used to do when she was upset. Maybe he truly was watching over her. She touched trembling fingers to her cheek. The thought gave her renewed strength.

Once she had composed herself, she whipped around to face Cliff, a mutinous cast to her lips. "If you tell Zach, I will deny it."

To her confusion, Cliff merely threw back his head and laughed. He unbuttoned his shirt and rolled up his sleeves. Grabbing a pair of tongs, he moved to Eugenia's side.

"Hope I ain't sorrier 'n an agin' whore without

367

a plug nickel saved for her old age for what I'm about to do, little lady. But show me how to work this here contraption. We got our work cut out for us if we're gonna get them oysters picked and get back before Kellogg finds out."

By the time she and Cliff had worked side-by-side most of the afternoon, Eugenia's spirits were soaring. Zach's partner not only had agreed to help her pick oysters, but he was going to cover for her while she took their harvest to Bruceport and sold them.

She had finally found a way to finance the repurchase of her father's oyster beds and give Zach a reason to remain as well.

For four days after Cliff had reassured Kellogg that Eugenia was remaining at the house, Cliff met Eugenia out at the oyster beds and worked until the baskets were brimming. Then he would rejoin Kellogg, who had been spending time in town, gathering all the information he could on those investors and the Garretts.

Maintaining his cover during the investigation had become even more complicated with so many men connected to the law in town. But thus far, Zach had moved among them almost freely without the beard they were accustomed to seeing him sport.

Each night Cliff excused himself after supper to saunter on over to Gertrude Englestrom's, leaving Zach and Eugenia alone. They made love for hours, exploring and experimenting with wild abandon. Afterwards, while she lay in his arms, she spun tall tales of domestic drudgery and ironed neckerchiefs, and she listened to the progress he was making on her father's case. Then they would fall asleep, entwined and sated.

"Wake up, my sweet Genie." Zach kissed each eyelid, and Eugenia smiled up at him.

She pulled his head down to her, kissing him thoroughly. Zach drew back. He sat up on the edge of the bed and stroked her cheek.

The serious expression on his face caused Eugenia to sit up. "Zach?"

"Eugenia, these past four days I've put off that talk we were supposed to have." Truth was after seeing her with that fancy lawyer, something had sparked inside him. He had not been able to bring himself to set her free to accept the company of someone like that.

But time was running out. "I've been guilty of—"

"No, you are not guilty of anything. The time we have spent together, we have shared responsibility."

"Eugenia—"

In utter panic that he was about to shatter the dream that had taken root and had been sprouting in her heart, Eugenia pressed a silencing finger to his lips. "Please. There is no need to have this talk you insist upon until the case is solved," she suggested with a nonchalance she did not feel.

"You know how I feel about the oyster beds, and I know how you feel about your work. We are both adults. Our lives are already set, so there is no longer a pressing reason," she added with a shade of forced indifference.

Zach's brow shoved up. The words she had just uttered were not characteristic of the Eugenia he knew. He did not have the right to continue to keep her with him, but something inside, her expression, her scent, the sound of her voice, encouraged him to wait. He settled on pure male selfishness.

"If you insist." He left her side and began to dress. Land and sea, he tried unsuccessfully to remind himself of an earlier decision. But the last week with Eugenia had been tempering and threatening that decision.

"Captain Derrick and I are going to spend a good part of the day practicing for tomorrow's regatta," he announced from the doorway. "Care to join us?"

"Thank you for the invitation, but I promised the Widow Garrett that I would help her in her yard today." She yawned and snuggled beneath the covers. "So I think I shall sleep in for a while longer."

"You probably could use the rest," he said and returned to her side and kissed her. "Our late nights have you looking a little drawn."

"Yes." Eugenia closed her eyes with visions of the long, hard days at the oyster beds. She heaved an inward sigh at her performance; it had staved off *that talk* and bought her time to finish selling enough oysters to reclaim the beds.

Despite a niggling sense that she was courting disaster, Eugenia left the bed and dressed in a plain shirt and pants the moment she heard the door slam. While she straightened the room, she picked up one of his shirts and rubbed it against her cheek, reveling in Zach's musky scent of masculine sweat.

She was so involved with her own plans and the need to hurry that she failed to glance out the window and see the Widow Garrett join Zach as he left for the wharf.

"You look like you may be dressed to do some sailing, young man," Ruth Garrett observed of Zach Kellogg's rain slicker when the weather was perfectly clear.

He fell in step beside the elderly widow outside of her picket fence. "And you look as if you're all decked out to meet some lucky juror," he remarked, keeping his face impassive.

"How did you guess?" She beamed, amazed. "You are such a perceptive young man. I have always found the trials intriguing to attend during Court Week. But this year they have taken on a personal significance since I met Judge Swensen. I am going to spend the entire day in town observing him preside over trials."

She let out a girlish giggle and took Zach's proffered arm. "Why, thank you, you are a gentleman. By the way, I'm giving a party tonight. I hope you will come."

Zach did not let on that he knew about the judge because he had been checking on her. He forced himself to exchange banal conversation with the widow, attentively listening to her sing Eugenia's praises and recommending he provide Eugenia escort tonight. Once he had left her at the courthouse, Zach's genial expression vanished as he headed down the boardwalk.

Eugenia had lied to him!

For some reason she had used helping the Widow

Garrett as an excuse not to be with him today. That little spitfire had to be up to something again, just when he'd felt assured that she had finally agreed to let him handle the case without interference.

The urge to head back to the house and confront her was nearly overwhelming. But he had to go out on that damned bay and practice sailing, even if it killed him, if he hoped to win the first place money offered tomorrow.

He had to win that money! For Eugenia. If nothing else, he wanted her to be able to keep her precious oyster beds.

His churning turmoil, inner rage and fear for her safety was pulling him in opposite directions when he spied Granger. His partner was standing behind Gertrude Englestrom while she unlocked her shop not more than three buildings in front of Zach.

Cliff Granger. The one man Zach would trust with his life. The one man capable of taking over in Zach's absence.

Zach stepped up his pace and hailed Granger just as he pressed a smacking kiss on a surprised Gertrude's mouth. "That's to keep you thinkin' 'bout what I'm gonna give you tonight, darlin'."

"I shall be waiting." Gertrude flushed before the milling throngs watching and hurried into her shop, leaving Cliff outside to wait for his partner.

Cliff removed a half-smoked cigarette he was accustomed to carrying in his shirt pocket and lit it. There was nothing like a good smoke to keep a nervous expression off his face. Although he was well schooled, the one man alive who could read him like a first grade McGuffey Reader was Zach Kellogg.

"Drink?" Zach suggested when he caught up with his partner.

Cliff glanced at the sun. It was still early morning, but during Court Week the saloons never seemed to close. "Sure, friend. Why not?"

They settled at the only unoccupied table in the rear corner of the Salty Dog, and Zach ordered two beers. Once the brews arrived, Zach sat and stared into the amber liquid topped with foam that reminded him of ocean waves. His finger circled the rim of the mug until a high-pitched hum issued from his efforts.

"We've been partners a long time, and it's farsight obvious, since you ain't drinkin' or talkin', that you didn't ask me in here to tip a few with you while we discuss the case. What's on your mind, Kellogg?" Cliff belted down most of his beer.

Cliff waited, but Kellogg's expression merely tightened. "Holy hot heaven, there's only one thin' that could make a perfectly sane man look like he could kill outright with no apparent cause; it's the woman, ain't it?" He hesitated a moment; Kellogg's face darkened.

"Christ's son Jesus, I should've knowed it. It's that little lady, Eugenia Whalen. Let me be buried alive at sea if I ain't right."

Kellogg's face clouded with dark, mushrooming thunderheads, and for an instant Cliff was sure lightning bolts were going to shoot from the man's eyes when he lifted his gaze.

"I want you to follow her today. Stick to her like

a tick on a deer. I want a detailed report," Kellogg said with such deadly calm that Cliff's throat suddenly dried up. Cliff had only seen Kellogg look like that once before; after he'd discovered his wife in bed with that Russian.

Cliff took a long swig on his beer to keep from giving himself away. Thank God he hadn't propositioned the little lady. He knew Eugenia was interested in nobody but Kellogg, so that wasn't the cause of whatever had Kellogg in such a foul mood. "There some reason you ain't doin' your own followin'?"

"I've got to be out on that frigging plunger with Derrick."

Cliff breathed an inner sigh of relief despite the ominous thunder in Kellogg's voice. Kellogg was going to be kept busy and out of the way. Cliff could help Eugenia without having to watch his own back. Of course, Kellogg couldn't know what he and Eugenia had been up to or he wouldn't have come to him.

Cliff rubbed his jaw. Something to do with the little lady had Kellogg mighty agitated. Cliff smiled to himself. It was a good sign that Kellogg had finally gotten that cheating ex-wife of his out of his blood.

"You care to let me in on why it is that you want me to stick to her tail today?" he carefully asked so as not to arouse distrust.

Zach was not prepared to share his inner torment or his suspicions. Slowly he unfolded his big frame from the chair and placed powerful fists on the table, leaning toward Granger. "Just do it."

The veins in Kellogg's neck stood out in suppressed fury, and his face was a turbulent mask.

Cliff grabbed Kellogg's untouched beer and guzzled it down as he watched Kellogg leave. There was barely leashed restraint in each pounding step. Cliff ordered another beer, wondering what the hell kind of detailed report he was going to come up with that Kellogg would accept.

Thirty-two

Strong winds whipped up choppy whitecaps on the bay, casting salty spray over the side of the plunger as Zach dropped anchor. He and the crew had just finished the practice course that Captain Derrick had set up for the third time.

To Zach's relief, as he waited for the white-haired captain to join him, he seemed to be developing a tolerance for the rolling motion of a ship. For a change, he was not experiencing the sick feeling that his gut was about to turn inside out and flop over, threatening to spill its contents.

Pocket watch in hand, Captain Derrick strode over to Kellogg. "Best time yet, man. But ye got to do a wee bit better if ye hope to win." Derrick grinned, although he did not understand the distant gleam of amusement in Kellogg's eyes as he stared at the watch. "Ready to give her another run?"

Snapped from his reverie over Eugenia's antics, Zach glanced up at the old man's face. "What?"

"Ye ain't goin' to be a winner if your mind's not on the race."

"Get me a horse 'n' saddle, and I'll give you a prizewinning race," Zach grumbled and wiped the sticky sea spray from his face. The salty drops reminded him of Eugenia and the taste of her soft flesh. It was ironic what lengths a man would go to for a woman. Even if he knew he had to leave her soon.

"Land versus the sea." The captain sighed. "Why be it that Man just can't resign himself to worshipping both fine mistresses?"

Land versus the sea. The captain's woeful remark might as well have been a knife which had stabbed Zach in the heart. He had been struggling with that very issue. Still was.

Zach gave a mirthless laugh. "Guess there's some of us who're tempted to bridge the two, only to realize that we're fated to keep our feet dry."

Captain Derrick had always had a keen eye, and silently questioned Kellogg's telling comment. He had been watching how the lass acted around the lawman. And he had observed how hard the lawman worked at mastering the plunger. No doubt for the lass, since it was obvious the lawman did not possess a longing for the watery life.

They would suit, he thought wryly, despite his land and her sea. If only they'd come to recognize it before it was too late.

"I'd say that if the sea starts at one end, and the land starts at the other, there be a definite chance that both could meet somewhere in the middle. Think on it. Land's surrounded by sea, and yet the two be managing to co-exist for eons, neither swallowing up the other."

Zach stared at the wily seafarer. The old man obviously had high hopes where there could be none. Zach could never make his living from the sea, and Eugenia would never be happy away from it. "Yeah, well, let's saddle up and spur this tub around the course one last time today."

"Aye. One last time before the race." The captain chuckled at Kellogg's phrasing. *Land.* "Remember, ye be a stubborn man; a quality fit for a stubborn lass."

Zach ignored the captain's blatant assertion and prepared the plunger for one last run. As he unfurled the sail, he caught a glimpse of Washer and Nelson on deck of a ship to the south of him. Then, as he was rounding the other side of the course, young Sweeney and Gertrude Englestrom aboard a smaller boat caught his eye. Not long after that, the sheriff and the elder Sweeney sailed by in one of Peter Holm's ships.

Zach's mind was churning as the pieces of the puzzle suddenly started to come together, and he had to fight to keep his mind on the plunger he was sailing.

Zach had nearly finished the course when he saw a plunger carrying Eugenia from the other side of the bay toward Oysterville. The unidentifiable man accompanying her was wearing a strangely familiar shirt, although Zach could not quite place it.

"Neptune's wrath must be upon us," the captain growled, pounding across the deck toward Zach.

"Ye be off by more than five minutes. That run be the biggest waste of time today."

Zach's brow shoved up. "I wouldn't say that."

"Then what would ye be sayin'?" the irritated captain shot back.

"I'd say that the run I just made may well be worth the jackpot," he said, but he was not thinking about tomorrow's regatta.

The captain snorted his disbelief at the lawman's reasoning. "With the time ye just clocked, ye ain't got no more a chance of being a winner than outswimming a riptide in freezing water."

The word "winner" sparked Zach's mind from the case to Eugenia. She had obviously snuck out to meet the man who was in the plunger with her after lying to him this morning. Zach wondered what the hell she was up to this time. But he knew Eugenia well enough that asking her outright for the truth would only garner a hastily concocted fabrication.

Miss Eugenia Huntley Whalen did not realize it, but he already had made arrangements to track her movements. He grinned to himself. At least he had made sure she would be safe.

"Ye be listening to a word I be speaking?" Derrick blustered. "When the race's over, ye'll be the last across the finish line unless ye keep your mind on the ship."

"Captain Derrick, the way I've always heard it told, it ain't over 'til it's over."

Zach was heading back toward the house, determined to locate Granger and learn the truth about what Eugenia had been up to when Judge Swensen, coming out of the courthouse, stopped him.

"Kellogg? Is that you?"

Damn! He had been in such a hurry, his mind full of Eugenia, that he had neglected his cover. He stopped and waited for the distinguished elderly juror to catch up with him. At least Swensen was one of the most honest and respected judges on the bench. He could be relied upon to be discreet.

"It is you, Kellogg." The men shook hands. "I wondered if it could be the same Zachary Kellogg I have known for years when Ruth mentioned your name."

Zach's brow shoved up. "Did you tell her about me?"

"Well, no. I had no reason to at the time. But now that I know—"

"I'd be obliged if you kept my identity confidential for the time being."

In order to get the judge away from the other men leaving the courthouse, Zach directed him away from the steps. While the juror listened, Zach described his reasons for needing to maintain his anonymity. He explained that he was close to solving Whalen's murder. What he did not say was that he was determined to participate in the regatta tomorrow before wrapping it up.

Before the men parted, the juror agreed to keep Zach's identity a secret, and offered to remain in town after the end of Court Week to hear the case.

Cliff was sitting at the kitchen table, munching on thick slices of ham, when Kellogg entered the house. "Honeyed beehives, you look like a bear 'bout to pounce, friend," Cliff said and stuffed another piece of ham into his mouth.

Zach frowned at his partner. Something about him disturbed Zach, but he could not quite put his finger on it. "What about Eugenia?"

"Somethin' to eat?" Cliff ignored Kellogg's question and held out a slice of meat. "You look like you could use somethin' to gnaw on."

Zach pulled up a chair and straddled it, his patience nearly spent. "All right, Granger, you've had your fun. Now, what about Eugenia?"

"What about Eugenia?" Eugenia mimicked, standing in the doorway.

Zach swung around. She took his breath away, she looked so beautiful in the flowing lemon yellow satin dress. She rarely wore such gowns, and Zach wondered why she was wearing it now.

"I was wondering where you were," he said, his eyes appreciatively roving over her gorgeous hourglass figure. Her auburn hair was swept up and adorned with matching ribbons. A darker yellow velvet sash was tied around her waist. He rubbed his fingers together; her bosoms were round and full, enough to fulfill any craving.

"Now you know." She pivoted around in order to give Zach a good look at her. She wanted to dazzle him, and from the expression on his face, she had.

"You don't look like you've been working out in Mrs. Garrett's yard all day. What's the occasion?"

Zach noted Eugenia and Granger exchange quick glances. Something clicked in the back of his mind, and his gaze settled on his partner's suddenly familiar shirt.

Granger had been the man in the boat with Eugenia.

Eugenia noticed Zach's scowl deepen, and recalled what Cliff had told her while they were picking oysters. Zach had wanted her followed. He was out on the bay. He may have seen them.

"Mrs. Garrett's party tonight is the occasion. I wanted to surprise you. Cliff came by and was kind enough to accompany me to Bruceport to purchase this special gown."

"Someone had to," Cliff offered with a shrug. The little lady was a pretty good storyteller when on the spot. "Wasn't it downright handy how I just happened to be nearby when the little lady really needed someone," he added with a wink to rile Kellogg.

Cliff knew the danger of his angling, but if he didn't light a fire under Kellogg soon, the man might very well be fool enough to let Eugenia get away. If Kellogg wasn't going to help himself, Cliff was going to give him a little nudge in the right direction.

"Real handy, Granger," Zach muttered, belatedly recalling the widow's invitation.

Cliff grinned and further courted a collision course with his partner. "You should know, Kellogg."

Zach's brow shoved up while his lips stretched into a feral snarl. "I should, shouldn't I? You always've liked the ladies, haven't you, Granger?"

"One 'n' all. Married, single, old or young. Never

been known to turn my back on a well-turned ankle aimed in my direction." Cliff smirked and let his eyes openly trail toward the hem of Eugenia's skirt. "Starts out one thin' and leads to another."

Zach followed Granger's eyes. "Eugenia? Granger, you bastard," Zach growled, sprang up, and landed a swift punch to Granger's face, knocking him clear off the chair.

Cliff sat on the floor, rubbing his jaw, looking up at his partner's black scowl. "Punchin' bags aplenty, I ain't never argued over the fact of my parentage. And lately you've been a mite free with those fists. But I ain't goin' to fight over 'em, neither one. Now, a lady's honor . . . that's another thin'."

"Get up!" Zach demanded. He was in a mood to make pulp out of Granger's grinning face. Hell, he had trusted Granger. Instead, the man had taken advantage of their friendship. Said as much. He grabbed Granger by the collar, hauling him to his feet.

One punch led to another, and soon the two men were grappling on the floor, upending the tidy kitchen.

Horrified, her hands clasping her mouth, Eugenia watched the two men beat each other until she could no longer stand it. "Stop it! Stop it right now!" she screamed.

Zach got the last punch in before the two men stilled and turned swollen eyes toward Eugenia. "Just look at the both of you. You are acting like foolish little boys! I will not have you fighting in the house. If you cannot stop this madness, at least take it outside where, with my blessing, you can proceed to kill each other without breaking the furniture."

A sudden vision blazed into Zach's mind. "What did Granger try with you?"

Eugenia threw up her hands. She wanted to scream at Zach that Cliff had been helping her. But she could not tell him yet, not until she had gathered the rest of the money.

"I knew it," Zach's voice rumbled, and he drew back a fist when she did not immediately offer an explanation.

"Cliff was the perfect gentleman," Eugenia cried, which caused Zach to lower his fist. "He never laid a hand on me. Unlike you, he merely rendered his assistance when I needed it."

Cliff feared that she was so distraught she was going to let on to Zach what they had been doing. He quickly took up the conversation. "I didn't do nothin' no red-blooded, all-American lawman wouldn't do."

"Careful, Granger," Zach snarled. "Remember, I've known more than a few red-blooded, all-American lawmen."

"At the moment, I wish I didn't," Eugenia snapped, disgust with both men clearly visible on her face.

Granger grinned. "Been one yourself, too. Huh, Kellogg."

"Will you two just stop it!" She threw up her hands. "Since neither of you have the slightest possibility of looking respectable tonight, I am going to the Widow Garrett's party alone. I hope you both will have the common decency to stay away and not create more talk with the way you look.

"The two of you can remain here and lick your wounds. You can either peacefully work out this foolishness or kill each other. Because at the moment, I do not give a single whit. I will not be forced to listen to such outrageous innuendos and then stand idly by while you two fight over me as if you were two rutting dogs."

She whipped around to leave, but Zach's soft voice halted her. "You will be attending the regatta tomorrow, won't you?"

"That depends," she said, her eyes still flashing like an angry green sea. "Will I have someone to cheer on?"

Zach suddenly felt guilty for the spectacle he had made of himself with Granger. He realized that his suspicions were groundless, and he had acted like some foolish, jealous swain. He was a seasoned lawman about to solve a case, and he had better remember that before he allowed his personal feelings to foul it up.

"I'll be at the starting line tomorrow." His male pride talking, he said, "Guess only you know for sure who you'll be rooting for."

A look of shock on her face, Eugenia sadly shook her head, grabbed a wrap, and fled from the house. As she crossed the walkway toward the Garrett house, which was gaily lit and bursting with laughter and music, she despaired.

Zach had not said what she had hoped to hear. She did not approve of his showing he cared for her by fighting his own partner over her. She was not a possession. But it seemed that he could not declare his intentions any other way. And at this rate, she feared that he never would.

Zach stood at the window. He watched Eugenia open the gate and disappear into the night before he went back to his partner. He hated himself at that moment. He should have ignored Granger, gone upstairs, changed, and escorted Eugenia to the party tonight. Instead, he was left with a mixture of aches and pains, bruises, and Granger's company.

"Blunted pig snouts, I ain't never stuck my nose in before, but—"

"Then don't start now," Zach shot back at Granger and explored the tenderness beneath his right eye.

Cliff climbed to his feet, wet a dishcloth and held it to his bleeding nose. "You're a dumb, blinded horse's ass, Kellogg."

Zach righted a chair they had knocked over and plunked down. "And I suppose you're going to be the one to tell me just how blind and how big of an ass I am?"

Cliff grabbed a chair and gingerly settled his battered body across the table from Kellogg just in case the man had another notion to start swinging. He leaned an elbow on the table.

"Way I see it, someone's got to."

Zach waved a sore arm, saying sarcastically, "Well, by all means, get whatever's on your mind off your chest so we can get back to work and finish solving the damned case that brought us here in the first place, unless you have forgotten."

"I ain't forgot. But you had no call to question me like you did, let alone accuse me. In case *you* forgot, you're the one who wanted me tailin' the little lady today."

"So?" Zach's brow shoved up.

"So, you know how Gertie feels about Eugenia. She ain't exactly made it a secret that she don't like her." Cliff was warming up now and decided to embellish the little fabrication he had planned to spin after seeing Kellogg while he and Eugenia were returning from Bruceport earlier.

"What does that have to do with why you were out on the bay with Eugenia after she said she was going to work in the widow's yard?"

"Gertie runs the best fancy dress shop in town. The little lady owes Gertie money. So when I followed Eugenia there, I overheard Gertie refuse to sell Eugenia another stitch until she paid her.

"Eugenia ran smack dab into me, stormin' from the shop. The poor little thing was frettin' that she wanted to surprise you and look her best tonight, so I agreed to go with her to Bruceport so she could get somethin' to wear from folks over there.

"If you wouldn't've gone off half-cocked and forced me to give you a taste of your own medicine, we both would've been at that shindig tonight with the rest of them and maybe picked up somethin' to help solve the case instead of makin' the little lady go all by her lonesome 'cuz we ain't presentable."

Zach almost felt remorse, but Granger had indeed goaded him beyond restraint, and there was the slightest twitch in Granger's eye that kept Zach from apologizing.

"It's just as well," Zach finally said, after mulling the explanation over a bit longer. "I think I'm getting close to figuring out who murdered Whalen. And with everyone occupied at that party tonight, there won't be any interference while we search for the stolen evidence Whalen claimed to have in his possession."

Zach stood. "Let's go get cleaned up, then on the way I'll fill you in on what I've come up with."

As Cliff followed Kellogg up the stairs, he had to wonder that when Kellogg mentioned being able to get the evidence without interference, he was referring to the murderer or Eugenia.

Thirty-three

Eugenia strolled among the clusters of partygoers, listening to the gaily dressed people discuss the cases tried this week. The longer she listened, the more her face became pinched. Horse thieves, trespassers, and a variety of other lawbreakers had been tried and sentenced. The person who had killed her father should have been on trial along with them.

"Eugenia, child," Ruth Garrett said, coming up from behind Eugenia. Eugenia swung around, her smile over bright. "I am so happy you decided to come tonight."

"It is a lovely party."

"It is, isn't it?" Ruth beamed in her pale blue ruffles. "Though I have not seen your young man yet?"

A look of unease squeezed Eugenia's features, and Ruth quickly sought to change the subject since she knew of their difficulties. Dropping a hand on Eugenia's forearm, Ruth said, "Have you met Judge Swensen?"

"Of course, how are you, sir?" Eugenia said, smiling at the elderly pair, their arms linked, obviously enjoying each other's company.

She spoke to them for a few moments, then made her excuses. Unable to maintain her usual animated demeanor, she inched past the sheriff, who was standing at the end of the refreshment table, busy upending a flask into a cup of punch. She gave a friendly nod to several others, then went out onto the porch and leaned against the rail.

For the first time in her life, she was feeling lonely, isolated, and adrift, despite being surrounded and welcomed by groups of friends and acquaintances. Secretly she wished Zach were there with her.

Wanting to be part of a pair was a new and painful experience, and Eugenia found herself wishing she could be a carefree child again, when life was so simple and uncomplicated by adult emotions.

Her thoughts naturally drifted back to Zach, and her gaze trailed toward her family home. She wondered if she should have stayed and tended his bruises. Her attention caught on a tight knot of partygoers mulling near the fence where her father's body was found; a place she had intentionally not gone near. Mr. Washer and the Sweeneys were laughing over some shared joke with Rube Nelson and Gertrude Englestrom.

Suddenly remembering how Zach had mentioned that whoever had broken into the house and ransacked the ship probably had been searching for the evidence her father had written to Zach about, Eugenia set aside her self-absorbed sadness.

Her mind working with new possibilities, she stealthily stepped from the porch so they wouldn't see her, and left the party.

With renewed determination in her stride, Eugenia decided to search each of their homes herself, ignoring Zach's earlier warning to leave the investigation to him. What better opportunity? she thought as she neared Nelson's house.

"Hobbled horse thieves, we're wastin' our time searchin' these houses," Cliff complained as they left the third house. "We've been through everythin' both Sweeneys and Gertie own, includin' that wall safe you cracked, and we came up empty. To my way of thinkin', if one of them's involved and found Whalen's evidence, it's already been destroyed."

Zach merely grunted and headed along the street.

"What we doin' now?"

"We're going to search Washer's house."

"Hell, Washer as well as the rest of them were with me the night the ship was ransacked. We're just chasin' our tails," Cliff complained bitterly.

"Did you keep track of every one of them at all times that night?"

"Well, no," Cliff admitted. He had been drinking pretty heavily that night. When the group he had arrived with left, he'd joined Derrick and his crew at the bar.

"And where did the Englestrom woman disappear to after someone shot out the parlor window?"

391

A dark grin came to Cliff's lips. "She explained that. I just forgot to tell you. Gertie broke down and admitted to goin' out to meet that snivelin' Gale Sweeney 'cuz she said I was so drunk she didn't think I was comin' back."

"And you believe her?" Zach questioned as flashbacks sparked of Sweeney and Gertrude together in the casket shop and on the bay.

"No reason not to."

"Doesn't bother you?"

Cliff shrugged. "Gertie don't mean nothin' to me like your little lady does to you."

Kellogg did not respond, which caused Cliff to say, "You so suddenly obsessed with solvin' this case 'cuz it's been draggin' on too long, or 'cuz you're afraid of your own feelin's for the little lady and want to get out of town before you're forced to confront them?"

Zach stopped and sent Granger a glare that could have frozen the Pacific Ocean. "Mind your own damned business."

"This case's my business," Cliff retorted, astounded by his partner's continued vehemence. "Hell, we're not goin' to turn up a thin'. All you're doin' is keepin' me from enjoyin' Gertie's many charms tonight."

Kellogg did not even bother to acknowledge Granger's remarks. Instead, he spun on his heel and started walking again.

Catching up with Kellogg, Cliff added, "We're only traipsin' around town tonight so you can keep yourself so busy that you don't got time to think 'bout that little lady. Why don't you just up and admit it so we can saunter on over to that shindig and do some serious drinkin' and skirt chasin'."

"Shut up, Granger." Although he was not about to admit it to his partner, Zach had been considering that very thing. But the simple fact was that no matter how busy he kept himself, Zach could not get Eugenia and his feelings for her out of his mind.

His hands in his pockets, Cliff grudgingly trudged along-side Kellogg. "You used to be fun to work with. We used to share a common interest in life's pleasures: boozin' and whorin'." Cliff groaned inwardly. "Since that little lady entered your life, everythin's changed. Your moods change faster'n the weather 'round here."

"Wait!" Zach snapped. Zach grabbed Granger's arm, nearly knocking him off his feet as Zach pulled him behind a huge alder tree. "Look."

At first Cliff thought Kellogg was going to start another fight, but he peered around the tree, then turned to Kellogg. "What am I s'pose to be lookin' at?"

"Washer's house. Look, there it is again; see that faint light? It's moving from room to room."

"So?"

"So Washer and his family're supposed to be at the widow's party. Even if they weren't, don't you think it's a mite strange that the house's dark except for that one dim light?"

"Could be somebody's breakin' in. Even if someone is, it's none of our business. We're investigatin' a murder, remember?"

"True. But a gut instinct tells me I ought to have

a looksee. You watch the front door while I go 'round back. Let's see what we can flush out."

As Kellogg crept from the tree through the shadows toward the house, Cliff griped, "And I thought I was the senior partner."

Cliff moved to the side of the house and peeked through the window. What he saw made him want to laugh out loud.

Eugenia had thrust open Washer's rolltop desk and was rummaging through it.

For an instant he considered hailing Kellogg, but Kellogg had made it his case. An idea came to Cliff. He strode toward the front of the house, pounded up onto the porch and rattled the doorknob. Peering through the lace covered window at the top of the door, Cliff watched the light dim, flickering toward the rear of the house.

A broad smile on his face, Cliff plunked down on the steps, crossed his arms over his chest, and waited for the fireworks to begin.

Zach pulled his six-shooter from his holster and crept through the darkness to the back door. Carefully he turned the knob and was slowly pushing open the door.

Suddenly the door slammed back, smashing into his nose.

"Damn son of a bitch!"

Zach grabbed the door and shoved. Whoever was on the other side was pushing back. "You might as well give up, you're under arrest."

The door quivered but did not budge.

Zach's nose throbbed, increasing his determination to catch whoever was inside the house. He holstered his gun, turned the knob and battered his shoulder against the door.

There was no escape. Realizing it was Zach, and probably Cliff at the front door, Eugenia bit her lip. She blew out her candle and stepped back.

Zach crashed through the door with such force that he landed at the intruder's feet.

Eugenia saw her chance to flee and jumped over him toward the open door. She was almost out the door when steely hands clamped around her ankle.

"Oh, no, you don't!" Zach snarled.

He yanked the intruder off his feet and pounced, easily pinioning the soft arms over the intruder's head. He drew his gun.

"See you got your *man*, Kellogg." Cliff laughed, lighting a lamp and holding it overhead. "Or should I say woman?"

In the light, Zach saw Eugenia's livid expression glaring up at him. She struggled. "You can get off me any time now," she seethed, embarrassed to be in such a position beneath Zach in front of his partner once again.

Despite his anger at having discovered Eugenia was interfering again, Zach's senses were responding to the perfect cradle her body formed for his. The more she struggled, the more his body hardened.

"I'll just wait outside." Cliff grinned ear to ear, set the lamp down, and stepped around the pair to leave the house.

Once they were alone, Eugenia hissed, "Let go of my wrists and get off me!"

"Did I tell you earlier how lovely you look tonight?" he murmured, gazing into her stormy green eyes. He could see the anger fading, transforming into a silent, warming glow. And her cheeks flushed.

If they had been elsewhere, she might have succumbed to the powerful draw he had for her. "Zach, please."

"All right," he said with regret and pulled her to her feet with him.

He extinguished the lamp and led her from the house out to the swing in the far corner of the back yard. Cliff had gone, leaving Zach alone with Eugenia. "Sit down," he directed.

"Shouldn't we get away from here first?" To her chagrin, he plunked down on the swing and patted the space next to him. It was so tempting, her breasts peaked against the satin fabric at the thought of sitting so close to him. The bushes rustled nearby, and a cat scooted past, reminding her how vulnerable they were out in the open.

"I am not going to remain here to be discovered by Mr. Washer when he returns home," she spat and swung on her heel.

Pity, Zach thought as he left the swing. It was such a pleasant evening to nestle Eugenia in the crook of his arm while they rocked in the moonlight.

Just as well, he grudgingly concluded, catching up with her; if he did not keep his distance, he'd never be able to leave.

"All right, Eugenia, what the hell were you up to this time?"

She kept walking until they were a safe distance

from Washer's house. Then she turned on him. "While you and Cliff were back at the house busy licking your wounds, I noticed all those investors were at the widow's party, so I decided to search their houses."

"What's the matter, Eugenia, do you want to get killed? The murderer could have been the one who discovered you instead of me."

Her chin tilted up in defiance. "Well, he or she didn't! As a matter of fact, Mr. Lawman, while you were busy fighting your own partner, I managed to get the proof on who murdered my father."

He grabbed her arm. "What're you talking about?"

Eugenia patted her bodice. "I found the evidence in Washer's house which proves he is guilty. And now I am going back to the party, locate the sheriff, and present it to him so he can arrest the bastard."

Zach's smile was one-sided, and he dropped his hand. "I thought the corset you had on was a mite stiff." Then he grew serious. "Give me the evidence you claim incriminates Washer, Eugenia."

"No. I am taking it directly to the sheriff."

She tried to step around him, but he blocked her way. She was going to ruin his investigation if she got to the sheriff. "Give me the evidence."

"No."

"I'm warning you," he demanded in a low growl. "I'll take it from you if I have to."

She stepped back, holding a protective arm across her bodice. "You wouldn't."

"Wouldn't I?" He took a step toward her. "Dare me, Eugenia."

"No." She knew better. Zachary Kellogg was not a man who did not follow through with a threat.

Zach's brow shoved up, and he held out a hand. "Eugenia. Now."

A couple unknown to her passed them on the other side of the street. "You would not try anything in front of witnesses." She took two more steps backward, placing her in the light spilling from a house.

"Wrong." In a flash he grabbed her and tossed her over his shoulder as if she were no more than a fishing net.

"Stop! No!" She reached out toward the couple. "Help me. He is going to ravish me. Get the sheriff—"

The couple stopped and were earnestly staring. Zach turned toward them. He sent them a pitiable smile. "Reluctant bride," he said with a sorrowful sigh.

He swung back toward the house, and Eugenia saw them shaking their heads in disapproval of her before continuing on their way. They were not going to help; they actually believed she was some recalcitrant newlywed.

"You better quit struggling, Genie. You're giving me ideas which have no connection with the case," he said in a husky voice.

"I will quit struggling, but I will not walk," she snapped to his back.

Zach took her around to the back door, avoiding the partygoers at the next house. He pounded up the stairs and dumped her onto his bed. She scooted against the headboard and glared at him, keeping her arms protectively across her bodice.

"You are not getting these papers," she bellowed in outrage.

His eyes were filled with passion's fire when he sat on the edge of the bed. In a silken voice, he murmured, "Oh, but I am. As a matter of fact, I may find great pleasure in tying your wrists and ankles to the bedposts so you won't be able to resist me. You see, there's nothing . . . nothing in this world I'd rather do than slowly undress you, Eugenia. Layer by layer."

He reached out and pulled a ribbon from her hair. He drew it across his wrist. "Velvet bindings so as not to bruise tender skin," he said in a sultry whisper.

The intensity in his eyes warned Eugenia that he meant to carry out his threat. Would indeed relish it. The thought frightened and intrigued her at the same time. The vision of herself bound to the bed, wide open and vulnerable to his touch, his every whim, caused a rush of liquid warmth at the apex of her thighs.

She glanced at the ribbon in his hand. Pale yellow blended against bronzed skin. She imagined it wrapped around her tanned wrists, binding her ankles. Velvet, like his intimate touch when he had set her flesh ablaze.

The rhythm of her breathing increased, and her heart raced with the arousing thoughts. She was sorely tempted to test his sensual threat when she heard the echo of voices drift through the window from the party, questioning her absence. What if someone came to check on her?

"Oh, all right," she choked out and dug the papers from her bodice. "Here." She thrust them at him.

"Can't say that I'm not terribly disappointed, and I can see that you are, too."

"Being rather presumptuous, aren't you?" She tried to sound indignant.

"No. Just very observant."

Eugenia felt a ruby red flush climb her face, and she dropped her gaze. Despite a stringent denial, he knew what she had been thinking. He knew!

After long moments, she ventured to peek at him from beneath her lashes. He was perusing the papers. For an instant, a pique of disappointment flowed over her that he had so easily shifted his attention.

"Morton Washer is guilty, isn't he? He murdered my father."

Zach looked up. Animosity now emanated from her every pore where a moment ago she had been ready to accept his touch. Pity Eugenia's face no longer carried that delectable flush. He secretly longed to put it there again soon. He quietly slipped the ribbon into his pocket.

"Well?" she prodded.

"These documents definitely appear to incriminate Washer. Points to him stealing from your father and hiring a schooner to ship his ill-gotten gain to San Francisco, then depositing the profits in a bank account at Astoria. These ledgers also seem to indicate that he has been stealing profits from that investment group as well. It appears that he even has been secretly trying to buy up the beds of other oystermen independent of the group."

"That explains everything. My father found out what Washer was up to, and when he confronted Washer with this irrefutable evidence, Washer killed him to protect his scheme from being disclosed."

She grabbed a handful of the evidence and flew off the bed to the door. "Come on, Washer is next door at the Widow Garrett's party. You can arrest him there, in front of everybody. Then I will be able to watch him swing from the end of a rope before Court Week concludes."

Her eyes glittered with such unhidden hatred that Zach wondered whether she would let the man come to trial without trying to kill him, she had loved her father that much. It was a dark side of her that he had only seen in a few men, and in himself when his wife had run off. Most kept it well hidden.

Eugenia was barely more than a girl; a woman only because he had made her one. But she had more strength, more determination, more grit, and more facets to her character than most men possessed. And more impetuous foolhardiness than was good for her.

He bounded to the door and put his shoulder against it, blocking her exit. "Eugenia, before you go off half-cocked with this bloodthirsty vengeance you're seeking, I want you to listen to me."

"No, Zach. I may have been born a woman, who is supposed to be soft and forgiving. But I cannot forgive. I am not going to turn the other cheek. Not this time. The Bible says an eye for an eye, and I aim to make sure it is a life for a life."

Zach shook his head. She was so all-fired wound up, he wasn't sure she could think rationally. "Listen to me. What you've got isn't enough to convict the man."

She opened her mouth to protest, but he raised a silencing hand. "No. Let me finish. I've spent a lot of time nosing around town, talking to folks and—"

"What did they say that would change my mind?" she demanded, unconvinced although the stiffness in her stance diminished.

"It's what they didn't say." He relaxed, confident he was making progress talking some sense into her. "I have a hunch, but I need a couple more days."

Eugenia stared into his eyes. Hope and something almost akin to love—or lust—the past were mirrored there. A couple more days. That is all he was asking.

A couple more days. In a couple more days, she could harvest enough oysters to buy back the beds, so he would not have to leave. A couple more days, she agonized.

She stared deeper into those intense blue eyes. She did not see her own future reflected there. She realized that she truly could have no future until the past was laid to rest. In her agitated state, she decided there was only one way to overcome the past.

She had to fulfill the vow she had made to herself. She had to see justice done to her father's murderer. If she agreed to a couple more days, Washer could escape. Then Zach would go after him, which meant he would leave. Maybe never to return.

Zach saw fear and doubt flicker into Eugenia's eyes. In an effort to reassure her, he offered, "You don't have to worry. I won't let the murderer get away. But I need a couple more days to finish sewing it up."

"No!" she cried and dashed around Zach, throwing open the door and skinning out. She slid down the banister. Barely managing to escape his grasp, she rushed from the house. "Eugenia, you little fool, come back here! Dammit, you'll rip the case wide open!"

She stumbled, but she kept running. Once outside the gate, she screamed back at Zach, "Washer is not going to get away with murdering my father!"

Thirty-four

Eugenia was nearly out of breath by the time she dashed through the widow's yard and bounded onto the porch. In a panic to avoid Zach, she frantically pushed open the front door and tripped into the house. The crumpled documents flew from her hands. She hurriedly kneeled down and started scooping up the scattered papers.

All the gay chatter and laughter in the crowded house suddenly ceased, and curious eyes swung toward Eugenia.

"Here, let me assist you," Morton Washer stepped forward and bent over.

"No!" Eugenia screamed and ripped an invoice out of his hand. "Get away from me, you . . . you murderer!"

"Eugenia, what has gotten into you? Have you lost your mind!" Washer sputtered, stunned. "You are talking utter nonsense." He looked around the room at the startled partygoers, expecting support against her accusation. Horrified gasps and whispers greeted him. Even his stout wife of twenty-three years stood still with a hand grasped at her throat.

"Am I?" Eugenia cried. She grabbed the remaining papers and awkwardly got to her feet, teetering precariously after stepping on the hem of her soiled gown.

She waved a fistful of papers at the red-haired man. "These documents prove you murdered my father after he found out you were cheating him and secretly trying to gain control of the oyster beds."

Zach had entered the house too late to stop the stubborn little spitfire. But he just might be able to use her outburst to his advantage. Silently, Zach shook his head, stopping Granger from advancing on Eugenia.

Zach leaned against the wall, scanning the crowd, keenly observing and gauging the reactions to Eugenia's stunning indictment. Doubt, disbelief, horror lined the faces. Some shook their heads, others nodded. But what registered most of all was shock. His sweet Genie's impetuousness had caused quite a mixed reaction.

Len Sweeney moved to Eugenia's side. He circled a meaty arm around Eugenia's trembling shoulders. "Out of respect for Eugenia's deceased father, we have a responsibility to at least have a look at the evidence she purports to have in her possession." He practically had to pry the documents from her fingers, she was gripping them so hard. He perused the various entries. When he looked up, his face was grave. "This is very incriminating evidence. Your name's all over these, Washer."

"That is impossible." Washer choked and snatched several of the pages, one a statement from a bank in Astoria. Sheer dismay colored his face when he finished reading them. "These documents are pure fabrication! I demand to know where you got them?"

"I searched your house and found them in your desk," she spat.

"You couldn't have," Washer snorted. Zach noted the blur of confusion cross the man's face. "I always keep my desk locked."

"Ain't it a pity you forgot for once," she mocked, each word delivered with crisp incrimination.

While Washer vented his outrage, Eugenia's gaze shifted to Zach. His face was void of emotion, and he stared back at her. She shifted feet, feeling that in a sense she had betrayed him. Despite his bland expression, she was sure his fury was merely banked.

I need a couple more days. You'll tear the case wide open. His words echoed in her mind, and she noted that he made no move to arrest Washer. Although she found it difficult, she felt that he must have his reasons. She had not been able to be patient and let Washer continue to go free another minute, but she did not have to expose Zach's cover. Not when he was planning to compete against the other oystermen in the Fourth of July regatta tomorrow.

Sheriff Dollard could arrest Washer.

Zach's brow shoved up as he stared back at Eugenia. He ought to be furious with her for interfering. And a part of him was. But part of him admired her will and strength. And part of him

406

envied and longed for the deep love and commitment she had for her pa that had supported her determination to seek justice.

His gaze left her. He scrutinized the sheriff exchanging glances with Sweeney before Dollard swaggered forward as if on cue. Obviously Dollard had been spending too much time at the punch bowl, guzzling the joy juice. His eyes were overbright and bloodshot, and his lopsided grin was a little too fevered for a mere drunk.

Liquor loosened the tongue. That could work to Zach's advantage later tonight.

"I'll take them papers, Miss Eugenia." She reluctantly passed the documents to him. He clamped a hand on Washer's arm. "Better you come with me."

Washer just kept shaking his head, loudly proclaiming his innocence while the sheriff led him from the house. Their exit left Eugenia the sole center of attention as censoring eyes stared at her.

Zach stepped within inches of Eugenia. Retaining a nonchalance, he leaned toward her ear. "And I suggest you come with me."

"I did not do anything wrong," she insisted, unable to comprehend why she should leave.

Zach's brow shoved up. But he was not going to enlighten her in front of a roomful of spectators.

Ruth glared at Eugenia, hissing, "How could you choose to create havoc at my party tonight with such wild allegations?" Moving to the center of the milling clusters of guests, Ruth raised her chin and clapped her hands. "Let's try not to allow Eugenia's ill-timed appearance to ruin our celebration."

Len Sweeney held up a hand when the murmurs continued. "We can all rest assured that Sheriff Dollard will take proper care of Washer."

Trying to swallow a cry, Washer's wife ran from the house.

Ruth's wrinkled face was pinched and pale as a newly laundered sheet despite a forced smile. "Please, everyone, let's attempt to put this dreadful incident behind us tonight. There is still plenty to eat and drink." Ruth turned her back on Eugenia and herded her guests toward a parlor table laden with a bountiful assortment of food.

"I think that's your cue to make a quiet exit," Zach drawled and pulled Eugenia from the house. He marched her across the yard.

"I do not understand," she said through tight lips. "Why was Mrs. Garrett so miffed at me? It was so unlike her."

He opened the door for her and followed her inside. "I'd say your timing left a little to be desired."

"But Washer is guilty and must be punished!"

"The murderer will be punished," he said without emotion. They ascended the stairs and stopped at her bedroom door. "Now, why don't you get some rest before the regatta tomorrow."

"I will be out in front tomorrow, rooting for you," she said to reassure him that she had not meant what she had said earlier.

He opened the door, and she stepped inside, but

he did not follow as she had expected. She turned and lingered in the doorway, waiting.

"Good night, Eugenia," he said in an even voice.

"Zach," she said in a puzzled whisper. "Aren't you going to rage at me or something for not waiting?"

"No, Eugenia." He headed down the hall. He needed to bridle her at arm's length tonight, keep his head clear and focused on what had to be done later tonight and tomorrow.

She leaned out the door. "Zach, people who care about each other fight out their differences. It gives them an excuse to spend time alone together making up."

Zach pivoted around, wanting her so bad he fought to keep from doubling over. "Not all men need to fight with the one they care about as an excuse to spend time alone together. Sleep well."

In his own room, Zach squeezed his eyes shut in an effort to block out the vision of the way she looked at him—with such wide-eyed naivete. She was so real, so genuine, so unfettered by society's strictures. It had taken all the self-control he possessed not to stay with her. Not to make passionate love to her all night. Not to lose himself in her.

Not to take her with him when he had to leave.

Eugenia was left with a myriad of emotions filling her breast when she climbed into bed alone. She felt small and lost in the bed that now seemed too large for one person. The bed was cold and empty without Zach filling it with his tender warmth. She hugged a pillow to her breast.

She had felt split between determination to find

her father's killer and her growing feelings for Zach. She sighed and buried her face in the cushion. Zach's scent lingered there, stealing any chance of solace she'd sought to find.

Part of her experienced a deep sense of relief now that Washer would be brought to justice; a crushing weight lifted from her shoulders. But another kind of weight remained, just as heavy and just as pressing—the burdening question of whether Zach would accept her gift of the oyster beds, an offering of love, and remain on the peninsula with her after the regatta tomorrow.

Sun glistened across the bay, a dozen plungers bobbing in the wind that whipped the pristine waters. It looked to be a fine day for the regatta. Zach's nerve endings were electrified as he waited for the race to begin along the thirty-mile triangular course. He glanced out at the spectators lining the banks of the bay and crowding boats near the finish line.

He was unable to pick Eugenia out from the throng. After he had joined Granger last night to trail Dollard, he had not had the opportunity to return to the house.

"Looking for Miss Eugenia?" one of the longtime oystermen called out from the plunger next to Zach's.

Zach merely nodded. Along with the crew, he busied himself with last minute preparations, but he kept an eye out for her.

"Don't see her anywhere," the man continued.

"Wouldn't worry none if I was you, Kellogg. That girl's life is so rooted in this peninsula and tangled up in the oyster business that she'd never miss a race intentionally. Never has before. May not be able to see her, but she's out there just the same, somewhere among those folks."

Somewhere. But where? The man's telling comment about Eugenia and the peninsula weighed on Zach's mind. She said she would be out in front where he could see her. An elemental urge, a longing down deep inside Zach, as well as a nagging warning, kept his eyes scanning the bystanders for her hourglass figure. He had to know without doubt that she was there, in the front of the crowd, cheering him on with an enthusiasm only Eugenia possessed.

The patriarch of Oysterville, the venerable founder, dressed in black broadcloth and beaver hat discharged the cannon.

The race was on!

Having overslept, Eugenia raced around her room, trying on dress after dress until she was satisfied that she looked her feminine best today in a ruffled rose muslin pinched at the waist. Letting her wild curls hang loose down her back, she smiled at her reflection while she threaded a pale yellow ribbon through her hair. The smoldering gaze Zach had pinned her with while he held one of her ribbons last night could only help serve as a reminder of the unguarded feelings she had glimpsed in his eyes.

411

She rearranged the ruffle off her shoulders. She wanted to look her most enticing when she offered Zach the oyster beds after the race. She did not quite have all the money, but that was a mere detail she would worry about later.

She grabbed the small American flag she intended to wave at the finish line, stuffed it in her reticule, rushed from her room, and knocked on Zach's door. When there was no answer, she peeked inside to reassure herself that he had already gone. She was about to close the door when she noticed the remaining evidence she had found against Washer piled on a bureau top.

Knowing that Sheriff Dollard had no interest in the annual Fourth of July event and seldom attended, she captured the documents and haphazardly stuffed them into her reticule. She glanced at the clock near his bed. "I have just enough time to deliver these to the sheriff before the race."

In a flurry to be at the finish line, rooting for Zach in front of everyone, Eugenia rushed from the house. She was in such a hurry, she did not notice Cliff lurking behind a nearby tree.

She was thankful the town was deserted and the citizens out at the bay as she lifted her skirts, practically running along the boardwalk. At least no one would be witness to her latest trespass against proper ladylike demeanor.

Just as she reached the jail, the strap on her reticule snapped. The overstuffed bag tipped to one side, spilling its contents. She dropped to her knees to retrieve the items.

The stars and stripes clutched in her hand, she suddenly froze.

Spiking through the door were familiar voices raised in anger.

"You'd be wise to accept my offer to buy out your share of the partnership," Len Sweeney said, pacing back and forth in front of Washer's cell. "I'm sure your widow will need the money."

"This is a frame up," Washer raged, his knuckles white from grasping the bars. "That evidence was planted in my desk, and you know it, Sweeney," he accused.

"I don't know what you are blathering about. The Whalen girl has always liked you; she had no reason to frame you. Send word through Dollard when you come to your senses and change your mind." Sweeney went to the door, ready to leave Washer time alone to contemplate his sealed fate.

"She did not frame me. That falsified evidence was carefully planted by someone who knows Whalen's daughter well enough to anticipate her movements."

Sweeney pivoted around slowly, his face a barely disguised mask. "Oh?"

"Nelson and I have been doing some checking," Washer said. "We knew that someone has been secretly buying up the oyster beds before our group had the chance, but the way the ownership was set up it was impossible to trace. And just the other day we paid a visit to our investments and noticed that more oysters had been harvested than were logged in the books.

"I serve as town banker. Why would I have a

413

bank account in Astoria? That faked document only made me think. Whoever is guilty just might have such an account somewhere, rather than keep all that money around the house. Nelson and I hadn't considered that."

"What are you suggesting? That the sheriff contact the bank in Astoria?"

"I'm sure that if some further digging in Astoria is done, no one would turn up a nickel. But since I was tossed in here last night, I've had time to ponder where just such an account might very well exist. And then I asked myself, who would benefit the most from adding Whalen's beds to his holdings. Who makes frequent trips to Bruceport?

"Shakespeare wrote something to the effect that 'methinks he doth protest too much.' Now, Sweeney, who is the most vocal partner—"

"No one's going to listen to your hastily concocted theories," Sweeney scoffed.

"Are you so sure?"

"You're nothing more than a desperate murderer trying to save his own hide," Sweeney sneered, but he was starting to sweat.

"Just desperate enough to remember where my wife got the desk. Odd, don't you think, that Whalen's daughter just happened on that incriminating *evidence* so conveniently left in an unlocked desk while the wife and I were out for the entire evening?"

"Boss, you want for me to shut his puss before he's got a chance to blab his story to someone who might lend a ear?" Sheriff Dollard offered from where he leaned back in his chair, his boots crossed at the ankle on his desk, polishing his gun.

"What do you have in mind?"

"I could save the fine folks of Oysterville the money of a trial 'n' hangin' if I was forced to shoot a murderin' dog who was tryin' to escape." His grin was evil. "Bet even the Whalen gal would thank me."

Off in the distance, the cannon blasted.

Eugenia's head snapped up. The race had begun. The bile of fear bubbled in her throat. She had to get to Zach. She had to get to that finish line.

She scrambled to her feet only to come face to face with Len Sweeney.

Thirty-five

Sweeney could hardly believe his eyes when he threw open the door to see Eugenia Whalen standing before him.

"Eugenia!" Len Sweeney snarled in astonishment.

A weak smile trembling on her lips, Eugenia did the only thing that came to mind. She stepped back and half-heartedly waved the flag she held back and forth.

"H-Happy Fourth of July?"

Sweeney reached out to grab her arm. Her heart pounding, Eugenia thrust the flag into his hand and fled. As she ran she could hear Sweeney shouting at her to stop. Then he ordered the sheriff to pursue her.

Boots beat against the wooden boards, pounding after her, but suddenly stopped. She glanced back over her shoulder; she was some distance in front of Dollard. Her chest was heaving, but she kept going. A little farther and she would be able to elude him, escaping into the trees and thick undergrowth where she could hide until she could reach Zach.

"You can't outrun a bullet!" the sheriff suddenly yelled. He raised his gun and took a potshot at her feet. Dust blasted around her heels, and she jumped. But the fool gal kept running. "The next shot's gonna be aimed at your back."

Panting with fear that he would indeed kill her, Eugenia immediately halted. Her heart pounding wildly, she pivoted around. The sheriff ordered her to return as Sweeney dashed the flag to the ground before joining him. Slowly, she forced her feet to move toward the lanky sheriff who held a gun pointed directly at her.

Sweeney was nervously wringing his hands as Dollard waved his gun and forced her into the jail.

Keeping her chin tilted in defiance despite being terrified, Eugenia spat, "Were you going to shoot me in the back the same way you shot my father, *Sheriff* Dollard?"

Dollard's lips curled back. "You mean you don't believe that the man you had arrested last night did the killin' no more?"

"I told you I did not kill your father," Washer interjected.

"Shut up, Washer!" Sweeney ordered. He took out a handkerchief and dabbed the perspiration from his forehead. "Toss her in the cell next to him, Dollard, until I can figure out what to do with them."

Dollard set his gun on the desk and roughly shoved Eugenia into the cell, locking it behind her.

"You will not get away with this!" she cried, shaking the bars.

"Have to admit, your presence further complicates things," Sweeney sneered in a shaky voice.

Dollard's hand suddenly lunged out and grabbed Eugenia's wrist. He yanked her arm through the bars. She bit her lip and swallowed a scream, refusing to give him the satisfaction of hearing her beg to relinquish his hurtful grip.

Dollard's lewd grin devoured her before he turned to Sweeney. "I got me a real good idea 'bout what to do with her."

"Oh? How'd you like to explain just exactly what this real good idea of yours is, Dollard?" Zach said in a deceptively silken voice.

"Zach!" Eugenia cried in relief and tried to glance past Dollard.

Sweeney and Dollard's eyes whipped to the door. Kellogg filled the doorway, two guns drawn and pointed in their direction. Dollard's gaze carefully trailed to his gun on the desk.

"Don't even think about it," Zach warned. " 'Cause I doubt there'd be many mourners at your funeral. Now, I suggest you let go of Eugenia and unlock her cell. Then I want you two *gentlemen* to trade places with her."

"Sure, Kellogg, but you're makin' a big mistake," Dollard said.

Zach grinned, but it did not reach his eyes. "I'll be the judge of that."

While Dollard grudgingly carried out Kellogg's demands, he whined, "I wasn't gonna harm her. The minute Sweeney left, I was gonna let her go."

Eugenia surged from the cell, rubbing her aching wrist, and kicked Dollard in the shin. "That's for pointing a gun at me."

"You—" he yelped, and his fist jerked up until he heard the click of a trigger.

Sweeney shuffled into the cell behind Dollard. While Eugenia turned the key in the lock, Sweeney burst out, "I admit to planting that evidence against Washer. Hell, Eugenia, you gave me the idea to use Washer that day you came to me for advice and mentioned your suspicions. And I came here this morning in an attempt to buy Washer's share in the oyster beds. I even admit to causing your father's financial setbacks, Eugenia. I—"

"Daddy must have discovered what you were doing and started gathering evidence against you." She turned pained filled eyes to Zach. "That must be when he wrote to you." Then she spun back around to face Sweeney. "You? My father's friend? You were not satisfied until you ransacked the house and ship and stole the evidence so you could blame the murder you committed on someone else?" she muttered, shaking her head. "You are responsible?"

Sweeney seemed to deflate. "Eugenia, listen. I confess that I altered the evidence after I had Dollard get it. I put the business on the auction block so I could have a stranger out-bid the others, and I could add it to my own holdings without anyone the wiser. But I was foiled from buying it when my man arrived late, and Kellogg showed up unexpectedly."

Sweeney's knees failed him, and he sank to the

hard bunk. "But so help me, Eugenia, may God strike me dead where I stand, I am not a murderer. I did not murder your father, Eugenia. I swear it. You've got to believe me."

Eugenia was too numb to move, although her mind recalled Sweeney's unease the day of the auction. All the years her father had worked with the man, her father was the only one to go out to the beds daily. She remembered his laughter when she asked about Sweeney. "Sweeney never was one to get his own hands dirty."

Eugenia's gaze shifted to Dollard.

"Hey, now, don't go givin' me your hard, icy look. I may've helped scare off a few oyster grubbers so Sweeney could buy their beds cheap, and I ain't above stealin', shadowin' or threatenin' like I done with Holm. But I ain't got no gut for murder; I ain't no backshooter."

"You shot at my back," Eugenia cried.

"I didn't put no hole in you, did I?"

"You threatened my life earlier," Washer added his two cents to the conversation while Eugenia took the keys and released him.

"And that's all I done. Hell, you can check, I ain't never shot no one the whole time I been sheriff . . . ever, I swear."

"Just like you swore to uphold the law," Zach commented dryly. But after his investigation last night he believed them.

Now that the sheriff was no longer a threat, Washer boldly strolled to Dollard's cell and snatched the badge from his chest. Dropping the badge into his pocket, Washer announced indignantly, "Since Sweeney has just cleared my good name, and you seem to be in control of the situation, Kellogg, I will head on out to the race. Perhaps I will be able to catch the end of it."

"I am sorry, Mr. Washer, I—"

He went to the door. "No need to apologize now, young woman," he said tightly. "A public apology later will suffice, as soon as the law is brought in to handle this matter."

"Zach is a territorial marshal," Eugenia announced to startled expressions. "He has been working undercover, investigating my father's murder."

"No doubt you spent a lot of time under covers, since you been livin' with her," Dollard snickered.

"And no doubt you're going to spend a lot of time behind bars living with women-starved men," Zach retorted glibly.

Dollard harumphed, "not for murder," but his long face had paled.

"I didn't do it either," Sweeney sniveled from the bunk.

Washer cleared his throat. "Well, Kellogg, since you are a lawman, I am sure I can speak for the town when I say, I am glad you're here. If what they say is true, I hope you will arrest the real murderer soon," he said beneath a raised brow directed pointedly at Eugenia.

Last thing he grumbled before exiting was, 'Pity you did not keep Eugenia on a leash during your investigation so innocent folks did not have to suffer."

Dollard stuck his face out between the bars and

snickered, "Bet she'd be real nice chained to your bed, huh Kellogg?"

Zach's fist thrust out so fast, smashing the grin off Dollard's face, that it sent him reeling against the back wall. He said no more as he held a palm against his bleeding mouth.

Eugenia plopped down on a chair and lifted troubled eyes to Zach. Her father had been murdered in a cowardly way, shot in the back. Sweeney and Dollard had proved to be cowards. She was just about to ask Zach if he thought they could be lying when gunshots rang out.

Guns ready, Zach grabbed the handcuffs off the desk and ran from the jail. Eugenia followed him. "Zach, wait! That means the regatta is over." A sudden realization hit her. As Zach walked back to her, she questioned, "Why weren't you in the race? Even Captain Derrick thought you had a chance to win."

Zach ringed an arm around her shoulders. He began directing her toward the house. "I was out on the bay, ready. When I couldn't see you out in front of the spectators, my gut warned me that you could be in trouble, so I ordered the crew to put me ashore."

He had foregone the race for her. Again his actions were speaking louder than the words she longed to hear. "But how did you know to come to the jail?"

"I didn't until I heard shots."

They continued toward the house while Zach explained that Sweeney and Dollard were not going anywhere and did not require supervision, since he did not believe they committed the murder. Eugenia reluctantly agreed and was sad he missed the race. But Zach reassured her that she was much more important than a single boat race. Although he silently wondered how he was going to buy back the oyster beds for her now before he had to leave.

When Eugenia realized where they were headed, she asked, "Wouldn't you at least like to join in the rest of the festivities? Everyone gets together and eats oysters and drinks lemonade. And later, after the banquet, we have a fancy-dress ball. It is really quite a celebration."

"I've got unfinished business first."

She wondered why they were going back to the house, but decided it wise to keep her own counsel for once. She had already created enough stir for one day. It was not until they entered his bedroom that she could no longer tolerate the suspense and asked.

"Because I'm locking you in this room. I want you out of the way when I arrest the murderer," he told her.

She was right behind him as he started to leave. "Who?" He ignored her demand. "I have a right to be there. It will not do you any good to lock the door," she hissed. "It will not stop me. I will simply climb out the window and follow you."

Zach stopped. "You would, wouldn't you?"

"Yes."

Without another word, he scooped her up and strode to his bed. He clamped the handcuffs he'd picked up at the jail around her wrist and to the bedpost. To her bellow of fury, he said with a grin,

"You know, Dollard's idea wasn't half bad. You will be real nice chained to my bed. You might wish to look out the window though."

Struggling against the cuff, she shook the bedpost. "There is nothing out there but a view of the Widow Garrett's house," she spat.

"True." He closed the door behind him against a passel of hurtled invectives.

Outside, Zach joined Granger, who was leaning against a tree. "Anything yet?"

"Nah. You sure you saw what you thought you saw last night after tailin' Dollard? You sure I ain't been wastin' my time lurkin' behind this tree all mornin'?"

"I'm sure." Zach explained what had transpired at the jail. He had missed the race, but Sweeney and Dollard were now in jail guilty of misdeeds involving greed, not murder. Washer had been vindicated and released to rejoin the citizens at the bay.

"Ruttin' elks, you mean Washer wasn't even grateful?"

Always alert, Zach kept one eye on the rear of the widow's house as he explained the details supporting his earliest theory that the case was more complicated than just murder. "Seems this case involves murder, greed and revenge. What threw me was the way in which the elements were related."

Then he informed Granger that he had convinced Eugenia to remain upstairs out of the way. He did not go into detail about the persuasive tactics he had been forced to resort to in order to accomplish that feat.

Zach noticed the movement of a shadow from behind a bush near the widow's back steps. He glanced up toward his bedroom window; something inside him was sorry he was about to wrap up the case.

He would have to leave shortly afterward.

The shadow shifted again, and Zach drew his gun. "Looks like it's time to close this case."

"It's your party." Cliff unholstered his gun and crept along behind Zach.

As they got closer, the door suddenly swung open, and a hooded figure dashed inside the house. Zach leapt over the picket fence and rushed the front door while Granger veered toward the rear.

Eugenia watched in astounded horror and disbelief at the scene unfolding next door. She gasped when Zach kicked the front door in and disappeared inside. "Not Ruth Garrett," she cried.

The elderly woman had been like a mother to Eugenia. Eugenia's mind worked overtime. Had the widow held Eugenia's father responsible for her husband's death? Had her father been murdered for revenge?

Unable to take her eyes from the window, she nevertheless continued to quake the bedpost in a desperate attempt to break free. She was frantic and determined to get inside that house with Zach.

Zach burst into the parlor to come face to face with a shotgun pointed at his gut. Ruth Garrett stood in the doorway of the kitchen, grasping a gun almost as big as she was. "You can stop right where you are, Mr. Kellogg," Ruth Garrett announced, her fingers trembling around the trigger. "Throw down your gun."

"You're making a big mistake, Mrs. Garrett," Zach said in a calming voice. He dropped the gun and took a step toward her.

An instant later, a wild-eyed young man with a six-shooter nervously appeared behind her. "Shoot him, Mother Garrett!" the man yelled. "Shoot him!"

"She's not a murderer, Gerard." Zach kept his voice soothing. "It is Gerard Hamlett, isn't it? Mrs. Garrett's son-in-law?"

"So you know. It won't do you no good," he sneered and shoved the old lady out of the way. His gun aimed at Kellogg, he laughed. "In case you're stalling so that other fool can jump me from behind, don't bother. I already took care of him."

Holding her bruised shoulder against the wall, Ruth pleaded with her son-in-law to give himself up. But his laughter only grew more high-pitched.

"You can't protect me for that precious daughter of yours any longer. I'm guilty. Whalen came home and caught me in his house while I was robbing the place." At her stunned look, he said, "Nothin' was left in this dump to sell so I had to go next door.

"Whalen demanded that I put back the stuff and then turn myself in. Can you imagine? Said it would go easier on me. When I waved a gun in the old man's face, he laughed and had the gall to say I didn't have the balls to shoot him. Then he turned his back on me and headed out the kitchen to get the law. Well, after I pulled the trigger, he didn't laugh no more."

"You said it was an accident," Ruth cried, and her shoulders slumped in despair. "I thought when I hid your presence here, withdrew my savings from Mr. Washer and gave it to you, that would be the end of it. Then I even tried to buy Eugenia's schooner so you would have the means to leave and start over somewhere else."

Gerard was shaking. "Don't you see? I tried to put a stop to it. I took aim at Whalen's whelp, but I missed. If I let him take me in, I'll hang. Just hurry up and get the rest of the money I know you got hidden around here so I can get out of the territory. You don't want your precious grandchildren to watch their pa hang, do you?"

"Oh, my sweet Lord," Ruth wept. "You tried to kill Eugenia, too? How could I have been so blind for so long to the kind of man my daughter married. I'm a silly, stupid old fool." Her face seemed to have aged ten years in the last ten minutes, and she looked wizened, pale and defeated.

"No more killing, Gerard," she pleaded. "I'll get your money so you'll get out of my poor daughter and her children's lives." Her head down, she accidently stepped between Hamlett and Kellogg.

It was the moment Zach had been waiting for. He lunged, grabbing his gun in the same instant that Hamlett shoved the old lady forward.

Thirty-six

Zach caught the widow and adeptly set her aside. He was determined that Hamlett would not get far. Zach stampeded through the kitchen and past Granger, who was sprawled in a heap beside the table. Slamming out the back door, Zach suddenly came to an abrupt halt. Drawing up short, he lowered his gun.

Hamlett was lying unconscious on the ground. Eugenia stood over him, her arms behind her back, rocking back and forth on her heels.

"What kept you?"

"How did you manage to get free?" he snapped, searching his pockets; he still had the key.

"At first I did not think I was going to. But it only took me a few minutes once I recalled that my mother used to hide her valuables in the hollowed bedpost you so kindly chained me to. I merely unscrewed it.

"See?" A triumphant smile on her face, she brought her arms from behind her back. One side of the handcuffs still encircled her wrist, the other bracelet hung freely, still locked. In her other hand was the barrel of the gun she had bought. "When he came running out the back door, I hit him over the head with the gun you taught me how to use."

"Except my lessons involved holding the other end," Zach remarked dryly.

"A mere detail."

"My God, I should have known." Zach shook his head. "With you anywhere nearby, the murdering son of a bitch didn't stand a chance."

Her eyes suddenly dropped to the unconscious man she had known for years. When she raised her head, her eyes were bright with unshed tears of pent-up cold fury. "Gerard murdered my father?"

"Yes," Zach answered, his gaze glued to the gun she had now shifted in her hand.

"I do not understand." Her fingers tightened around the butt of the gun and curled over the trigger. "Even after Daddy was forced to fire him, Daddy arranged for him and his family to have a fresh start in Astoria."

Zach intently watched her. She was valiantly fighting back tears, gulping in big breaths of air. "He's a rabid dog who bit the hand that fed him," Zach said softly in a soothing voice, cautiously inching closer to her.

"Sometimes no matter how much good folks do for others, it isn't enough. Truth is some folks are plain rotten all the way through. I'm sorry, Eugenia, your pa was unfortunate to get hooked up with one of them."

"How did you know it was Gerard?" she asked,

429

fighting to hold back the flood of emotions that she had suppressed.

"I had a hunch after we talked to Dollard at the sheriff's office. That's why I told you I needed a couple more days; I wanted to check it out.

"Last night at the party I noticed Dollard and Sweeney exchange looks that confirmed another suspicion I got while I was practicing on the bay. I saw Sweeney and Dollard sail by together in one of Holm's boats.

"While Granger and I were tailing Dollard to Holm's, I noticed someone sneak into the widow's house. But I wasn't absolutely sure until Sweeney's confession fit with Peter Holm's last night."

Zach kept his voice steady, his eyes on her trigger finger. "Holm broke down and confessed that Sweeney had threatened him with financial ruin unless he allowed Sweeney to use Holm's schooners as part of his scheme to gain control of the oyster beds. That's why Peter Holm was so nervous.

"If Sweeney were a murderer, he could've just as easily killed Holm to keep him quiet. So, that excluded Sweeney. And Sweeney's confession at the jail reinforced my hunch. The leftover pieces of the puzzle just fit after that."

Zach described how he had thought it was more than just a murder and defined the steps that led him to that conclusion. He had ruled out Gertrude and Gale after he learned of their affair, and Gertrude's awkward attempts to procure the schooner. Rube Nelson merely followed Washer's lead.

Keeping his eyes on the gun she had raised an inch, Zach kept talking to occupy her mind. He explained how he could not understand how the person who had shot out the window was able to vanish so fast without a trace unless he had somewhere nearby to go.

He recounted the widow's visit that day in Washer's shop to withdraw a large sum of money. And he added it in with Eugenia's comments about the widow's behavior change and offer to purchase the schooner, although her house was nearly bare.

"An eye for an eye," she whispered and pointed the gun at Gerard.

"Eugenia! No!" Zach reached out his open palm to her. Softly, but with the strength of conviction, Zach said, "Hamlett will pay with his life. Trust me."

She was openly crying now, her hand trembling.

"Trust me, Eugenia," he repeated and carefully wrapped his fingers around the gun barrel. With a mournful cry, Eugenia released the gun, and Zach gathered her into his arms. He tossed the weapon away and held her against his chest, supporting her and smoothing a hand down the back of her head while she sobbed.

Rubbing his head, Cliff stumbled from the house accompanied by a very distraught Ruth Garrett. While Zach explained everything to Cliff, he unlocked the cuffs from Eugenia's wrists and cradled her back within his embrace.

When she stepped away from him, Zach asked, "Eugenia, are you okay?"

"Finally, I think in time I may be. Mrs. Garrett needs me now." She went to the widow and consoled her.

"Mrs. Garrett, I am so sorry," Eugenia tried to wrap her arms around the elderly widow, who now seemed so frail and so much older.

Ruth instead hugged Eugenia, then held her at arm's length. "Eugenia, child, I am the one who is so sorry. I pray you can find it in your heart to forgive me. I didn't know that Gerard did . . . was the one who . . . he swore to me it was an accident. He's kin.

"Inside I had to believe him for my daughter's sake. Then just now I found out that he was using me, that he intentionally murdered your father after he went there to rob him. Gerard—"

Eugenia stepped back and shook her raised palms. "No. Please, Mrs. Garrett," she sniffled. "No more." Her temples were pounding with blinding pain as she dropped her eyes to Gerard's pathetic prone figure.

It was over. Her father's murderer would now be brought to justice; he would reap in kind that which he had sown.

Suddenly the cold reality hit her hard, and the urge to visit her father's grave became overwhelming.

"Eugenia, are you all right?" Zach asked, sensing an abrupt change in her.

She turned and fled.

Zach started after her, but Ruth grabbed his arm. "Let her go, son. She's headed toward the cemetery. I suspect the reality of her father's death has finally caught up with her, and she is going to visit his grave. She needs time alone."

At Zach's strained expression, she forced herself

432

to add, "Eugenia refused to say good-bye to her father until the m-murderer was caught."

Gathering clouds blocked the sun as Zach reluctantly watched Eugenia disappear. Then he hauled Hamlett to his feet.

Eugenia chewed on her bottom lip to keep it from trembling when she entered the cemetery. Memories of the girl she had been, her small hand clutched in her father's large one, while her mother was buried met her. Her trembling fingers squeezed tighter around the blooms she had picked along the way.

She briefly stopped at her mother's grave to lay a petaled remembrance there. Her eyes misted. "You are no longer alone."

Tears rolled down her cheeks.

Forever gone from this earth.

First her mother. Then her father.

She moved to the simple wooden headstone marking her father's burial site and dropped to her knees. Solemnly, she ran quivering fingers over the freshly carved letters before placing the flower on the ground.

"Oh, Daddy," she sobbed. "I didn't even have the chance to say good-bye. I miss you so much." She sniffled and wiped the back of her hand under her nose. "I love you"—her eyes trailed to her mother's grave—"both."

For a long while she remained, quietly sobbing, finally able to grieve, to allow all the pain and sorrow and misery she had locked inside to pour forth.

She cried until there were no more tears left within her. Feeling cold, empty and alone, she lingered there until she felt the presence of someone standing nearby.

She glanced up.

Zach was quietly standing a short distance behind her, his hands clasped in front of him.

She was pale, her eyes swollen and ringed in red. "Hope I'm not intruding." He had locked Hamlett away and waited as long as he could stand it before getting directions. "Had to make sure you were all right."

"I don't know."

"I remember when I lost my folks. I think I understand the depth of your torment. Grief's a heavy burden often borne alone. I know it's your sorrow, but I came in case you needed someone to help you bear it."

Unable to speak, she nodded and reached out to him. Zach stepped forward and closed reassuring fingers around hers, pulling her up into his embrace. She seemed so small, so vulnerable, so fragile that he wanted to hold and protect her forever.

While they stood silently together, the sun broke through the clouds. Eugenia looked down, a sad smile curving the corners of her lips. The sun was shining down on her parents' final resting place.

Her parents had been reunited; they were together now; they had each other and were wrapped in God's loving arms. Suddenly she no longer felt so cold nor alone. With his arms wrapped tenderly around her, Zach was filling the void.

"Would you like to stay for awhile?"

"No," she whispered, a weak smile breaking through her sadness. "I remember when my mother died twelve years ago after a long illness, Daddy told me not to mourn. He said we should be happy and rejoice because she had no more pain; she was with God, watching over us. Now they are together, watching over me."

Zach ringed a supporting arm around her, leading her from the cemetery. "You know, Daddy said that life naturally passes from generation to generation. After my mother died, I remember him advising me that when he passed on, I should celebrate his life, not mourn and grieve over his death."

"He sounds like he was a very wise man."

"He never openly mourned my mother in front of me. You know what he said when I asked him about it?" Zach squeezed her shoulder. She needed to talk. "Daddy said that was reserved for parents who must bury a child, because children are the future."

"You're their future, Eugenia," he said softly.

"Daddy said that even after they were both gone, part of them would continue to live through the love that produced me . . ."

While Zach escorted Eugenia back toward the house, he quietly listened without interruption as she continued to talk about her family. She was carrying out her pa's wishes; through her memories, she was celebrating her parents' lives. Her reminiscences slowly swung from the past toward plans for the future. He noted the sadness begin to fade and a hint of animation return to her voice.

A short distance from the festivities, she suddenly stopped when the bay came into sight. She stood staring at the glistening blue waters.

He squeezed her hand. "Eugenia, I'm sorry about the oyster beds."

"You do not have to be." A renewed, although somewhat tempered, excitement filled her. "I almost have enough money to buy them back." She explained how she had been harvesting the oysters and selling them.

His brow shoved up. Her undauntable spirit was returning. "You've been stealing?"

"Only from the government. It is not the same as if I had taken them from the other oystermen."

"You broke the law. You'll have to give the money back."

The time had come. Zach may very well leave if she did not speak up. She took a deep breath, feeling a new strength possess her.

"I did it so I could buy the beds for you."

For the first time since she'd encountered Zach, he truly appeared stunned.

"For me?" he said in an astounded voice. "I only entered that regatta so I could buy them back from the government for you."

Her sad heart suddenly buoyed. "You mean so you could remain on the peninsula with me? So we—"

"Eugenia." She held her breath when she noticed a curtain begin to drop over his eyes, and he held her at arm's length. "I told you once that I'm a lawman. It's all I know. It's all I want to know."

436

Then softer. "My feet're planted—rooted—firmly on dry land."

Her heart plummeted. It was *that talk,* the one she had dreaded. "What about us?"

She waited, hoping that he would speak his heart. When he remained silent, she said, "Was I too impetuous again to believe that you felt there could be an us?"

"Oh God," he groaned and hugged her to him, pressing a kiss to the top of her head.

He wanted to throw her on the back of his horse and take her away with him. But he recalled what the oysterman waiting for the regatta to start had said. Eugenia's roots were here, her life, her future.

"Eugenia!" came the screeching voice of Aunt Iris. The sudden caterwauling broke the tension, only to replace it with tension of another kind.

Eugenia pulled away from Zach. Her aunt, accompanied by her uncle, cousin, and a whole bevy of the town's citizens were marching toward them.

Of all moments, why did her kin manage to reach Oysterville today! Her aunt's usually impeccable dress was smudged, her hat drooped over a pinched face and narrowed eyes which glared at her. Having not fared much better, her uncle and cousin stood stiffly in the background.

Captain Derrick hurried to the forefront of the crowd. "I be sorry, lass. They came in from Ilwaco on the stage this morning."

"After you made arrangements for us to be way-laid!" Iris accused Eugenia. "Oh, yes, I learned that you were the one responsible for rudely causing your own relatives to be sent to Bruceport and Astoria."

Iris waited for an apology. When one was not forthcoming, she raised her chin into an impervious line. "Well, despite the fact that you obviously are not repentant, we have endured a dreadful journey just to render our assistance as family should."

Zach noted Eugenia's spirit seem to shrivel under the weight of the overbearing woman's tongue. The old crow was the first person he had seen who was able to intimidate Eugenia. He ringed a buttressing arm around Eugenia's sagging shoulders. It was the least he could do before he had to leave.

Iris slapped a hand to her chest. "Move away from him, Eugenia." She glared at the huge man. "Unhand her!" Zach ignored her demands and pulled Eugenia closer to him. "Where is the law in this godforsaken outpost? I insist that this person be arrested for attempting to . . . to molest my dear dead sister's daughter."

Washer cleared his throat and stepped from the crowd to join the ranting woman. "Excuse me, ma'am, but he is the law."

"Well, I never!" she huffed, feeling faint. She leaned against her husband for support.

"See here, Sheriff." Eduardo puffed out his ample chest and barked at the man. "As Eugenia's only living family, we have a responsibility for her welfare. We have traveled all this way, taken the burden upon ourselves to settle the matter of her inheritance—"

"It's already been settled," Zach said in a clipped

tone. "Captain Derrick, get your crew together and assist Eugenia's *relatives* so they take it upon themselves to sail with the tide back to wherever they came from. She doesn't need them."

"Aye, aye, lad. I be most happy to." A triumphant smile on his weathered face, the white-haired captain saluted. He grabbed Iris and Eduardo by the arms and pointed them in the direction of the schooner. Surprise on her face, Mildred trailed behind them.

"Eugenia!" Iris screeched over her shoulder, holding her hat as she was so rudely being dismissed and manhandled.

Eugenia glanced up at Zach. His face was an immovable granite wall. Her heart fluttered. A grin on her lips, she waved at her aunt. "Have a pleasant voyage home, Auntie."

Washer waited until the outsiders had been escorted from view before he awkwardly stepped forward again. "Kellogg, after I informed everyone of your background and how you handled yourself at the jail, we took a vote."

Kellogg did not appear impressed or interested, causing Washer to fumble in his vest pocket. "Well, if you're interested, Oysterville could use a man like you as sheriff."

Washer pulled out Dollard's badge and held it out in his palm. "What do you say, Kellogg?"

Dead silence fell over the crowd. Tension built as eager faces waited. Eugenia was still, not daring to breathe. Cliff appeared from the back of the mass and sent a nod of approval, along with a wink. She noticed Gale and Gertrude then, arm in arm, their noses in the air. She still had Gertrude's debt to worry about.

"You serve as the town's banker, don't you, Washer?" Zach finally said, piercing the thick silence.

"Of sorts, yes. But now look here," Washer blustered. "If you are trying to hold us up for a hefty raise just because we are in dire need of a sheriff, we are not—"

Zach held up a hand. "I'm not holding you up for a raise. Eugenia requires a temporary business loan until her oyster beds are harvested," he said without emotion.

"Ah, I-I thought you owned the beds." His eyes suddenly brightened. "But if you are a territorial marshal and was working undercover, that means you must have purchased them with government money. If that is the case, anyone can bid on them now."

Eugenia gasped. Gertrude and Gale suddenly brightened. Rube Nelson looked expectant. The rest of the faces watching became a blur as Eugenia fought the cloying pressure.

"I wouldn't advise it," Zach snarled. "As I said, Eugenia requires monetary assistance for *her* oyster beds. If it weren't for Eugenia, you might still be rotting in a cell."

"She put me there," Washer sputtered, then shrank under Kellogg's biting stare. Kellogg was not moved.

"Well, I suppose I could see my way clear to make you a loan, Kellogg, if you were our sheriff." He took a deep breath and ventured to lean toward the big man. Taking a chance, he dropped the shiny star into Kellogg's coat pocket. "Then what you do with the money is your business. That's the best I can do."

"I see."

Washer waited. When the moments stretched out, Washer awkwardly stepped backwards toward the expectant crowd. "We all will return to the festivities and let you think it over."

"Don't worry, Eugenia, one way or another, you'll get your money," Zach said softly, then turned back toward the crowd. He and Granger held each other's eyes for a moment before the lanky man lit a smoke, turned and walked away.

Eugenia gazed at Zach's magnificent profile while the crowd dispersed. It was set in an unmoving line. Her mind was a jumble of emotions.

Zach had defended her against the one person able to intimidate her and sent the mean-spirited woman packing. He would arrange to borrow money so she could keep her oyster beds. He would go into debt for her, defend her, rescue her, comfort her, bed her. But he would not . . . or . . . could not say he loved her.

Eugenia bit her tongue to keep from commenting on the hard-driven proposition Zach put to Washer until the last of the crowd had left them standing alone. Angry, she swung on him. "I do not need you interceding on my behalf."

"You're a perfectly capable young woman," he said evenly.

"Exactly." Her hands were on her hips, her chin jutting forward.

"I made the statement. I agree, so there's no argument. The money from the oysters I shipped is in your name in a bank in Astoria."

"You've been stealing?" she mimicked an earlier remark he'd made.

"Only from the government," he in turn echoed with a hint of amusement. "I'll get the rest of the money from Washer tomorrow."

"No, you won't. I will not take any money from you. I can manage just fine by myself," she announced, although she was secretly touched to learn what he had done for her.

Her stubbornness would try the patience of a saint, and God knew he would never qualify. "Like you did with Sweeney and Dollard?" His voice now had a sharp edge to it. "And how, pray tell, do you plan to pay back that Englestrom woman? Why do you think she showed you those notes from your pa and allowed you to run up such a big bill at her shop?"

"I have no doubt you are going to enlighten me."

"Seems somebody has to." His anger exploded. "I checked her out. She and her latest lover, your ex-fiance, have formed a partnership and plan to become enterprising entrepreneurs on their own.

"Hell, they'll be first in line to get their claws on those precious oyster beds, even if you do manage to buy them back from the government. If you don't, I hope you remember her demand that you sell your schooner."

"And I suppose everything would be simply grand if you loaned me the money, then mounted your horse and rode off in search of dry land where your feet are firmly planted and rooted?" she practically shouted, angrily gesturing toward the east.

He suddenly realized she was tossing his very own words back in his face. It gave him pause. His hand brushed his coat pocket, and his glance dropped to his boots.

Hell, if he had only bothered to look, he was already standing on dry land.

"I love you," he said softly.

"Well, I love you, too," she retorted. The lines of anger around her eyes and mouth smoothed as the momentum of their argument lost sail, and comprehension of their last exchange struck her.

She threw up her hands and walked in a complete circle, frantically trying to think. He had finally said the words she had been longing to hear. Now what would happen? Would he ask her to leave with him? Could she beg him to stay?

She stopped before him. "Despite our feelings for each other, how ever are we going to resolve this?"

Without her voicing the conflicting emotions marching across her face, he knew exactly what she was thinking. "I do believe the perfect solution to this seeming impasse of ours has come to me," he said simply.

She kept her gaze glued to his. Silently she prayed she saw a gleam there, a glimmer on which she could fasten her hope. "It has? Just now?"

She leaned into him. She could feel the pounding of his heart, the tightening of his muscles, matched only by her own. His arms went around her, and she experienced the tension, the raw power of his embrace.

"My solution isn't exactly some hidden divine intervention, although I must admit I've been giving a number of possibilities some serious consideration lately."

"You have?" The suspense was threatening to overcome her.

"Absolutely." He stepped back, took her hand, and started walking toward the festivities. Reaching into his pocket with his free hand, he removed the badge and pinned it on his chest.

"What better way to put an end to our predicament and resolve the ownership of the oyster beds than with the marriage bed."

Dear Readers,

PETTICOAT PIRATE is a fictional work. Therefore, for those of you familiar with the rich history of this marvelous corner of the world, I hope you will forgive the literary license taken with several of the dates. For instance, the courthouse was actually built in 1875. Prior to that time the county recorder maintained the records books at his home until the frugal commissioners provided the building funds. The first regatta was held in 1876 in celebration of America's centennial. The Lightning Express Stageline was not introduced until 1877.

Oysters were a relished delicacy, allowing Oysterville to parallel the richest gold mining towns in California and Colorado known to pioneer history. Unfortunately, the native oysters began to die out by 1881 due to eelgrass, pests and cold. And like so many of our natural resources, they were gathered indiscriminately. Soon thereafter the native oyster had forever disappeared from the bay. Today the bay (now called Willapa Bay) teems with the Pacific oyster introduced from Japan in 1931.

Oysterville was the county seat until 1893. In February of that year, eighty-five men from across the bay stole the county records and removed them to South Bend. Although Oysterville's citizens protested, the county offices remained in South Bend. Today, historic Oysterville is a sleepy, quaint little reminder of those glorious times past.

I hope you have enjoyed Eugenia and Zach's story as much as I enjoyed writing it. Laughter is wonderful medicine, and I sincerely trust I have provided you, my dearly cherished readers, with a few hours of pleasurable entertainment in which you can sit back, escape and revel in a love story set against the delightful setting such as was Oysterville in the nineteenth century. Your suggestions and comments are always appreciated. You may write to me at the address below:

Love to you all . . .
Gwen Cleary
Zebra Books
475 Park Avenue South
New York, New York 10016

SASE appreciated.

About the Author

GWEN CLEARY, winner of the Romantic Times Reviewers Choice Love and Laughter Award, has delighted many readers with her original tales filled with passion and humor. A native of Southern California, Gwen enjoys traveling to the exciting locales she writes about and rummaging through museums. She is the author of RIVERBOAT TEMPTATION, NEVADA TEMPTATION, COLORADO TEMPTATION, MISSOURI FLAME, PASSIONATE POSSESSION, ECSTASY'S MASQUERADE, and VICTORIA'S ECSTASY.

Gwen loves to hear from readers. You can write to her c/o Zebra Books, 475 Park Avenue South, New York, New York 10016. Please include a self addressed, stamped envelope for a reply.